NOT SAFE AFTER DARK

AND OTHER WORKS

ALSO BY PETER ROBINSON

The Inspector Banks series

GALLOWS VIEW

A DEDICATED MAN

A NECESSARY END

THE HANGING VALLEY

PAST REASON HATED

WEDNESDAY'S CHILD

DRY BONES THAT DREAM

INNOCENT GRAVES

DEAD RIGHT

IN A DRY SEASON

COLD IS THE GRAVE

AFTERMATH

THE SUMMER THAT NEVER WAS

PLAYING WITH FIRE

and

CAEDMON'S SONG

PETER ROBINSON

NOT SAFE AFTER DARK

AND OTHER WORKS

MACMILLAN

For Sheila

Collection first published 2004 by Macmillan
an imprint of Pan Macmillan Ltd
Pan Macmillan, 20 New Wharf Road, London N1 9RR
Oxford and Basingstoke
Associated companies throughout the world
www.panmacmillan.com

ISBN 1 4050 2111 X HB
ISBN 1 4050 2112 8 PB

1 3 5 7 9 8 6 4 2

A CIP catalogue record for this book is available from
the British Library.

Typeset by IntypeLibra Ltd
Printed and bound in Great Britain by
Mackays of Chatham plc, Chatham, Kent

CONTENTS

ACKNOWLEDGEMENTS

Individual stories first published in different form as: 'Summer Rain' © *Ellery Queen's Mystery Magazine*, New York, December 1994. An Inspector Banks story; 'Fan Mail' © *Cold Blood II*, ed. Peter Sellers (Mosaic Press: Oakville, Canada, 1989); 'Innocence' © *Cold Blood III*, ed. Peter Sellers (Mosaic Press: Oakville, Canada, 1990); 'Murder in Utopia' © *Crime Through Time III*, ed. Sharan Newman (Berkeley, New York, July 2000); 'Not Safe After Dark' © *Criminal Shorts*, ed. Howard Engel and Eric Wright (Macmillan: Toronto, Canada, 1992); 'Just My Luck' © *Bouchercon XXII Souvenir Programme Book*, Toronto, 1992; 'Anna Said. . .' © *Cold Blood IV*, ed. Peter Sellers (Mosaic Press: Oakville, Canada, 1992). An Inspector Banks story; 'Missing in Action' © *Ellery Queen's Mystery Magazine*, New York, November 2000; 'Memory Lane' © *Blue Lightning*, edited by John Harvey, Slow Dancer Press (UK), 1998; 'Carrion' © *No Alibi*, ed. Maxim Jakubowski (Ringpull: Manchester, 1995); 'April in Paris' © *Love and Death*, ed. Carolyn Hart (Berkley, New York), February 2001; 'The Good Partner' © *Ellery Queen's Mystery Magazine*, New York, March 1994. An Inspector Banks story; 'Some Land in Florida' © *Ellery Queen's Mystery Magazine*, New York, Christmas issue, 1996; 'The Wrong Hands' © *Ellery Queen's Mystery Magazine*, New York, April 1998; 'The Two Ladies of Rose Cottage' © *Malice Domestic 6*, ed. Anne Perry (New York: Pocket Books, 1997); 'Lawn Sale' © *Cold Blood V*, ed. Peter Sellers and John North (Mosaic Press: Oakville, Canada, 1994); 'Gone to the Dawgs' © *The Mighty Johns*, ed. Otto Penzler (New Millenium Press, Beverly Hills, CA), summer 2002; 'In Flanders Fields' © First published in *Not Safe After Dark and Other Stories*, by Peter Robinson, Crippen & Landru (Virginia), October 1998; 'The Duke's Wife' © *Much Ado About Murder*, ed. Anne Perry (Berkley, New York, December 2002).

'Going Back' first published 2004; © Eastvale Enterprise Inc.

INTRODUCTION

I remember once talking to a famous crime writer about getting a short story out of my home being burgled, and she replied, 'I get a short story out of everything.' That certainly put me in my place. It also serves as useful opening to this introduction because some writers I know find that short stories come easily, whereas I don't.

I think this is partly because I have become so used to thinking in terms of the novel, with the broad canvas it offers, that it's hard to work in miniature. I carry a novel around in my head for a long time – at least a year, waking and sleeping – and this gives me time to get under the skin of the characters *and* the story. Also, plotting is probably the most difficult part of writing for me, and being asked to write a short story, which so often depends on a plot twist, a clever diversion or a surprising revelation, guarantees that I'll get the laundry done and probably the ironing, too.

That said, there is nevertheless a great deal of satisfaction to be had from writing short stories. Partly, of course, it's the quick payoff. A short story is, by definition, *short*. Consequently, you get that wonderful rush of having *finished* something far more quickly than you do with a novel.

But it isn't only the instant gratification that makes short stories so attractive to me, it's also the new possibilities they offer. When you work primarily as a series writer, as I do, most of your time goes into the creation of that series. That, of course, is as it should be: I wouldn't be writing the Inspector Banks books if I didn't want to. But there's always the temptation to try something different, and to risk a week or so doing this is a lot easier than to risk a year or more on a project that might easily meet with rejection.

Short stories also offer a wonderful opportunity for the series writer to spread his or her wings and fly to new, exotic places, to meet different people and to try out different techniques. The Inspector Banks series is set, for the most part, in Yorkshire, but these stories range from Toronto to Paris, from Florida to California. The Banks books are third-person narratives, while many of the stories are first-person. Banks is a policeman, but you'll find very few policemen between these covers. A number of the stories, such as 'Murder in Utopia' and 'Missing in Action', are set in different periods of history.

While short stories come from the same seeds as novels, usually they come as ideas that can *only* be developed into short stories. 'Innocence' was one exception to this rule. After writing the story, I couldn't let go and went on to write an entire novel from Reed's point of view, expanding the events of the story, but my publishers turned it down. I put it aside for a while, then thought that perhaps if Banks was there it might work better. Thus, Reed became Owen and 'Innocence' (1990) became *Innocent Graves* (1996). Both the short story and the novel won Arthur Ellis awards in Canada.

A sense of place has always been important in my work and is no less so here. In Florida one December I witnessed a Christmas singalong around the swimming pool, Santa in his usual outfit leading the crowd on electric piano. Only this took place in twenty-seven degree heat and they were singing 'White Christmas', something I think they don't usually have down there. Needless to say, the absurdity of the scene was not lost on me, and in 'Some Land in Florida' Santa ends up in the pool with his electric piano thrown after him – still plugged in!

The first historical story I wrote, 'The Two Ladies of Rose Cottage', was inspired by both a place and by my interest in Thomas Hardy. I once paid a visit to the house where he was born in Bockhampton, Dorset, and stood in the room where he was cast aside as dead by the doctor who delivered him, only to be revived by a quick-thinking nurse. As I looked out of his upstairs window on much the same view he often enjoyed as he wrote his early books, this short story of murder and deceit ranging over more than a hundred years began to form in my mind, and Hardy himself even makes a brief appearance in it.

Other stories have their origins in such diverse sources as an unusual piece of information ('Carrion'), fragments of dreams ('Fan Mail'), stories recounted by others ('The Wrong Hands' and 'Memory Lane') and research for other works. I doubt that I would ever have written 'In Flanders Field' or 'Missing in Action', for example, if I hadn't spent so much time researching the Second World War for *In a Dry Season*.

Sometimes, as in 'Gone to the Dawgs' and 'The Duke's Wife', I was asked for a story on a specific topic – in these cases, American Football and Shakespeare respectively. But no matter how much or how little is given, or demanded, there is always a lot to change and more to add, all subjected to the constant 'What if?' of the writer's imagination.

While I did mention earlier that most of the stories here represent a break from Inspector Banks, there are three Banks short stories in the collection. In a way, they were the hardest for me to write because I'm so used to giving Banks plenty of space. There's little room for significant character or plot development in a short story, or for the creation of multiple points of view. Still, it was impossible to resist the temptation to try, especially to have Banks attempt to solve the mystery of a man who claims to have been murdered in a previous lifetime, as happens in 'Summer Rain'. You'll have to judge the results for yourself.

Finally, the Inspector Banks novella 'Going Back' is a special case and has never been published before. I wrote it early in 1999, so it came between *In a Dry Season* and *Cold Is the Grave*. At that point I didn't know that I was going to send Banks home to deal with his old school friend's disappearance in *The Summer that Never Was* (2003) and I wanted to show him interacting with his family and responding to the place where he grew up. In manuscript, it reached 106 pages, too long for any of the magazines or anthologies that regularly published my stories, and too short for separate book publication. And so it sat there gathering dust until I came to write *The Summer that Never Was,* when I incorporated parts of the novella into the novel – mostly details about the street Banks grew up on, his relationship with his parents, the music he listened to and the books he read as an adolescent.

When I came to revise 'Going Back' for this collection, I had to shift it chronologically, so that it now falls between *The Summer that Never Was* and *Playing with Fire*. I also had to try to avoid too much repetition of details I had cannibalized for the novel without spoiling the original conception. It was a difficult balancing act, but I hope you enjoy the final result, along with the rest of the stories in this collection.

PETER ROBINSON
FEBRUARY, 2004

SUMMER RAIN

AN INSPECTOR BANKS STORY

1

'And exactly how many times have you died, Mr Singer?'

'Fourteen. That's fourteen I've managed to uncover. They say that each human being has lived about twenty incarnations. But it's the last one I'm telling you about. See, I died by violence. I was murdered.'

Detective Constable Susan Gay made a note on the yellow pad in front of her. When she looked down, she noticed that she had doodled an intricate pattern of curves and loops, a bit like Spaghetti Junction, during the few minutes she had been talking to Jerry Singer.

She tried to keep the scepticism out of her voice. 'Ah-hah. And when was this, sir?'

'Nineteen sixty-six. July. That makes it exactly thirty-two years ago this week.'

'I see.'

Jerry Singer had given his age as thirty-one, which meant that he had been murdered a year before he was born.

'How do you know it was nineteen sixty-six?' Susan asked.

Singer leaned forward. He was a remarkably intense young man, Susan noticed, thin to the point of emaciation, with glittering green eyes behind wire-rimmed glasses. He looked as if the lightest breeze would blow him away. His fine red hair had a gossamer quality that reminded Susan of spiders' webs. He wore jeans, a red T-shirt and a grey anorak, its shoulders darkened by the rain. Though he said he came from San Diego, California, Susan could detect no trace of suntan.

'It's like this,' he began. 'There's no fixed period between incarnations, but my channeller told me—'

'Channeller?' Susan interrupted.

'She's a kind of spokesperson for the spirit world.'

'A medium?'

'Not quite.' Singer managed a brief smile. 'But close enough. More of mediator, really.'

'Oh, I see,' said Susan, who didn't. 'Go on.'

'Well, she told me there would be a period of about a year between my previous incarnation and my present one.'

'How did she know?'

'She just *knows*. It varies from one soul to another. Some need a lot of time to digest what they've learned and make plans for the next incarnation. Some souls just can't wait to return to another body.' He shrugged. 'After some lifetimes, you might simply just get tired and need a long rest.'

After some mornings, too, Susan thought, 'OK,' she said, 'let's move on. Is this your first visit to Yorkshire?'

'It's my first trip to England, period. I've just qualified in dentistry, and I thought I'd give myself a treat before I settled down to the daily grind.'

Susan winced. Was that a pun? Singer wasn't smiling. A New Age dentist, now there was an interesting combination, she thought. Can I read your tarot cards for you while I drill? Perhaps you might like to take a little astral journey to Neptune while I'm doing your root canal? She forced herself to concentrate on what Singer was saying.

'So, you see,' he went on, 'as I've never been here before, it *must* be real, mustn't it?'

Susan realized she had missed something. 'What?'

'Well, it was all so familiar, the landscape, everything. And it's not only the *déjà vu* I had. There was the dream, too. We haven't even approached this in hypnotic regression yet, so—'

Susan held up her hand. 'Hang on a minute. You're losing me. What was so familiar?'

'Oh, I thought I'd made that clear.'

'Not to me.'

'The place. Where I was murdered. It was near here. In Swainsdale.'

2

Banks was sitting in his office with his feet on the desk and a buff folder open on his lap when Susan Gay popped her head around the door. The top button of his white shirt was undone and his tie hung askew.

That morning, he was supposed to be working on the monthly crime figures, but instead, through the half-open window, he listened to the summer rain as it harmonized with Michael Nyman's soundtrack from *The Piano*, playing quietly on his portable cassette. His eyes were closed and he was daydreaming of waves washing in and out on a beach of pure white sand. The ocean and sky were the brightest blue he could imagine, and tall palm trees dotted the landscape. The pastel village that straddled the steep hillside looked like a cubist collage.

'Sorry to bother you, sir,' Susan said, 'but it looks like we've got a right one here.'

Banks opened his eyes and rubbed them. He felt as if he were coming back from a very long way. 'It's all right,' he said. 'I was getting a bit bored with the crime statistics, anyway.' He tossed the folder onto his desk and linked his hands behind his head. 'Well, what is it?'

Susan entered the office. 'It's sort of hard to explain, sir.'

'Try.'

Susan told him about Jerry Singer. As he listened, Banks's blue eyes sparkled with amusement and interest. When Susan had finished, he thought for a moment, then sat up and turned off the music. 'Why not?' he said. 'It's been a slow week. Let's live dangerously. Bring him in.' He fastened his top button and straightened his tie.

A few moments later, Susan returned with Jerry Singer in tow. Singer looked nervously around the office and took the seat opposite Banks. The two exchanged introductions, then Banks leaned back and lit a cigarette. He loved the mingled smells of smoke and summer rain.

'Perhaps you'd better start at the beginning,' he said.

'Well,' said Singer, turning his nose up at the smoke, 'I've been involved in regressing to past lives for a few years now, partly through hypnosis. It's been a fascinating journey, and I've discovered a great deal about myself.' He sat forward and rested his hands on the desk. His fingers were short and tapered. 'For example, I was a merchant's wife in Venice in the fifteenth century. I had seven children and died giving birth to the eighth. I was only twenty-nine. In my next incarnation, I was an actor in a troupe of Elizabethan players, the Lord Chamberlain's Men. I remember playing Bardolph in *Henry V* in 1599. After that, I—'

'I get the picture,' said Banks. 'I don't mean to be rude, Mr Singer, but maybe we can skip to the twentieth century?'

Singer paused and frowned at Banks. 'Sorry. Well, as I was telling Detective Constable Gay here, it's the least clear one so far. I was a hippie. At least, I think I was. I had long hair, wore a caftan, bell-bottom jeans. And I had this incredible sense of déjà vu when I was driving through Swainsdale yesterday afternoon.'

'Where, exactly?'

'It was just before Fortford. I was coming from Helmthorpe, where I'm staying. There's a small hill by the river with a few trees on it, all bent by the wind. Maybe you know it?'

Banks nodded. He knew the place. The hill was, in fact, a drumlin, a kind of hump-backed mound of detritus left by the retreating ice age. Six trees grew on it, and they had all bent slightly to the south-east after years of strong north-westerly winds. The drumlin was about two miles west of Fortford.

'Is that all?' Banks asked.

'All?'

'Yes.' Banks leaned forward and rested his elbows on the desk. 'You know there are plenty of explanations for déjà vu, don't you, Mr Singer? Perhaps you've seen a place very similar before and only remembered it when you passed the drumlin?'

Singer shook his head. 'I understand your doubts,' he said, 'and I can't offer concrete *proof*, but the *feeling* is unmistakable. I have been there before, in a previous life. I'm certain of it. And that's not all. There's the dream.'

'Dream?'

'Yes. I've had it several times. The same one. It's raining, like today, and I'm passing through a landscape very similar to what I've seen in Swainsdale. I arrive at a very old stone house. There are people and their voices are raised, maybe in anger or laughter, I can't tell. But I start to feel tense and claustrophobic. There's a baby crying somewhere and it won't stop. I climb up some creaky stairs. When I get to the top, I find a door and open it. Then I feel that panicky sensation of endlessly falling, and I usually wake up frightened.'

Banks thought for a moment. 'That's all very interesting,' he said, 'but have you considered that you might have come to the wrong place? We're not usually in the business of interpreting dreams and visions.'

Singer stood his ground. 'This is real,' he said. 'A crime has been committed. Against me.' He poked himself in the chest with his thumb. 'The crime of murder. The least you can do is do me the courtesy of checking your records.' His odd blend of naivety and intensity charged the air.

Banks stared at him, then looked at Susan, whose face showed sceptical interest. Never having been one to shy away from what killed the cat, Banks let his curiosity get the better of him yet again. 'All right,' he said, standing up. 'We'll look into it. Where did you say you were staying?'

3

Banks turned right by the whitewashed sixteenth-century Rose and Crown in Fortford, and stopped just after he had crossed the small stone bridge over the River Swain.

The rain was still falling, obscuring the higher green dale sides and their latticework of drystone walls. Lyndgarth, a cluster of limestone cottages and a church huddled around a small village green, looked like an Impressionist painting. The rain-darkened ruins of Devraulx Abbey, just up the hill to his left, poked through the trees like a setting for *Camelot*.

Banks rolled his window down and listened to the rain slapping against leaves and dancing on the river's surface. To the west he could see the drumlin that Jerry Singer had felt so strongly about.

Today it looked ghostly in the rain, and it was easy to imagine the place as some ancient barrow where the spirits of Bronze Age men lingered. But it wasn't a barrow; it was a drumlin created by glacial deposits. And Jerry Singer hadn't been a Bronze Age man in his previous lifetime; he had been a sixties hippie, or so he believed.

Leaving the window down, Banks drove through Lyndgarth and parked at the end of Gristhorpe's rutted driveway, in front of the squat limestone farmhouse. Inside, he found Gristhorpe staring gloomily out of the back window at a pile of stones and a half-completed drystone wall. The superintendent, he knew, had taken a week's holiday and hoped to work on the wall, which went nowhere and closed in nothing. But he hadn't bargained for the summer rain, which had been falling nonstop for the past two days.

He poured Banks a cup of tea so strong you could stand a spoon up in it, offered some scones, and they sat in Gristhorpe's study. A paperback copy of Trollope's *The Vicar of Bullhampton* lay on small table beside a worn and scuffed brown leather armchair.

'Do you believe in reincarnation?' Banks asked.

Gristhorpe considered the question a moment. 'No. Why?'

Banks told him about Jerry Singer, then said, 'I wanted your opinion. Besides, you were here then, weren't you?'

Gristhorpe's bushy eyebrows knit in a frown. 'Nineteen sixty-six?'

'Yes.'

'I was here, but that's over thirty years ago, Alan. My memory's not what it used to be. Besides, what makes you think there's anything in this other than some New Age fantasy?'

'I don't know that there is,' Banks answered, at a loss how to explain his interest, even to the broad-minded Gristhorpe. Boredom, partly, and the oddness of Singer's claim, the certainty the man seemed to feel about it. But how could he tell his superintendent that he had so little to do he was opening investigations into the supernatural? 'There was a sort of innocence about him,' he said. 'And he seemed so sincere about it, so intense.'

'"The best lack all conviction, while the worst / Are full of passionate intensity." W. B. Yeats,' Gristhorpe replied.

'Perhaps. Anyway, I've arranged to talk to Jenny Fuller about it later today.' Jenny was a psychologist who had worked with the Eastvale police before.

'Good idea,' said Gristhorpe. 'All right, then, just for argument's sake, let's examine his claim objectively. He's convinced he was a hippie murdered in Swainsdale in summer, nineteen sixty-six, right?'

Banks nodded.

'And he thinks this because he believes in reincarnation, he had a déjà vu and he's had a recurring dream?'

'True.'

'Now,' Gristhorpe went on, 'leaving aside the question of whether you or I believe in reincarnation, or, indeed, whether there is such a thing – a philosophical speculation we could hardly settle over tea and scones, anyway – he doesn't give us a hell of a lot to go on, does he?'

'That's the problem. I thought you might remember something.'

Gristhorpe sighed and shifted in his chair. The scuffed leather creaked. 'In nineteen sixty-six, I was a thirty-year-old detective sergeant in a backwoods division. In fact, we were nothing but a sub-division then, and I was the senior detective. Most of the time I investigated burglaries, the occasional outbreak of sheep stealing, market-stall owners fencing stolen goods.' He sipped some tea. 'We had one or two murders – really interesting ones I'll tell you about someday – but not a lot. What I'm saying, Alan, is that no matter how poor my memory is, I'd remember a murdered hippie.'

'And nothing fits the bill?'

'Nothing. I'm not saying we didn't have a few hippies around, but none of them got murdered. I think your Mr Singer must be mistaken.'

Banks put his mug down on the table and stood up to leave. 'Better get back to the crime statistics, then,' he said.

Gristhorpe smiled. 'So *that's* why you're so interested in this cock and bull story? Can't say I blame you. Sorry I can't help. Wait a minute, though,' he added as they walked to the door. 'There was old Bert Atherton's lad. I suppose that was around the time you're talking about, give or take a year or two.'

Banks paused at the door. 'Atherton?'

'Aye. Owns a farm between Lyndgarth and Helmthorpe. Or did. He's dead now. I only mention it because Atherton's son, Joseph, was something of a hippie.'

'What happened?'

'Fell down the stairs and broke his neck. Family never got over it. As I said, old man Atherton died a couple of years back, but his missis is still around.'

'You'd no reason to suspect anything?'

Gristhorpe shook his head. 'None at all. The Athertons were a decent, hard-working family. Apparently the lad was visiting them on his way to Scotland to join some commune or other. He fell down the stairs. It's a pretty isolated spot, and it was too late when the ambulance arrived, especially as they had to drive a mile down country lanes to the nearest telephone box. They were really devastated. He was their only child.'

'What made him fall?'

'He wasn't pushed, if that's what you're thinking. There was no stair carpet and the steps were a bit slippery. According to his dad, Joseph was walking around without his slippers on and he slipped in his stockinged feet.'

'And you've no reason to doubt him?'

'No. I did have one small suspicion at the time, though.'

'What?'

'According to the post-mortem, Joseph Atherton was a heroin addict, though he didn't have any traces of the drug in his system at the time of his death. I thought he might have been smoking marijuana or something up in his room. That might have made him a bit unsteady on his feet.'

'Did you search the place?'

Gristhorpe snorted. 'Nay, Alan. There was no sense bringing more grief on his parents. What would we do if we found something, charge *them* with possession?'

'I see your point.' Banks opened the door and put up his collar against the rain. 'I might dig up the file anyway,' he called, running over to the car. 'Enjoy the rest of your week off.'

Gristhorpe's curse was lost in the sound of the engine starting up and the finale of Mussorgsky's 'Great Gate of Kiev' on Classic FM, blasting out from the radio, which Banks had forgotten to switch off.

4

In addition to the cells and the charge room, the lower floor of Eastvale Divisional Headquarters housed old files and records. The dank room was lit by a single bare light bulb and packed with dusty files. So far, Banks had checked nineteen sixty-five and sixty-six but found nothing on the Atherton business.

Give or take a couple of years, Gristhorpe had said. Without much hope, Banks reached for nineteen sixty-four. That was a bit too early for hippies, he thought, especially in the far reaches of rural North Yorkshire.

In nineteen sixty-four, he remembered, the Beatles were still recording ballads like 'I'll Follow the Sun' and old rockers like 'Long Tall Sally'. John hadn't met Yoko, and there wasn't a sitar within earshot. The Rolling Stones were doing 'Not Fade Away' and 'It's All Over Now', the Kinks had a huge hit with 'You Really Got Me', and the charts were full of Dusty Springfield, Peter and Gordon, the Dave Clark Five and Herman's Hermits.

So nineteen sixty-four was a write-off as far as dead hippies were concerned. Banks looked anyway. Maybe Joseph Atherton had been way ahead of his time. Or perhaps Jerry Singer's channeller had been wrong about the time between incarnations. Why was this whole charade taking on such an aura of unreality?

Banks's stomach rumbled. Apart from that scone at Gristhorpe's, he hadn't eaten since breakfast, he realized. He put the file aside. Though there hardly seemed any point looking further ahead than nineteen sixty-six, he did so out of curiosity. Just as he was feeling success slip away, he came across it: Joseph Atherton. Coroner's verdict: accidental death. There was only one problem: it had happened in 1969.

According to the Athertons' statement, their son wrote to say he was coming to see them en route to Scotland. He said he was on his way to join some sort of commune and arrived at Eastvale station on the London train at three forty-five in the afternoon, 11 July 1969. By ten o'clock that night he was dead. He didn't have transport of his own, so his father had met him at the station in the Land Rover and driven him back to the farm.

Banks picked up a sheet of lined writing paper, yellowed around the edges. A separate sheet described it as an anonymous note received at the Eastvale police station about a week after the coroner's verdict. All it said, in block capitals, was, 'Ask Atherton about the red Volkswagen.'

Next came a brief interview report, in which a PC Wythers said he had questioned the Athertons about the car and they said they didn't know what he was talking about. That was that.

Banks supposed it was remotely possible that whoever was in the red Volkswagen had killed Joseph Atherton. But why would his parents lie? According to the statement, they spent the evening together at the farm eating dinner, catching up on family news, then Joseph went up to his room to unpack and came down in his stockinged feet. Maybe he'd been smoking marijuana, as Gristhorpe suggested. Anyway, he slipped at the top of the stairs and broke his neck. It was tragic, but hardly what Banks was looking for.

He heard a sound at the door and looked up to see Susan Gay.

'Found anything, sir?' she asked.

'Maybe,' said Banks. 'One or two loose ends. But I haven't a clue what it all means, if anything. I'm beginning to wish I'd never seen Mr Jerry Singer.'

Susan smiled. 'Do you know, sir,' she said, 'he almost had me believing him.'

Banks put the file aside. 'Did he? I suppose it always pays to keep an open mind,' he said. 'That's why we're going to visit Mrs Atherton.'

5

The Atherton farm was every bit as isolated as Gristhorpe had said, and the relentless rain had muddied the lane. At one point Banks thought they would have to get out and push, but on the third try the wheels caught and the car lurched forward.

The farmyard looked neglected: bedraggled weeds poked

through the mud; part of the barn roof had collapsed; and the wheels and tines of the old hayrake had rusted.

Mrs Atherton answered their knock almost immediately. Banks had phoned ahead so their arrival wouldn't frighten her. After all, a woman living alone in such a wild place couldn't be too careful.

She led them into the large kitchen and put the kettle on the Aga. The stone-walled room looked clean and tidy enough, but Banks noted an underlying smell, like old greens and meat rotting under the sink.

Mrs Atherton carried the aura of the sickroom about with her. Her complexion was as grey as her sparse hair; her eyes were dull yellow with milky blue irises; and the skin below them looked dark as a bruise. As she made the tea, she moved slowly, as if measuring the energy required for each step. How on earth, Banks wondered, did she manage up here all by herself? Yorkshire grit was legendary, and as often close to fool hardiness as anything else, he thought.

She put the teapot on the table. 'We'll just let it mash a minute,' she said. 'Now, what is it you want to talk to me about?'

Banks didn't know how to begin. He had no intention of telling Mrs Atherton about Jerry Singer's 'previous lifetime', or of interrogating her about her son's death. Which didn't leave him many options.

'How are you managing?' he asked first.

'Mustn't grumble.'

'It must be hard, taking care of this place all by yourself?'

'Nay, there's not much to do these days. Jack Crocker keeps an eye on the sheep. I've nobbut got a few cows to milk.'

'No poultry?'

'Nay, it's not worth it any more, not with these battery farms. Anyway, seeing as you're a copper, I don't suppose you came to talk to me about the farming life, did you? Come on, spit it out, lad.'

Banks noticed Susan look down and smile. 'Well,' he said, 'I hate to bring up a painful subject, but it's your son's death we want to talk to you about.'

Mrs Atherton looked at Susan as if noticing her for the first time. A shadow crossed her face. Then she turned back to Banks. 'Our Joseph?' she said. 'But he's been dead nigh on thirty years.'

'I know that,' said Banks. 'We won't trouble you for long.'

'There's nowt else to add.' She poured the tea, fussed with milk and sugar, and sat down again.

'You said your son wrote and said he was coming?'

'Aye.'

'Did you keep the letter?'

'What?'

'The letter. I've not seen any mention of it anywhere. It's not in the file.'

'Well, it wouldn't be, would it? We don't leave scraps of paper cluttering up the place.'

'So you threw it out?'

'Aye. Bert or me.' She looked at Susan again. 'That was my husband, God rest his soul. Besides,' she said, 'how else would we know he was coming? We couldn't afford a telephone back then.'

'I know,' said Banks. But nobody had asked at the railway station whether Bert Atherton actually *had* met his son there, and now it was too late. He sipped some tea; it tasted as if the teabag had been used before. 'I don't suppose you remember seeing a red Volkswagen in the area around that time, do you?'

'No. They asked us that when it first happened. I didn't know owt about it then, and I don't know owt now.'

'Was there anyone else in the house when the accident occurred?'

'No, of course there weren't. Do you think I wouldn't have said if there were? Look, young man, what are you getting at? Do you have summat to tell me, summat I should know?'

Banks sighed and took another sip of weak tea. It didn't wash away the taste of decay that permeated the kitchen. He signalled to Susan and stood up. 'No,' he said. 'No, I've nothing new to tell you, Mrs Atherton. Just chasing will o' the wisps, that's all.'

'Well, I'm sorry, but you'll have to go chase 'em somewhere else, lad. I've got work to do.'

6

The Queen's Arms was quiet late that afternoon. Rain had kept the tourists away, and at four o'clock most of the locals were still at work in the offices and shops around the market square. Banks ordered a pork pie, then he and Jenny Fuller took their drinks to an isolated corner table and settled down. The first long draught of Theakston's bitter washed the archive dust and the taste of decay from Banks's throat.

'Well,' said Jenny, raising her glass of lager in a toast. 'To what do I owe the honour?'

She looked radiant, Banks thought: thick red hair tumbling over her shoulders, emerald green eyes full of humour and vitality, a fresh scent that cut through the atmosphere of stale smoke and made him think of childhood apple orchards. Though Banks was married, he and Jenny had once come very close to getting involved, and every now and then he felt a pang of regret for the road not taken.

'Reincarnation,' said Banks, clinking glasses.

Jenny raised her eyebrows. 'You know I'll drink to most things,' she said, 'but really, Alan, isn't this going a bit far?'

Banks explained what had happened so far that day. By the time he had finished, the barman delivered his pork pie, along with a large pickled onion. As Jenny mulled over what he had said, he sliced the pie into quarters and shook a dollop of HP Sauce onto his plate to dip them in.

'Fantasy,' she said finally.

'Would you care to elaborate?'

'If you don't believe in reincarnation, then there are an awful lot of strange phenomena you have to explain in more rational ways. Now, I'm no expert on parapsychology, but most people who claim to have lived past lifetimes generally become convinced through hypnosis, dreams and déjà vu experiences, like the ones you mentioned, or by spontaneous recall.'

'What's that?'

'Exactly what it sounds like. Remembering past lifetimes out of the blue. Children playing the piano without lessons, people suddenly speaking foreign languages, that kind of thing. Or any memory you have but can't explain, something that seems to have come from beyond your experience.'

'You mean if I'm walking down the street and I suddenly think of a Roman soldier and remember some sort of Latin phrase, then I'm recalling a previous lifetime?'

Jenny gave him a withering look. 'Don't be so silly, Alan. Of course *I* don't think that. Some people might, though. People are limitlessly gullible, it seems to me, especially when it comes to life after death. No, what I mean is that this is the kind of thing believers try to put forward as proof of reincarnation.'

'And how would a rational psychologist explain it?'

'She might argue that what a person recalls under hypnosis, in dreams, or wherever, is simply a web of fantasy woven from things that person has already seen or heard and maybe forgotten.'

'But he says he's never been here before.'

'There's television, books, films.'

Banks finished his pork pie, took a swig of Theakston's and lit a Silk Cut. 'So you're saying that maybe our Mr Singer has watched one too many episodes of *All Creatures Great and Small*?'

Jenny tossed back her hair and laughed, 'It wouldn't surprise me.' She looked at her watch, then drained her glass. 'Look, I'm sorry, but I must dash.' And with that, she jumped up, pecked him on the cheek and left. Jenny was always dashing, it seemed. Sometimes he wondered where.

Banks thought over what she had said. It made sense. More sense than Singer's reincarnation theory and more sense than suspecting Joseph Atherton's parents of covering up their son's murder.

But there remained the unsubstantiated story of the letter and the anonymous note about the red Volkswagen. If somebody else *had* driven Joseph Atherton to the farm, then his parents had been lying about the letter. Why? And who could it have been?

7

Two days later, sorting through his post, Banks found a letter addressed to him in longhand. It stood out like a sore thumb among the usual bundle of circulars and official communications. He spread it open on his desk in front of him and read.

Dear Mr Banks,

I'm not much of a one for letter writing so you must forgive me any mistakes. I didn't get much schooling due to me being a sickly child but my father always told us it was important to read and write. Your visit last week upset me by raking up the past I'd rather forget. I don't know what made you come and ask those questions but they made me think it is time to make my peace with God and tell the truth after all these years.

What we told the police was not true. Our Joseph didn't write to say he was coming and Bert didn't pick him up at the station. Joseph just turned up out of the blue one afternoon in that red car. I don't know who told the police about the car but I think it might have been Len Grimond in the farm down the road because he had fallen out with Bert over paying for repairs to a wall.

Anyway, it wasn't our Joseph's car. There was an American lass with him called Annie and she was driving. They had a baby with them that they said was theirs. I suppose that made him our grandson but it was the first time we ever heard about him. Our Joseph hadn't written or visited us for four years and we didn't know if he was alive or dead. He was a bonny little lad about two or three with the most solemn look on his face.

Well it was plain from the start that something was wrong. We tried to behave like good loving parents and welcome them into our home but the girl was moody and she didn't want to stay. The baby cried a lot and I don't think he had been looked after properly, though it's not my place to say. And Joseph was behaving very peculiar. His eyes looked all glassy with tiny pupils. We didn't know what was the matter. I think from what he said that he just wanted money.

They wouldn't eat much though I cooked a good roast for them, and Yorkshire puddings too, but our Joseph just picked at his food and the girl sat there all sulky holding the baby and wanting to go. She said she was a vegetarian. After we'd finished the dinner Joseph got very upset and said he had to go to the toilet. By then Bert was wondering what was going on and also a bit angry at how they treated our hospitality even if Joseph was our son.

Joseph was a long time in the toilet. Bert called up to him but he didn't answer. The girl said something about leaving him alone and laughed, but it wasn't a nice laugh. We thought something might be wrong with him so Bert went up and found Joseph with a piece of string tied around his arm heating something in a spoon with a match. It was one of our silver anniversary spoons he had taken from the kitchen without asking. We were just ignorant farmers and didn't know what was happening in crime and drugs and everything like you do, Mr Banks, but we knew our Joseph was doing something bad.

Bert lost his temper and pulled Joseph out of the toilet. When they were at the top of the stairs, Joseph started swearing at his father, using such words I've never heard before and would blush to repeat. That's when Bert lost his temper and hit him. On God's honour, he didn't mean to hurt him. Joseph was our only son and we loved him even though he was breaking my heart. But when Bert hit him Joseph fell down the stairs and when he got to the bottom his head was at such a funny angle I knew he must have broken his neck.

The girl started screaming then took the baby and ran outside and drove away. We have never seen her again or our grandson and don't know what has become of him. There was such a silence like you have never heard when the sound of the car engine vanished in the distance and Joseph was laying at the bottom of the stairs all twisted and broken. We tried to feel his pulse and Bert even put a mirror to his mouth to see if his breath would mist it but there was nothing.

I know we should have told the truth and we have regretted it for all those years. We were always brought up to be decent honest folk respecting our parents and God and the law. Bert was ashamed that his son was a drug addict and didn't want it in the papers. I didn't want him to go to jail for what he had done because it was really an accident and it wasn't fair. He was suffering more than enough anyway because he had killed his only son.

So I said we must throw away all the drugs and needle and things and take our Joseph's shoes off and say he slipped coming down the stairs. We knew that the police would believe us because we were good people and we had no reason to lie. That was the hardest part. The laces got tied in knots and I broke my fingernails and in the end I was shaking so much I had to use the scissors.

And that is God's honest truth, Mr Banks. I know we did wrong but Bert was never the same after. Not a day went by when he didn't cry about what he'd done and I never saw him smile ever again. To this day we still do not know what has become of our grandson but whatever it is we hope he is healthy and happy and not as foolish as his father.

By the time you read this letter I'll be gone to my resting place too. For two years now I have had cancer and no matter what operations they do it is eating me away. I have saved my tablets. Now that I have taken the weight off my conscience I can only hope that the good Lord sees fit to forgive me my sins and take me unto his bosom.

Yours sincerely,
Betty Atherton

Banks put the letter aside and rubbed his left eye with the back of his hand. Outside, the rain was still falling, providing a gentle background for Finzi's Clarinet Concerto on the portable cassette. Banks stared at the sheets of blue vellum covered in Betty Atherton's crabbed hand, then he cursed, slammed his fist on the desk, went to the door and shouted for Susan Gay.

8

'Her name is Catherine Anne Singer,' said Susan the next afternoon. 'And she was relieved to talk to me as soon as I told her we weren't after her for leaving the scene of a crime. She comes from somewhere called Garden Grove, California. Like a lot of young Americans, she came over to "do" Europe in the sixties.'

The three of them – Banks, Susan and Jenny Fuller – sat over drinks at a dimpled, copper-topped table in the Queen's Arms listening to the summer rain tap against the diamonds of coloured glass.

'And she's Jerry Singer's mother?' Banks asked.

Susan nodded. 'Yes. I just asked him for her telephone number. I didn't tell him why I wanted it.'

Banks nodded. 'Good. Go on.'

'Well, she ended up living in London. It was easy enough to get jobs that paid under the counter, places where nobody asked too many questions. Eventually, she hooked up with Joseph Atherton and they lived together in a bedsit in Notting Hill. Joseph fancied himself as a musician then—'

'Who didn't?' said Banks. He remembered taking a few abortive guitar lessons himself. 'Sorry. Go on.'

'There's not a lot to add, sir. She got pregnant, wouldn't agree to an abortion, though apparently Joseph tried to persuade her. She named the child Jerry, after some guitarist Joseph liked called Jerry Garcia. Luckily for Jerry, Annie wasn't on heroin. She drew the line at hash and LSD. Anyway, they were off to join some Buddhist commune in the wilds of Scotland when Joseph said they should drop in on his parents on the way and try to get some money. She didn't like the idea, but she went along with it anyway.

'Everything happened exactly as Mrs Atherton described it. Annie got scared and ran away. When she got back to London, she decided it was time to go home. She sold the car and took out all her savings from the bank, then she got the first flight she could and settled back in California. She went to university and ended up working as a marine biologist in San Diego. She never married, and she never mentioned her time in England, or that night at the Atherton farm, to Jerry. She told him his father had left them when Jerry was still a baby. He was only two and a half at the time of Atherton's death, and as far as he was concerned he had spent his entire life in southern California.'

Banks drained his pint and looked at Jenny.

'Cryptomnesia,' she said.

'Come again?'

'Cryptomnesia. It means memories you're not consciously aware of, a memory of an incident in your own life that you've forgotten. Jerry Singer was present when his grandfather knocked his father down the stairs, but as far as he was concerned *consciously*, he'd never been to Swainsdale before, so how could he remember it? When he got mixed up in the New Age scene, these memories he didn't know he had started to seem like some sort of proof of reincarnation.'

Sometimes, Banks thought to himself, things are better left alone. The thought surprised him because it went against the grain of both his job and his innate curiosity. But what good had come from Jerry Singer presenting himself at the station three days ago? None at all. Perhaps the only blessing in the whole affair was that Betty Atherton had passed away peacefully, as she had intended, in her pill-induced sleep. Now she wouldn't suffer any more in this world. And if there were a God, Banks thought, he surely couldn't be such a bastard as to let her suffer in the next one, either.

'Sir?'

'Sorry, Susan, I was miles away.'

'I asked who was going to tell him. You or me?'

'I'll do it,' said Banks, with a sigh. 'It's no good trying to sit on it all now. But I need another pint first. My shout.'

As he stood up to go to the bar, the door opened and Jerry Singer walked in. He spotted them at once and walked over. He had that strange naive, intense look in his eyes. Banks instinctively reached for his cigarettes.

'They told me you were here,' Singer said awkwardly, pointing back through the door towards the Tudor-fronted police station across the street. 'I'm leaving for home tomorrow and I was just wondering if you'd found anything out yet?'

FAN MAIL

The letter arrived one sunny Thursday morning in August, along with a Visa bill and a royalty statement. Dennis Quilley carried the mail out to the deck of his Beaches home, stopping by the kitchen on the way to pour himself a gin and tonic. He had already been writing for three hours straight and he felt he deserved a drink.

First he looked at the amount of the royalty cheque, then he put aside the Visa bill and picked up the letter carefully, as if he were a forensic expert investigating it for prints. Postmarked Toronto and dated four days earlier, it was addressed in a small, precise hand and looked as if it had been written with a fine-nibbed calligraphic pen. But the post code was different; that had been hurriedly scrawled in with a ballpoint. Whoever it was, Quilley thought, had probably got his name from the telephone directory and had then looked up the code in the post office just before mailing.

Pleased with his deductions, Quilley opened the letter. Written in the same neat and mannered hand as the address, it said:

Dear Mr Quilley,

Please forgive me for writing to you at home like this. I know you must be very busy, and it is inexcusable of me to intrude on your valuable time. Believe me, I would not do so if I could think of any other way.

I have been a great fan of your work for many years

now. As a collector of mysteries, too, I also have first editions of all your books. From what I have read, I know you are a clever man and, I hope, just the man to help me with my problem.

For the past twenty years, my wife has been making my life a misery. I put up with her for the sake of the children, but now they have all gone to live their own lives. I have asked her for a divorce, but she just laughed in my face. I have decided, finally, that the only way out is to kill her and that is why I am seeking your advice.

You may think this is insane of me, especially saying it in a letter, but it is just a measure of my desperation. I would quite understand it if you went straight to the police, and I am sure they would find me and punish me. Believe me, I've thought about it. Even that would be preferable to the misery I must suffer day after day.

If you can find it in your heart to help a devoted fan in his hour of need, please meet me on the roof lounge of the Park Plaza Hotel on Wednesday, 19 August at two p.m. I have taken the afternoon off work and will wait longer if for any reason you are delayed. Don't worry, I will recognize you easily from your photo on the dust jacket of your books.

Yours, in hope,
A Fan

The letter slipped from Quilley's hand. He couldn't believe what he'd just read. He was a mystery writer – he specialized in devising ingenious murders – but for someone to assume that he did the same in real life was absurd. Could it be a practical joke?

He picked up the letter and read through it again. The man's whining tone and clichéd style seemed sincere enough, and the more Quilley thought about it, the more certain he became that none of his friends was sick enough to play such a joke.

Assuming that it was real, then, what should he do? His impulse was to crumple up the letter and throw it away. But should he go to the police? No. That would be a waste of time. The real police were a terribly dull and literal-minded lot. They would probably think he was seeking publicity.

He found that he had screwed up the sheet of paper in his fist, and he was just about to toss it aside when he changed his mind. Wasn't there another option? Go. Go and meet the man. Find out more about him. Find out if he was genuine. Surely there would be no obligation in that? All he had to do was turn up at the Park Plaza at the appointed time and see what happened.

Quilley's life was fine – no troublesome woman to torment him, plenty of money (mostly from American sales), a beautiful lakeside cottage near Huntsville, a modicum of fame, the esteem of his peers – but it had been rather boring of late. Here was an opportunity for adventure of a kind. Besides, he might get a story idea out of the meeting. Why not go and see?

He finished his drink and smoothed the letter on his knee. He had to smile at that last bit. No doubt the man would recognize him from his book-jacket photo, but it was an old one and had been retouched in the first place. His cheeks had filled out a bit since then and his thinning hair had acquired a sprinkling of grey. Still, he thought, he was a handsome man for fifty: handsome, clever and successful.

Smiling, he picked up both letter and envelope and went back to the kitchen in search of matches. There must be no evidence.

•

Over the next few days Quilley hardly gave a thought to the mysterious letter. As usual in summer, he divided his time between writing in Toronto, where he found the city worked as a stimulus, and weekends at the cottage. There he walked in the woods, chatted to locals in the lodge, swam in the clear lake and idled around getting a tan. Evenings, he would open a bottle of Chardonnay, reread P. G. Wodehouse and listen to Bach. It was an ideal life: quiet, solitary, independent.

When Wednesday came, though, he drove downtown, parked in the multi-storey at Cumberland and Avenue Road, then walked to the Park Plaza. It was another hot day. The tourists were out in force across Bloor Street by the Royal Ontario Museum, many of them Americans from Buffalo, Rochester or Detroit: the men in loud-checked shirts photographing everything in sight, their wives in tight shorts looking tired and thirsty.

Quilley took the elevator up to the nineteenth floor and wandered through the bar, an olde-worlde place with deep armchairs and framed reproductions of old Colonial scenes on the walls. It was busier than usual, and even though the windows were open, the smoke bothered him. He walked out onto the roof lounge and scanned the faces. Within moments he noticed someone looking his way. The man paused for just a split second, perhaps to translate the dust-jacket photo into reality, then beckoned Quilley over with raised eyebrows and a twitch of the head.

The man rose to shake hands, then sat down again, glancing around to make sure nobody had paid the two of them undue attention. He was short and thin, with sandy hair and a pale grey complexion, as if he had just come out of hospital. He wore wire-rimmed glasses and had a habit of rolling his tongue around in his mouth when he wasn't talking.

'First of all, Mr Quilley,' the man said, raising his glass, 'may I say how honoured I am to meet you.' He spoke with a pronounced English accent.

Quilley inclined his head. 'I'm flattered, Mr . . . er . . . ?'

'Peplow, Frank Peplow.'

'Yes . . . Mr Peplow. But I must admit I'm puzzled by your letter.'

A waiter in a burgundy jacket came over to take Quilley's order. He asked for an Amstel.

Peplow paused until the waiter was out of earshot. 'Puzzled?'

'What I mean is,' Quilley went on, struggling for the right words, 'whether you were serious or not, whether you really do want to—'

Peplow leaned forward. Behind the lenses, his pale blue eyes looked sane enough. 'I assure you, Mr Quilley, that I was, that I *am* entirely serious. That woman is ruining my life and I can't allow it to go on any longer.'

Speaking about her brought little spots of red to his cheeks. Quilley held his hand up. 'All right, I believe you. I suppose you realize I should have gone to the police?'

'But you didn't.'

'I could have. They might be here, watching us.'

Peplow shook his head. 'Mr Quilley, if you won't help, I'd even welcome prison. Don't think I haven't realized that I might get caught, that no murder is perfect. All I want is a chance. It's worth the risk.'

The waiter returned with Quilley's drink and they both sat in silence until he had gone. Quilley was intrigued by this drab man sitting opposite him, a man who obviously didn't even have the imagination to dream up his own murder plot. 'What do you want from me?' he asked.

'I have no right to ask anything of you, I understand that,' Peplow said. 'I have absolutely nothing to offer in return. I'm not rich. I have no savings. I suppose all I want really is advice, encouragement.'

'If I were to help,' Quilley said, 'if I were to help, then I'd do nothing more than offer advice. Is that clear?'

Peplow nodded. 'Does that mean you will?'

'If I can.'

And so Dennis Quilley found himself helping to plot the murder of a woman he'd never met with a man he didn't even particularly like. Later, when he analysed his reasons for playing along, he realized that that was exactly what he had been doing – playing. It had been a game, a cerebral puzzle, just like thinking up a plot for a book, and he never, at first, gave a thought to real murder, real blood, real death.

Peplow took a handkerchief from his top pocket and wiped the thin film of sweat from his brow. 'You don't know how happy this makes me, Mr Quilley. At last I have a chance. My life hasn't amounted to much and I don't suppose it ever will. But at least I might find some peace and quiet in my final years. I'm not a well man.' He placed one hand solemnly over his chest. 'Ticker. Not fair, is it? I've never smoked, I hardly drink, and I'm only fifty-three. But the doctor has promised me a few years yet if I live right. All I want is to be left alone with my books and my garden.'

'Tell me about your wife,' Quilley prompted.

Peplow's expression darkened. 'She's a cruel and selfish woman,' he said. 'And she's messy, she never does anything around the place. Too busy watching those damn soap operas on television day and night. She cares about nothing but her own comfort, and she never overlooks an opportunity to nag me or taunt me. If I try to escape to my collection, she mocks me and calls me dull and boring. I'm not even safe from her in my garden. I realize I have no imagination, Mr Quilley, and perhaps even less courage, but even a man like me deserves some peace in his life, don't you think?'

Quilley had to admit that the woman really did sound awful – worse than any he had known, and he had met some shrews in his time. He had never had much use for women, except for occasional sex in his younger days. Even that had become sordid, and now he stayed away from them as much as possible. He found, as he listened, that he could summon up remarkable sympathy for Peplow's position.

'What do you have in mind?' he asked.

'I don't really know. That's why I wrote to you. I was hoping you might be able to help with some ideas. Your books . . . you seem to know so much.'

'In my books,' Quilley said, 'the murderer always gets caught.'

'Well, yes,' said Peplow, 'of course. But that's because the genre demands it, isn't it? I mean, your Inspector Baldry is much smarter than any real policeman. I'm sure if you'd made him a criminal, he would always get away.'

There was no arguing with that, Quilley thought. 'How do you want to do it?' he asked. 'A domestic accident? Electric shock, say? Gadget in the bathtub? She must have a hair curler or a dryer?'

Peplow shook his head, eyes tightly closed. 'Oh no,' he whispered, 'I couldn't. I couldn't do anything like that. No more than I could bear the sight of her blood.'

'How's her health?'

'Unfortunately,' said Peplow, 'she seems obscenely robust.'

'How old is she?'

'Forty-nine.'

'Any bad habits?'

'Mr Quilley, my wife has nothing *but* bad habits. The only thing she won't tolerate is drink, for some reason, and I don't think she has other men – though that's probably because nobody will have her.'

'Does she smoke?'

'Like a chimney.'

Quilley shuddered. 'How long?'

'Ever since she was a teenager, I think. Before I met her.'

'Does she exercise?'

'Never.'

'What about her weight, her diet?'

'Well, you might not call her fat, but you'd be generous in saying she was full-figured. She eats too much junk food. I've always said that. And eggs. She loves bacon and eggs for breakfast. And she's always stuffing herself with cream cakes and tarts.'

'Hmmm,' said Quilley, taking a sip of Amstel. 'She sounds like a prime candidate for a heart attack.'

'But it's me who—' Peplow stopped as comprehension dawned. 'Yes, I see. You mean one could be *induced*?'

'Quite. Do you think you could manage that?'

'Well, I could if I didn't have to be there to watch. But I don't know how.'

'Poison.'

'I don't know anything about poison.'

'Never mind. Give me a few days to look into it. I'll give you advice, remember, but that's as far as it goes.'

'Understood.'

Quilley smiled. 'Good. Another beer?'

'No, I'd better not. She'll be able to smell this one on my breath and I'll be in for it already. I'd better go.'

Quilley looked at his watch. Two-thirty. He could have done with another Amstel, but he didn't want to stay there by himself. Besides, at three it would be time to meet his agent at the Four Seasons, and there he would have the opportunity to drink as much as he wanted. To pass the time, he could browse in Book City. 'Fine,' he said, 'I'll go down with you.'

Outside on the hot, busy street, they shook hands and agreed to meet in a week's time on the back patio of the Madison Avenue Pub. It wouldn't do to be seen together twice in the same place.

Quilley stood on the corner of Bloor and Avenue Road among the camera-clicking tourists and watched Peplow walk off towards the St George subway station. Now that their meeting was over and the spell was broken, he wondered again what the hell he was doing helping this pathetic little man. It certainly wasn't altruism. Perhaps the challenge appealed to him; after all, people climb mountains just because they're there.

And then there was Peplow's mystery collection. There was just a chance that it might contain an item of great interest to Quilley and that Peplow might be grateful enough to part with it.

Wondering how to approach the subject at their next meeting, Quilley wiped the sweat from his brow with the back of his hand and walked towards the bookshop.

•

Atropine, hyoscyamine, belladonna . . . Quilley flipped through Dreisbach's *Handbook of Poisoning* one evening at the cottage. Poison seemed to have gone out of fashion these days, and he had only used it in one of his novels, about six years ago. That had been the old standby, cyanide, with its familiar smell of bitter almonds, which he had so often read about but never experienced. The small black handbook had sat on his shelf gathering dust ever since.

Writing a book, of course, one could generally skip over the problems of acquiring the stuff – give the killer a job as a pharmacist or in a hospital dispensary, for example. In real life, getting one's hands on poison might prove more difficult.

So far, he had read through the sections on agricultural poisons, household hazards and medicinal poisons. The problem was that whatever Peplow used had to be easily available. Prescription drugs were out. Even if Peplow could persuade a doctor to give him barbiturates, for example, the prescription would be on record and any death in the household would be regarded as suspicious. Barbiturates wouldn't do, anyway, and nor would such common products as paint thinner, insecticides and weed killers – they didn't reproduce the symptoms of a heart attack.

Near the back of the book was a list of poisonous plants that shocked Quilley by its sheer length. He hadn't known just how much deadliness there was lurking in fields, gardens and woods. Rhubarb leaves contained oxalic acid, for example, and caused nausea, vomiting and diarrhoea. The bark, wood, leaves or seeds of the yew had a similar effect. Boxwood leaves and twigs caused convulsions; celandine could bring about a coma; hydrangeas contained cyanide; and laburnums brought on irregular pulse, delirium, twitching and unconsciousness. And so the list went on – lupins, mistletoe, sweet peas, rhododendron – a poisoner's delight. Even the beautiful poinsettia, which brightened up so many Toronto homes each Christmas, could cause gastroenteritis. Most of these plants were easy to get hold of, and in many cases the active ingredients could be extracted simply by soaking or boiling in water.

It wasn't long before Quilley found what he was looking for. Beside 'Oleander' the note read, 'See *digitalis*, 374.' And there it was, set out in detail. Digitalis occurred in all parts of the common foxglove, which grew on waste ground and woodland slopes, and flowered from June to September. Acute poisoning would bring about death from ventricular fibrillation. No doctor would consider an autopsy if Peplow's wife appeared to die of a heart attack, given her habits, especially if Peplow fed her a few smaller doses first to establish the symptoms.

Quilley set aside the book. It was already dark outside, and the downpour that the humid, cloudy day had been promising had just begun. Rain slapped against the asphalt roof tiles, gurgled down the drainpipe and pattered on the leaves of the overhanging trees. In the background, it hissed as it fell on the lake. Distant flashes of lightning and deep rumblings of thunder warned of the coming storm.

Happy with his solitude and his cleverness, Quilley linked his hands behind his head and leaned back in the chair. Out back, he heard the rustling of a small animal making its way through the undergrowth – a raccoon, perhaps, or even a skunk. When he closed his eyes, he pictured all the trees, shrubs and wild flowers around the cottage and marvelled at the deadly potential so many of them contained.

•

The sun blazed down on the back patio of the Madison, a small garden protected from the wind by high fences. Quilley wore his sunglasses and nursed a pint of Conner's Ale. The place was packed. Skilled and pretty waitresses came and went, trays laden with baskets of chicken wings and golden pints of lager.

The two of them sat out of the way at a white table in a corner by the metal fire escape. A striped parasol offered some protection, but the sun was still too hot and too bright. Peplow's wife must have given him hell about drinking the last time because today he had ordered only a Coke.

'It was easy,' Quilley said. 'You could have done it yourself. The only setback was that foxgloves don't grow wild here like they do in England. But you're a gardener; you grow them.'

Peplow shook his head and smiled. 'It's the gift of clever people like yourself to make difficult things seem easy. I'm not particularly resourceful, Mr Quilley. Believe me, I wouldn't have known where to start. I had no idea that such a book existed, but you did because of your art. Even if I had known, I'd hardly have dared buy it or take it out of the library for fear that someone would remember. But you've had your copy for years. A simple tool of the trade. No, Mr Quilley, please don't underestimate your contribution. I was a desperate man. Now you've given me a chance at freedom. If there's anything at all I can do for you, please don't hesitate to say. I'd consider it an honour.'

'This collection of yours,' Quilley said. 'What does it consist of?'

'British and Canadian crime fiction, mostly. I don't like to boast, but it's a very good collection. Try me. Go on, just mention a name.'

'E. C. R. Lorac.'

'About twenty of the Inspector MacDonalds. First editions, mint condition.'

'Anne Hocking?'

'Everything but *Night's Candles*.'

'Trotton?'

Peplow raised his eyebrows. 'Good Lord, that's an obscure one. Do you know, you're the first person I've come across who's ever mentioned that.'

'Do you have it?'

'Oh, yes.' Peplow smiled smugly. 'X. J. Trotton, *Signed in Blood*, published 1942. It turned up in a pile of junk I bought at an auction some years ago. It's rare, but not very valuable. Came out in Britain during the war and probably died an immediate death. It was his only book, as far as I can make out, and there is no biographical information. Perhaps it was a pseudonym for someone famous?'

Quilley shook his head. 'I'm afraid I don't know. Have you read it?'

'Good Lord, no! I don't read them. It could damage the spines.

Many of them are fragile. Anything I want to read – like your books – I also buy in paperback.'

'Mr Peplow,' Quilley said slowly, 'you asked if there was anything you could do for me. As a matter of fact, there *is* something you can give me for my services.'

'Yes?'

'The Trotton.'

Peplow frowned and pursed his thin lips. 'Why on earth . . . ?'

'For my own collection, of course. I'm especially interested in the war period.'

Peplow smiled. 'Ah! So that's how you knew so much about them? I'd no idea you were a collector too.'

Quilley shrugged modestly. He could see Peplow struggling, visualizing the gap in his collection. But finally the poor man decided that the murder of his wife was more important to him than an obscure mystery novel. 'Very well,' he said gravely. 'I'll mail it to you.'

'How can I be sure . . . ?'

Peplow looked offended. 'I'm a man of my word, Mr Quilley. A bargain is a bargain.' He held out his hand. 'Gentleman's agreement.'

'All right.' Quilley believed him. 'You'll be in touch when it's done?'

'Yes. Perhaps a brief note in with the Trotton, if you can wait that long. Say two or three weeks?'

'Fine. I'm in no hurry.'

Quilley hadn't examined his motives since the first meeting, but he had realized, as he passed on the information and instructions, that it was the challenge he responded to more than anything else. For years he had been writing crime novels, and in providing Peplow with the means to kill his slatternly, overbearing wife, Quilley had derived some vicarious pleasure from the knowledge that he – Inspector Baldry's creator – could bring off in real life what he had always been praised for doing in fiction.

Quilley also knew that there were no real detectives who

possessed Baldry's curious mixture of intellect and instinct. Most of them were thick plodders, and they would never realize that dull Mr Peplow had murdered his wife with a bunch of foxgloves, of all things. Nor would they ever know that the brains behind the whole affair had been none other than his, Dennis Quilley's.

The two men drained their glasses and left together. The corner of Bloor and Spadina was busy with tourists and students lining up for charcoal-grilled hot dogs from the street vendor. Peplow turned towards the subway and Quilley wandered among the artsy crowd and the rollerbladers on Bloor Street West for a while, then he settled at an open-air cafe over a daiquiri and a slice of kiwi-fruit cheesecake to read the *Globe and Mail*.

Now, he thought as he sipped his drink and turned to the arts section, all he had to do was wait. One day soon a small package would arrive for him. Peplow would be free of his wife, and Quilley would be the proud owner of one of the few remaining copies of X. J. Trotton's one and only mystery novel, *Signed in Blood*.

•

Three weeks passed and no package arrived. Occasionally, Quilley thought of Mr Peplow and wondered what had become of him. Perhaps he had lost his nerve after all. That wouldn't be surprising. Quilley knew that he would have no way of finding out what had happened if Peplow chose not to contact him again. He didn't know where the man lived or where he worked. He didn't even know if Peplow was his real name. Still, he thought, it was best that way. No contact. Even the Trotton wasn't worth being involved in a botched murder for.

Then, at ten o'clock one warm Tuesday morning in September, the doorbell chimed. Quilley looked at his watch and frowned. Too early for the postman. Sighing, he pressed the SAVE command on his PC and walked down to answer the door. A stranger stood there, an overweight woman in a yellow polka-dot dress with short sleeves and a low neck. She had piggy eyes set in a round face and dyed red hair that looked limp and lifeless after a cheap perm. She carried an imitation crocodile-skin handbag.

Quilley must have stood there looking puzzled for too long. The woman's eyes narrowed and her rosebud mouth tightened so much that white furrows radiated from the red circle of her lips.

'May I come in?' she asked.

Stunned, Quilley stood back and let her enter. She walked straight over to a wicker armchair and sat down. The basketwork creaked under her. From there, she surveyed the room, with its waxed parquet floor, stone fireplace and antique Ontario furniture.

'Nice,' she said, clutching her handbag on her lap. Quilley sat down opposite her. Her dress was a size too small and the material strained over her red, fleshy upper arms and pinkish bosom. The hem rode up as she crossed her legs, exposing a wedge of fat, mottled thigh. Primly, she pulled it down again over her dimpled knees.

'I'm sorry to appear rude,' said Quilley, regaining his composure, 'but who the hell are you?'

'My name is Peplow,' the woman said. 'Gloria Peplow. I'm a widow.'

Quilley felt a tingling sensation along his spine, the way he always did when fear began to take hold of him.

He frowned and said, 'I'm afraid I don't know you, do I?'

'We've never met,' the woman replied, 'but I think you knew my husband.'

'I don't recall any Peplow. Perhaps you're mistaken?'

Gloria Peplow shook her head and fixed him with her piggy eyes. He noticed they were black, or as near as. 'I'm not mistaken, Mr Quilley. You didn't only know my husband, you also plotted with him to murder me.'

Quilley flushed and jumped to his feet. 'That's absurd! Look, if you've come here to make insane accusations like that, you'd better go.' He stood like an ancient statue, one hand pointing dramatically towards the door.

Mrs Peplow smirked. 'Oh, sit down. You look very foolish standing there like that.'

Quilley continued to stand. 'This is *my* home, Mrs Peplow, and I insist that you leave. Now!'

Mrs Peplow sighed and opened the gilded plastic clasp on her purse. She took out a Shoppers Drug Mart envelope, picked out two colour photographs and dropped them next to the Wedgwood dish on the antique wine table by her chair. Leaning forward, Quilley could see clearly what they were: one showed him standing with Peplow outside the Park Plaza, and the other caught the two of them talking outside the Scotiabank at Bloor and Spadina. Mrs Peplow flipped the photos over, and Quilley saw that they had been date-stamped by the processors.

'You met with my husband at least twice to help him plan my death.'

'That's ridiculous. I do remember him now I've seen the picture. I just couldn't recollect his name. He was a fan. We talked about mystery novels. I'm very sorry to hear that he's passed away.'

'He had a heart attack, Mr Quilley, and now I'm all alone in the world.'

'I'm very sorry, but I don't see . . .'

Mrs Peplow waved his protests aside. Quilley noticed the dark sweat stain on the tight material around her armpit. She fumbled with the catch on her purse again and brought out a pack of Export Lights and a book of matches.

'I don't allow smoking in my house,' Quilley said. 'It doesn't agree with me.'

'Pity,' she said, lighting the cigarette and dropping the spent match in the Wedgwood bowl. She blew a stream of smoke directly at Quilley, who coughed and fanned it away.

'Listen to me, Mr Quilley,' she said, 'and listen good. My husband might have been stupid, but I'm not. He was not only a pathetic and boring little man, he was also an open book. Don't ask me why I married him. He wasn't even much of a man, if you know what I mean. Do you think I haven't known for some time that he was thinking of ways to get rid of me? I wouldn't give him a divorce because the one thing he did – the *only* thing he did – was provide for me and he didn't even do that very well. I'd have got half if we divorced, but half of what he earned isn't enough to keep a bag lady. I'd have had to go to work and I don't like that idea. So I watched him. He got more and more desperate, more and more secretive. When he started looking smug, I knew he was up to something.'

'Mrs Peplow,' Quilley interrupted, 'this is all very well, but I don't see what it has to do with me. You come in here and pollute my home with smoke, then you start telling me some fairy tale about your husband, a man I met casually once or twice. I'm busy, Mrs Peplow, and quite frankly I'd rather you left and let me get back to work.'

'I'm sure you would.' She flicked a column of ash into the Wedgwood bowl. 'As I was saying, I knew he was up to something, so I started following him. I thought he might have another woman, unlikely as it seemed, so I took my camera along. I wasn't really surprised when he headed for the Park Plaza instead of going back to the office after lunch one day. I watched the elevator go up to the nineteenth floor, the bar, so I waited across the street in the crowd for him to come out again. As you know, I didn't have to wait very long. He came out with you. And it was just as easy the next time.'

'I've already told you, Mrs Peplow, he was a mystery buff, a fellow collector, that's all—'

'Yes, yes, I know he was. Him and his stupid catalogues and collection. Still,' she mused, 'it had its uses. That's how I found out who you were. I'd seen your picture on the book covers, of course. If I may say so, it does you more than justice.' She looked him up and down as if he were a side of beef hanging in a butcher's window. He cringed. 'As I was saying, my husband was obvious. I knew he must be chasing you for advice. He spends so much time escaping to his garden or his little world of books that it was perfectly natural he would go to a mystery novelist for advice rather than to a real criminal. I imagine you were a bit more accessible, too. A little flattery and you were hooked. Just another puzzle for you to work on.'

'Look, Mrs Peplow—'

'Let me finish.' She ground out her cigarette butt in the bowl. 'Foxgloves, indeed! Do you think he could manage to brew up a dose of digitalis without leaving traces all over the place? Do you know what he did the first time? He put just enough in my Big Mac to make me a bit nauseous and make my pulse race, but he left the leaves and stems in the garbage! Can you believe that? Oh, I became very careful in my eating habits after that, Mr Quilley. Anyway, your little plan didn't work. I'm here and he's dead.'

Quilley paled. 'My God, you killed him, didn't you?'

'He was the one with the bad heart, not me.' She lit another cigarette.

'You can hardly blackmail me for plotting with your husband to kill you when *he's* the one who's dead,' said Quilley. 'And as for evidence, there's nothing. No, Mrs Peplow, I think you'd better go, and think yourself lucky I don't call the police.'

Mrs Peplow looked surprised. 'What are you talking about? I have no intention of blackmailing you for plotting to kill me.'

'Then what . . . ?'

'Mr Quilley, my husband was blackmailing you. That's why *you* killed *him*.'

Quilley slumped back in his chair. 'I what?'

She took a sheet of paper from her purse and passed it over to him. On it were just two words: 'Trotton – Quilley.' He recognized the neat handwriting. 'That's a photocopy,' Mrs Peplow went on. 'The original's where I found it, slipped between the pages of a book called *Signed in Blood* by X. J. Trotton. Do you know that book, Mr Quilley?'

'Vaguely. I've heard of it.'

'Oh, have you? It might also interest you to know that along with that book and the slip of paper, locked away in my husband's files, is a copy of your own first novel. I put it there.'

Quilley felt the room spinning around him. 'I . . . I . . .' Peplow had given him the impression that Gloria was stupid, but that was turning out to be far from the truth.

'My husband's only been dead for two days. If the doctors look, they'll *know* that he's been poisoned. For a start, they'll find high levels of potassium and then they'll discover *eosinophilia*. Do you know what they are, Mr Quilley? I looked them up. They're a kind of white blood cell, and you find lots of them around if there's been any allergic reaction or inflammation. If I was to go to the police and say I'd been suspicious about my husband's behaviour over the past few weeks, that I had followed him and photographed him with you, and if they were to find the two books and the slip of paper in his files . . . Well, I think you know what they'd make of it, don't you? Especially if I told them he came home feeling ill after a lunch with you.'

'It's not fair,' Quilley said, banging his fist on the chair arm. 'It's just not bloody fair.'

'Life rarely is. But the police aren't to know how stupid and unimaginative my husband was. They'll just look at the note, read the books, and assume he was blackmailing you.' She laughed. 'Even if Frank had read the Trotton book, I'm sure he'd have only noticed an "influence", at the most. But you and I know what really went on, don't we? It happens more often than people think. A few years ago I read in the newspaper about similarities between a book by Colleen McCullough and *The Blue Castle* by Lucy Maud Montgomery. I'd say that was a bit obvious, wouldn't you? It was much easier in your case, much less dangerous. You were very clever, Mr Quilley. You found an obscure novel and you didn't only adapt the plot for your own first book, you even stole the character of your series detective. There was some risk involved, certainly, but not much. Your book is better, without a doubt. You have some writing talent, which X. J. Trotton completely lacked. But he did have the germ of an original idea, and it wasn't lost on you, was it?'

Quilley groaned. Thirteen solid police procedurals, twelve of them all his own work, but the first, yes, a deliberate adaptation of a piece of ephemeral trash. He had seen what Trotton could have done and had done it himself. Serendipity, or so it had seemed when he found the dusty volume in a second-hand bookshop in Victoria years ago. All he had had to do was change the setting from London to Toronto, alter the names and set about improving upon the original. And now . . . ? The hell of it was that he would have been perfectly safe without the damn book. He had simply given in to the urge to get his hands on Peplow's copy and destroy it. It wouldn't have mattered, really. *Signed in Blood* would have remained unread on Peplow's shelf. If only the bloody fool hadn't written that note . . .

'Even if the police can't make a murder charge stick,' Mrs Peplow went on, 'I think your reputation would suffer if this got out. Oh, the great reading public might not care. Perhaps a trial would even increase your sales – you know how ghoulish people are – but the plagiarism would at the very least lose you the respect of your peers. I don't think your agent and publisher would be very happy either. Am I making myself clear?'

Pale and sweating, Quilley nodded. 'How much?' he whispered.

'Pardon?'

'I said how much. How much do you want to keep quiet?'

'Oh, it's not your money I'm after, Mr Quilley, or may I call you Dennis? Well, not *only* money, anyway. I'm a widow now. I'm all alone in the world.'

She looked around the room, her piggy eyes glittering, then gave Quilley one of the most disgusting looks he'd ever had in his life.

'I've always fancied living near the lake,' she said, reaching for another cigarette. 'Live here alone, do you?'

INNOCENCE

Francis must be late, surely, Reed thought as he stood waiting on the bridge by the railway station. He was beginning to feel restless and uncomfortable; the handles of his holdall bit into his palm, and he noticed that the rain promised in the forecast that morning was already starting to fall.

Wonderful! Here he was, over two hundred miles away from home, and Francis hadn't turned up. But Reed couldn't be sure about that. Perhaps *he* was early. They had made the same arrangement three or four times over the past five years, but for the life of him Reed couldn't remember the exact time they'd met.

Reed turned and noticed a plump woman in a threadbare blue overcoat come struggling against the wind over the bridge towards him. She pushed a large pram, in which two infants fought and squealed.

'Excuse me,' he called out as she neared him, 'could you tell me what time school gets out?'

The woman gave him a funny look – either puzzlement or irritation, he couldn't decide which – and answered in the clipped, nasal accent peculiar to the Midlands, 'Half past three.' Then she hurried by, giving Reed a wide berth.

He was wrong. For some reason he had got it into his mind that Francis finished teaching at three o'clock. It was only twenty-five past now, so there would be at least another fifteen minutes to wait before the familiar red Escort came into sight.

The rain was getting heavier and the wind lashed it hard

against Reed's face. A few yards up the road from the bridge was the bus station, which was attached to large modern shopping centre, all glass and escalators. Reed could stand in the entrance there just beyond the doors, where it was warm and dry, and still watch for Francis.

At about twenty-five to four, the first schoolchildren came dashing over the bridge and into the bus station, satchels swinging, voices shrill and loud with freedom. The rain didn't seem to bother them, Reed noticed: hair lay plastered to skulls; beads of rain hung on the tips of noses. Most of the boys' ties were askew, their socks hung loose around their ankles and their shoelaces snaked along the ground. It was a wonder they didn't trip over themselves. Reed smiled, remembering his own schooldays.

And how alluring the girls looked as they ran smiling and laughing out of the rain into the shelter of the mall. Not the really young ones, the unformed ones, but the older, long-limbed girls, newly aware of their breasts and the swelling of their hips. They wore their clothes carelessly: blouses hanging out, black woolly tights twisted or torn at the knees. To Reed, there was something wanton in their disarray.

These days, of course, they probably all knew what was what, but Reed couldn't help but feel that there was also a certain innocence about them: a naive, carefree grace in the way they moved and a casual freedom in their laughter and gestures. Life hadn't got to them yet; they hadn't felt its weight and seen the darkness at its core.

Mustn't get carried away, Reed told himself, with a smile. It was all very well to joke with Bill in the office about how sexy the schoolgirls who passed the window each day were, but it was positively unhealthy to mean it, or (God forbid!) attempt to do anything about it. He couldn't be turning into a dirty old man at thirty-five, could he? Sometimes the power and violence of his fantasies worried him, but perhaps everyone else had them too. It wasn't something you could talk about at work. He didn't really think he was abnormal; after all, he hadn't acted them out, and you couldn't be arrested for your fantasies, could you?

Where the hell was Francis? Reed peered out through the glass. Wind-blown rain lashed across the huge plate windows and distorted the outside world. All detail was obliterated in favour of the overall mood: grey-glum and dream-like.

Reed glanced at his watch again. After four o'clock. The only schoolchildren left now were the stragglers, the ones who lived nearby and didn't have to hurry for a bus. They sauntered over the bridge, shoving each other, playing tag, hopping and skipping over the cracks in the pavement, oblivious to the rain and the wind that drove it.

Francis ought to be here by now. Worried, Reed went over the arrangements again in his mind. He knew that he'd got the date right because he'd written it down in his appointment book. Reed had tried to call the previous evening to confirm, but no one had answered. If Francis had been trying to get in touch with him at work or at home, he would have been out of luck. Reed had been visiting another old friend – this one in Exeter – and Elsie, the office receptionist, could hardly be trusted to get her own name right.

When five o'clock came and there was still no sign of Francis, Reed picked up his holdall again and walked back down to the station. It was still raining, but not so fast, and the wind had dropped. The only train back home that night left Birmingham at nine-forty and didn't get to Carlisle until well after midnight. By then the local buses would have stopped running and he would have to get a taxi. Was it worth it?

There wasn't much alternative, really. A hotel would be too expensive. Still, the idea had its appeal: a warm room with a soft bed, shower, colour television and maybe even a bar downstairs, where he might meet a girl. He would just have to decide later. Anyway, if he did want to catch the train, he would have to take the eight-fifty from Redditch to get to Birmingham in time. That left three hours and fifty minutes to kill.

As he walked over the bridge and up towards the town centre in the darkening evening, Reed noticed two schoolgirls walking in front of him. They must have been kept in detention, he thought, or perhaps they'd just finished games practice. No doubt they had to do that, even in the rain. One looked dumpy from behind, but her friend was a dream: long wavy hair tumbling messily over her shoulders; short skirt flicking over her long, slim thighs; white socks fallen around her ankles, leaving her shapely calves bare. Reed watched the tendons at the back of her knees flex and loosen as she walked and thought of her struggling beneath him, his hands on her soft throat. They turned down a side street and Reed carried on ahead, shaking off his fantasy.

Could Francis have got lumbered with taking detention or games? he wondered. Or perhaps he had passed by without even noticing Reed sheltering from the rain. He didn't know where Francis's school was, or even what it was called. Somehow, the subject had just never come up. Also, the village where Francis lived was about eight miles away from Redditch and the local bus service was terrible. Still, he could phone. If Francis were home, he'd come out again and pick Reed up.

After phoning and getting no answer, Reed walked around town for a long time looking in shop windows and wondering about how to get out of the mess he was in. His holdall weighed heavy in his hand. Finally, he got hungry and ducked out of the light rain into the Tandoori Palace. It was still early, just after six, and the place was empty apart from a young couple absorbed in one another in a dim corner. Reed had the waiter's undivided attention. He ordered pakoras, tandoori and dhal. The food was very good and Reed ate it too fast.

After the spiced tea, he took out his wallet to pay. He had some cash, but he had decided to have pint or two, and he might have to take a taxi home from the station. Best hang onto the paper money. The waiter didn't seem to mind taking plastic, even for so small a sum, and Reed rewarded him with a generous tip.

Next he tried Francis again, but the phone just rang and rang.

Why didn't the bugger invest in an answering machine? Reed cursed. Then he realized he didn't even have one himself, hated the things. Francis no doubt felt the same way. If you were out, tough tittie; you were out and that was that.

Outside, the street lights reflected in oily puddles on the roads and pavements. After walking off his heartburn for half an hour, thoroughly soaked and out of breath, Reed ducked into the first pub he saw. The locals eyed him suspiciously at first, then ignored him and went back to their drinks.

'Pint of bitter, please,' Reed said, rubbing his hands together. 'In a sleeve glass, if you've got one.'

'Sorry, sir,' the landlord said, reaching for a mug. 'The locals bring their own.'

'Oh, very well.'

'Nasty night.'

'Yes,' said Reed. 'Very.'

'From these parts?'

'No. Just passing through.'

'Ah.' The landlord passed over a brimming pint mug, took Reed's money and went back to the conversation he'd been having with a round-faced man in a pin-stripe suit. Reed took his drink over to a table and sat down.

Over the next hour and a half he phoned Francis four more times, but still got no reply. He also changed pubs after each pint, but got very little in the way of a friendly greeting. Finally, at about twenty to nine, knowing he couldn't bear to wake up in such a miserable town even if he could afford a hotel, he went back to the station and took the train home.

•

Because of his intended visit to Francis, Reed hadn't planned anything for the weekend at home. The weather was miserable, anyway, so he spent most of his time indoors reading and watching television, or down at the local. He tried Francis's number a few more times, but still got no reply. He also phoned Camille, hoping that her warm, lithe body and her fondness for experiment might brighten up his Saturday night and Sunday morning, but all he got was her answering machine.

On Monday evening, just as he was about to go to bed after a long day catching up on boring paperwork, the phone rang. Grouchily, he picked up the receiver: 'Yes?'

'Terry?'

'Yes.'

'This is Francis.'

'Where the hell—'

'Did you come all the way down on Friday?'

'Of course I bloody well did. I thought we had an—'

'Oh God. Look, I'm sorry, mate, really I am. I tried to call. That woman at work – what's her name?'

'Elsie?'

'That's the one. She said she'd give you a message. I must admit she didn't sound as if she quite had her wits about her, but I'd no choice.'

Reed softened a little. 'What happened?'

'My mother. You know she's been ill for a long time?'

'Yes.'

'Well, she died last Wednesday. I had to rush off back to Manchester. Look, I really am sorry, but you can see I couldn't do anything about it, can't you?'

'It's me who should be sorry,' Reed said. 'To hear about your mother, I mean.'

'Yes, well, at least there'll be no more suffering for her. Maybe we could get together in a few weeks?'

'Sure. Just let me know when.'

'All right. I've still got stuff to do, you know, things to organize. How about if I call you back in a couple of weeks?'

'Great, I'll look forward to it. Bye.'

'Bye. And I'm sorry, Terry, really.'

Reed put the phone down and went to bed. So that was it – the mystery solved.

•

The following evening, just after he'd arrived home from work, Reed heard a loud knock at his door. When he opened it, he saw two strangers standing there. At first he thought they were Jehovah's Witnesses – who else came to the door in pairs, wearing suits? – but these two didn't quite look the part. True, one did look a bit like a bible salesman – chubby, with a cheerful, earnest expression on a face fringed by a neatly trimmed dark beard – but the other, painfully thin, with a long, pock-marked face, looked more like an undertaker, except for the way his sharp blue eyes glittered with intelligent suspicion.

'Mr Reed? Mr Terence J. Reed?' the cadaverous one said, in a deep, quiet voice, just like the way Reed imagined a real undertaker would speak. And wasn't there a hint of the Midlands nasal quality in the way he slurred the vowels?

'Yes, I'm Terry Reed. What is it? What do you want?' Reed could already see, over their shoulders, his neighbours spying from their windows: little corners of white net-curtain twitched aside to give a clear view.

'We're police officers, sir. Mind if we come in for a moment?' They flashed their identity cards, but put them away before Reed had time to see what was written there. He backed into the hallway and they took their opportunity to enter. As soon as they had closed the door behind them, Reed noticed the one with the beard start glancing around him, taking everything in, while the other continued to hold Reed's gaze. Finally, Reed turned and led them into the living room. He felt some kind of signal pass between them behind his back.

'Nice place you've got,' the thin one said, while the other prowled the room, picking up vases and looking inside, opening drawers an inch or two, then closing them again.

'Look, what is this?' Reed said. 'Is he supposed to be poking through my things? I mean, do you have a search warrant or something?'

'Oh, don't mind him,' the tall one said. 'He's just like that. Insatiable curiosity. By the way, my name's Bentley, Detective

Superintendent Bentley. My colleague over there goes by the name of Inspector Rodmoor. We're from the Midlands Regional Crime Squad.' He looked to see Reed's reactions as he said this, but Reed tried to show no emotion at all.

'I still don't see what you want with me,' he said.

'Just routine,' said Bentley. 'Mind if I sit down?'

'Be my guest.'

Bentley sat in the rocker by the fireplace and Reed sat opposite on the sofa. A mug of half-finished coffee stood between them on the glass-topped table, beside a couple of unpaid bills and the latest *Radio Times*.

'Would you like something to drink?' Reed offered.

Bentley shook his head.

'What about him?' Reed glanced over nervously towards Inspector Rodmoor, who was looking through his bookcase, pulling out volumes that caught his fancy and flipping through them.

Bentley folded his hands on his lap: 'Just try to forget he's here.'

But Reed couldn't. He kept flicking his eyes edgily from one to the other, always anxious about what Rodmoor was getting into next.

'Mr Reed,' Bentley went on, 'were you in Redditch on the evening of 9 November? Last Friday, that was.'

Reed put his hand to his brow, which was damp with sweat. 'Let me think now . . . Yes, yes, I believe I was.'

'Why?'

'What? Sorry . . . ?'

'I asked why. Why were you in Redditch? What was the purpose of your visit?'

He sounded like an immigration control officer at the airport, Reed thought. 'I was there to meet an old university friend,' he answered. 'I've been going down for a weekend once a year or so ever since he moved there.'

'And did you meet him?'

'As a matter of fact, no, I didn't.' Reed explained the communications breakdown with Francis.

Bentley raised an eyebrow. Rodmoor rifled through the magazine rack by the fireplace.

'But you still went there?' Bentley persisted.

'Yes. I told you, I didn't know he'd be away. Look, do you mind telling me what this is about? I think I have a right to know.'

Rodmoor fished a copy of *Mayfair* out of the magazine rack and held it up for Bentley to see. Bentley frowned and reached over for it. The cover showed a shapely blonde in skimpy pink lace panties and camisole, stockings and a suspender belt. She was on her knees on a sofa, and her round behind faced the viewer. Her face was also turned towards the camera, and she looked as if she'd just been licking her glossy red lips. The thin strap of the camisole had slipped over her upper arm.

'Nice,' Bentley said. 'Looks a bit young, though, don't you think?'

Reed shrugged. He felt embarrassed and didn't know what to say.

Bentley flipped through the rest of the magazine, pausing over the colour spreads of naked women in fetching poses.

'It's not illegal you know,' Reed burst out. 'You can buy it in any newsagent's. It's not pornography.'

'That's a matter of opinion, isn't it, sir?' said Inspector Rodmoor, taking the magazine back from his boss and replacing it.

Bentley smiled. 'Don't mind him, lad,' he said. 'He's a Methodist. Now where were we?'

Reed shook his head.

'Do you own a car?' Bentley asked.

'No.'

'Do you live here by yourself?'

'Yes.'

'Ever been married?'

'No.'

'Girlfriends?'

'Some.'

'But not to live with?'

'No.'

'Magazines enough for you, eh?'

'Now just a minute—'

'Sorry,' Bentley said, holding up his skeletal hand. 'Pretty tasteless of me, that was. Out of line.'

Why couldn't Reed quite believe the apology? He sensed very strongly that Bentley had made the remark on purpose to see how he would react. He hoped he'd passed the test. 'You were going to tell me what all this was about . . .'

'Was I? Why don't you tell me about what you did in Redditch last Friday evening first? Inspector Rodmoor will join us here by the table and take notes. No hurry. Take your time.'

And slowly, trying to remember all the details of that miserable, washed-out evening five days ago, Reed told them. At one point, Bentley asked him what he'd been wearing, and Inspector Rodmoor asked if they might have a look at his raincoat and holdall. When Reed finished, the heavy silence stretched on for seconds. What were they thinking about? he wondered. Were they trying to make up their minds about him? What was he supposed to have done?

Finally, after they had asked him to go over one or two random points, Rodmoor closed his notebook and Bentley got to his feet. 'That'll be all for now, sir.'

'For now?'

'We might want to talk to you again. Don't know. Have to check up on a few points first. We'll just take the coat and the holdall with us, if you don't mind, sir. Inspector Rodmoor will give you a receipt. Be available, will you?'

In his confusion, Reed accepted the slip of paper from Rodmoor and did nothing to stop them taking his things. 'I'm not planning on going anywhere, if that's what you mean.'

Bentley smiled. He looked like an undertaker consoling the

bereaved. 'Good. Well, we'll be off then.' And they walked towards the door.

'Aren't you going to tell me what it's all about?' Reed asked again as he opened the door for them. They walked out onto the path, and it was Inspector Rodmoor who turned and frowned. 'That's the funny thing about it, sir,' he said, 'that you don't seem to know.'

'Believe me, I don't.'

Rodmoor shook his head slowly. 'Anybody would think you don't read your papers.' And they walked down the path to their Rover.

Reed stood for a few moments watching the curtains opposite twitch and wondering what on earth Rodmoor meant. Then he realized that the newspapers had been delivered as usual the past few days, so they must have been in with magazines in the rack, but he had been too disinterested, too tired, or too busy to read any of them. He often felt like that. News was, more often than not, depressing, the last thing one needed on a wet weekend in Carlisle. Quickly, he shut the door on the gawping neighbours and hurried towards the magazine rack.

He didn't have far to look. The item was on the front page of yesterday's paper, under the headline, MIDLANDS MURDER SHOCK. It read,

> The quiet Midlands town of Redditch is still in shock today over the brutal slaying of schoolgirl Debbie Harrison. Debbie, 15, failed to arrive home after a late hockey practice on Friday evening. Police found her partially clad body in an abandoned warehouse close to the town centre early Saturday morning. Detective Superintendent Bentley, in charge of the investigation, told our reporter that police are pursuing some positive leads. They would particularly like to talk to anyone who was in the area of the bus station and noticed a strange man hanging around the vicinity late that afternoon. Descriptions are vague so far, but the man was wearing a light tan raincoat and carrying a blue holdall.

He read and reread the article in horror, but what was even worse than the words was the photograph that accompanied it. He couldn't be certain because it was a poor shot, but he thought it was the schoolgirl with the long wavy hair and the socks around her ankles, the one who had walked in front of him with her dumpy friend.

The most acceptable explanation of the police visit would be that they needed him as a possible witness, but the truth was that the 'strange man hanging around the vicinity' wearing 'a light tan raincoat' and carrying a 'blue holdall' was none other than himself, Terence J. Reed. But how did they know he'd been there?

•

The second time the police called Reed was at work. They marched right into the office, brazen as brass, and asked him if he could spare some time to talk to them down at the station. Bill only looked on curiously, but Frank, the boss, was hardly able to hide his irritation. Reed wasn't his favourite employee anyway; he hadn't been turning enough profit lately.

Nobody spoke during the journey, and when they got to the station one of the local policemen pointed Bentley towards a free interview room. It was a bare place: grey metal desk, ashtray, three chairs. Bentley sat opposite Reed, and Inspector Rodmoor sat in a corner, out of his line of vision.

Bentley placed the folder he'd been carrying on the desk and smiled his funeral director's smile. 'Just a few further points, Terry. Hope I don't have to keep you long.'

'So do I,' Reed said. 'Look, I don't know what's going on, but shouldn't I call my lawyer or something?'

'Oh, I don't think so. It isn't as if we've charged you or anything. You're simply helping us with our enquiries, aren't you? Besides, do you actually have a solicitor? Most people don't.'

Come to think of it, Reed didn't have one. He knew one, though. Another old university friend had gone into law and practised nearby. Reed couldn't remember what he specialized in.

'Let me lay my cards on the table, as it were,' Bentley said, spreading his hands on the desk. 'You admit you were in Redditch last Friday evening to visit your friend. We've been in touch with him, by the way, and he verifies your story. What puzzles us is what you did between, say, four and eight-thirty. A number of people saw you at various times, but there's at least an hour or more here and there that we can't account for.'

'I've already told you what I did.'

Bentley consulted the file he had set on the desk. 'You ate at roughly six o'clock, is that right?'

'About then, yes.'

'So you walked around Redditch in the rain between five and six, and between six-thirty and seven? Hardly a pleasant aesthetic experience, I'd imagine.'

'I told you, I was thinking things out. I looked in shops, got lost a couple of times . . .'

'Did you happen to get lost in the vicinity of Simmons Street?'

'I don't know the street names.'

'Of course. Not much of a street, really, more an alley. It runs by a number of disused warehouses—'

'Now wait a minute! If you're trying to tie me in to that girl's murder, then you're way off beam. Perhaps I *had* better call a solicitor, after all.'

'Ah!' said Bentley, glancing over at Rodmoor. 'So you *do* read the papers?'

'I did. After you left. Of course I did.'

'But not before?'

'I'd have known what you were on about, then, wouldn't I? And while we're on the subject, how the hell did you find out I was in Redditch that evening?'

'You used your credit card in the Tandoori Palace,' Bentley said. 'The waiter remembered you and looked up his records.'

Reed slapped the desk. 'There! That proves it. If I'd done what you seem to be accusing me of, I'd hardly have been as daft as to leave my calling card, would I?'

Bentley shrugged. 'Criminals make mistakes, just like everybody else. Otherwise we'd never catch any. And I'm not accusing you of anything at the moment. You can see our problem, though, can't you? Your story sounds thin, very thin.'

'I can't help that. It's the truth.'

'What state would you say you were in when you went into the Tandoori Palace?'

'State?'

'Yes. Your condition.'

Reed shrugged. 'I was wet, I suppose. A bit fed up. I hadn't been able to get in touch with Francis. Hungry, too.'

'Would you say you appeared agitated?'

'Not really, no.'

'But someone who didn't know you might just assume that you were?'

'I don't know. Maybe. I was out of breath.'

'Oh? Why?'

'We'll I'd been walking around for a long time carrying my holdall. It was quite heavy.'

'Yes, of course. So you were wet and breathless when you ate in the restaurant. What about the pub you went into just after seven o'clock?'

'What about it?'

'Did you remain seated long?'

'I don't know what you mean.'

'Did you just sit and sip your drink, have a nice rest after a heavy meal and a long walk?'

'Well, I had to go the toilet, of course. And I tried phoning Francis a few more times.'

'So you were up and down, a bit like a yo-yo, eh?'

'But I had good reason! I was stranded. I desperately wanted to get in touch with my friend.'

'Yes, of course. Cast your mind back a bit earlier in the afternoon. At about twenty past three, you asked a woman what time the schools came out.'

'Yes. I . . . I couldn't remember. Francis is a teacher, so naturally I wanted to know if I was early or late. It was starting to rain.'

'But you'd visited him there before. You said so. He'd picked you up at the same place several times.'

'I know. I just couldn't remember if it was three o'clock or four. I know it sounds silly, but it's true. Don't you ever forget little things like that?'

'So you asked the woman on the bridge? That *was* you?'

'Yes. Look, I'd hardly have done that, would I, if . . . I mean . . . like with the credit card. I'd hardly have advertised my intentions if I was going to . . . you know . . .'

Bentley raised a beetle-black eyebrow. 'Going to *what*, Terry?'

Reed ran his hands through his hair and rested his elbows on the desk. 'It doesn't matter. This is absurd. I've done nothing. I'm innocent.'

'Don't you find schoolgirls attractive?' Bentley went on in a soft voice. 'After all, it would only be natural, wouldn't it? They can be real beauties at fifteen or sixteen, can't they? Proper little temptresses, some of them, I'll bet. Right prick-teasers. Just think about it – short skirts, bare legs, firm young tits. Doesn't it excite you, Terry? Don't you get hard just thinking about it?'

'No, it doesn't,' Reed said tightly. 'I'm not a pervert.'

Bentley laughed. 'Nobody's suggesting you are. It gets *me* going, I don't mind admitting. Perfectly normal, I'd say, to find a fifteen-year-old schoolgirl sexy. My Methodist inspector might not agree, but you and I know different, Terry, don't we? All that sweet innocence wrapped up in a soft, desirable young body. Doesn't it just make your blood sing? And wouldn't it be easy to get a bit carried away if she resisted, put your hands around her throat . . . ?'

'No!' Reed said again, aware of his cheeks burning.

'What about those women in the magazine, Terry? The one we found at your house?'

'That's different.'

'Don't tell me you buy it just for the stories.'

'I didn't say that. I'm normal. I like looking at naked women, just like any other man.'

'Some of them seemed very young to me.'

'For Christ's sake, they're models. They get paid for posing like that. I told you before, that magazine's freely available. There's nothing illegal about it.' Reed glanced over his shoulder at Rodmoor, who kept his head bent impassively over his notebook.

'And you like videos, too, don't you? We've had a little talk with Mr Hakim in your corner shop. He told us about one video in particular you've rented lately. Soft porn, I suppose you'd call it. Nothing illegal, true, at least not yet, but a bit dodgy. I'd wonder about a bloke who watches stuff like that.'

'It's a free country. I'm a normal single male. I have a right to watch whatever kind of videos I want.'

'*School's Out*,' Bentley said quietly. 'A bit over the top, wouldn't you say?'

'But they weren't *real* schoolgirls. The lead was thirty if she was a day. Besides, I only rented it out of curiosity. I thought it might be a bit of a laugh.'

'And was it?'

'I can't remember.'

'But you see what I mean, don't you? It looks bad: the subject-matter, the image. It all looks a bit odd. Fishy.'

'Well it's not. I'm perfectly innocent, and that's the truth.'

Bentley stood up abruptly and Rodmoor slipped out of the room. 'You can go now,' the superintendent said. 'It's been nice to have a little chat.'

'That's it?'

'For the moment, yes.'

'But don't leave town?'

Bentley laughed. 'You really must give up those American cop shows. Though it's a wonder you find time to watch them with all those naughty videos you rent. They warp your sense of reality – cop shows and sex films. Life isn't like that at all.'

'Thank you. I'll bear that in mind,' Reed said. 'I take it I *am* free to go?'

'Of course.' Bentley gestured towards the door.

Reed left. He was shaking when he got out onto the wet, chilly street. Thank God the pubs were still open. He went into the first one he came to and ordered a double Scotch. Usually he wasn't much of a spirits drinker, but these, he reminded himself as the fiery liquor warmed his belly, were unusual circumstances. He knew he should go back to work, but he couldn't face it: Bill's questions, Frank's obvious disapproval. No. He ordered another double, and after he'd finished that, he went home for the afternoon. The first thing he did when he got into the house was tear up the copy of *Mayfair* and burn the pieces in the fireplace one by one. After that, he tore up his video club membership card and burned that too. Damn Hakim!

•

'Terence J. Reed, it is my duty to arrest you for the murder of Deborah Susan Harrison . . .'

Reed couldn't believe this was happening. Not to him. The world began to shimmer and fade before his eyes, and the next thing he knew Rodmoor was bent over him offering a glass of water, a benevolent smile on his bible salesman's face.

The next few days were a nightmare. Reed was charged and held until his trial date could be set. There was no chance of bail, given the seriousness of his alleged crime. He had no money anyway, and no close family to support him. He had never felt so alone in his life as he did those long dark nights in the cell. Nothing terrible happened. None of the things he'd heard about in films and documentaries: he wasn't sodomized; nor was he forced to perform fellatio at knife point; he wasn't even beaten up. Mostly he was left alone in the dark with his fears. He felt all the certainties of his life slip away from him, almost to the point where he wasn't even sure of the truth any more: guilty or innocent? The more he proclaimed his innocence, the less people seemed to believe him. Had he done it? He might have done.

He felt like an inflatable doll, full of nothing but air, manoeuvred into awkward positions by forces he could do nothing about. He had no control over his life any more. Not only couldn't he come and go as he pleased, he couldn't even think for himself any more. Solicitors and barristers and policemen did that for him. And in the cell, in the dark, everything seemed to close in on him and some nights he had to struggle for breath.

When the trial date finally arrived, Reed felt relief. At least he could breathe in the large, airy courtroom, and soon it would be all over, one way or another.

In the crowded court, Reed sat still as stone in the dock, steadily chewing the edges of his newly grown beard. He heard the evidence against him – all circumstantial, all convincing.

If the police surgeon had found traces of semen in the victim, an expert explained, then they could have tried for a genetic match with the defendant's DNA, and that would have settled Reed's guilt or innocence once and for all. But in this case it wasn't so easy: there had been no seminal fluid found in the dead girl. The forensics people speculated, from the state of her body, that the killer had tried to rape her, found he was impotent and strangled her in his ensuing rage.

A woman called Maggie, with whom Reed had had a brief fling a year or so ago, was brought onto the stand. The defendant had been impotent with her, it was established, on several occasions towards the end of their relationship, and he had become angry about it more than once, using more and more violent means to achieve sexual satisfaction. Once he had gone so far as to put his hands around her throat.

Well, yes he had. He'd been worried. During the time with Maggie, he had been under a lot of stress at work, drinking too much as well, and he hadn't been able to get it up. So what? Happens to everyone. And she'd wanted it like that, too, the rough way. Putting his hands around her throat had been her idea, something she'd got from a kinky book she'd read, and he'd gone along with her because she told him it might cure his impotence. Now she made the whole sordid episode sound much worse than it had been. She also admitted she had been just eighteen at the time, as well, and, as he remembered, she'd said she was twenty-three.

Besides, he had been impotent and violent only with Maggie. They could have brought on any number of other women to testify to his gentleness and virility, though no doubt if they did, he thought, his promiscuity would count just as much against him. What did he have to do to appear as normal as he needed to be, as he had once thought he was?

The witnesses for the prosecution all arose to testify against Reed like the spirits from Virgil's world of the dead. Though they were still alive, they seemed more like spirits to him: insubstantial, unreal. The woman from the bridge identified him as the shifty-looking person who had asked her what time the schools came out; the Indian waiter and the landlord of the pub told how agitated Reed had looked and acted that evening; other people had spotted him in the street, apparently following the murdered girl and her friend. Mr Hakim was there to tell the court what kind of videos Reed had rented lately – including *School's Out* – and even Bill told how his colleague used to make remarks about the schoolgirls passing by: 'You know, he'd get all excited about glimpsing a bit of black knicker when the wind blew their skirts up. It just seemed like a bit of a lark. I thought nothing of it at the time.' Then he shrugged and gave Reed a pitying look. And as if all that weren't enough, there was Maggie, a shabby Dido, refusing to look at him as she told the court of the way he had abused and abandoned her.

Towards the end of the prosecution case, even Reed's barrister was beginning to look depressed. He did his best in cross-examination, but the damnedest thing was that they were all telling the truth, or their versions of it. Yes, Mr Hakim admitted, other people had rented the same videos. Yes, he might have even watched some of them himself. But the fact remained that the man on trial was Terence J. Reed, and Reed had recently rented a video called *School's Out*, the kind of thing, ladies and gentlemen of the jury, that you wouldn't want to find your husbands or sons watching.

Reed could understand members of the victim's community appearing against him, and he could even comprehend Maggie's hurt pride. But why Hakim and Bill? What had he ever done to them? Had they never really liked him? It went on and on, a nightmare of distorted truth. Reed felt as if he had been set up in front of a funfair mirror, and all the jurors could see was his warped and twisted reflection. I'm innocent, he kept telling himself as he gripped the rail, but his knuckles turned whiter and whiter and his voice grew fainter and fainter.

Hadn't Bill joined in the remarks about schoolgirls? Wasn't it all in the spirit of fun? Yes, of course. But Bill wasn't in the dock. It was Terence J. Reed who stood accused of killing an innocent fifteen-year-old schoolgirl. *He* had been in the right place at the right time, and *he* had passed remarks on the budding breasts and milky thighs of the girls who had crossed the road in front of their office every day.

Then, the morning before the defence case was about to open – Reed himself was set to go into the dock, and not at all sure by now what the truth was – a strange thing happened.

Bentley and Rodmoor came softly into the courtroom, tiptoed up to the judge and began to whisper. Then the judge appeared to ask them questions. They nodded. Rodmoor looked in Reed's direction. After a few minutes of this, the two men took seats and the judge made a motion for the dismissal of all charges against the accused. Pandemonium broke out in court: reporters dashed for phones and the spectators' gallery buzzed with speculation. Amidst it all, Terry Reed got to his feet, realized *what* had happened, if not *how*, and promptly collapsed.

•

Nervous exhaustion, the doctor said, and not surprising after the ordeal Reed had been through. Complete rest was the only cure.

When Reed felt well enough, a few days after the trial had ended in uproar, his solicitor dropped by to tell him what had happened. Apparently, another schoolgirl had been assaulted in the same area, only this one had proved more than a match for her attacker. She had fought tooth and nail to hang onto her life, and in doing so had managed to pick up a half brick and crack the man's skull with it. He hadn't been seriously injured, but he'd been unconscious long enough for the girl to get help. When he was arrested, the man had confessed to the murder of Debbie Harrison. He had known details not revealed in the papers. After a night-long interrogation, police officers had no doubt whatsoever that he was telling the truth. Which meant Reed couldn't possibly be guilty. Hence motion for dismissal, end of trial. Reed was a free man again.

He stayed at home for three weeks, hardly venturing out of the house except for food, and even then he always went further afield for it than Hakim's. His neighbours watched him walk by, their faces pinched with disapproval, as if he were some kind of monster in their midst. He almost expected them to get up a petition to force him out of his home.

During that time he heard not one word of apology from the undertaker and the bible salesman; Francis still had 'stuff to do . . . things to organize'; and Camille's answering machine seemed permanently switched on.

At night Reed suffered claustrophobic nightmares of prison. He couldn't sleep well and even the mild sleeping pills the doctor gave him didn't really help. The bags grew heavier and darker under his eyes. Some days he wandered the city in a dream, not knowing where he was going, or, when he got there, how he had arrived.

The only thing that sustained him, the only pure, innocent, untarnished thing in his entire life, was when Debbie Harrison visited him in his dreams. She was alive then, just as she had been when he saw her for the first and only time, and he felt no desire to rob her of her innocence, only to partake of it himself. She smelled of apples in autumn and everything they saw and did together became a source of pure wonder. When she smiled, his heart almost broke with joy.

At the end of the third week, Reed trimmed his beard, got out his suit and went in to work. In the office he was met with an embarrassed silence from Bill and a redundancy cheque from Frank, who thrust it at him without a word of explanation. Reed shrugged, pocketed the cheque and left.

Every time he went into town, strangers stared at him in the street and whispered about him in pubs. Mothers held more tightly onto their daughters' hands when he passed them by in the shopping centres. He seemed to have become quite a celebrity in his home town. At first, he couldn't think why, then one day he plucked up the courage to visit the library and look up the newspapers that had been published during his trial.

What he found was total character annihilation, nothing less. When the headline about the capture of the real killer came out, it could have made no difference at all; the damage had already been done to Reed's reputation, and it was permanent. He might have been found innocent of the girl's murder, but he had been found guilty too, guilty of being a sick consumer of pornography, of being obsessed with young girls, unable to get it up without the aid of a struggle on the part of the female. None of it was true, of course, but somehow that didn't matter. It had been made so. As it is written, so let it be. And to cap it all, his photograph had appeared almost every day, both with and without the beard. There could be very few people in England who would fail to recognize him in the street.

Reed stumbled outside into the hazy afternoon. It was warming up towards spring, but the air was moist and grey with rain so fine it was closer to mist. The pubs were still open, so he dropped by the nearest one and ordered a double Scotch. The other customers looked at him suspiciously as he sat hunched in his corner, eyes bloodshot and puffy from lack of sleep, gaze directed sharply inwards.

Standing on the bridge in the misty rain an hour later, Reed couldn't remember making the actual decision to throw himself over the side, but he knew that was what he had to do. He couldn't even remember how he had ended up on this particular bridge, or the route he'd taken from the pub. He had thought, drinking his third double Scotch, that maybe he should go away and rebuild his life, perhaps abroad. But that didn't ring true as a solution. Life is what you have to live with, what you are, and now his life was what it had become, or what it had been turned into. It was what being in the wrong place at the wrong time had made it, and *that* was what he had to live with. The problem was he couldn't live with it; therefore, he had to die.

He couldn't actually see the river below – everything was grey – but he knew it was there. The River Eden, it was called. Reed laughed harshly to himself. It wasn't his fault that the river that runs through Carlisle is called the Eden, he thought; it was just one of life's little ironies.

Twenty-five to four on a wet Wednesday afternoon. Nobody about. Now was as good a time as any.

Just as he was about to climb onto the parapet, a figure emerged from the mist. It was the first girl on her way home from school. Her grey pleated skirt swished around her long, slim legs, and her socks hung over her ankles. Under her green blazer, the misty rain had wet the top of her white blouse so much that it stuck to her chest. Reed gazed at her in awe. Her long blonde hair had darkened and curled in the rain, sticking in strands over her cheek. There were tears in his eyes. He moved away from the parapet.

As she neared him, she smiled shyly.

Innocence.

Reed stood before her in the mist and held his hands out, crying like a baby.

'Hello,' he said.

MURDER IN UTOPIA

I had just finished cauterizing the stump of Ezekiel Metcalfe's left arm, which I had had to amputate after it was shredded in one of the combing machines, when young Billy Ratcliffe came running in to tell me that a man had fallen over the weir.

Believing my medical skills might be required, I left my assistant Benjamin to take care of Ezekiel and tried to keep up with young Billy as he led me down Victoria Road at a breakneck pace. I was not an old man at that time, but I fear I had led a rather sedentary life, and I was panting by the time we passed the allotment gardens in front of the mill. A little more slowly now, we crossed the railway lines and the canal before arriving at the cast-iron bridge that spanned the River Aire.

Several men had gathered on the bridge, and they were looking down into the water, some of them pointing at a dark shape that seemed to bob and twist in the current. As soon as I got my first look at the scene, I knew that none of my skills would be of any use to the poor soul, whose coat had snagged on a tree root poking out from the river bank.

'Did anyone see him fall?' I asked.

They all shook their heads. I picked a couple of stout lads and led them down through the bushes to the river bank. With a little manoeuvring, they were able to lie on their bellies and reach over the shallow edge to grab hold of an arm each. Slowly they raised the dripping body from the water.

When they had completed their task, a gasp arose from the

crowd on the bridge. Though his white face was badly marked with cuts and bruises, there could be hardly a person present who didn't recognize Richard Ellerby, one of Sir Titus Salt's chief wool buyers.

•

Saltaire, where the events of which I am about to speak occurred in the spring of 1873, was then a 'model' village, a mill workers' Utopia of some four or five thousand souls, built by Sir Titus Salt in the valley of the River Aire between Leeds and Bradford. The village, laid out in a simple grid system, still stands, looking much the same as it did then, across the railway lines a little to the south-west of the colossal, six-storey woollen mill to which it owes its existence.

As there was no crime in Utopia, no police force was required, and we relied on constables from nearby townships in the unlikely event that any real unpleasantness or unrest should arise. There was certainly no reason to suspect foul play in Richard Ellerby's death, but legal procedures must be followed in all cases where the circumstances of death are not immediately apparent.

My name is Dr William Oulton, and I was then employed by the Saltaire hospital both as a physician and as a scientist, conducting research into the link between raw wool and anthrax. I also acted as coroner; therefore, I took it as my responsibility to enquire into the facts of Richard Ellerby's death.

In this case, I also had a personal interest, as the deceased was a close acquaintance of mine, and I had dined with him and his charming wife Caroline on a number of occasions. Richard and I both belonged to the Saltaire Institute – Sir Titus's enlightened alternative to the evils of public houses – and we often attended chamber-music concerts there together, played a game of billiards or relaxed in the smoking room, where we had on occasion discussed the possible health problems associated with importing wool. I wouldn't say I knew Richard *well* – he was, in many ways, reserved and private in my company – but I knew him to be an honest and industrious man who believed wholeheartedly in Sir Titus's vision.

My post-mortem examination the following day indicated only that Richard Ellerby had enough water in his lungs to support a verdict of death by drowning. Let me repeat: *there was no reason whatsoever to suspect foul play*. People had fallen over the weir and died in this way before. Assault and murder were crimes that rarely crossed the minds of the denizens of Utopia. That the back of Richard's skull was fractured, and that his face and body were covered with scratches and bruises, could easily be explained by the tumble he took over the weir. It was May and the thaw had created a spate of meltwater, which thundered down from its sources high in the Pennines with such force as easily to cause those injuries I witnessed on the body.

Of course, there *could* be another explanation, and that, perhaps, was why I was loath to let matters stand.

If you have imagined from my tone that I was less fully convinced of Saltaire's standing as a latterday Utopia than some of my contemporaries, then you may compliment yourself on your sensitivity to the nuances of the English language. As I look back on those days, though, I wonder if I am not allowing my present opinions to cloud the glass through which I peer at the past. Perhaps a little. I do know that I certainly believed in Sir Titus's absolute commitment to the idea, but I also think that even back then, after only thirty years on this earth, I had seen far too much of human nature to believe in Utopias like Saltaire.

Besides, I had another quality that would not permit me to let things rest: if I were a cat, believe me, I would be dead by now, nine lives notwithstanding.

•

It was another fine morning when I left Benjamin in charge of the ward rounds and stepped out of the hospital on a matter that had been occupying my mind for the past two days. The almshouses over the road made a pretty sight, set back behind their broad swathe of grass. A few pensioners sat on the benches smoking their pipes under trees bearing pink and white blossoms. Men of 'good moral character', they benefited from Sit Titus's largesse to the extent of free accommodation and a pension of seven shillings and six pence per week, but only as long as they continued to show their 'good moral character'. Charity, after all, is not for everyone, but only for those who merit it.

Lest you think I was a complete cynic at such an early age, I must admit that I found much to admire about Saltaire. Unlike the cramped, airless and filthy back-to-back slums of Bradford, where I myself had seen ten or more people sharing a dark, dank cellar that flooded every time it rained, Saltaire was designed as an open and airy environment. The streets were all paved and well drained, avoiding the filthy conditions that breed disease. Each house had its own outdoor lavatory, which was cleared regularly, again averting the possibility of sickness caused by the sharing of such facilities. Sir Titus also insisted on special measures to reduce the output of smoke from the mill, so that we didn't live under a pall of suffocating fumes, and our pretty sandstone houses were not crusted over with a layer of grime. Still, there is a price to pay for everything, and in Saltaire it was the sense of constantly living out another man's moral vision.

I turned left on Titus Street, passing by the house with the 'spy' tower on top. This extra room was almost all windows, like the top of a lighthouse, and I had often spotted a shadowy figure up there. Rumour has it that Sir Titus employed a man with a telescope to survey the village, to look for signs of trouble and report any infringements to him. I thought I saw someone up there as I passed, but it could have been a trick of sunlight on the glass.

Several women had hung out their washing to dry across Ada Street, as usual. Though everyone knew that Sir Titus frowned on this practice – indeed, he had generously provided public wash houses in an attempt to discourage it – this was their little way of asserting their independence, of cocking a snook at authority.

As befitted a wool buyer, Richard Ellerby had lived with his wife and two children in one of the grander houses on Albert Road, facing westwards, away from the mill towards the open country. According to local practice after bereavement, the upstairs curtains were drawn.

I knocked on the door and waited. Caroline Ellerby opened it herself, wearing her widow's black, and bade me enter. She was a handsome woman, but today her skin was pale and her eyes red-rimmed from weeping. When I was seated in her spacious living room, she asked me if I would care for a small sherry. While Sir Titus would allow no public houses in Saltaire, convinced that they encouraged vice, idleness and profligacy, he held no objection to people serving alcohol in their own homes. Indeed, he was known to keep a well-stocked wine cellar himself. On this occasion I declined, citing the earliness of the hour and the volume of work awaiting me back at the hospital.

Caroline Ellerby smoothed her voluminous black skirts and sat on the chesterfield. After I had expressed my sorrow over her loss and she had inclined her head in acceptance, I moved on to the business that had been occupying my thoughts.

'I need to ask you a few questions about Richard's accident,' I explained to her, 'only if, that is, you feel up to answering them.'

'Of course,' she said, folding her hands on her lap. 'Please continue.'

'When did you last see your husband?'

'The evening before . . . before he was discovered.'

'He was away from the house all night?'

She nodded.

'But surely you must have noticed he was missing?' I realized I was perhaps on the verge of being offensive, or even well beyond the verge, but the matter puzzled me, and when things puzzle me I worry away at them until they yield a solution. I could no more help myself than a tiger can change its stripes.

'I took a sleeping draught,' she said. 'I'm afraid I wouldn't have woken up if you'd set me down in the weaving shed.'

Given that the weaving shed contained twelve hundred power

looms, all thrumming and clattering at once, I suspected Caroline of hyperbole, but she got her point across.

'Believe me,' she went on, 'I have been tormenting myself ever since . . . *If* I hadn't taken the sleeping draught. *If* I had noticed he hadn't come home. *If* I had tried to find him . . .'

'It wouldn't have helped, Caroline,' I said. 'His death must have been very swift. There was nothing you could have done. There's no use torturing yourself.'

'You're very kind, but even so . . .'

'When *did* you notice that Richard hadn't come home?'

'Not until George Walker from the office came to tell me.'

I paused before going on, uncertain how to soften my line of enquiry. 'Caroline, believe me, I don't mean to pry unnecessarily or to cause you any distress, but do you have any idea where Richard went that night?'

She seemed puzzled at my question. 'Went? Why, he went to the Travellers' Rest, of course, out on the Otley Road.'

It was my turn to be surprised. I thought I had known Richard Ellerby, but I didn't know he was a frequenter of public houses; the subject had simply never come up between us. 'The Travellers' Rest? Did he go there often?'

'Not *often*, no, but he enjoyed the atmosphere of a good tavern on occasion. According to Richard, the Travellers' Rest was a respectable establishment. I had no reason not to believe him.'

'Of course not.' I knew of the place, and had certainly heard nothing to blacken its character.

'You seem puzzled, Dr Oulton.'

'Only because your husband never mentioned it to me.'

Caroline summoned up a brief smile. 'Richard comes from humble origins, as I'm sure you know. He has worked very hard, both in Bradford and here at Saltaire, to achieve the elevated position he has attained. He is a great believer in Mr Samuel Smiles and his doctrine of self-help. Despite his personal success and advancement, though, he is not a snob. He has never lost touch with his origins. Richard enjoys the company of his fellow working men in the cheery atmosphere of a good tavern. That is all.'

I nodded. There was nothing unusual in that. I myself ventured to the Shoulder of Mutton, up on the Bingley Road, on occasion. After all, the village was not intended as a prison. It was beginning to dawn on me, though, that Richard probably assumed I was above such things as public houses because I was a member of the professional classes, or that I disapproved of them on health grounds because I was a doctor. I felt a pang of regret that we had never been able to get together over a pipe and a pint of ale. Now that he was dead, we never would.

'Did he ever overindulge?' I went on. 'I ask only because I'm searching for a reason for what happened. If Richard had, perhaps, had too much to drink that night and missed his footing . . .?'

Caroline pursed her lips and frowned, deep in thought for a moment. 'I'll not say he's *never* had a few too many,' she admitted, 'but I *can* say that he was not in the habit of overindulging.'

'And there was nothing on his mind, nothing that might tempt him to have more than his share that night?'

'There were many things on Richard's mind, especially as regarded his work, but nothing unusual, nothing that would drive him to drink, of that I can assure you.' She paused. 'Dr Oulton, is there anything else? I'm afraid I'm very tired. Even with the sleeping draught . . . the past couple of nights . . . I'm sure you can understand. I've had to send the children to mother's. I just can't handle them at the moment.'

I got to my feet. 'Of course. You've been a great help already. Just one small thing?'

She tilted her head. 'Yes?'

'Did Richard have any enemies?'

'Enemies? No. Not that I know of. Surely you can't be suggesting someone did this to him?'

'I don't know, Caroline. I just don't know. That's the problem. Please, stay where you are. I'll see myself out.'

As I walked back to the hospital, I realized that *was* the problem:

I *didn't know*. I also found myself wondering what on earth Richard was doing by the weir if he was coming home from the Travellers' Rest. The canal towpath would certainly be an ideal route to the tavern and back, but the river was north of the canal, and Richard Ellerby's house was south.

•

On my way to the Travellers' Rest that evening, I considered the theory that Richard might have attracted the attention of a villain, or a group of villains, who had subsequently followed him, robbed him and tossed his body over the weir. The only problem with my theory, as far as I could see, was that he still had several gold sovereigns in his pocket, and no self-respecting thieves would have overlooked a haul that big.

As it turned out, the Travellers' Rest was as respectable a tavern as Richard had told his wife, and as cheery a one as I could have hoped for after my gloomy thoughts. It certainly didn't seem to be a haunt of cutpurses and ruffians. On the contrary, the gas-lit public bar was full of warm laughter and conversation, and I recognized several groups of mill workers, many of whom I had treated for one minor ailment or another. Some of them looked up, surprised to see me there, and muttered sheepish hellos. Others were brash and greeted me more loudly, taking my presence as an endorsement of their own indulgence. Jack Liversedge was there, sitting alone in a corner nursing his drink. My heart went out to him; poor Jack had been severely depressed ever since he lost his wife to anthrax two months before, and there seemed nothing anyone could do to console him. He didn't even look up when I entered.

I made my way to the bar and engaged the landlord's attention. He was a plump man with a veined red nose, rather like a radish, which seemed to me to indicate that he was perhaps a whit too fond of his own product. He nodded a crisp greeting, and I asked for a pint of ale. When I had been served, noticing a slight lull in business, I introduced myself and asked him if he remembered

Richard Ellerby's last visit. Once I had described my late colleague, he said that he did.

'Proper gentleman, Mr Ellerby was, sir. I were right sorry to hear about what happened.'

'I was wondering if anything unusual happened that evening.'

'Unusual?'

'Did he drink too much?'

'No, sir. Two or three ales. That's his limit.'

'So he wasn't drunk when he left here, unsteady in his gait?'

'No, sir. Excuse me a moment.' He went to serve another customer then came back. 'No, sir, I can't say as I've ever seen Mr Ellerby inebriated.'

'Were there any rough elements in here that night?'

He shook his head. 'Any rough elements I send packing, up to the Feathers on the Leeds Road. That's a proper rough sort of place, that is. But this is a respectable establishment.' He leaned forward across the bar. 'I'll tell thee summat for nowt, if Mr Salt won't have public houses in his village, there's no better place for his workers to pass an hour or two than the Travellers' Rest, and that's God's honest truth.'

'I'm sure you're right,' I said, 'but surely things must get a little out of hand on occasion?'

He laughed. 'Nothing I can't handle.'

'And you're sure nothing strange happened the last night Mr Ellerby was here?'

'You'd be better off asking him over there about that.' He nodded towards Jack Liversedge, who seemed engaged in a muttered dispute with himself. 'I've as much pity as the next man for a fellow who's lost his wife, poor beggar, but the way he's carrying on . . .' He shook his head.

'What happened?'

'They got into a bit of a barney.'

'What about?'

He shrugged. 'I heard Mr Liversedge call Mr Ellerby no better than a murderer, then he finished his drink and walked out.'

'How much longer before Mr Ellerby left?'

'Five minutes, mebbe. Not long.'

I mulled this over as he excused himself to serve more customers. Jack Liversedge's wife, Florence, a wool sorter, had died of anthrax two months ago. It is a terrible disease, and one we were only slowly coming to understand. Through my own research, I had been in correspondence with two important scientists working in the field: M. Casimir-Joseph Davaine, in France, and Herr Robert Koch, in Germany. Thus far we had been able to determine that the disease is caused by living micro-organisms, most likely hiding in the alpaca wool of the South American llamas and the mohair of the Angora goats, both of which Sir Tutus imported to make his fine cloths, but we were a long way from finding a prevention or a cure.

As I sipped my ale and looked at Jack Liversedge, I began to wonder. Richard Ellerby was a wool buyer. Had Jack, in his distraught and confused state, considered him culpable of Florence's death? Certainly from what I had seen and heard of Jack's erratic behaviour since her death, it was possible, and he was a big, strong fellow.

I was just about to go over to him, without having any clear plan in mind of what to say, when he seemed to come to a pause in his argument with himself, slammed his tankard down and left, bumping into several people on his way out. I decided to go after him.

•

I followed Jack down the stone steps to the towpath and called out his name, at which he turned and asked who I was. I introduced myself.

'Ah,' he said, ''tis thee, Doctor.'

The towpath was unlit, but the canal was straight, and the light of a three-quarter moon lay on the still water like a shroud. It was enough to enable us to see our way.

'I saw you in the Travellers' Rest,' I said. 'You seemed upset. I thought we might share the walk home, if that's all right?'

'As you will.'

We walked in silence, all the while growing closer to the mill, which rose ahead in the silvery light, a ghostly block of sandstone against the black, starlit sky. I didn't know how to broach the subject that was on my mind, fearing that if I were right, Jack would put up a fight, and if I were wrong he would be justly offended. Finally, I decided to muddle along as best I could.

'I hear Richard Ellerby was in the Travellers' the other night, Jack.'

'Is that so?'

'Yes. I hear you argued with him.'

'Mebbe I did.'

'What was it about, Jack? Did you get into a fight with him?'

Jack paused on the path to face me, and for a moment I thought he was going to come at me. I braced myself, but nothing happened. The mill loomed over his shoulder. I could see a number of emotions cross his features in the moonlight, from fear and sorrow to, finally, resignation. He seemed somehow *relieved* that I had asked him about Richard.

'He were the wool buyer, weren't he?' he said, with gritted anger in his voice. 'He should've known.'

I sighed. 'Oh, Jack. Nobody could have known. He just buys the wool. There are no tests. There's no way of *knowing*.'

'It's not right. He bought the wool that killed her. Someone had to pay.'

He turned his back to me and walked on. I followed. We got to bottom of Victoria Road, and I could hear the weir roaring to our right. Jack walked to the cast-iron bridge, where he stood gazing into the rushing water. I went and stood beside him. 'And whose place is it to decide who pays, Jack?' I asked, raising my voice over the water's roar. 'Whose job do you think it is to play God? Yours?'

He looked at me with pity and contempt, then shook his head and said, 'You don't understand.'

I looked down into water, its foam tipped with moonlight. 'Did you kill him?' I asked. 'Did you kill Richard Ellerby because you blamed him for Florence's death?'

He said nothing for a moment, then gave a brief, jerky nod. 'There he were,' he said, 'standing there in his finest coat, drinking and laughing, while my Florence were rotting in her grave.'

'How did it happen?'

'I told him he were no better than a murderer, buying up wool that kills people. I mean, it weren't the first time, were it? He said it weren't his fault, that nobody could've known. Then, when I told him he should take more care, he said I didn't understand, that it were just a hazard of the job, like, and that she should've known she were taking a risk before she took it on.'

If Richard really *had* spoken that way to Jack, then he had certainly been guilty of exhibiting a gross insensitivity I had not suspected to be part of his character. Even if that was the case, we are all capable of saying the wrong thing at the wrong time, especially if we are pushed as far as Jack probably pushed Richard. What he had done had certainly not justified his murder.

'*How* did it happen, Jack?' I asked him.

After a short pause, he said, 'I waited for him on the towpath. All the way home we argued and in the end I lost my temper. There were a long bit of wood from a packing crate or summat by the bushes. He turned his back on me and started walking away. I picked it up and clouted him and down he went.'

'But why the weir?'

'I realized what I'd done.' He gave a harsh laugh. 'It's funny, you know, especially now it doesn't matter. But back then, when I'd just done it, when I knew I'd *killed* a man, I panicked. I thought if I threw his body over the weir then people would think he'd fallen. It weren't far, and he weren't a heavy man.'

'He wasn't dead, Jack,' I said. 'He had water in his lungs. That meant he was alive when he went into the water.'

'It's no matter,' said Jack. 'One way or another, it was me who killed him.'

The water roared in my ears. Jack turned towards me. I flinched and stepped back again, thrusting my arm out to keep him at a distance.

He shook his head slowly, tears in his eyes, and spoke so softly I had to strain to hear him. 'Nay, Doctor, you've nowt to fear from me. It's me who's got summat to fear from you.'

I shook my head. I really didn't know what to do, and my heart was still beating fast from the fear that he had been going to tip me over the railing.

'Well,' he said, 'all I ask is that you leave it till morning. One more night in the house me an Florence shared. Will you do that for me, at least, Doctor?'

As I nodded numbly, he turned and began to walk away.

•

Early the following morning, after a miserable night spent tossing and turning, grappling with my conscience, I was summoned from the hospital to the works office building, attached to the west side of the mill. I hurried down Victoria Road, wondering what on earth it could be about, and soon found myself ushered into a large, well-appointed office with a thick Turkish carpet, dark wainscoting and a number of local landscapes hanging on the walls. Sitting behind the huge mahogany desk was Sir Titus himself, still a grand, imposing figure despite his years and his declining health.

'Dr Oulton,' he said, without looking up from his papers. 'Please sit down.'

I wondered what had brought him the twelve miles or so from Crows Nest, where he lived. He rarely appeared at the mill in those days.

'I understand,' he said in his deep, commanding voice, still not looking at me, 'that you have been enquiring into the circumstances surrounding Richard Ellerby's death?'

I nodded. 'Yes, Sir Titus.'

'And what, pray, have you discovered?'

I took a deep breath, then told him everything. As I spoke, he stood up, clasped his hands behind his back and paced the room, head hanging so that his grey beard almost reached his waist. Though his cheeks and eyes looked sunken, as if he was ill, his presence dominated the room. When I had finished, he sat down again and treated me to a long silence before he said, 'And what are we going to do about it?'

'The police will have to be notified.'

'As yet, then, you and I are the only ones who know the full truth?'

'And Jack himself.'

'Yes, of course.' Sir Titus stroked his beard. I could hear the muffled noise of the mill and feel the vibrations of the power looms shaking the office. It was a warm day, and despite the open window the room was stuffy. I felt the sweat gather on my brow and upper lip. I gazed out of the window and saw the weir, where Richard Ellerby had met his death. 'This is not good,' Sir Titus said finally. 'Not good at all.'

'Sir?'

He gestured with his arm to take in the whole of Saltaire. 'What I mean, Dr Oulton, is that this could be very bad for the village. Very bad. Do you have faith in the experiment?'

'The experiment, sir?'

'The moral experiment that is Saltaire.'

'I have never doubted your motive in wanting to do good, sir.'

Sir Titus managed a thin smile. 'A very revealing answer.' Another long silence followed. He got up and started pacing again. 'If a man visits a public house and becomes so intoxicated that he falls in a river and drowns, then that is an exemplary tale for all of us, wouldn't you say?'

'I would, sir.'

'And if a man, after visiting a public house, is followed by a group of ruffians who attack him, rob him and throw him in a river to drown, then again we have an exemplary – nay, a *cautionary* – tale, do we not?'

'We do, sir. But Richard Ellerby wasn't robbed.'

He waved his hand impatiently. 'Yes, yes, of course. I know that. I'm merely thinking out loud. Please forgive an old man his indulgence. This place – Saltaire – means the world to me, Dr Oulton. Can you understand that? The *world*.'

'I think I can, sir.'

'It's not just a matter of profits, though I'll not deny it's profitable enough. But I think I have created something unique. I call it my "experiment", of course, yet for others it is a home, a way of life. At least I hope it is. It was my aim to make Saltaire everything Bradford was not. It was designed to nurture self-improvement, decency, orderly behaviour and good health among my workers. I wanted to prove that making my own fortune was not incompatible with the material and spiritual wellbeing of the working classes. I saw it as my duty, my God-given duty. If the Lord looks so favourably upon me, then I take that as an obligation to look favourably upon my workers. Do you follow me?'

'Yes, sir.'

'And now this. Murder. Manslaughter. Call it what you will. It disrupts the fabric of things. It could destroy any trust that might have built up in the community. No doubt you remember the troubles we had over anthrax some years ago?'

'I do, sir.' In 1868 a man called Sutcliffe Rhodes had garnered much support from the village in his campaign against anthrax, and Sir Titus had been seriously embarrassed by the whole matter. 'But surely you can't expect me to ignore what I know, sir?' I said. 'To lie.'

Sir Titus smiled grimly. 'I could never ask a man to go against his beliefs, Doctor. All I ask is that you follow the dictates of your own conscience, but that you please bear in mind the consequences. If this issue surfaces again, especially in this way, then we're done for. Nobody will *believe* in the goodness of Saltaire any more, and I meant it to be a *good* place, a place where there would never be any reason for murder to occur.'

He shook his head in sadness and let the silence stretch again. Above the noise of the mill I suddenly heard men shouting. Someone hammered on the door and dashed into the office without ceremony. I couldn't be certain, but my first impression was that it was the same shadowy figure I had seen in the 'spy' tower.

'Sir Titus,' the interloper said, after a quick bow, 'my apologies for barging in like this, but you must come. There's a man on the mill roof.'

Sir Titus and I frowned at one another, then we followed him outside. I walked slowly, in deference to Sir Titus's age, and it took us several minutes to get around to the allotment gardens, from where we had a clear view.

The man stood atop the mill roof, full six storeys up, between its two decorative lanterns. I could also make out another figure inside one of the lanterns, perhaps talking to him. But the man on the roof didn't appear to be listening. He stood right at the edge and, even as we watched, he spread out his arms as if attempting to fly, then he sprang off the roof and seemed to hover in the air for a moment before falling with a thud to the forecourt.

It was a curious sensation. Though I knew in my heart and mind that I was witnessing the death of a fellow human being, there was a distant quality about the event. The figure was dwarfed by the mill, for a start, and just in front of us, a dog scratched at the dirt, as if digging for its bone, and it didn't cease during the man's entire fall to earth.

A mill hand came running up and told us that the man who had jumped was Jack Liversedge. Again it was an eerie feeling, but I suppose, in a way, I already knew that.

'An accident and a suicide,' muttered Sir Titus, fixing me with his deep-set eyes. 'It's bad enough, but we can weather it, wouldn't you say, Doctor?' There was hope in his voice.

My jaw tensed. I was tempted to tell him to go to hell, that his vision, his *experiment*, wasn't worth lying for. But I saw in front of me a sick old man who had at least tried to do *something* for the people who made him rich. Whether it was enough or not was not for me to say. Saltaire wasn't perfect – perfection is a state we will never find on this earth – but it was better than most mill towns.

Swallowing my bile, I gave Sir Titus a curt nod and set off back up Victoria Road to the hospital.

•

In the days and weeks that followed, I tried to continue with my work – after all, the people of Saltaire still needed a hospital and a doctor – but after Jack Liversedge's pointless death, my heart just didn't seem to be in it any more. Jack's dramatic suicide lowered the morale of the town for a short while – there were long faces everywhere and some mutterings of dissent – but eventually it was forgotten, and the townspeople threw themselves back into their work: weaving fine cloths of alpaca and mohair for those wealthy enough to be able to afford them.

Still, no matter how much I tried to convince myself to put the matter behind me and carry on, I felt there was something missing from the community; something more than a mere man had died the day Jack killed himself.

One day, after I had spent a wearying few hours tending to one of the wool sorters dying of anthrax, I made my decision to leave. A month later, after sorting out my affairs and helping my replacement settle in, I left Saltaire for South Africa, where I eventually met the woman who was to become my wife. We raised our three children, and I practised my profession in Cape Town for thirty years. After my retirement, we decided to move back to England, where we settled comfortably in a small Cornish fishing village. Now, my children are grown up, married and gone away, my wife is dead and I am an old man who spends his days wandering the cliffs above the sea watching the birds soar and dip.

And sometimes the sound of the waves reminds me of the roar of the Saltaire weir.

More than forty years have now passed since that night by the weir, when Jack Liversedge told me he had killed Richard Ellerby; more than forty years have passed since Sir Titus and I stood by the allotments and saw Jack's body fall and break on the forecourt of the mill.

Forty years. Long enough to keep a secret.

Besides, the world has changed so much since then that what happened that day long ago in Saltaire seems of little consequence now. Sir Titus died three years after Jack's fall, and his dream died with him. Fashions changed, and the ladies no longer wanted the bright, radiant fabrics that Sir Titus had produced. His son, Titus junior, struggled with the business until he, too, died in 1887, and the mill was taken over by a consortium of Bradford businessmen. Today, Saltaire is no longer a moral experiment or a mill workers' Utopia; it is merely another business.

And today, in July 1916, nobody believes in Utopias any more.

NOT SAFE AFTER DARK

He had only gone out to the convenience store for cigarettes, but the park across the intersection looked inviting. It seemed to offer a brief escape from the heat and dirt and noise of the city. Cars whooshed by, radios blasting rock and funk and rap into the hot summer night. Street lights and coloured neons looked smeared and blurry in the humid heat. A walk among the trees by the lake might cool him down a little.

He knew he shouldn't, knew it was dangerous. What was it the guidebooks always said about big city parks? *Not safe after dark*. That was it. No matter which park they talked about – Central Park, Golden Gate Park – they were always *not safe after dark*.

He wondered why. Parks were quiet, peaceful places, a few acres of unspoilt nature in the heart of the city. People took their dogs for walks; children played on swings and teeter-totters. Parks provided retreats for meditation and the contemplation of nature, surely, not playgrounds for the corrupt and the delinquent.

There was more danger, he thought, among the dregs of humanity that haunted the vast urban sex and drug supermarkets like Times Square or the Tenderloin. There you got mugged, beaten up, raped, even murdered, for no good reason at all.

Hoodlums and thugs weren't into nature; they were happier idling on street corners harassing passers-by, starting fights in strip clubs or rock bars, and selling drugs in garbage-strewn alleys. If they wanted to mug someone, they had more chance downtown, where the crowds were thick and some fool always took a short cut down a dark alley. If they just wanted to scare and hurt people for the fun of it, crowded places like shopping malls guaranteed them both the victims and the audience.

Or so he found himself reasoning as he stood there by the traffic lights. Should he risk it? Over the road, the dark, tangled mass of branches tossed in the hot breeze like billowing black smoke against the starlit sky. A yellowish full moon, surrounded by a halo, gilded the tree tops. The traffic lights changed to green, and after only a moment's hesitation, he began to cross. Why not? What could possibly happen? The entrance, a long, tree-lined avenue, seemed rolled out like a tongue ready to lick him up and draw him into the park's dark mouth. Maybe he had a death wish, though he didn't think so.

Muted, wrought-iron street lamps flanked the broad cinder path, which led under a small imitation Arc de Triomphe gate overgrown with weeds and lichen. Beyond that, the branches swayed slowly in the muggy gusts, leaves making a wet, hissing sound. The dimly lit path, he noticed, was lined with statues. He went over to see if he could make out any of the names. Writers: Shakespeare, Sir Walter Scott, Tennyson, Wordsworth. What on earth were they doing there?

The avenue ended at a small boating pool. In the water, a child's yacht with a white sail turned in slow circles. The sight brought a lump to his throat. He didn't know why, but somewhere, perhaps buried deep in his memories, was just such a feeling of loss or of drifting aimlessly in circles, never arriving. It made him feel suddenly, inexplicably sad.

Beyond the pond the park stretched, rising and falling down to the lake. Here were no broad avenues, only tarmac paths and dirt trails. He took one of the main paths that wound deeper into the woods. He could always take a side path later if he wanted. So far he had seen no one, and the traffic sounds from the main road sounded more and more distant behind him. It was much darker now, away from the dim antique lights of the entrance. Only the jaundiced and haze-shrouded moon shone through the trees and slicked the path with oily gold. But as he walked, he found his eyes soon adjusted. At least he could make out shapes, if not details.

After he had been walking a few minutes, he noticed a playground to his left. There was nobody in it at this time of night, but one of the swings was rocking back and forth gently in the wind, creaking where its chains needed greasing. He felt like sitting on one of the wooden seats and shooting himself high, aiming his feet at the moon. But it would only draw unwelcome attention. Just being here was supposed to be dangerous enough, without asking for trouble. Somewhere, back on the road, he heard the whine of a police siren.

Off to the right, a path wound up the hillside between the trees. He took it. It was some kind of fitness trail. Every so often, he could make out wooden chin bars where the joggers were encouraged to pause and do a few pull-ups. Occasionally, he would hear a scuttling sound in the undergrowth. At first, it scared him, but he figured it was only a harmless squirrel, or a chipmunk running away.

The path straightened out at the top of the short hill, and almost before he knew it he was in a clearing surrounded by trees. He thought he heard a different sound now, a low moan or a sigh. He pulled back quickly behind a tree. In the clearing stood a number of picnic benches, and at one of them he could just make out a couple of human figures. It took him a few seconds to focus clearly in the poor light, but when he realized what was happening, his throat constricted and his heart seemed to start thumping so loudly he was sure they could hear him.

There were two of them. One half-sat on the table edge, hands stretched behind, supporting himself as he arched backwards. The other knelt at his feet, head bowed forward. They seemed to freeze for a moment, as if they had heard him, then the one on the table said something he couldn't quite catch and the one on his knees continued slowly moving his head forward and back.

He felt sick and dizzy. He clutched onto the tree tightly and tried to control the swimming feeling in his head. He couldn't afford to faint – not here, not now, with those two so close. After a few deep breaths, he turned as quietly as he could and hurried down a dirt track that forked off in another direction.

After he had covered a good distance as fast as he dare go, he squatted in the ferns at the side of the trail, head in hands, and waited for his heart to still and his breathing to become regular. An insect crawled up his bare arm; he shuddered and brushed it off.

He was beginning to feel really scared now. He had no idea where he was, which direction he was travelling in. Like that yacht back in the pond a million miles away, he could be going in circles. Again he fought back the panic and walked on. Now he cursed his stupidity. Why had he come here? It hadn't been a good idea at all. He would wander round and round, then end up back where he started. He would collapse with exhaustion and those two men from the picnic table would find him and . . . Maybe he did have a death wish, after all. He should have taken notice of the guidebooks. He told himself to stop panicking and calm down.

Before he had got much further, he heard voices just off the path over to his left. He paused. Someone was singing an old Neil Young song. Someone else said 'Shut up,' then a girl giggled. After that came more singing, then a loud yell. They were drunk; that was it. As if to confirm his suspicions, he heard the sound of a bottle smashing on a road. He decided he had better lie low and keep out of their way. There was no telling what a gang of drunks might do to someone walking alone in the park. So he waited, behind a tree, as their voices faded slowly into the distance. He stayed where he was until he could hear them no longer, then set off again.

When he crested the next hill, he could see the lights of houses to his right and left. The park had narrowed to a kind of deep ravine now, and the path he was on ran parallel to its bottom, about halfway up one side. If he left the path and walked all the way up the side, he would probably soon find himself in someone's back garden.

He could see the moonlight gleaming on the surface of the narrow stream that flowed along the bottom. Across the other side, he could make out the lights of a police car flashing along a road that skirted the ravine's edge. The hillside was thickly wooded and the spaces between trees filled with ferns and shrubbery. At least now, he thought, he ought to be able to find his way back to civilization easily enough.

He heard a noise lower down the hillside and realized there was another path, running parallel to his, about fifty yards below, closer to the water. Again, he froze. This sound was far too loud to be a squirrel or a bird; it certainly wasn't the sound of a small animal running away, but more like a large one coming *towards* him.

He crouched by the edge of the dirt path and peered down through the bushes. He couldn't make much out at first, but something was moving through the undergrowth. A few moments later, his heart beating fast again, he saw the eyes, not more than thirty yards away down the slope. What was it? A fox? A wolf? Then he heard the woman's voice: 'Jason! Jason! Where are you, boy? Come on.' And she whistled. So it was a dog! But Jason took no notice of her. It seemed to have caught his scent and was making its way cautiously up the hillside to check him out.

He couldn't tell from that distance in the dark, but he was worried that it might be a pit bull or a Rottweiler. Surely no woman would go walking alone in the park at night without a vicious dog to guard her? He felt beside him on the path and his hand grasped a large stone, just big enough to hold. The dog came closer. 'Come on, Jason,' he whispered. 'Come on, boy!' The dog barked and made the last few yards in a dash. He swung the rock hard at its head, and the dog whimpered, then let out a low wail and collapsed.

'Jason?' the woman called from below. 'Jason! Where are you?' She sounded worried now. He could just about make her out in the faint light. She looked youngish, with long hair tied behind her neck in a ponytail, and she was wearing shorts and a T-shirt. She called for the dog again, then left the path and started climbing the hill through the shrubbery to the place she'd heard it wail.

Thirty yards. Twenty-five. Twenty. He could see the moonlight glint on her bracelet. Fifteen. He could hear her panting with effort. Ten. She ran the back of her hand over her brow and pushed back a stray tress of hair. 'Jason?' Five. He glanced around and listened. Nothing. So close to civilization, yet so far. There was nobody around but him and her.

Four. He held his breath. Three yards. She slipped back but managed to grasp a root and keep her balance. Two. He gripped the rock tight in his hand and felt it sticky and warm with the dog's blood. She was almost there now. Just a few more steps. One. He gripped the rock tighter, raising his arm. Suddenly he felt himself filled with strange joy and he knew he was grinning like an idiot. So this was why he had come. He didn't have a death wish, after all. What on earth had those fools who wrote the guidebooks meant? Of course it was safe after dark. Perfectly safe.

JUST MY LUCK

Los Angeles was the last place Walter Dimchuk would have chosen for the convention. A confirmed Torontonian, Walter had never been able to take California seriously. It seemed to him that the people there merely played at life under the palm trees and came up with loony-tune ideas.

Take the cuisine, if you could call it that: it was either Mexican, which gave Walter the runs, or so-called 'Californian': watercress, alfalfa sprouts and avocado with everything, even a burger. Faggot food, more like. He'd had a house salad just yesterday in which he hadn't recognized one single ingredient. Cilantro, arugula, fresh basil, sun-dried tomatoes and goat's cheese, the waiter had told him. With a dressing of tarragon, balsamic vinegar, cardamom oil and toasted pine nuts, for Christ's sake. Just his luck. Couldn't a person get a simple grilled cheese sandwich and a glass of milk in this state?

Smog, killer freeways, serial-killer bubblegum cards, earthquakes, Rodney King riots, more fruit loops per square mile than an asylum . . . the list went on. He hadn't been happy about leaving Kate and Maria alone in the house either. They might not be as close a family as they had once been – what could you expect after thirty-five years of marriage and three children grown up to adults – but they still got on all right, mostly thanks to Maria, a late blessing when Kate was forty-five, and now a gawky thirteen-year-old.

The only good thing about the trip that Walter had been able to come up with on the plane over (Air Canada, three hours late, sweet Jesus, just Walter's fucking luck) was a brief respite from a cool Toronto October.

But he hadn't banked on the Santa Ana. When Toronto got hot, you sweated; here you dried to dust, dehydrated in seconds. He had once read a story about the hot, desert wind, the way it made meek wives feel the edge of the carving knife and study their husbands' necks. The writer was right: it *did* make you edgy and crazy. Walter felt as if he'd had a steel band around his forehead for two days. It was getting tighter.

'Wally!'

Walter came out of his reverie. He was sitting in the hotel lobby taking a smoke break between sessions. Nobody seemed to smoke these days. In California it was hardly surprising: you couldn't find many places where it was legal to do so. Damn government health warnings on everything now, even the wine. And he had seen the way the young hotshots with their white teeth turned up their noses when he lit up, even if they were sitting in a goddamn bar. Christ, who was this coming towards him, hand outstretched, teeth bared in a predatory smile? Should he remember? Awkwardly, he got to his feet.

'Hi, good to see you,' he said.

'Good to see *you*!' the stranger said. 'It's been years.'

'Yeah.' Walter scratched the side of his right eye and frowned. 'Now where the hell was it . . . ?'

'Baltimore. Baltimore, 'seventy-nine. Jimmy Lavalli. Remember, we closed down that bar together?'

'Yeah, of course. How you doing, Jimmy?'

And so it went on, the empty greetings, inane conversations, tales of triple bypasses, and all the time Walter knew, deep inside, that they were all out to get him, were all laughing at him. 'Oh, old Wally Woodchuk, Wally Dump-truck, Wally Up-chuck, fucking dinosaur, sales have been down for years.' No one had said it to his face, but they didn't need to. Wally knew. At fifty-nine, he was too old for the pool supplies business. And it was obvious from the number of tanned young men around the convention that the company thought so too. You'd almost think the new breed were chosen because they'd look good sitting around a swimming pool, like the way auto manufacturers used curvaceous women to sell cars. Wally's curves were in all the wrong places. Ungrateful bastards. He'd given his life to Hudson's Pools and Supplies, and this was how they paid him back. He felt like that salesman in the play must have done, the one that guy who'd been married to Marilyn Monroe – not the baseball player, one of the others – had written for Dustin Hoffman.

He had heard the talk around the office, noticed the muted conversations and insincere greetings as he passed couples chatting in the corridor. They were putting him out to pasture. That was why they sent him to California. He wouldn't be surprised if his office – if you could call a screened-off corner in an open plan an office – was cleaned out when he got back and someone else was sitting there in his place. Some tanned young asshole with white teeth and a wolfish smile. Maybe called Scott.

He got rid of Jimmy with promises to look him up if he was ever in Baltimore (not if he could help it!) and looked at his watch. Five o'clock. Shit. Time for another boring session, then up to get changed for the convention banquet. Tofu burgers again, most likely. Maybe grab a few minutes in between and call Kate . . .

•

Thank God that was over with, Walter thought, as he waved goodnight to the stragglers in the Pasadena Ballroom and headed for the elevator. What a fucking ordeal. And typical California, too – no smoking, not *anywhere* in the dining hall. Not tofu burgers, but almost as bad: Cornish game hen or some such skinny little bird stuffed with grapes and olives and jalapeno peppers, basted in lemon, garlic and the ubiquitous cilantro, of course. And they had to put him at the table with that loud-mouthed jerk Carson, from United. Just his luck. Still, Walter had kept his end up. He had been nice to the right people, managed a smile, passed his company card around, even if the recipients did absently slip it into their side pockets where they'd throw it out with the lint and the hotel matches.

A funny business these conventions, he thought as went into his room. Hours of manic glad-handing, hurried conversations in lobbies and men's rooms, talking business even with your dick in your hand, then when you finally got to be alone at the end of the night, all you felt was an incredible loneliness descend. At least Walter did.

So there you are in your strange hotel room alone miles from home after the party. Oh, the guys were setting up all-night poker sessions, planning trips to strip joints and bars, but Walter had had enough of all that, and of his colleagues. He wanted to *be* alone, but he didn't want to *feel* alone.

It was the wind, he thought, that goddamn Santa Ana. And the air-conditioner had quit. Just his luck. He lay down on the bed with his hands behind his head and tried to relax. He couldn't. He hadn't drunk much. That was one thing he had under control these days. That was why he couldn't for the life of him remember closing any bar with Jimmy Lavalli in Baltimore. If those tanned bastards knew what they looked like after they'd had a few too many . . . anyway, those days were past. As he lay there restless in the heat, feeling the band tighten around his head, the heartburn start to kick in, the resentment and fear churn inside him, he became aware of one feeling he would never have expected. God dammit, Walter Dimchuk was horny!

Not that it had never happened before, of course, but never with such a keen, urgent edge, not for a long time. He remembered the outing he'd had with Al and Larry yesterday afternoon. Given a couple of spare hours, they had driven to Santa Monica, walked on the pier, the boardwalk towards Venice. And now as he lay trying to find sleep, all Walter could find were the disturbing images of those girls in their bikinis, all that smooth, firm, tanned flesh.

He turned over. This was ridiculous. His lust felt so strong it was gripping his heart, making him squirm. The images churned in his mind, spurring him on. It was the damn heat, he knew it. Maybe if he could get out for a while. Tell someone at the desk to fix his air-conditioning while he took a little drive around town.

He sat up and slid his shoes back on. Yeah, that was the thing to do. Maybe drive to the ocean and cool off a little. That or a cold shower. He looked at his watch. Still only eleven o'clock. OK, car keys, jacket . . .

•

Such romantic-sounding street names they had: La Cienega, Sepulveda, La Brea. But they weren't so fucking romantic when you were on them; they were either freeways or roads running past shitty little Spanish-style stucco houses with graffiti all over the stucco and postage-stamp gardens full of junk.

It was cool in the rental, but Walter still couldn't shake the horniness. He'd pass a row of stores set back from the road and see a gang of kids there, girls in cut-off jeans and halter tops drinking Coke from the bottle, breasts jutting out. It was getting worse, as if the Santa Ana somehow slipped in through the air-conditioning and messed with his brain.

He found himself on Hollywood Boulevard. Walter loved old movies, the black and white kind, and the real stars they had back then like Cary Grant, Garbo, Bogie, Gable, Jimmy Stewart. Christ, he must have seen *It's a Wonderful Life* about twenty times, and then they went and colourized the motherfucker. But the boulevard, with all those stars in the sidewalk, had gone to porn theatres, dirty bookstores with barred windows, hookers, pimps, muggers, losers.

He was stopped at a red light when he heard the tap on his window. If it had been a man, he would have burnt rubber driving away, even through a stop light. It wasn't. Nervously, he rolled down the window.

'Wann' good time, mister? Wann' have some fun?'

He looked at her. She must have been all of sixteen, going on forty, but she was pretty, a Latino with that honey skin and lustrous black hair. From what he could see of the rest of her, it looked pretty good too.

Walter hesitated. He had never been with a hooker before. He knew it happened at conventions, and somehow the guys thought it was all right, playing away from home like that. What the old lady doesn't know won't hurt her, hey Wally? But Walter had never done it. Now, though, with this girl hanging in his window practically spilling her tits onto his lap, with the lights changing, someone blowing a horn behind him and the desire sharp as knife cutting away inside him . . . Well, he opened the door.

The hooker got in and Walter drove off. She was wearing a short black skirt, way up around her thighs, and a tight pink halter made of material so thin he could see her nipples poking though. Her bare midriff was flat, with an outie belly button.

His mouth was dry. 'Where?' he croaked.

She directed him to a rundown hotel off Sunset, and he followed her up the stairs in a daze, aware only of the smell of disinfectant and rotting meat in the dim lobby and of the scuffed, stained linoleum on the stairs.

In the shaded light, the room didn't look too bad. What did it matter, anyway? She took his money first, then Walter watched as she wriggled out of the halter and her honey breasts with the dark hard nipples quivered as they fell free. Grinning at him, the tip of her tongue between her small, white teeth, she unzipped her skirt and let it fall. She was wearing only white panties now. He could see the dark shadow of her pubic hair, and some of the hairs curled around the edges of the silky material.

'You no undress?' she asked. 'Wann' me take your clothes off?'

Walter nodded. Deftly, she took off his jacket, shirt, pants.

'Oh, my, you so big,' she said, touching his erection. 'So big and hard. Safe,' she said, reaching for a condom from her bag. 'Always safe.'

Walter felt glad of that. AIDS had crossed his mind more than once between Hollywood Boulevard and the hotel, but if she always insisted on a condom she was bound to be clean, he thought. Desire seared like the sharp, hot desert wind inside him, driving him recklessly and thoughtlessly on.

She put her hands on his chest and pushed him gently down on the bed, then she straddled him, felt for his penis between her legs and thrust down on it slowly. Walter groaned and reached for her breasts as she moved back and forth on him. Dimly, he was aware of the bed springs creaking, but it didn't matter. Nothing mattered but this moist, warm tightness all around him, sucking him in, hooking onto his desire and channelling it, concentrating it. He couldn't have held back if he'd tried. It seemed like no time at all when everything burst and warmth flooded his veins. The woman moaned. He knew she was faking, but he didn't care.

Then it was all over. Walter thanked her and hurried out to his car and his shame. At first, he sat there breathing hard and cranked up the air-conditioner. His stomach clenched, his loins felt dry and empty, but the steel band was still there, tightening around his skull. Lighting a cigarette, he turned onto the boulevard and headed back to the hotel.

•

They still hadn't fixed the air-conditioning, he noticed, and when he phoned down to complain, the desk clerk said no one would be able to do it till the morning. Just his fucking luck. He should have felt better after sating his desire, he knew, but when he lay down and relived what he had just done he was appalled.

It was only midnight. No more than an hour ago he had been an innocent, a virtuous man. Now he had been tainted. How little time it took. And now he was worried, too. Condom or no condom, he could still get AIDS. That was a fact. The wind had done this to him, the wind and the palm trees and the hooker with the wonderful breasts and the sweet, warm place inside her. He'd been suckered. Jesus Christ, he wept, how could he face Kate and Maria again, after he'd been corrupted? That hooker hadn't been much older than his daughter. The goddamn hot wind had made him fuck his own daughter. Even if they didn't know, *he* knew. He couldn't face them. His marriage was over, his family broken, all because of some two-bit whore who had tempted him and given him a disease. He ground his teeth. The heat seemed to bore into his bones the way the damp cold did in England that time he went with Kate, so many years ago. He was burning up. Maybe he was already showing symptoms of whatever disease that whore had given him. But that was ridiculous. Maybe he'd got flu. Or maybe it was the Santa Ana.

He turned over and tried to sleep, but the steel band tightened and the guilt hammered away at him, making sleep impossible. His life was ruined. All because of fucking California. He couldn't think straight any more. Nothing but images shot through his mind, disjointed images: Kate crying; Maria slipping her panties off and rubbing her hand between her legs; the tanned assholes with the two-thousand-dollar smiles who were going to have his job. He couldn't take it any more. He had to do something. Christ, they'd walked over old Walter Dimchuk for long enough, pushed him around, used him for a doormat, laughed behind his back. Now they'd corrupted his soul. God dammit, enough was enough. His luck was going to change.

Hardly thinking, he got dressed quickly and picked up his car keys. At the last moment, just before the door shut behind him, he went back and picked up the ice pick from the dish by the television.

•

This time it was a Caucasian girl: blonde hair, clean-cut looks, but the same style, tight short skirt and halter top. And she wanted to make a quick phone call before she got into his car and directed him to a different hotel. It was a step up from the last one, he noticed, for Wally was noticing things clearly now, like the old-fashioned bell on the wooden desk, the discreet damask armchairs in the lobby, the wood-panelling look, the hovering scent of sandalwood. In fact, Walter felt strangely calm and in control now he knew what he was going to do. The steel band had loosened.

He smiled to himself as she went through her undressing routine, a bit more elaborate and drawn out than the last one, with slow gestures and teasing glances. He felt no desire now; it was all gone. He let her continue.

Outside, the hot wind huffed and puffed at the windows. The halter revealed white, droopy breasts, the kind that fold over like envelope flaps. Her eyes were unfocused and dull, as if she were on drugs. She had a large bruise on the outside of her right thigh and a little scar just under her navel. Appendicitis? he wondered. But the appendix was further to the right, wasn't it? No matter. She stood naked before him finally, and he still felt no desire, only disgust and hatred. It wasn't the same one who had ruined him, corrupted him, but they were all the same underneath. Whores. They all shared the same tainted, rotten soul. She would do. He let her unbutton his shirt, then he moved her gently away and asked her to lie face down on the bed.

'Wanna come in from behind, hey, honey?' she said, and grinned lasciviously, lying down and hugging the pillow.

'No, that's not it.' Walter's voice felt strange – dry and stuck deep in his chest. 'That's not it at all.'

'S'OK by me.'

Walter slipped the ice pick from his jacket pocket and felt its point cool in his dry hand. He was just about to raise it above his head and plunge into the back of her neck when he heard a sound behind him.

Everything happened so fast. First, the door opened, and Walter saw a huge man blocking the exit, a giant with blond hair hanging over his massive shoulders, a tanned face carved of rock and veins thick as cables snaking down his thick arms. The man, he also noticed, was wearing a sleeveless white T-shirt and baggy, flowered pants held up by elastic.

Shit, Walter thought, glancing back at the girl for a second, then at his jacket over the back of a chair, they're going to rip me off, rob me. That's what the phone call was about. Just my fucking luck.

But what Walter didn't really register until it was much too late was that when he turned towards the doorway, he had an ice pick still raised above his head, and the other man had a gun.

Walter never did get a chance to explain. The giant raised his gun and, without a word, fired two shots right into Walter Dimchuk's angry, corrupt and unlucky heart.

ANNA SAID

AN INSPECTOR BANKS STORY

1

'I'm not happy with it, laddie,' said Dr Glendenning, shaking his head. 'Not happy at all.'

'So the super told me,' said Banks. 'What's the problem?'

They sat at a dimpled, copper-topped table in the Queen's Arms, Glendenning over a glass of Glenmorangie and Banks over a pint of Theakston's. It was a bitterly cold evening in February. Banks was anxious to get home and take Sandra out to dinner as he had promised, but Dr Glendenning had asked for help, and a Home Office pathologist was too important to brush off.

'One of these?' Glendenning offered Banks a Senior Service.

Banks grimaced. 'No. No thanks. I'll stick with tipped. I'm trying to give up.'

'Aye,' said Glendenning, lighting up. 'Me, too.'

'So what's the problem?'

'She should never have died,' the doctor said, 'but that's by the way. These things happen.'

'Who shouldn't have died?'

'Oh, sorry. Forgot you didn't know. Anna, Anna Childers is – was – her name. Admitted to the hospital this morning.'

'Any reason to suspect a crime?'

'No-o, not on the surface. That's why I wanted an informal chat first.' Rain lashed at the window; the buzz of conversation rose and fell around them.

'What happened?' Banks asked.

'Her boyfriend brought her in at about ten o'clock this

morning. He said she'd been up half the night vomiting. They thought it was gastric flu. Dr Gibson treated the symptoms as best he could, but . . .' Glendenning shrugged.

'Cause of death?'

'Respiratory failure. If she hadn't suffered from asthma, she might have had a chance. Dr Gibson managed at least to get the convulsions under control. But as for the cause of it all, don't ask me. I've no idea yet. It could have been food poisoning. Or she could have taken something, a suicide attempt. You know how I hate guesswork.' He looked at his watch and finished his drink. 'Anyway, I'm off to do the post-mortem now. Should know a bit more after that.'

'What do you want me to do?'

'You're the copper, laddie. I'll not tell you your job. All I'll say is the circumstances are suspicious enough to worry me. Maybe you could talk to the boyfriend?'

Banks took out his notebook. 'What's his name and address?'

Glendenning told him and left. Banks sighed and went to the telephone. Sandra wouldn't like this at all.

2

Banks pulled up outside Anna Childers's large semi in south Eastvale, near the big roundabout, and turned off the tape of Furtwängler conducting Beethoven's Ninth. It was the 1951 live Bayreuth recording, mono but magnificent. The rain was still falling hard, and Banks fancied he could feel the sting of hail against his cheek as he dashed to the door, raincoat collar turned up.

The man who answered his ring, John Billings, looked awful. Normally, Banks guessed, he was a clean-cut, athletic type, at his best on a tennis court, perhaps, or a ski slope, but grief and lack of sleep had turned his skin pale and his features puffy. His shoulders slumped as Banks followed him into the living room, which looked like one of the package designs advertised in the Sunday colour supplements. Banks sat down in a damask-upholstered armchair and shivered.

'I'm sorry,' muttered Billings, turning on the gas fire. 'I didn't . . .'

'It's understandable,' Banks said, leaning forward and rubbing his hands.

'There's nothing wrong, is there?' Billings asked. 'I mean, the police . . . ?'

'Nothing for you to worry about,' Banks said. 'Just some questions.'

'Yes.' Billings flopped onto the sofa and crossed his legs. 'Of course.'

'I'm sorry about what happened,' Banks began. 'I just want to get some idea of how. It all seems a bit of a mystery to the doctors.'

Billings sniffed. 'You can say that again.'

'When did Anna start feeling ill?'

'About four in the morning. She complained of a headache, said she was feeling dizzy. Then she was up and down to the toilet the rest of the night. I thought it was a virus or something. I mean, you don't go running off to the doctor's over the least little thing, do you?'

'But it got worse?'

'Yes. It just wouldn't stop.' He held his face in his hands. Banks heard the hissing of the fire and the pellets of hail against the curtained window. Billings took a deep breath. 'I'm sorry. At the end she was bringing up blood, shivering, and she had problems breathing. Then . . . well, you know what happened.'

'How long had you known her?'

'Pardon?'

Banks repeated the question.

'A couple of years in all, I suppose. But only as a business acquaintance at first. Anna's a chartered accountant and I run a small consultancy firm. She did some auditing work for us.'

'That's how you met her?'

'Yes.'

Banks looked around at the entertainment centre, the framed Van Gogh print. 'Who owns the house?'

If Billings was surprised at the question, he didn't show it. 'Anna. It was only a temporary arrangement, my living here. I had a flat. I moved out. We were going to get married, buy a house together somewhere in the dale. Helmthorpe, perhaps.'

'How long had you been going out together?'

'Six months.'

'Living together?'

'Three.'

'Getting on all right?'

'I told you. We were going to get married.'

'You say you'd known her two years, but you've only been seeing each other six months. What took you so long? Was there someone else?'

Billings nodded.

'For you or her?'

'For Anna. Owen was still living with her until about seven months ago. Owen Doughton.'

'And they split up?'

'Yes.'

'Any bitterness?'

Billings shook his head. 'No. It was all very civilized. They weren't married. Anna said they just started going their different ways. They'd been together about five years and they felt they weren't really going anywhere together, so they decided to separate.'

'What did the two of you do last night?'

'We went out for dinner at that Chinese place on Kendal Road. You don't think it could have been that?'

'I really can't say. What did you eat?'

'The usual. Egg rolls, chicken chow mein, a Szechuan prawn dish. We shared everything.'

'Are you sure?'

'Yes. We usually do. Anna doesn't really like spicy food, but she'll have a little, just to keep me happy. I'm a curry nut, myself. The hotter the better. I thought at first maybe that was what made her sick, you know, if it wasn't the flu, the chillies they use.'

'Then you came straight home?'

'No. We stopped for a drink at the Red Lion. Got home just after eleven.'

'And Anna was feeling fine?'

'Yes. Fine.'

'What did you do when you got home?'

'Nothing much, really. Pottered around a bit, then we went to bed.'

'And that's it?'

'Yes. I must admit, I felt a little unwell myself during the night. I had a headache and an upset stomach, but Alka-Seltzer soon put it right. I just can't believe it. I keep thinking she'll walk in the door at any moment and say it was all mistake.'

'Did Anna have a nightcap or anything?' Banks asked after a pause. 'A cup of Horlicks, something like that?'

He shook his head. 'She couldn't stand Horlicks. No, neither of us had anything after the pub.'

Banks stood up. The room was warm now and his blotched raincoat had started to dry out. 'Thanks very much,' he said, offering his hand. 'And again, I'm sorry for intruding on your grief.'

Billings shrugged. 'What do you think it was?'

'I don't know yet. There is one more thing I have to ask. Please don't take offence.'

Billings stared at him. 'Go on.'

'Was Anna upset about anything? Depressed?'

He shook his head vigorously. 'No, no. Quite the opposite. She was happier than she'd ever been. She told me. I know what you're getting at, Inspector – the doctor suggested the same thing – but you can forget it. Anna would never have tried to take her own life. She just wasn't that kind of person. She was too full of life and energy.'

Banks nodded. If he'd had a pound for every time he'd heard that about a suicide he would be a rich man. 'Fair enough,' he said. 'Just for the record, this Owen, where does he live?'

'I'm afraid I don't know. He works at that big garden centre just off North Market Street, over from the Town Hall.'

'I know it. Thanks very much, Mr Billings.'

Banks pulled up his collar again and dashed for the car. The hail had turned to rain again. As he drove, windscreen wipers slapping, he pondered his talk with John Billings. The man seemed genuine in his grief, and he had no apparent motive for harming Anna Childers; but, again, all Banks had to go on was what he had been told. Then there was Owen Doughton, the ex live-in lover. Things might not have been as civilized as Anna Childers had made out.

The marvellous fourth movement of the symphony began just as Banks turned into his street. He sat in the parked car with the rain streaming down the windows and listened until Otto Edelmann came in with 'O Freunde, nicht diese Töne . . .' then turned off the tape and headed indoors. If he stayed out any longer he'd be there until the end of the symphony, and Sandra certainly wouldn't appreciate that.

3

Banks found Owen Doughton hefting bags of fertilizer around in the garden centre early the next morning. Doughton was a short, rather hangdog-looking man in his early thirties with shaggy dark hair and a droopy moustache. The rain had stopped overnight, but a brisk, chill wind was fast bringing in more cloud, so Banks asked if they could talk inside. Doughton led him to a small, cluttered office that smelled faintly of paraffin. Doughton sat on the desk and Banks took the swivel chair.

'I'm afraid I've got some bad news for you, Mr Doughton,' Banks started.

Doughton studied his cracked, dirty fingernails. 'I read about Anna in the paper this morning, if that's what you mean,' he said. 'It's terrible, a tragedy.' He brushed back a thick lock of hair from his right eye.

'Did you see much of her lately?'

'Not a lot, no. Not since we split up. We'd have lunch occasionally if neither of us was too busy.'

'So there were no hard feelings?'

'No. Anna said it was just time to move on, that we'd outgrown each other. We both needed more space to grow.'

'Was she right?'

He shrugged. 'Seems so. But I still cared for her. I don't want you to think I didn't. I just can't take this in.' He looked Banks in the eye for the first time. 'What's wrong, anyway? Why are the police interested?'

'It's just routine,' Banks said. 'I don't suppose you'd know anything about her state of mind recently?'

'Not really.'

'When did you see her last?'

'A couple of weeks ago. She seemed fine, really.'

'Did you know her new boyfriend?'

Doughton returned to study his fingernails. 'No. She told me about him, of course, but we never met. Sounded like a nice bloke. Probably better for her than me. I wished her every happiness. Surely you can't think she did this herself? Anna just wasn't the type. She had too much to live for.'

'Most likely food poisoning,' Banks said, closing his notebook, 'but we have to cover the possibilities. Nice talking to you, anyway. I don't suppose I'll be troubling you again.'

'No problem,' Doughton said, standing up.

Banks nodded and left.

4

'If we split up,' Banks mused aloud to Sandra over an early lunch in the new McDonald's that day, 'do you think you'd be upset?'

Sandra narrowed her eyes, clear blue under the dark brows and blonde hair. 'Are you trying to tell me something, Alan? Is there something I should know?'

Banks paused, Big Mac halfway to his mouth, and laughed. 'No. No, nothing like that. It's purely hypothetical.'

'Well, thank goodness for that.' Sandra took a bite of her McChicken sandwich and pulled a face. 'Yuck. Have you really developed a taste for this stuff?'

Banks nodded. 'It's all right, really. Full of nutrition.' And he took a big bite as if to prove it.

'Well,' she said, 'you certainly know how to show a woman a good time, I'll say that for you. And what on earth are you talking about?'

'Splitting up. It's just something that puzzles me, that's all.'

'I've been married to you half my life,' Sandra said. 'Twenty years. Of course I'd be bloody upset if we split up.'

'You can't see us just going our separate ways, growing apart, needing more space?'

'Alan, what's got into you? Have you been reading those self-help books?' She looked around the place again, taking in the plastic decor. 'I'm getting worried about you.'

'Well, don't. It's simple really. I know twenty years hardly compares with five, but do you believe people can just disentangle their lives from one another and carry on with someone new as if nothing had happened?'

'Maybe they could've done in 1967,' Sandra answered. 'And maybe some people still can, but I think it cuts a lot deeper than that, no matter what anyone says.'

'Anna said it was fine,' Banks muttered, almost to himself. 'But Anna's dead.'

'Is this that investigation you're doing for Dr Glendenning, the reason you stood me up last night?'

'I didn't stand you up. I phoned to apologize. But, yes. I've got a nagging feeling about it. Something's not quite right.'

'What do you mean? You think she was poisoned or something?'

'It's possible, but I can't prove it. I can't even figure out how.'

'Then maybe you're wrong.'

'Huh.' Banks chomped on his Big Mac again. 'Wouldn't be the first time, would it?' He explained about his talks with John Billings and Owen Doughton. Sandra thought for a moment, sipping her Coke through a straw and picking at her chips, sandwich abandoned on her tray. 'Sounds like a determined woman, this Anna. I suppose it's possible she just made a seamless transition from one to the other, but I'd bet there's a lot more to it than that. I'd have a word with both of them again, if I were you.'

'Mmm,' said Banks. 'Thought you'd say that. Fancy a sweet?'

5

'**The tests** are going to take time,' Glendenning said over the phone, 'but from what I could see there's severe damage to the liver, kidneys, heart and lungs, not to mention the central nervous system.'

'Could it be food poisoning?' Banks asked.

'It certainly looks like some kind of poisoning. A healthy person doesn't usually die just like that. I suppose at a pinch it could be botulism,' Glendenning said. 'Certainly some of the symptoms match. I'll get the Board of Trade to check out that Chinese restaurant.'

'Any other possibilities?'

'Too damned many,' Glendenning growled. 'That's the problem. There's enough nasty stuff around to make you that ill if you're unlucky enough to swallow it: household cleaners, pesticides, industrial chemicals. The list goes on. That's why we'll have to wait for the test results.' And he hung up.

Cantankerous old bugger, Banks thought with a smile. How Glendenning hated being pinned down. The problem was, though, if someone - Owen, John or some undiscovered enemy - had poisoned Anna, how had he done it? John Billings could have doctored her food at the Chinese restaurant, or her drink in the pub, or perhaps there was something she had eaten that he had simply failed to mention. He certainly had the best opportunity.

But John Billings seemed the most unlikely suspect: he loved the woman; they were going to get married. Or so he said. Anna Childers was quite well off and upwardly mobile, but it was unlikely that Billings stood to gain, or even needed to gain, financially from her death. It was worth looking into, though. She had only been thirty, but she night have made a will in his favour. And Billings's consultancy could do with a bit of scrutiny.

Money wouldn't be a motive with Owen Doughton, though. According to both the late Anna and to Owen himself, they had parted without rancour, each content to get on with life. Again, it might be worth asking a few of their friends and acquaintances if they had reason to think any differently. Doughton had seemed gentle, reserved, a private person, but who could tell what went on in his mind? Banks walked down the corridor to see if either Detective Constable Susan Gay or Detective Sergeant Philip Richmond was free for an hour or two.

6

Two hours later, DC Susan Gay sat in front of Banks's desk, smoothed her grey skirt over her lap and opened her notebook. As usual, Banks thought, she was well dressed: tight blonde curls; just enough make-up; the silver hoop earrings; black scoop-necked top; and a mere whiff of Miss Dior cutting the stale cigarette smoke in his office.

'There's not much, I'm afraid,' Susan started, glancing up from her notes. 'No will, as far as I can discover, but she did alter the beneficiary on her insurance policy a month ago.'

'In whose benefit?'

'John Billings. Apparently she has no family.'

Banks raised his eyebrows. 'Who was the previous beneficiary?'

'Owen Doughton.'

'Odd that, isn't it?' Banks speculated aloud. 'A woman who changes her insurance policy with her boyfriends.'

'Well she wouldn't want it to go to the government, would she?' Susan said. 'And I don't suppose she'd want to make her ex rich either.'

'True,' said Banks. 'It's often easier to keep a policy going than let it lapse and apply all over again later. And they *were* going to get married. But why change it so soon? How much is it for?'

'Fifty thousand.'

Banks whistled.

'Owen Doughton's poor as a church mouse,' Susan went on, 'but he doesn't stand to gain anything.'

'But did he know that? I doubt Anna Childers would have told him. What about Billings?'

Susan gnawed the tip of her Biro and hesitated. 'Pretty well off,' she said. 'Bit of an up-and-comer in the consultancy world. You can see why a woman like Anna Childers would want to attach herself to him.'

'Why?'

'He's going places, of course. Expensive places.'

'I see,' said Banks. 'And you think she was a gold-digger?'

Susan flushed. 'Not necessarily. She just knew what side her bread was buttered on, that's all. Same as with a lot of new businesses, though, Billings has a bit of a cash-flow problem.'

'Hmm. Any gossip on the split up?'

'Not much. I had a chat with a couple of locals in the Red Lion. Anna Childers always seemed cheerful enough, but she was a tough nut to crack, they said, strong protective shell.'

'What about Doughton?'

'He doesn't seem to have many friends. His boss says he's noticed no real changes, but he says Owen keeps to himself, always did. I'm sorry. It's not much help.'

'Never mind,' Banks said. 'Look, I've got a couple of things to do. Can you find Phil for me?'

7

'**Did you** know that Anna had an insurance policy?' Banks asked Owen Doughton. They stood in the cold yard while Doughton stacked some bags of peat moss.

Doughton stood up and rubbed the small of his back. 'Aye,' he said. 'What of it?'

'Did you know how much it was for?'

He shook his head.

'All right,' Banks said. 'Did Anna tell you she'd changed the beneficiary, named John Billings instead of you?'

Doughton paused with his mouth open. 'No,' he said. 'No, she didn't.'

'So you know now that you stand to gain nothing, that it all goes to John?'

Doughton's face darkened, then he looked away and Banks swore he could hear a strangled laugh or cry. 'I don't believe this,' Doughton said, facing him again. 'I can't believe I'm hearing this. You think *I* might have killed Anna? And for money? This is insane. Look, go away, please. I don't have to talk to you, do I?'

'No,' said Banks.

'Well, bugger off then. I've got work to do. But remember one thing.'

'What's that?'

'I loved her. I loved Anna.'

8

John Billings looked even more wretched than he had the day before. His eyes were bloodshot, underlined by black smudges, and he hadn't shaved. Banks could smell alcohol on his breath. A suitcase stood in the hallway.

'Where are you going, John?' Banks asked.

'I can't stay here, can I? I mean, it's not my house, for a start, and . . . the memories.'

'Where are you going?'

He picked up the case. 'I don't know. Just away from here, that's all.'

'I don't think so.' Gently, Banks took the case from him and set it down. 'We haven't got to the bottom of this yet.'

'What do you mean? For Christ's sake, man!'

'You'd better come with me, John.'

'Where?'

'Police station. We'll have a chat there.'

Billings stared angrily at him, then seemed to fold. 'Oh, what the hell,' he muttered. 'What does it matter?' And he picked his coat off the rack and followed Banks. He didn't see DS Philip Richmond watching from the window of the cafe over the road.

9

It was after seven o'clock, dark, cold and windy outside. Banks decided to wait in the bedroom, on the chair wedged in the corner between the wardrobe and the dressing table. From there, with the door open, he could see the staircase, and he would be able to hear any sounds in the house.

He had just managed to get the item on the local news show at six o'clock, only minutes after Dr Glendenning had phoned with more detailed information: 'Poison suspected in death of Eastvale woman. Police baffled. No suspects as yet.' Of course, the killer might not have seen it, or might have already covered his tracks, but if Anna Childers *had* been poisoned, and Glendenning now seemed certain she had, then the answer had to be here.

Given possible reaction times, Glendenning had said in his late afternoon phone call, there was little chance she could have taken the poison into her system before eight o'clock the previous evening, at which time she had gone out to dine with John Billings.

The house was dark and silent save for the ticking of a clock on the bedside table and the howling wind rattling the window. Eight o'clock. Nine. Nothing happened except Banks got cramp in his left calf. He massaged it, then stood up at regular intervals and stretched. He thought of DS Richmond down the street in the unmarked car. Between them, they'd be sure to catch anyone who came.

Finally, close to ten o'clock, he heard it, a scraping at the lock on the front door. He drew himself deep into the chair, melted into the darkness and held his breath. The door opened and closed softly. He could see a torch beam sweeping the wall by the staircase, coming closer. The intruder was coming straight up the stairs. Damn! Banks hadn't expected that. He wanted whoever it was to lead him to the poison, not walk right into him.

He sat rigid in the chair as the beam played over the threshold of the bedroom, mercifully not falling on him in his dark corner. The intruder didn't hesitate. He walked around the bed, within inches of Banks's feet, and over to the bedside table. Shining his torch, he opened the top drawer and picked something up. At that moment Banks turned on the light. The figure turned sharply, then froze.

'Hello, Owen,' said Banks. 'What brings you here?'

10

'**If it** was anyone, it had to be either you or him, John,' Banks said later back in his office, while Owen Doughton was being charged downstairs. 'Only the two of you were intimate enough with Anna to know her habits, her routines. And Owen had lived with her until quite recently. There was a chance he still had a key.'

John Billings shook his head. 'I thought you were arresting *me*.'

'It was touch and go, I won't deny it. But at least I thought I'd give you a chance, the benefit of the doubt.'

'And if your trap hadn't worked?'

Banks shrugged. 'Down to you, I suppose. The poison could have been anywhere, in anything. Toothpaste, for example. I knew if it wasn't you, and the killer heard the news, he'd try to destroy any remaining evidence. He wouldn't have had a chance to do so yet because you were in the house.'

'But I was at the hospital nearly all yesterday.'

'Too soon. He had no idea anything had happened at that time. This wasn't a carefully calculated plan.'

'But why?'

Banks shook his head. 'That I can't say for certain. He's a sick man, an obsessed man. It's my guess it was his warped form of revenge. It had been eating away at him for some time. Anna didn't treat him very well, John. She didn't really stop to take his feelings into account when she kicked him out and took up with you. She just assumed he would understand, like he always had, because he loved her and had her welfare at heart. He was deeply hurt, but he wasn't the kind to make a fuss or let his feelings show. He kept it all bottled up.'

'She could be a bit blinkered, could Anna,' John mumbled. 'She was a very focused woman.'

'Yes. And I'm sure Doughton felt humiliated when she dumped him and turned to you. After all, he didn't have much of a financial future, unlike you.'

'But it wasn't that, not with Anna,' Billings protested. 'We just had so much in common. Goals, tastes, ambitions. She and Owen had nothing in common any more.'

'You're probably right,' Banks said. 'Anyway, when she told him a couple of weeks ago that she was going to get married to you, it was the last straw. He said she expected him to be happy for her.'

'But why did he keep on seeing her if it hurt him so much?'

'He was still in love with her. It was better seeing her, even under those circumstances, than not at all.'

'Then why kill her?'

Banks looked at Billings. 'Love and hate, John,' he said. 'They're not so far apart. Besides, he doesn't believe he did kill her, that wasn't really his intention at all.'

'I don't understand. You said he did. How did he do it?'

Banks paused and lit a cigarette. This wasn't going to be easy. Rain blew against the window and a draught rattled the Venetian blind.

'How?' Billings repeated.

Banks looked at his calendar, trying to put off the moment; it showed a woodland scene, snowdrops blooming near The Strid at Bolton Abbey. He cleared his throat. 'Owen came to the house while you were both out,' Banks began. 'He brought a syringe loaded with a strong pesticide he got from the garden centre. Remember, he knew Anna intimately. Did you and Anna make love that night, John?'

Billings reddened. 'For Christ's sake—'

'I'm not asking whether the earth moved, I'm just asking if you did. Believe me, it's relevant.'

'All right,' said Billings after a pause. 'Yes, we did, as a matter of fact.'

'Owen knew Anna well enough to know that she was frightened of getting pregnant,' Banks went on, 'but she wouldn't take the pill because of the side effects. He knew she insisted on condoms, and he knew she liked to make love in the dark. It was easy enough to insert the needle into a couple of packages and squirt in some pesticide. Not much, but it's very powerful stuff, colourless and odourless, so even an infinitesimal coating would have some effect. The condoms were lubricated, so they'd feel oily anyway, and nobody would notice a tiny pinprick in the package. You absorbed a little into your system, too, and that's why you felt ill. You see, it's easily absorbed through skin or membranes. But Anna got the lion's share. Dr Glendenning would have found out eventually how the poison was administered from tissue samples, but further tests would have taken time. Owen could easily have nipped back to the house and removed the evidence by then. Or we might have decided that you had better access to the method.'

Billings paled. 'You mean it could just as easily have been me either killed or arrested for murder?'

Banks shrugged. 'It could have turned out any way, really. There was no way of knowing accurately what would happen, and certainly there was a chance that either you would die or the blame would fall on you. As it turned out, Anna absorbed most of it, and she had asthma. In Owen's twisted mind, he wanted your love-making to make you sick. That was his statement, if you like, after suffering so long in silence, pretending it was OK that Anna had moved on. But that's all. It was a sick joke, if you like. We found three poisoned condoms. Certainly if one hadn't worked the way it did, there could have been a build up of the pesticide, causing chronic problems. I did read about a case once,' Banks went on, 'where a man married rich women and murdered them for their money by putting arsenic on his condoms, but they were made of goatskin back then. Besides, he was French. I've never come across a case quite as strange as this.'

Billings shook his head slowly. 'Can I go now?' he asked.

'Where to?'

'I don't know. A hotel, perhaps, until . . .'

Banks nodded and stood up. As they went down the stairs, they came face to face with Owen Doughton, handcuffed to a large constable. Billings stiffened. Doughton glared at him and spoke to Banks. 'He's the one who killed her,' he said, with a toss of his head. 'He's the one you should be arresting.' Then he looked directly at Billings. 'You're going to have to live with that, you know, Mr Moneybags. It was you who killed her. Hear that, Mr Yuppie Moneybags? *You* killed her. You killed Anna.'

Banks couldn't tell whether he was laughing or crying as the constable led him down to the cells.

MISSING IN ACTION

People go missing all the time in war, of course, but not usually nine-year-old boys. Besides, the war had hardly begun. It was only 20 September 1939 when Mary Critchley came hammering on my door at about three o'clock, interrupting my afternoon nap.

It was a Wednesday, and normally I would have been teaching the fifth formers Shakespeare at Silverhill Grammar School (a thankless task if ever there was one), but the Ministry had just got around to constructing air-raid shelters there, so the school was closed for the week. We didn't even know if it was going to reopen because the plan was to evacuate all the children to safer areas in the countryside. Now I would be among the first to admit that a teacher's highest aspiration is a school without pupils, but in the meantime the government, in its eternal wisdom, put us redundant teachers to such complex, intellectual tasks as preparing ration cards for the Ministry of Food. (After all, *they* knew what was coming.)

All this was just a small part of the chaos that seemed to reign at that time. Not the chaos of war, the kind I remembered from the trenches at Ypres in 1917, but the chaos of government bureaucracies trying to organize the country for war.

Anyway, I was fortunate enough to become a Special Constable, which is a rather grandiose title for a sort of part-time dogsbody, and that was why Mary Critchley came running to me. That and what little reputation I had for solving people's problems.

'Mr Bashcombe! Mr Bashcombe!' she cried. 'It's our Johnny. He's gone missing. You musht help.'

My name is actually *Bascombe*, Frank Bascombe, but Mary Critchley has a slight speech impediment, so I forgave her the mispronunciation. Still, with half the city's children running wild in the streets and the other half standing on crowded station platforms clutching their Mickey Mouse gas-masks in little cardboard boxes, ready to be herded into trains bound for such nearby country havens as Graythorpe, Kilsden and Acksham, I thought perhaps she was overreacting a tad, and I can't say I welcomed her arrival after only about twenty of my allotted forty winks.

'He's probably out playing with his mates,' I told her.

'Not my Johnny,' she said, wiping the tears from her eyes. 'Not since . . . you know . . .'

I knew. Mr Critchley, Ted to his friends, had been a Royal Navy man since well before the war. He had also been unfortunate enough to serve on the aircraft carrier *Courageous*, which had been sunk by a German U-boat off the south-west coast of Ireland just three days before. Over five hundred men had been lost, including Ted Critchley. Of course, no body had been found, and probably never would be, so he was only officially 'missing in action'.

I also knew young Johnny Critchley, and thought him to be a serious boy, a bit too imaginative and innocent for his own good. (Well, many are at that age, aren't they, before the world grabs them by the balls and shakes some reality into them.) Johnny trusted everyone, even strangers.

'Johnny's not been in much of a mood for playing with his mates sinsh we got the news about Ted's ship,' Mary Critchley went on.

I could understand that well enough – young Johnny was an only child, and he always did worship his father – but I still didn't see what I could do about it. 'Have you asked around?'

'What do you think I've been doing sinsh he didn't come home at twelve o'clock like he was supposed to? I've ashked everyone in the street. Last time he was seen he was down by the canal at about eleven o'clock. Maurice Richards saw him. What can I do, Mr Bashcombe? Firsht Ted, and now . . . now my Johnny!' She burst into tears.

After I had managed to calm her down, I sighed and told her I would look for Johnny myself. There certainly wasn't much hope of my getting the other twenty winks now.

•

It was a glorious day, so warm and sunny you would hardly believe there was a war on. The late afternoon sunshine made even our narrow streets of cramped brick terraced houses look attractive. As the shadows lengthened, the light turned to molten gold. First, I scoured the local rec, where the children played cricket and football, and the dogs ran wild. Some soldiers were busy digging trenches for air-raid shelters. Just the sight of those long, dark grooves in the earth gave me the shivers. Behind the trenches, barrage balloons pulled at their moorings on the breeze like playful porpoises, orange and pink in the sun. I asked the soldiers, but they hadn't seen Johnny. Nor had any of the other lads.

After the rec, I headed for the derelict houses on Gallipoli Street. The landlord had let them go to rack and ruin two years ago, and they were quite uninhabitable, not even fit for billeting soldiers. They were also dangerous and should have been pulled down, but I think the old skinflint was hoping a bomb would hit them so he could claim insurance or compensation from the government. The doors and windows had been boarded up, but children are resourceful, and it wasn't difficult even for me to remove a couple of loose sheets of plywood and make my way inside. I wished I had my torch, but I had to make do with what little light slipped through the holes. Every time I moved, my feet stirred up clouds of dust, which did my poor lungs no good at all.

I thought Johnny might have fallen or got trapped in one of the houses. The staircases were rotten, and more than one lad had fallen through on his way up. The floors weren't much better, either, and one of the fourth-formers at Silverhill had needed more than fifteen stitches a couple of weeks before when one of his legs went right through the rotten wood and the splinters gouged his flesh.

I searched as best I could in the poor light, and I called out Johnny's name, but no answer came. Before I left, I stood silently and listened for any traces of harsh breathing or whimpering.

Nothing.

After three hours of searching the neighbourhood, I'd had no luck at all. Blackout time was seven forty-five p.m., so I still had about an hour and a half left, but if Johnny wasn't in any of the local children's usual haunts, I was at a loss as to where to look. I talked to the other boys I met here and there, but none of his friends had seen him since the family got the news of Ted's death. Little Johnny Critchley, it seemed, had vanished into thin air.

•

At half past six, I called on Maurice Richards, grateful for his offer of a cup of tea and the chance to rest my aching feet. Maurice and I went back a long time. We had both survived the first war, Maurice with the loss of an arm, and me with permanent facial scarring and a racking cough that comes and goes, thanks to the mustard gas leaking through my mask at the Third Battle of Ypres. We never talked about the war, but it was there, we both knew, an invisible bond tying us close together while at the same time excluding us from so much other, normal human intercourse. Not many had seen the things we had, and thank God for that.

Maurice lit up a Passing Cloud one-handed, then he poured the tea. The seven o'clock news came on the radio, some rot about us vowing to keep fighting until we'd vanquished the foe. It was still very much a war of words at that time, and the more rhetorical the language sounded, the better the politicians thought they were doing. There had been a couple of minor air skirmishes, and the sinking of the *Courageous*, of course, but all the action was taking place in Poland, which seemed as remote as the moon to most people. Some clever buggers had already started calling it the 'Bore War'.

'Did you hear Tommy Handley last night, Frank?' Maurice asked.

I shook my head. There'd been a lot of hoopla about Tommy Handley's new radio programme, *It's That Man Again*, or *ITMA*, as people called it. I was never a fan. Call me a snob, but when evening falls I'm far happier curling up with a good book or an interesting talk on the radio than listening to Tommy Handley.

'Talk about laugh,' said Maurice. 'They had this one sketch about the Ministry of Aggravation and the Office of Twerps. I nearly died.'

I smiled. 'Not far from the truth,' I said. There were now so many of these obscure ministries, boards and departments involved in so many absurd pursuits – all for the common good, of course – that I had been thinking of writing a dystopian satire. I proposed to set it in the near future, which would merely be a thinly disguised version of the present. So far, all I had was a great idea for the title: I would reverse the last two numbers in the current year, so instead of 1939, I'd call it *1993*. (Well, *I* thought it was a good idea!)

'Look, Maurice,' I said, 'it's about young Johnny Critchley. His mother tells me you were the last person to see him.'

'Oh, aye,' Maurice said. 'She were round asking about him not long ago. Still not turned up?'

'No.'

'Cause for concern, then.'

'I'm beginning to think so. What was he doing when you saw him?'

'Just walking down by the canal, by old Woodruff's scrapyard.'

'That's all?'

'Yes.'

'Was he alone?'

Maurice nodded.

'Did he say anything.'

'No.'

'You didn't say anything to him?'

'No cause to. He seemed preoccupied, just staring in the water, like, hands in his pockets. I've heard what happened to his dad. A lad has to do his grieving.'

'Too true. Did you see anyone else? Anything suspicious?'

'No, nothing. Just a minute, though . . .'

'What?'

'Oh, it's probably nothing, but just after I saw Johnny, when I was crossing the bridge, I bumped into Colin Gormond, you know, that chap who's a bit . . . you know.'

Colin Gormond. I knew him all right. And that wasn't good news; it wasn't good news at all.

•

Of all the policemen they could have sent, they had to send Detective bloody Sergeant Longbottom, a big, brutish-looking fellow with a pronounced limp and a Cro-Magnon brow. Longbottom was thick as two short planks. I doubt he could have found his own arse even if someone nailed a sign on it, or detected his way out of an Anderson shelter if it were in his own back yard. But that's the calibre of men this wretched war has left us with at home. Along with good ones like me, of course.

DS Longbottom wore a shiny brown suit and a Silverhill Grammar School tie. I wondered where he'd got it from; he probably stole it from a schoolboy he caught nicking sweets from the corner shop. He kept tugging at his collar with his pink sausage fingers as we talked in Mary Critchley's living room. His face was flushed with the heat, and sweat gathered on his thick eyebrows and trickled down the sides of his neck.

'So he's been missing since lunchtime, has he?' DS Longbottom repeated.

Mary Critchley nodded. 'He went out at about half past ten, just for a walk like. Said he'd be back at twelve. When it got to three . . . well, I went to see Mr Bashcombe here.'

DS Longbottom curled his lip at me and grunted. 'Mr Bascombe.

Special Constable. I suppose you realize that gives you no real police powers, don't you?'

'As a matter of fact,' I said, 'I thought it made me your superior. After all, you're not a *special* sergeant, are you?'

He looked at me as if he wanted to hit me. Perhaps he would have done if Mary Critchley hadn't been in the room. 'Enough of your lip. Just answer my questions.'

'Yes, sir.'

'You say you looked all over for this lad?'

'All his usual haunts.'

'And you found no trace of him?'

'If I had, do you think we'd have sent for you?'

'I warned you. Cut the lip and answer the questions. This, what's his name, Maurice Richards, was he the last person to see the lad?'

'Johnny's his name. And yes is the answer, as far as we know.' I paused. He'd have to know eventually, and if I didn't tell him, Maurice would. The longer we delayed, the worse it would be in the long run. 'There was someone else in the area at the time. A man called Colin Gormond.'

Mary Critchley gave a sharp gasp. DS Longbottom frowned, licked the tip of his pencil and scribbled something in his notebook. 'I'll have to have a word with him,' he said. Then he turned to her. 'Recognize the name, do you, ma'm?'

'I know Colin,' I answered, perhaps a bit too quickly.

DS Longbottom stared at Mary Critchley, whose lower lip started quivering, then turned slowly back to me. 'Tell me about him.'

I sighed. Colin Gormond was an oddball. Some people said he was a bit slow, but I'd never seen any real evidence of that. He lived alone and he didn't have much to do with the locals; that was enough evidence against him for some people.

And then there were the children.

For some reason, Colin preferred the company of the local lads to that of the rest of us adults. To be quite honest, I can't say I blame him, but in a situation like this it's bound to look suspicious. Especially if the investigating officer is someone with the sensitivity and understanding of a DS Longbottom.

Colin would take them trainspotting on the hill overlooking the main line, for example, or he'd play cricket with them on the rec, or hand out conkers when the season came. He sometimes bought them sweets and ice creams, even gave them books, marbles and comics.

To my knowledge, Colin Gormond had never once put a foot out of line, never laid so much as a finger on any of the lads, either in anger or in friendship. There had, however, been one or two mutterings from some parents – most notably from Jack Blackwell, father of one of Johnny's pals, Nick – that it somehow *wasn't right*, that it was *unnatural* for a man who must be in his late thirties or early forties to spend so much time playing with young children. There must be something not quite right in his head, he must be up to *something*, Jack Blackwell hinted, and as usual when someone starts a vicious rumour, there is no shortage of willing believers. Such a reaction was only to be expected from someone, of course, but I knew it wouldn't go down well with DS Longbottom. I don't know why, but I felt a strange need to *protect* Colin.

'Colin's a local,' I explained. 'Lived around here for years. He plays with the lads a bit. Most of them like him. He seems a harmless sort of fellow.'

'How old is he?'

I shrugged. 'Hard to say. About forty, perhaps.'

DS Longbottom raised a thick eyebrow. 'About forty and he plays with the kiddies, you say?'

'Sometimes. Like a schoolteacher, or a youth club leader.'

'Is he a schoolteacher?'

'No.'

'Is he a youth club leader?'

'No. Look, what I meant—'

'I know exactly what you meant, Mr Bascombe. Now you just listen to what *I* mean. What we've got here is an older man who's known to hang around with young children, and he's been placed near the scene where a young child has gone missing. Now, don't you think that's just a wee bit suspicious?'

Mary Critchley let out a great wail and started crying again. DS Longbottom ignored her. Instead, he concentrated all his venom on me, the softie, the liberal, the defender of child molesters. 'What do you have to say about *that*, Mr Special Constable Bascombe?'

'Only that Colin was a friend to the children and that he had no reason to harm anyone.'

'*Friend*,' DS Longbottom sneered, struggling to his feet. 'We can only be thankful you're not regular police, Mr Bascombe,' he said, nodding to himself, in acknowledgement of his own wisdom. 'That we can.'

'So what are you going to do?' I asked.

DS Longbottom looked at his watch and frowned. Either he was trying to work out what it meant when the little hand and the big hand were in the positions they were in, or he was squinting because of poor eyesight. 'I'll have a word with this here Colin Gormond. Other than that, there's not much more we can do tonight. First thing tomorrow morning, we'll drag the canal.' He got to the door, turned, pointed to the windows and said, 'And don't forget to put up your blackout curtains, ma'm, or you'll have the ARP man to answer to.'

Mary Critchley bust into floods of tears again.

•

Even the soft dawn light could do nothing for the canal. It oozed through the city like an open sewer, oil slicks shimmering like rainbows in the sun, brown water dotted with industrial scum and suds, bits of driftwood and paper wrappings floating along with them. On one side was Ezekiel Woodruff's scrapyard. Old Woodruff was a bit of an eccentric. He used to come around the streets with his horse and cart, yelling, 'Any old iron,' but now the government had other uses for scrap metal – supposedly to be used in aircraft manufacture – poor old Woodruff didn't have a way to make his living any more. He'd already sent old Nell the carthorse to the knacker's yard, where she was probably doing her bit for the war effort by helping to make the glue to stick the aircraft together. Old mangles and bits of broken furniture stuck up from the ruins of the scrapyard like shattered artillery after a battle.

On the other side, the bank rose steeply towards the backs of the houses on Canal Road, and the people who lived there seemed to regard it as their personal tip. Flies and wasps buzzed around old hessian sacks and paper bags full of God knew what. A couple of buckled bicycle tires and a wheel-less pram completed the picture.

I stood and watched as Longbottom supervised the dragging, a slow and laborious process that seemed to be sucking all manner of unwholesome objects to the surface – except Johnny Critchley's body.

I felt tense. At any moment I half expected the cry to come from one of the policemen in the boats that they had found him, half expected to see the small, pathetic bundle bob above the water's surface. I didn't think Colin Gormond had done anything to Johnny – nor Maurice, though DS Longbottom had seemed suspicious of him too – but I did think that, given how upset he was, Johnny might just have jumped in. He never struck me as the suicidal type, but I have no idea whether suicide enters the minds of nine-year-olds. All I knew was that he *was* upset about his father, and he *was* last seen skulking by the canal.

So I stood around with DS Longbottom and the rest as the day grew warmer, and there was still no sign of Johnny. After about three hours, the police gave up and went for bacon and eggs at Betty's Cafe over on Chadwick Road. They didn't invite me, and I was grateful to be spared both the unpleasant food and company. I stood and stared into the greasy water a while longer, unsure whether it was a good sign or not that Johnny wasn't in the canal, then I decided to go and have a chat with Colin Gormond.

•

'What is it, Colin?' I asked him gently. 'Come on. You can tell me.'

But Colin continued to stand with his back turned to me in the dark corner of his cramped living room, hands to his face, making eerie snuffling sounds, shaking his head. It was bright daylight outside, but the blackout curtains were still drawn tightly, and not a chink of light crept between their edges. I had already tried the light switch, but either Colin had removed the bulb or he didn't have one.

'Come on, Colin. This is silly. You know me. I'm Mr Bascombe. I won't hurt you. Tell me what happened.'

Finally Colin turned silent and came out of his corner with his funny, shuffling way of walking. Someone said he had a club foot, and someone else said he'd had a lot of operations on his feet when he was a young lad, but nobody knew for certain why he walked the way he did. When he sat down and lit a cigarette, the match light illuminated his large nose, shiny forehead and watery blue eyes. He used the same match to light a candle on the table beside him, and then I saw them: the black eye, the bruise on his left cheek. DS Longbottom. The bastard.

'Did you say anything to him?' I asked, anxious that DS Longbottom might have beaten a confession out of Colin, without even thinking that Colin probably wouldn't still be at home if that were the case.

He shook his head mournfully. 'Nothing, Mr Bascombe. Honest. There was nothing I *could* tell him.'

'Did you see Johnny Critchley yesterday, Colin?'

'Aye.'

'Where?'

'Down by the canal.'

'What was he doing?'

'Just standing there chucking stones in the water.'

'Did you talk to him?'

Colin paused and turned away before answering, 'No.'

I had a brief coughing spell, his cigarette smoke working on my gassed lungs. When it cleared up, I said, 'Colin, there's something you're not telling me, isn't there? You'd better tell me. You know I won't hurt you, and I just might be the only person who can help you.'

He looked at me, pale eyes imploring. 'I only called out to him, from the bridge, like, didn't I?'

'What happened next?'

'Nothing. I swear it.'

'Did he answer?'

'No. He just looked my way and shook his head. I could tell then that he didn't want to play. He seemed sad.'

'He'd just heard his dad's been killed.'

Colin's already watery eyes brimmed with tears. 'Poor lad.'

I nodded. For all I knew, Colin might have been thinking about *his* dad, too. Not many knew it, but Mr Gormond senior had been killed in the same bloody war that left me with my bad lungs and scarred face. 'What happened next, Colin?'

Colin shook his head and wiped his eyes with the back of his hand. 'Nothing,' he said. 'It was such a lovely day I just went on walking. I went to the park and watched the soldiers digging trenches, then I went for my cigarettes and came home to listen to the wireless.'

'And after that?'

'I stayed in.'

'All evening?'

'That's right. Sometimes I go down to the White Rose, but . . .'

'But what, Colin?'

'Well, Mr Smedley, you know, the air raid precautions man?'

I nodded. 'I know him.'

'He said my blackout cloth wasn't good enough and he'd fine me if I didn't get some proper stuff by yesterday.'

'I understand, Colin.' Good-quality, thick, impenetrable blackout cloth had become both scarce and expensive, which was no doubt why Colin had been cheated in the first place.

'Anyway, what with that and the cigarettes . . .'

I reached into my pocket and slipped out a few bob for him.

Colin looked away, ashamed, but I put it on the table and he didn't tell me to take it back. I knew how it must hurt his pride to accept charity, but I had no idea how much money he made, or how he made it. I'd never seen him beg, but I had a feeling he survived on odd jobs and lived very much from hand to mouth.

I stood up. 'All right, Colin,' I said. 'Thanks very much.' I paused at the door, uncertain how to say what had just entered my mind. Finally I blundered ahead. 'It might be better if you kept a low profile till they find him, Colin. You know what some of the people around here are like.'

'What do you mean, Mr Bascombe?'

'Just be careful, Colin, that's all I mean. Just be careful.'

He nodded gormlessly and I left.

•

As I shut Colin's front door, I noticed Jack Blackwell standing on his doorstep, arms folded, a small crowd of locals around him, their shadows intersecting on the cobbled street. They kept glancing towards Colin's house, and when they saw me come out they all shuffled off except Jack himself, who gave me a grim stare before going inside and slamming his door. I felt a shiver go up my spine, as if a goose had stepped on my grave, as my dear mother used to say, bless her soul, and when I got home I couldn't concentrate on my book one little bit.

•

By the following morning, when Johnny had been missing over thirty-six hours, the mood in the street had started to turn ugly. In my experience, when you get right down to it, there's no sorrier spectacle, nothing much worse or more dangerous, than the human mob mentality. After all, armies are nothing more than mobs, really, even when they are organized to a greater or lesser degree. I'd been at Ypres, as you know, and there wasn't a hell of a lot you could tell me about military organization. So when I heard the muttered words on doorsteps, saw the little knots of people here and there, Jack Blackwell flitting from door to door like a political canvasser, I had to do something, and I could hardly count on any help from DS Longbottom.

One thing I had learned both as a soldier and as a schoolteacher was that, if you had a chance, your best bet was to take out the ringleader. That meant Jack Blackwell. Jack was the nasty type, and he and I had had more than one run-in over his son Nick's bullying and poor performance in class. In my opinion, young Nick was the sort of walking dead loss who should probably have been drowned at birth, a waste of skin, sinew, tissue and bone, and it wasn't hard to see where he got it from. Nick's older brother, Dave, was already doing a long stretch in the Scrubs for beating a night watchman senseless during a robbery, and even the army couldn't find an excuse to spring him and enlist his service in killing Germans. Mrs Blackwell had been seen more than once walking with difficulty, with bruises on her cheek. The sooner Jack Blackwell got his call-up papers, the better things would be all around.

I intercepted Jack between the Deakins' and the Kellys' houses, and it was clear from his gruff, 'What do you want?' that he didn't want to talk to me.

But I was adamant.

'Morning, Jack,' I greeted him. 'Lovely day for a walk, isn't it?'

'What's it to you?'

'Just being polite. What are you up to, Jack? What's going on?'

'None of your business.'

'Up to your old tricks? Spreading poison?'

'I don't know what you're talking about.' He made to walk away, but I grabbed his arm. He glared at me but didn't do anything. Just as well. At my age, and with my lungs, I'd hardly last ten seconds in a fight. 'Jack,' I said, 'don't you think you'd all be best off using your time to look for the poor lad?'

'Look for him! That's a laugh. You know as well as I do where that young lad is.'

'Where? Where is he, Jack?'

'You know.'

'No, I don't. Tell me.'

'He's dead and buried, that's what.'

'Where, Jack?'

'I don't know the exact spot. If he's not in the canal, then he's buried somewhere not far away.'

'Maybe he is. But you don't *know* that. Not for certain. And even if you believe that, you don't know who put him there.'

Jack wrenched his arm out of my weakening grip and sneered. 'I've got a damn sight better idea than you have, Frank Bascombe. With all your *book* learning!' Then he turned and marched off.

Somehow I got the feeling that I had just made things worse.

•

After my brief fracas with Jack Blackwell, I was at a loose end. I knew the police would still be looking for Johnny, asking questions, searching areas of waste ground, so there wasn't much I could do to help them. Feeling impotent, I went down to the canal, near Woodruff's scrapyard. Old Ezekiel Woodruff himself was poking around in the ruins of his business, so I decided to talk to him. I kept my distance, though, for even on a hot day such as this Woodruff was wearing his greatcoat and black wool gloves with the fingers cut off. He wasn't known for his personal hygiene, so I made sure I didn't stand downwind of him. Not that there was much of a wind, but then it didn't take much.

'Morning, Ezekiel,' I said. 'I understand young Johnny Critchley was down around here the day before yesterday.'

'So they say,' muttered Ezekiel.

'See him, did you?'

'I weren't here.'

'So you didn't see him?'

'Police have already been asking questions.'

'And what did you tell them?'

He pointed to the other side of the canal, the back of the housing estate. 'I were over there,' he said. 'Sometimes people chuck out summat of value, even these days.'

'But you did see Johnny?'

He paused, then said, 'Aye.'

'On this side of the canal?'

Woodruff nodded.

'What time was this?'

'I don't have a watch, but it weren't long after that daft bloke had gone by.'

'Do you mean Colin Gormond?'

'Aye, that's the one.'

So Johnny was still alone by the canal *after* Colin had passed by. DS Longbottom had probably known this, but he had beaten Colin anyway. One day I'd find a way to get even with him. The breeze shifted a little and I got a whiff of stale sweat and worse. 'What was Johnny doing?'

'Doing? Nowt special. He were just walking.'

'Walking? Where?'

Woodruff pointed. 'That way. Towards the city centre.'

'Alone?'

'Aye.'

'And nobody approached him?'

'Nope. Not while I were watching.'

I didn't think there was anything further to be got from Ezekiel Woodruff, so I bade him good morning. I can't say the suspicion didn't enter my head that *he* might have had something to do with Johnny's disappearance, though I'd have been hard pushed to say exactly why or what. Odd though old Woodruff might be, there had never been any rumour or suspicion of his being overly interested in young boys, and I didn't want to jump to conclusions the way Jack Blackwell had. Still, I filed away my suspicions for later.

A fighter droned overhead. I watched it dip and spin through the blue air and wished I could be up there. I'd always regretted not being a pilot in the war. A barge full of soldiers drifted by, and I moved aside on the towpath to let the horse that was pulling it pass by. For my troubles I got a full blast of sweaty horseflesh and a pile of steaming manure at my feet. That had even Ezekiel Woodruff beat.

Aimlessly I followed the direction Ezekiel had told me Johnny had walked in – towards the city centre. As I walked, Jack Blackwell's scornful words about my inability to find Johnny echoed in my mind. *Book learning*. That was exactly the kind of cheap insult you would expect from a moron like Jack Blackwell, but it hurt nonetheless. No sense telling him I'd been buried in the mud under the bodies of my comrades for two days. No sense telling him about the young German soldier I'd surprised and bayoneted to death, twisting the blade until it snapped and broke off inside him. Jack Blackwell was too young to have seen action in the last war, but if there was any justice in the world, he'd damn well see it in *this* one.

The canal ran by the back of the train station, where I crossed the narrow bridge and walked through the crowds of evacuees out front to City Square. Mary Critchley's anguish reverberated in my mind, too: '*Mr Bashcombe! Mr Bashcombe!*' I heard her call.

Then, all of a sudden, as I looked at the black facade of the post office and the statue of the Black Prince in the centre of City Square, it hit me. I thought I knew what had happened to Johnny Critchley, but first I had to go back to the street and ask just one important question.

•

It was late morning. The station smelt of damp soot and warm oil. Crowds of children thronged around trying to find out where they were supposed to go. They wore name tags and carried little cardboard boxes. Adults with clipboards, for the most part temporarily unemployed schoolteachers and local volunteers, directed them to the right queue, and their names were ticked off as they boarded the carriages.

Despite being neither an evacuated child nor a supervisor, I managed to buy a ticket and ended up sharing a compartment with a rather severe-looking woman in a brown uniform I didn't recognize, and a male civilian with a brush moustache and a lot of Brylcreem on his hair. They seemed to be in charge of several young children, also in the compartment, who couldn't sit still. I could hardly blame them. They were going to the alien countryside, to live with strangers, far away from their parents, for only God knew how long, and the idea scared them half to death.

The buttoned cushions were warm and the air in the carriage still and close, despite the open window. When we finally set off, the motion stirred up a breeze, which helped a little. On the wall opposite me was a poster of the Scarborough seafront, and I spent most of the journey remembering the carefree childhood holidays I had enjoyed there with my parents in the early years of the century: another world, another time. The rest of the trip I glanced out of the window, beyond the scum-scabbed canal, and saw the urban industrial landscape drift by: back gardens, where some people had put in Anderson shelters half-covered with earth to grow vegetables on; the dark mass of the town hall clock tower behind the city centre buildings; a factory yard, where several men were loading heavy crates onto a lorry, flushed and sweating in the heat.

Then we were in the countryside, where the smells of grass, hay and manure displaced the reek of the city. I saw small, squat farms, drystone walls, sheep and cattle grazing. Soon train tracks and canal diverged. We went through a long noisy tunnel, and the children whimpered. Later, I was surprised to see so many army convoys winding along the narrow roads, and the one big aerodrome we passed seemed buzzing with activity.

All in all, the journey took a little over two hours. Only about ten or eleven children were shepherded off at the small country station, and I followed as they were met and taken to the village hall, where the men and women who were to care for them awaited. It was more civilized than some of the evacuation systems I'd heard about, which sounded more like the slave markets of old, where farmers waited on the platforms to pick out the strong lads, and local dignitaries whisked away the nicely dressed boys and girls.

I went up to the volunteer in charge, an attractive young country woman in a simple blue frock with a white lace collar and a belt around her slim waist, and asked her if she had any record of an evacuee called John, or Johnny, Critchley. She checked her records then shook her head, as I knew she would. If I were right, Johnny wouldn't be here under his own name. I explained my problem to the woman, who told me her name was Phyllis Rigby. She had a yellow ribbon in her long wavy hair and smelled of fresh apples. 'I don't see how anything like that could have happened,' Phyllis said. 'We've been very meticulous. But there again, things *have* been a little chaotic.' She frowned in thought for a moment, then she delegated her present duties to another volunteer.

'Come on,' she said, 'I'll help you go from house to house. There weren't that many evacuees, you know. Far fewer than we expected.'

I nodded. I'd heard how a lot of parents weren't bothering to evacuate their children. 'They can't see anything happening yet,' I said. 'Just you wait. After the first air raid you'll have so many you won't have room for them all.'

Phyllis smiled. 'The poor things. It must be such an upheaval for them.'

'Indeed.'

I took deep, welcome breaths of country air as Phyllis and I set out from the village hall to visit the families listed on her clipboard. There were perhaps a couple of hundred houses, and less than fifty per cent had received evacuees. Even so, we worked up quite a sweat calling at them all. Or I did, rather, as sweating didn't seem to be in Phyllis's nature. We chatted as we went, me telling her about my school teaching, and she telling me about her husband, Thomas, training as a fighter pilot in the RAF. After an hour or so with no luck, we stopped in at her cottage for a refreshing cup of tea, then we were off again.

At last, late in the afternoon, we struck gold.

•

Mr and Mrs Douglas, who were billetting Johnny Critchley, seemed a very pleasant couple, and they were sad to hear that they could not keep him with them for a while longer. I explained everything to them and assured them that they would get someone else as soon as we had the whole business sorted out.

'He's *not* here,' Johnny said as we walked with Phyllis to the station. 'I've looked everywhere, but I couldn't find him.'

I shook my head. 'Sorry, Johnny. You know your mum's got a speech impediment. That was why I had to go back and ask her exactly what she said to you before I came here. She said she told you your father was missing in action, which, the way it came out, sounded like missing in *Acksham*, didn't it? That's why you came here, wasn't it, to look for your father?'

Young Johnny nodded, tears in his eyes. 'I'm sorry,' he said. 'I couldn't understand why *she* didn't come and look for him. She must be really vexed with me.'

I patted his shoulder. 'I don't think so. More like she'll be glad to see you. How did you manage to sneak in with the real evacuees, by the way?'

Johnny wiped his eyes with his grubby sleeve. 'At the station. There were so many people standing around, at first I didn't know . . . Then I saw a boy I knew from playing cricket on the rec.'

'Oliver Bradley,' I said. The boy whose name Johnny was registered under.

'Yes. He goes to Broad Hill.'

I nodded. Though I had never heard of Oliver Bradley, I knew the school; it was just across the valley from us. 'Go on.'

'I asked him where he was going, and he said he was being sent to Acksham. It was perfect.'

'But how did you get him to change places with you?'

'He didn't want to. Not at first.'

'How did you persuade him?'

Johnny looked down at the road and scraped at some gravel with the scuffed tip of his shoe. 'It cost me a complete set of "Great

Cricketers" cigarette cards. Ones my dad gave me before he went away.'

I smiled. It would have to be something like that.

'And I made him promise not to tell anyone, just to go home and say there wasn't room for him, and he'd have to try again in a few days. I just needed enough time to find Dad . . . you know.'

'I know.'

We arrived at the station, where Johnny sat on the bench and Phyllis and I chatted in the late afternoon sunlight, our shadows lengthening across the tracks. In addition to the birds singing in the trees and hedgerows, I could hear grasshoppers chirruping, a sound you rarely heard in the city. I had often thought how much I would like to live in the country and, perhaps when I retired from teaching a few years in the future, I would be able to do so.

We didn't have long to wait for our train. I thanked Phyllis for all her help, told her I wished her husband well, and she waved to us as the old banger chugged out of the station.

•

It was past blackout when I finally walked into our street holding Johnny's hand. He was tired after his adventure and had spent most of the train journey with his head on my shoulder. Once or twice, from the depths of a dream, he had called his father's name.

I could sense that something was wrong as soon as I turned the corner. It was nothing specific, just a sudden chill at the back of my neck. Because of the blackout, I couldn't see anything clearly, but I got a strong impression of a knot of shifting shadows, just a little bit darker than the night itself, milling around outside Colin Gormond's house.

I quickened my step, and as I got nearer I heard a whisper pass through the crowd when they saw Johnny. Then the shadows began to disperse, slinking and sidling away, disappearing like smoke into the air. From somewhere, Mary Critchley lurched forward with a cry and took young Johnny in her arms. I let him go.

I could hear her thanking me between sobs, but I couldn't stop walking.

The first thing I noticed when I approached Colin's house was that the window was broken and half the blackout curtain had been ripped away. Next I saw that the door was slightly ajar. I was worried that Colin might be hurt, but out of courtesy I knocked and called out his name.

Nothing.

I pushed the door open and walked inside. It was pitch dark. I didn't have a torch with me, and I knew that Colin's light didn't work, but I remembered the matches and the candle on the table. I lit it and held it up before me as I walked forward.

I didn't have far to look. If I hadn't had the candle, I might have bumped right into him. First I saw his face, about level with mine. His froth-specked lips had turned blue, and a trickle of dried blood ran from his left nostril. The blackout cloth was knotted around his neck in a makeshift noose, attached to a hook screwed into the lintel over the kitchen door. As I stood back and examined the scene further, I saw that his down-turned toes were about three inches from the floor, and there was no sign of an upset chair or stool.

Harmless Colin Gormond, friend to the local children. Dead.

I felt the anger well up in me, along with the guilt. It was my fault. I shouldn't have gone dashing off to Acksham like that in search of Johnny, or I should at least have taken Colin with me. I knew the danger he was in; I had talked to Jack Blackwell before I left. How could I have been so stupid, so careless as to leave Colin to his fate with only a warning he didn't understand?

Maybe Colin *had* managed to hang himself somehow, without standing on a stool, though I doubted it. But whether or not Jack Blackwell or the rest had actually laid a finger on him, they were all guilty of driving him to it in my book. Besides, if Jack or anyone else from the street *had* strung Colin up, there would be evidence – fibres, fingerprints, footprints, whatever – and even DS bloody Longbottom wouldn't be able to ignore that.

I stumbled outside and made my way towards the telephone box on the corner. Not a soul stirred now, but as I went I heard one door – Jack Blackwell's door – close softly this time, as if he thought that too much noise might wake the dead, and the dead might have a tale or two to tell.

MEMORY LANE

Another shitty gig. In more ways than one. I can smell the colostomy bags the minute we walk in the front doors. I shudder, as I always do when we enter a place like this. One day, and it might not be long, I know I won't be coming out.

The Recreation Director is waiting to greet us, crisp blue suit and Morningside accent. Why do RDs all have Scottish accents, even in Vancouver? A gold name tag just above the swell of her left breast tells me her name is Emily. Actually, if you look closely, our Emily's not that bad at all, despite the ill-fitting glasses and lifeless hair.

'You'll be the musicians, then?' Nervously eyeing her wristwatch.

Why does it sound like an insult?

'We'll be the musicians,' I admit. Then I introduce the band: Memory Lane. There are five of us, three of us expat Brits. Kit Stark, a washed-up hippie, is our drummer. Kit took one too many hits of acid on the Isle of Wight ferry nearly thirty years ago. When they'd fished him out of the Solent and done artificial respiration, he spent the next twenty years in and out of the nut house hallucinating plankton before washing up on the shores of Nova Scotia. Then there's Benny Leiberman, our morose, alcoholic bass player from Des Moines. Taffy Lloyd plays trumpet and trombone, and when he's not doing that, he's our vocalist. He looks like Harry Secombe but sounds more like one of the Spice Girls. The Hunchback of Notre Band, Geoff Carroll, plays piano, guitar and vibes and does most of our arrangements. He's so short-sighted that he has developed a permanent hunch from leaning over the keyboard to read the music.

Last but not least, there's me, Dex Hill (well, my real name is William Hill, but wouldn't *you* change that for something a bit more jazzy-sounding?), apple of my music teacher's eye, future clarinet soloist for the London Symphony Orchestra (failed), the next John Coltrane (failed) and husband to the beautiful, sexy and cruel Andrea (also failed).

Get the picture?

'I suppose you'd like to tune up, then?' suggests Emily.

Tune up? You don't tune up a clarinet or a saxophone. Or a trumpet for that matter. Perhaps Benny wants to mess around with his bass strings, though the way he's shaking he looks more as if he needs a drink.

I nod.

'Follow me. I'll show you the dressing room.'

We follow Emily's gently swaying hips down the corridor. If we exude a general aroma of booze and smoke, especially with those filthy French cigarettes Benny smokes, she affects not to notice. What does she go home to, my Emily, I wonder? How does she get the aura of death and disease out of her system when she leaves here? Sex? Drugs? Maybe I'll ask her.

Once we're settled in the broom closet they call a dressing room, Emily-less, Benny takes out a fifth of Jim Beam and inhales. He doesn't offer it around. He never does. Some people might think that's rude, but we're used to him and his strange lonely ways by now. Kit and I share a spliff. Just another little smell lost among the faeces and sour sweat. Taffy, as is his wont, puffs on a Rothman's and does a few vocal exercises. Geoff studies the music as if it's the first time he's ever set eyes on it. He always does. In a way, I feel sorry for Geoff because wherever we go the poor sod *always* gets stuck with an out-of-tune piano. Still, he takes it in his stride. Very phlegmatic is Geoff. Lots of sangfroid. You have to have with a hunchback like his.

Anyway, after a few minutes of this and a chat about the order of songs, Emily returns and we're ready to face the chanting crowds.

'They've been looking forward to this all week, you know,' she says, with a tight, Morningside smile. 'A lot of them were in the war, with the Canadian armed forces, or with the RAF. It'll mean a lot to them, hearing those old songs played again.'

Well, there are about twenty people in the recreation room, which is quite a crowd for this sort of gig. I remember one RD apologizing – I think it was in Swift Current or Red Deer – that there would have been more people in the audience only two of them croaked during the night. That seemed a bit excessive to me. I mean, one, maybe, you might expect, but *two*?

There they sit, a pathetic bunch of losers waiting to die. It gives me the shivers just to look at them. Empty husks. Nothing left except bodily functions. Even those who have arses left probably need someone to wipe them. Most sit in wheelchairs, reptilian talons plucking at the tartan blankets spread over their knees. Some have the head shakes, some drool and twitch every now and then.

Still, I suppose I've seen worse audiences in Toronto jazz clubs.

A quick count, and we're off: 'Tennessee Waltz', always a nice easy swinger to start with. Intro done, Taffy comes in with the vocals, sounding more like Tiny Tim than Sporty Spice today. One, two, three, here we go . . . Hey up, there's one bloke on the nod already.

'I was dancing with my darling . . .'

•

I was the best dancer. That's why she chose me. I was the best dancer. She wasn't Carl's to start with. Wasn't anyone's. Just another girl at a forces dance on a Saturday night. Carl was the handsomest; he always got the pick of the girls. But not this time. I was the best dancer. Just put his nose out of joint a little, that's all. I didn't steal her from anyone. She melted in my arms, her shape moulded against me; we were missing halves of a whole and the purpose the music had been waiting for; we completed it, carried it away from its airy pointlessness to something more profound; we gave the music meaning.

Bullshit, O'Farrell. You stole your best friend's sweetheart, pure and simple. And all the rest, all this about profundity and meaning, is bullshit. Lust, that's all it was. Lust. And revenge for all those times when Carl got the girl. And look what happened. A two-week honeymoon, then you took her thousands of miles away from her family and friends, spent the next fifty years in and out of the bottle and drove the poor bitch to an early grave.

No . . . no . . . it wasn't like that. I'm tired, so tired of arguing with myself . . .

•

On the nod, just as we're going into 'Cheek to Cheek'. Christ, how stimulating we must be, what fucking exciting memories we must invoke. Still, he's twitching a bit in his wheelchair, so I suppose he must still be alive. His mouth seems to be moving. Maybe he's trying to sing along. Sometimes they do. But no, this one looks more as if he's having a conversation with himself, only half-mouthing the words, hardly daring to give them full breath. A little string of drool hangs from his chin. Shit, I hate this job. Solo time, man. Remember what Geoff told you, 'Stick real close to the melody line, Dex. You're not Coltrane playing "My Favourite Things" you know.' Thanks a lot, Geoff. And fuck you . . .

•

Heaven. I'm in heaven. Dancing cheek to cheek. A hot night in late July 1943. A little dance hall in a small town near the base, maybe used to be the church hall or the Women's Institute. A few rickety tables, a makeshift bar selling warm beer and weak scotch, weak beer and warm scotch, whatever. Dim air thick with smoke hanging in the lights: blue straight from the cigarette, grey when it comes out of the lungs. Everyone smoked then. All of us. It was the least of our worries. 'Cheek to Cheek' was the first song we danced to, the first time the magic hit.

But why does my memory smell of burning rubber and leather instead of her perfume? Why do flames and smoke blossom when I close my eyes and lean into her? I'm holding her close enough that she could almost be a part of me and I'm smelling hot metal and engine oil.

Bombenbrandschrumpfleichen.

My God, Carl, where did that come from? Not now. Not yet. That was later. Back to the dance. Holding her. Some of her face powder rubbed off when my lips brushed her cheek. It tasted like chalk. Carl was pissed, I could tell, but I was flying that night (funny, I was flying the night before, too) and it was my turn for once. They'd only been out together a couple of times. It wasn't serious. Besides, how was I to know that Mary and I would fall in love? It was just another dance, for crying out loud. We'd been to hundreds of them and Carl always got the best-looking women. But I was the best dancer and Carl had no chance this time when she and I were dancing cheek to cheek, me tasting chalk (or was it stardust?), smelling rubber burn and hearing those crackling noises arcing in my brain from ear to ear.

•

Christ, just look at them, will you? Half of them are asleep, about a third are deaf and three-quarters have no faculties left at all. What does that make? Is anyone out there listening at all? And that hunchbacked bastard Geoff gives me the evil eye for wandering too far on the 'Stardust' solo. As if anyone notices. Poor bastard's piano is so out of tune it sounds like a warped LP. Funny, all of a sudden I'm thinking of that bitch Andrea. Was 'Stardust' playing when we met, on our first date? I'm damned if I remember. 'Stairway to Heaven', more likely, or maybe 'Bitches Brew'. All I remember is ripping her panties off and fucking her hard up against the apartment door the minute we got back from the gig.

Play it Dex. 'All the Things You Are.' Bird, Trane, lead the way. And to hell with Geoff's evil eye . . .

•

Carl wouldn't talk to me. All the next day. And the next. He'd really wanted Mary the way a boy wants candy and he was jealous as hell. I didn't tell him anything. Didn't tell him about the softness of her body as we made love in the warm field that July night, the taste of the beet juice on her lips, the smooth warm skin, nipples hard as berries on my tongue, between her legs like warm, wet silk and how she cried out my name when she came. Not his. Mine. And clung to me afterwards for dear life as we lay against the dry-stone wall and watched squadron after squadron of Lancasters pass over the half-moon, blotting out its light like the plague of locusts, armadas from hell. Held me tighter as the roar of the bombers filled the sky.

Bombenbrandschrumpfleichen.

No. That wasn't till later. We didn't know then, the same way we didn't know smoking was killing us. We didn't know. But does that really make it any different in the end?

•

Another evil look from Geoff. Well, to hell with him. Let the miserable bastard fire me. I've had it with this, anyway. 'In the Middle of a Kiss.' Taffy always does a good job on this one. You just don't expect that alto voice to come out of someone so fat. Look at that guy, the way his head's swaying. If it's the shakes, at least he's in time with the music. Maybe some of them are capable of getting a little simple pleasure out of us, after all. Christ, if Andrea could see me now. She'd laugh until she pissed herself and tell me I'd found my true destiny. Here we go, man, 'Blowing Up a Storm'.

•

Firestorm. They had to invent new names for the way people died.

Bombenbrandschrumpfleichen.

Incendiary-bomb-shrunken bodies. Then there were the ones who melted, asphyxiated, baked or just plain roasted. And the human torches running down streets on fire, arms flailing.

These were the important factories and docks we were told we destroyed. The firestorm sucked in all the surrounding air, made winds rage fast as cyclones, suffocated all the people hiding in shelters, cellars and bunkers. Fifteen hundred degrees Fahrenheit at the core. Spontaneous combustion.

Bombenbrandschrumpfleichen.

And the night after that I stole my best friend's girl because I was the best dancer. That was the night we clung to one another watching the bombers set out again. Six raids. Day and night. Night and day. 41,800 killed. 37,439 injured, burned, maimed. Her skin warm and smooth, wet silk between her thighs, bombers blanking out the stars and the moon. Making Bombenbrandschrumpfleichen. *And the night after that, Carl bought it . . .*

•

'Blue Flame.' That should slow them down a bit before our fiery finale, and a nice searing blues solo for me. Most of them are asleep now anyway. There's even one old dear snoring in the far corner by the vase of flowers. And there's Emily, hands clasped on her lap, thin smile on her face. Is she enjoying us? As a matter of fact, I wouldn't mind fucking Emily, stick it to her hard, right up that tight Morningside arse of hers and take that smile off her face. Bet she's a screamer. That old guy's having a real struggle with himself now. Ought to be in a fucking nuthouse not a rest home. Drooling and muttering, arguing with himself . . .

•

It wasn't fair, we'd finished, we were heading home successful, looking forward to a hot cup of tea and a long sleep, no fighters in sight. But then it never is fair, is it? We'd dropped our load, made more Bombenbrandschrumpfleichen, *got out of the flack unscathed, and all of sudden there it was, a lone Messerschmitt.*

Whether he was lost or just scavenging, looking for stragglers, I don't know, but he buzzed at us like an angry wasp and let rip. He could outmanoeuvre us easily and his machine-gun fire ripped through the plane as if our fuselage were made of paper. I could smell the fires breaking out behind us. Me and Clarky, my co-pilot. We started spewing smoke and losing altitude. One of our gunners hit the 'Schmitt and it exploded at ten o'clock. We were bucking and swinging to starboard like an old Short Stirling. God knows how we made it, but we did, Clarky and me, we came limping in the minute we got beyond the old white cliffs and crash-landed in a field. The tail section broke off and flames leapt up all around us. Within minutes we were surrounded by a crowd of gaping yokels right out of a Thomas Hardy novel. Whether they wore smocks and carried pitchforks I can't be certain, but that's how I see them when I look now. And when I went back to see how Carl was doing, that's when I found him. He was dead. Along with the others in back. All black and burned up, uniform and skin fused, welded into one, his knees crooked and his arms tightened up and fists clenched like a boxer, aimed at me. For one of those stupid moments, before reality's cold blade pierced the back of my brain, I thought he was getting ready to fight me. We hadn't spoken for three days because of Mary and I knew he was still pissed. But he was dead. Burned and shrivelled.

Bombenbrandschrumpfleichen.

Just like the people of Hamburg. Carl, you poor, sad, cocky, two-left-footed bastard. You were the handsomest, the most charming; you were the lady killer. But come waltz, tango or jitterbug, goddamnit, I was the best dancer. I was the best dancer!

•

'I was the best dancer! I was the best dancer!'

One, two, three, and blow that bugle, Taffy! Let's wake the buggers up. 'Bugle Call Rag' and Jesus Christ, will you look at him, the old bastard's on his feet. Taffy flashes me a big grin and we get in the groove. I can feel Geoff's eyes boring into the back of my head. Fuck him. Things are jumping now. Taffy and I are trading licks like we haven't done in years. Trumpet and sax. Dizzy and Bird. Miles and Trane. Look at the guy go, he's out of his chair and jumping up and down, yelling at the top of his lungs, baggy pants slipping down his hips.

'I was the best dancer! I was the best dancer!'

Sure you were, buddy!

All of sudden he seems to reach some sort of inner peak or crescendo as my sax and Taffy's trumpet join in some of weirdest harmonies we've ever found. He's on tiptoe, stretching his arms as high as he can, reaching for the ceiling, or for heaven.

Then his whole body starts shaking. Taffy trails off to take a break and I blow harder, urging the old guy higher, but he's out of synch with us now. Whatever he's into, eyes closed, head tilted towards the ceiling, it's nothing to do with our music. His pants are down around his ankles, his shrivelled scrotum and shrunken penis there for all to see. I stop the solo and turn to catch Geoff's dagger gaze. I grin at him and shrug; he leads us back to the opening riff in a few spare, tight-assed chords.

The old man stiffens, then drops to the floor, spent. One by one, we let the music dribble away from us. Then there's the strangest sensation. The room seems to draw in on him, as if all its energy focuses on that single inert figure. Everything feels tight, like a corked bottle about to blow. The room fills with pressure, and it's hard against my eardrums, that deaf and fuzzy feeling before your ears pop on an airplane, everything silent and in slow motion.

Then it pops, the air hisses out, and he's just someone lying on the floor.

'Jesus,' whispers the man beside him. 'When I go, I want to go just like that.'

Then the smooth, practised staff breeze in like a team of office cleaners, or scene changers between the acts of a play, and start to tidy up the mess in a silence as heavy as prayer. Someone in white checks the old man's pulse and takes out a stethoscope. The other inmates, dazed, mumbling and drooling, are all wheeled back to their rooms. And it's getting to look like nothing ever happened.

Before they're done, Emily starts leading us back to the dressing room. 'I think it would probably be best all around if you left now, don't you think?' she says. 'Then we can get everyone calmed down. They take it hard, some of them, when one of them passes on, you know. See their own future, I suppose, poor things. Don't worry, you'll be paid your normal rate, of course. It wasn't your fault, after all, was it?'

I nod dumbly, walking beside her. She's right, of course. It wasn't our fault, no reason why we shouldn't get paid. But even so. *See their own future, I suppose*. Somehow that echoes, gets to me so much that I forget to ask for her phone number. And I remember it afterwards in the van. But this time Benny passes around the Jim Beam and Kit rolls another spliff and soon it's just another memory of just another shitty gig, after all, just another slice of turd on the nursing-home circuit.

This story was suggested by an anecdote told to me by Rick Scott, musician, in Sechelt, BC, August 1997. Rick gave me the bare outline, and the rest is pure invention.

CARRION

Isn't it strange the way two strangers might strike up a casual acquaintance due simply to a quirk of fate? And isn't it even stranger how that innocent meeting might so completely alter the life of one of them? That was exactly what happened when Edward Grainger and I met in a pub one wet September lunchtime, only weeks before his tragic loss.

I work in a bank in the City. It's a dull job, enlivened only by the occasional surge of adrenalin when the pound takes yet another plunge on the foreign exchange markets, and most lunchtimes I like to get out of the office and take refuge in the Mason's Arms.

As a rule, I will drink half a pint of Guinness with a slice of quiche or a cheese roll, say, and perhaps, once in a while, treat myself to a steak and kidney pie. As I eat, I work at *The Times* crossword, which I never seem able to finish before my glass is empty, and after my meal I enjoy a cigarette. I know the vile things are bad for me, but I can't quite seem to give them up. Besides, how bad can one cigarette a day be? And only five days a week, at that.

Given its location in the City, the Mason's Arms is generally busy, noisy and smoky by half past twelve on a weekday, and that suits me just fine. Lost in the crowd, buffeted by conversation and laughter that require no response on my part, I can concentrate on my crossword or allow my mind to drift in directions that the constant application of little grey cells to columns of figures precludes.

That particular lunchtime I found myself leaving the office a few minutes later than usual due to an important telephone conversation with an overseas client. The short walk also took longer because I had to struggle against the wind and rain with my rather flimsy umbrella. When I got to the Arms, as I had taken to calling it, I found my usual little corner table already taken by a stranger in a pinstripe suit. I could hardly tell him to sod off, so I carried my drink over and sat opposite him.

As he read his *Times*, I studied his features closely. I would guess his age at about forty-five – mostly because of the wrinkles around his eyes and the grey hair around his temples and ears – but having said that, I would have to admit that the overall effect of his face was one of youthfulness. He had bright blue eyes and a healthy, ruddy complexion, and he showed no sign of that dark, shadowy stubble that makes so many men look downright repulsive, not to mention sinister.

After I had finished my ham roll, I lit my cigarette and wrestled with eight down, letting the ebb and flow of conversation drift over me until a voice seemed to single itself out from the crowd and speak directly to me.

Startled, I noticed the man opposite looking at me in a way that suggested he had just spoken.

'Pardon?' I said. 'I was miles away.'

'"Crippen,"' he said. 'Eight down. "Quiet prince upset for this murderer." It's an anagram of "prince" and "p" for silent.'

'Yes, I do see that, thank you very much.' If my tone was a little frosty, it served the bugger right. I hate it when people solve my crossword clues for me, the same way I hate anyone reading over my shoulder. Takes all the fun out of it.

His face dropped when he saw the look I gave him.

'I'm sorry,' he said. 'Very rude of me. Didn't think.'

'It's all right.' I put the crossword aside and flicked a column of ash at the floor.

'Look, you wouldn't happen to know anything about septic tanks, would you?' he asked.

'I'm afraid not.' As far as conversational gambits went, this fellow wasn't exactly heading for the top of the class in my book.

'Oh. Pity. You see, we're having one installed in a couple of weeks, my wife Harriet and I. I'm just not sure what kind of mess to expect.'

'Well, I suppose they'll have to dig the garden up,' I told him. 'But I can't honestly say I've ever seen one, so I don't know how big they are.'

He smiled. 'Well, that's the point, isn't it? You're not supposed to *see* them. We're moving to the country, you know, to Hampshire.'

'Why are you moving?' I asked. And though I surprised myself by asking such a personal question of a complete stranger, it felt natural enough.

He sipped his gin and tonic before replying. 'It's for Harriet, mostly,' he said. 'Wants the country air. Not that I'd knock it, mind you. And it's a beautiful cottage, or it will be after the renovations. Seventeenth century. I'll keep the flat in town, of course, go down to the country at weekends. Yes, I'm sure it'll work out.'

'I hope so,' I told him. Then I excused myself and headed back to the bank, it being almost one-thirty and Mr Beamish, the branch manager, being a real stickler for punctuality.

•

As time went on, our conversations became a regular feature of my lunchtime visits to the Arms, though I would be hard pushed now to think of everything we discussed: politics, of course, on which we disagreed; books, on which we agreed far more than we would have imagined; and marriage, about which we couldn't quite make up our minds. Sometimes, we would just work on the crossword together in silence.

He also talked about weekends at the country house, of autumn walks in the woods, the occasional hovercraft trip to the Isle of Wight, quiet nights with a good bottle of claret, a hefty volume of Trollope, and a log fire crackling in the hearth.

Though I had never fancied country living myself, I must admit that Edward's accounts made me quite envious. So much so that when Evelyn brought up the subject at home after watching a documentary on the Cotswolds, I thought it might become a real possibility for us, too, in a year or two's time.

Edward and I never met at any other times or places – ours was a purely casual arrangement – but I like to think that a sort of friendship developed. Sometimes he didn't turn up at all. He worked in international finance, he told me, and now and then he had to sacrifice his lunch hour for emergency meetings or telephone calls from strange time zones. Occasionally, he had to go abroad for a few days. But when he did come, we usually contrived to sit together and chat over our drinks and rolls for half an hour or so.

During that time, I didn't find out very much more about his private life, and if I were to come to any conclusions they would be due entirely to my reading between the lines.

I didn't ask Edward about his wife's occupation, for example, but somehow I got the impression that she spent most of her time at home cooking, cake-decorating, cleaning, sewing, knitting and such. What people used to call a 'housewife' in the old days. I suppose now she could call herself an 'estate manager' down in Hampshire. As far as their relationship went, it sounded perfectly normal to me.

Though I had never met Harriet, I'm sure you can imagine how shocked I was on that bright, windy Thursday in early October when Edward came in a quarter of an hour later than usual, looking drawn and haggard, and told me that his wife had disappeared.

•

Naturally, I tried to comfort him as best I could over the following weeks, at least as far as our brief and irregular meetings allowed. But there was little I could do. For the most part, I could only look on sadly as Edward lost weight and his former ruddy complexion turned wan. Soon he came to remind of the wretched youth in Keats's poem: 'Alone and palely loitering.'

Weeks passed, and still there was no sign of Harriet. Theories as to her disappearance varied, as they do in cases like this. One tabloid speculated that she had been abducted by a serial killer, then chopped up and buried somewhere. A local doctor suggested that she could have suffered some form of amnesia. If so, he went on, she might easily have wandered off and ended up living on the streets of London with the thousands of other lost and lonely souls. One neighbour, Edward told me, speculated that Harriet could have been actually *planning* her escape for some time and had simply taken off for America, Ireland or France to start a new life under a new name. With a new man, of course. Astonishingly, Edward also told me that even *he* had come under police suspicion at one time, albeit not for long.

Christmas came and went. It was about as cheerful as a wet weekend in July, the way it usually is for families whose children have all grown up and left home. Edward seemed to have gained a little colour when I saw him after the holidays. Or perhaps the Arctic winds we had that January had rubbed his skin raw. Anyway, it was around then that he started dropping in at the Arms for lunch less and less frequently.

By the beginning of February I hadn't seen him for three weeks, and I was slipping easily back into my old routine of doing the crossword over lunch. I missed his company, of course, and I was certainly curious about Harriet, but we are creatures of habit, are we not? And old habits are deeply ingrained.

It was near the end of March when I saw him next, but it wasn't in the Arms. No, I had come into the West End to shop one Saturday afternoon, mostly to get out of the way while Evelyn was busy planting the herbaceous borders. I hate gardening, and if I'm around I usually get roped in.

Anyway, I was browsing downstairs in the fiction section of Waterstone's on Charing Cross Road, when I saw Edward across the table of new releases. It took me a moment to recognize him because he was wearing casual clothes and seemed to have done something to remove the grey from his hair. He was also fingering the new Will Self paperback, which one would hardly expect of a Trollope man.

On second glance, though, I realized it was definitely Edward and that the pretty young blonde with the prominent breasts didn't just happen to be standing beside him; she was *with* him. Surely this couldn't be the elusive Harriet?

Then a strange thing happened. Edward caught my eye as I walked over, and I saw a very odd look pass over his features. For a moment, I could have sworn, he wanted to turn tail and avoid me. But I got to him before he could retreat.

'Edward,' I said. 'It's good to see you.' Then I looked at the blonde. I could see her roots. 'I see Harriet has turned up, then,' I said with a smile.

Edward cleared his throat and the blonde merely frowned. 'Well . . . er . . .' he said. 'Not exactly. I mean, no, she hasn't. This is Joyce.' He put his arm around the blonde's shoulders and looked down at her with obvious pride and passion.

I said hello to Joyce as Edward haltingly explained our relationship, such as it was, then he made excuses and they hurried up the stairs as if the place were on fire. That was the last time I ever clapped eyes on Edward Grainger.

•

About a year after the incident in Waterstone's, something so profound, so shocking and so unexpected happened to me that my life was never to be the same again. I fell in love.

Like most people my age, I had long thought myself immune to powerful passions, long settled into a sedate and comfortable existence with little in the way of strong emotion to upset its even keel. If I have unsatisfied or unrequited hopes and wishes, then I am in good company, for who hasn't? If I regret some of the sacrifices I have made for the comforts I have gained, who doesn't? And if I sometimes feel that my life lacks adventure, lacks spice, then again, who doesn't? In all that, I felt, I was perfectly normal.

Life, it had come to seem to me, was a slow betrayal of the dreams of one's youth and a gradual decline from the desires of one's adolescence. Little did I know what a fragile illusion all that was until I met Katrina.

Imagine, if you can, my utter amazement when the bells started to ring, the earth moved and a sudden spring came into my step every time I saw her. Absurd, I told myself, she'll never pay the least attention to an old fuddy-duddy like you. But she did. Oh, indeed she did. Love truly must be blind if such a gorgeous creature as Katrina could give herself to me.

Katrina came to work for the branch in summer, and by autumn we were meeting clandestinely whenever we could. She lived alone in a tiny bedsit in Kennington, which was convenient, if a bit cramped. But what is a little discomfort to a pair of lovers? We were consumed with a passion that could no more be stopped than an avalanche or a tidal wave. It picked us up, tossed us about like rag dolls and threw us back on the ground dazed, dazzled and breathless. I couldn't get enough of her sad eyes, her soft red lips, her small breasts with the nipples hard as acorns when we made love, her skin like warm brown silk.

Needless to say, this affair made life very difficult both at work and at home, but I think I managed to cope well enough under the circumtances. I know I succeeded in hiding it from Evelyn, for I surely would have felt the repercussions had I not.

We went on meeting furtively for almost a year, during which time our passion did not abate in the least. Katrina never once asked me to abandon my marriage and live with her, but I wanted to. Oh God, how I wanted to. Only the thought of all the trouble, all the upheaval, that such a move would cause prevented me. For Evelyn wouldn't take it lying down. So, like many others embroiled in affairs, I simply let it run on, perhaps hoping vaguely that some *deus ex machina* would come along and solve my problems for me.

Then, one day, after an excruciatingly painful Christmas spent away from Katrina, Evelyn reminded me of a conversation we had had some time ago about getting a country cottage, and pointed out the ideal place in an estate agent's brochure: a rundown, isolated cottage in Oxfordshire, going for a song.

Furiously, I began to think of how such a move might prevent me from seeing Katrina as often as I needed to. We would have to sell the Dulwich house, of course, but the Oxfordshire cottage was indeed going for such an unbelievably low price that I might be able to afford a small flat in town.

At a pinch, however, Evelyn might suggest I could commute. The thought of that was unbearable. Though Katrina and I wouldn't be separated totally, anything other than a quick session after work before the train home would be impossible. And neither of us wanted to live like that. A quickie in the back of a car is so sordid, and we were passionately, romantically in love.

On the other hand, I could hardly crush Evelyn's dreams of a place in the country without thinking up a damn good explanation as to why we should simply stay put. And I couldn't. The price was right, and we might not have another chance for years. Even with the renovations that would need to be done, we worked out, we could still easily afford it.

And so we took the plunge and bought the cottage. To say I was a soul in torment might sound like an exaggeration, but believe me, it doesn't even come close to describing how wretched I really felt as I signed on the dotted line.

•

We had sent Sam Halsey, a jack-of-all-trades in the renovation business, over to Oxfordshire on a number of occasions to assess what needed doing and how it could be done to our liking *and* to our budget. One of his complaints was that, due to its isolation and to the odd whims of its previous owners, the toilet arrangements were far from adequate.

After much deliberation, one afternoon at the house in Dulwich, Sam said, 'Of course, you could have a septic tank put in.'

'A what?' I said.

'A septic tank. Perfectly respectable. Lots of country folk have them. Of course, you'll need some carrion.'

'I'm sorry, Sam, I don't follow you.'

'Carrion. To get the whole process going. Now, some of the younger chaps in the business will tell you a bit of compost will do the job just fine, but don't believe them. Don't you believe them. My old boss told me—'

Sam's voice faded into the background as, suddenly, it hit me. I thought of my old lunchtime companion, Edward Grainger, and that guilty look that flitted across his features the time I saw him in Waterstone's with Joyce, the blonde.

I remembered the tragedy of his wife's disappearance, and how, after that, I saw less and less of him.

And I remembered how the disappearance occurred around the time they were having a septic tank installed at their cottage in Hampshire. Carrion, indeed.

And then I thought of my Katrina, my beautiful, beautiful Katrina, who took my breath away with her sad eyes and her skin like warm brown silk.

And, lastly, I thought of Evelyn. Life just isn't fair, is it? Some people don't simply fade away quietly into the obscurity from whence they came when you want rid of them, do they? No, they have to cause trouble, create scenes, make unreasonable demands and generally do their damnedest to ruin your hopes of a decent and happy future without them. They just *won't go away*. Well, as I have already explained, Evelyn is one of those people. I'm certain of it.

On the other hand, people disappear all the time, don't they? And people change. Harriet changed into Joyce, didn't she? Sometimes you just have to give a little kick-start to get the process going, like the carrion in the septic tank, and then nature takes care of the rest.

'Penny for them?'

'What? Oh, I'm sorry, Sam. Miles away.'

'That's all right. I was just saying as how you'll need some carrion for the septic tank. My old boss swore by it, he did.'

At that moment, Evelyn passed by the open French windows in his shabby beige cardigan, secateurs in hand. Wisps of grey hair blew in the March wind like spiders' webs, and his glasses had slipped down his nose. Yes, people disappear all the time, don't they? And if it can happen to wives, I thought, then it can bloody well happen to husbands too.

'Yes, Sam,' I said slowly. 'Yes, I suppose we will. Don't worry. I'll take care of it.'

APRIL IN PARIS

The girl sitting outside the cafe reminds me of April. She has the same long hennaed hair, which she winds around her index finger in the same abstracted way. She is waiting for someone clearly – a lover perhaps – and as she waits she smokes, holding her cigarette in the same way, taking the same short, hurried puffs, that April used to do. With her free hand, she alternates between taking sips of milky *pastis* and tapping her cigarette packet on the table. She is smoking Marlboro, as everyone in Paris seems to do these days. Back then it was all Gitanes, Gauloises and Disque Bleus.

Still, it wasn't smoking that killed April; it was love.

•

It is late September, and though the weather is mild, it is still too cold outside for an old man like me, with blood as thin and as lacking in nutrients as workhouse gruel. Instead, I sit inside the little cafe on the Boulevard St Germain over a *pichet* of red wine, just watching the people come and go. The young people. I have spent most of my life surrounded by the young, and though I grow inexorably older every year, they always seem to stay young. *Immortal youth.* Like Tithonus, I am 'a white-haired shadow roaming like a dream'. But unlike Tennyson's luckless narrator, who gained eternal life but not eternal youth, I am not immortal.

Six months, perhaps less, the doctors say. Something is growing inside me; my cells are mutating. As yet I feel little pain, though my appetite has diminished and I often suffer from extreme weariness.

Dying, I find, lends an edge to living, gives a clarity and a special, golden hue to the quotidian scenes parading before me: a swarthy man with a briefcase, glancing at his watch, speeding up, late for an important appointment; a woman chastising her little girl at the corner, wagging her finger, the girl crying and stamping her foot; a distracted priest stumbling briefly as he walks up the steps to the church across the boulevard.

Dying accentuates the beauty of the young, sets their energy in relief, enhances the smooth glow of their unwrinkled skin. But dying does not make me bitter. I am resigned to my fate; I have come to the end of my threescore and ten; I have seen enough. If you wish to travel, my doctors told me, do it now while you're still strong enough. So here I am, revisiting the scene of my one and only great *amour*.

April. She always pronounced it *Ap-reel*. When I think of her, I still hear Thelonious Monk playing 'April in Paris', hesitantly at first, feeling his way into the song, reluctant to define the theme, then worrying away at it and, once finding it, altering it so much that the music becomes his own, only to be abandoned finally.

Of course, April didn't give a tinker's for Thelonious Monk. She listened to him dutifully, as they all did, for they were the heirs of Kerouac, Ginsberg and Burroughs, to whom Monk, Bird, Trane, Miles and Mingus were gods, sacred and cool. But April's generation had its own gods – the Doors, Cream, Jimi Hendrix, Bob Dylan – gods of words and images as well as of music, and it was they who provided the soundtrack to which I lived during my year as a visiting lecturer in American literature at the Sorbonne in 1968.

This cafe hasn't changed much. A lick of paint, perhaps, if that. It probably hasn't changed much since Hemingway and Fitzgerald used to hang out around here. Even the waiters are probably the same. It was here I first met April, of course (why else would I come here?), one fine evening towards the end of March that year, when I was still young enough to bear the slight chill of a clear spring evening.

•

That April was beautiful almost goes without saying. I remember her high cheekbones, her smooth, olive complexion, dark, watchful eyes and rich, moist lips, downturned at the edges, often making her look sulky or petulant when she was far from it. I remember also how she used to move with grace and confidence when she remembered, but how the gaucheness of late adolescence turned her movements into a country girl's gait when she was at her most unselfconscious. She was tall, slim and long-legged, and her breasts were small, round and high. The breasts of a Cranach nude.

We met, as I say, one late March evening in 1968 at this cafe, the Café de la Lune, where I was then sitting with the usual group: Henri, Nadine, Brad, Brigitte, Alain and Paul. This was only days after Daniel Cohn-Bendit and seven other students had occupied the dean's office at Nanterre to protest against the recent arrest of six members of the National Vietnam Committee, an event that was to have cataclysmic effects on us all not long afterwards. Much of the time in those days we spoke of revolution, but that evening we were discussing, I remember quite clearly, F. Scott Fitzgerald's *Tender Is the Night,* when in she walked, wearing a woolly jumper and close-fitting, bell-bottomed jeans with flowers embroidered around the bells. She was carrying a bulky leather shoulder bag, looking radiant and slightly lost, glancing around for someone she knew.

It turned out that she knew Brad, an American backpacker who had attached himself to our group. People like Brad had a sort of fringe, outlaw attraction for the students. They seemed, with their freedom to roam and their contempt for rules and authority, to embody the very principles that the students themselves, with their heavy workloads, exams and future careers, could only imagine, or live vicariously. There were always one or two Brads around. Some dealt in drugs to make a living; Brad, though he spoke a good revolution, lived on a generous allowance wired regularly by his wealthy Boston parents via Western Union.

April went up to Brad and kissed him on both cheeks, a formal French gesture he seemed to accept with thinly veiled amusement. In his turn, Brad introduced her to the rest of us. That done, we resumed our discussion over another bottle of wine, the tang of Gauloises and *café noir* infusing the chill night air, and April surprised me by demonstrating that she had not only read *Tender Is the Night*, but that she had thought about it, too, even though she was a student of history, not of literature.

'Don't you think those poor young girls are terribly *used*?' she said. 'I mean, Nicole is Dick's *patient*. He should be healing her, not sleeping with her. And the way Rosemary is manipulated by her mother . . . I'd go so far as to say that the mother seems to be *pimping* for her. Those films she made –' and here April gave her characteristic shrug, no more than a little shiver rippling across her shoulders – 'they were no doubt made to appeal to older men.' She didn't look at me as she said this, but my cheeks burned nonetheless.

'Have you read *Day of the Locust*?' Henri, one of the other students chimed in. 'If you want to know about how Hollywood warps people, that's your place to start. There's a mother in there who makes Rosemary's look like a saint.'

'Huxley?' asked Nadine, not our brightest.

'No,' said April. 'That was *After Many a Summer. Day of the Locust* was Nathanael West, I think. Yes?'

Here, she looked directly at me, the professor, for the first time, turned on me the full blaze of her beauty. She knew she was right, of course, but she still deferred to me out of politeness.

'That's right,' I said, smiling, feeling my heart lurch and my soul tingle inside its chains of flesh. 'Nathanael West wrote *Day of the Locust*.'

And from that moment on I was smitten.

•

I told myself not to be a fool, that April was far too young for me, and that a beautiful woman like her couldn't possibly be interested in a portly, forty-year-old lecturer, even if he did wear faded denim jeans, had a goatee and grew those wisps of hair that remained a little longer than some of his colleagues thought acceptable. But after that first meeting I found myself thinking about April a lot. In fact I couldn't get her out of my mind. It wasn't mere lust – though, Lord knows, it was that too – but I loved the sound of her voice, loved the way she twisted strands of hair around her finger as she spoke, the way she smoked her cigarette, loved the passion of her arguments, the sparkle of her laughter, the subtle jasmine of her perfume.

Love.

That night, she had left the cafe after about an hour, arm in arm with Brad – young, handsome, rich, footloose and fancy-free Brad – and I had lain awake tormented by images of their passionate love making. I had never felt like that before, never felt so consumed by desire for someone and so racked by pain at the thought of someone else having her. It was as if an alien organism had invaded my body, my very soul, and wrought such changes there that I could hardly cope with more mundane matters, such as teaching and writing, eating and sleeping.

The second time I met her it was raining. I was walking along the *quai* across from Notre Dame, staring distractedly at the rain pitting the river's steely surface, thinking of her, when she suddenly ducked under my umbrella and took my arm.

I must have gasped out loud.

'Professor Dodgson,' she said. Not a question. She *knew* who I was. 'Sorry I startled you.'

But that wasn't why I gasped, I wanted to tell her. It was the sudden apparition of this beautiful creature I had been dreaming about for days. I looked at her. The driving rain had soaked her hair and face. Like Dick in *Tender Is the Night*, I wanted to drink the rain that ran from her cheeks. 'How did you recognize me under this?' I asked her.

She gave that little shrug that was no more than a ripple and smiled up at me. 'Easy. You're carrying the same old briefcase you had last week. It's got your initials on it.'

'How sharp of you,' I said. 'You should become a detective.'

'Oh, I could never become a fascist pig.' She said this with a completely straight face. People said things like that back then.

'Just a joke,' I said. 'Where are you going?'

'Nowhere special.'

'Coffee?'

She looked at me again, chewing on her lower lip for a moment as she weighed up my invitation. 'All right,' she said finally. 'I know a place.' And her gentle pressure on my arm caused me to change direction and enter the narrow alleys that spread like veins throughout the Latin Quarter. 'Your French is very good,' she said as we walked. 'Where did you learn?'

'School, mostly. Then university. I seem to have a facility for it. We used to come here when I was a child, too, before the war. Brittany. My father fought in the first war, you see, and he developed this love for France. I think the fighting gave him a sort of stake in things.'

'Do you, too, have this stake in France?'

'I don't know.'

She found the cafe she was looking for on the Rue St Severin, and we ducked inside. 'Can you feel what's happening?' she asked me, once we were warm and dry, sitting at the zinc counter with hot, strong coffees before us. She lit a Gauloise and touched my arm. 'Isn't it exciting?'

I couldn't believe what I was hearing. *She* thought something was happening between us. I could hardly disguise my joy. But I was also so tongue-tied that I couldn't think of anything wise or witty to say. I probably sat there, my mouth opening and closing like a guppy's before saying, 'Yes. *Yes*, it is exciting.'

'There'll be a revolution before spring's over, you mark my words. We'll be rid of de Gaulle and ready to start building a new France.'

Ah, yes. *The revolution*. I should have known. It was the topic on everyone's mind at the time. Except mine, that is. I tried not to show my disappointment. Not that I wasn't interested – you couldn't be in Paris in the spring of 1968 and *not* be interested in the revolution one way or another – but I had been distracted from politics by my thoughts of April. Besides, as radical as I might have appeared to some people, I was still a foreign national, and I had to do my best to keep a low political profile, difficult though it was. One false step and I'd not only be out of a job but out of the country, and far away from April, for ever. And I had answered her question honestly; I didn't know whether I had a stake in France or not.

'What does Brad think?' I asked.

'Brad?' She seemed surprised by my question. 'Brad is an anarchist.'

'And you?'

She twisted her hair around her finger. 'I'm not sure. I know I want change. I think I'm an anarchist too, though I'm not sure I'd want to be completely without any sort of government at all. But we want the same things. Peace. A new, more equal society. He is an American, but they have had many demonstrations there, too, you know. Vietnam.'

'Ah, yes. I remember some of them.'

We passed a while talking about my experiences in California, which seemed to fascinate April, though I must admit I was far more interested in tracing the contours of her face and drinking in the beauty of her eyes and skin than I was in discussing the war in Vietnam.

In the end she looked at her watch and said she had to go to a lecture but would probably see me later at the cafe. I said I hoped so and watched her walk away.

•

You will have gathered that I loved April to distraction, but did she love me? I think not. She liked me well enough. I amused her, entertained her, and she was perhaps even flattered by my attentions, but ultimately brash youth wins out over suave age. It was Brad she loved. Brad, whose status in my mind quickly changed from that of a mildly entertaining, reasonably intelligent hanger-on to the bane of my existence.

He always seemed to be around, and I could never get April to myself. Whether this was deliberate – whether he was aware of my interest and made jealous by it – I do not know. All I know is that I had very few chances to be alone with her. When we were together, usually at a cafe or walking in the street, we talked – talked of what was happening in France, of the future of the university, of literature, of the Anarchists, Maoists, Trotskyists and Communists, talked about all these, but not, alas, of love.

Perhaps this was my fault. I never pushed myself on her, never tried to make advances, never tried to touch her, even though my cells ached to reach out and mingle with hers, and even though the most casual physical contact – a touch on the arm, for example – set me aflame with desire. After our first few meetings, she would greet me with kisses on each cheek, the way she greeted all her friends, and my cheeks would burn for hours afterwards. One day she left a silk scarf at the cafe, and I took it home and held it to my face like a lovesick schoolboy, inhaling April's subtle jasmine perfume as I tried to sleep that night.

But I did not dare make a pass; I feared her rejection and her laughter far more than anything else. While we do not have the capacity to choose our feelings in the first place, we certainly have the ability to choose not to *act* on them, and that was what I was trying to do, admittedly more for my own sake than for hers.

•

When I did see April alone again it was late in the morning of 3 May, and I was still in bed. I had been up late the night before, trying to concentrate on a Faulkner paper I had to present at a conference in Brussels that weekend, and as I had no actual classes on Fridays I had slept in.

The soft but insistent tapping at my door woke me from a dream about my father in the trenches (why is it we never seem to dream at night about those we dream about all day?) and I rubbed the sleep out of my eyes.

I must explain that at the time, like the poor French workers, I wasn't paid very much and consequently, as I didn't need very much either, I lived in small *pension* in a cobbled alley off the Boulevard St Michel, between the university and the Luxembourg Gardens. As I could easily walk from the *pension* to my office at the Sorbonne, as I usually ate at the university or at a cheap local bistro, and as I spent most of my social hours in the various bars and cafes of the Latin Quarter, I didn't really need much more than a place to lay my head at night.

I stretched, threw on my dressing gown and opened the door. I'm sure you can imagine my shock on finding April standing there. *Alone.* She had been to the room only once previously, along with Brad and a couple of others for a nightcap of cognac after a Nina Simone concert, but she clearly remembered where I lived.

'Oh, I'm sorry, Richard—' She had started calling me by my first name, at my insistence, though of course she pronounced it in the French manner, and it sounded absolutely delightful to me every time she spoke it. 'I didn't know . . .'

'Come in,' I said, standing back. She paused a moment in the doorway, smiled shyly, then entered. I lay back on the bed, mostly because there was hardly enough room for two of us to sit together.

'Shall I make coffee?' she asked.

'There's only instant.'

She made a typical April moue at the idea of instant coffee, as any true French person would, but I directed her to the tiny kitchenette behind the curtain and she busied herself with the kettle, calling out over her shoulder as she filled it and turned on the gas.

'There's trouble at the university,' she said. 'That's what I came to tell you. It's happening at last. Everything's boiling over.'

I remembered that there was supposed to be a meeting about the 'Nanterre Eight', who were about to face disciplinary charges the following Monday, and I assumed that was what she meant.

'What's happening?' I asked, still not quite awake.

April came back into the bedroom and sat demurely on the edge of my only chair, trying not to look at me lying on the bed. 'The revolution,' she said. 'There's already a big crowd there. Students and lecturers together. They're talking about calling the police. Closing down the university.'

This woke me up a little more. 'They're what?'

'It's true,' April went on. 'Somebody told me that the university authorities said they'd call in the police if the crowds didn't disperse. But they're not dispersing, they're getting bigger.' She lit a Gauloise and looked around for an ashtray. I passed her one I'd stolen from the Café de la Lune. She smiled when she saw it and took those short little puffs at her cigarette, hardly giving herself time to inhale and enjoy the tobacco before exhaling and puffing again. 'Brad's already there,' she added.

'Then he'd better be careful,' I said, getting out of bed. 'He's neither a student nor a French citizen.'

'But don't you see? This is everybody's struggle!'

'Try telling that to the police.'

'You can be so cynical sometimes.'

'I'm sorry, April,' I said, not wanting to offend her. 'I'm just concerned for him, that's all.' Of course, I was lying. Nothing would have pleased me better than to see Brad beaten to a pulp by the police or, better still, deported, but I could hardly tell April that. The kettle boiled and she gave me a smile of forgiveness and went to make the coffee. She only made one cup – for me – I noticed, and as I sipped it she talked on about what had happened that morning and how she could feel change in the air. Her animation and passion excited me and I had to arrange my position carefully to avoid showing any obvious evidence of my arousal.

Even in the silences she seemed inclined to linger, and in the end I had to ask her to leave while I got dressed, as there was nowhere for her retain her modesty, and the thought of her standing so close to me, facing the wall, as I took off my dressing gown was too excruciating for me to bear. She pouted and left, saying she'd wait for me outside. When I rejoined her we walked to the Sorbonne together, and I saw that she was right about the crowds. There was defiance in the air.

We found Brad standing with a group of Anarchists, and April went over to take his arm. I spoke with him briefly for a while, alarmed at some of the things he told me. I found some colleagues from the literature department, and they said the police had been sent for. By four o'clock in the afternoon the university was surrounded by the Compagnies Républicaines de Sécurité – the CRS, riot police – and a number of students and lecturers had been arrested. Before long even more students arrived and started fighting with the CRS to free those who had been arrested. Nobody was backing down this time.

The revolution had begun.

•

I took the train to Brussels on Saturday morning and didn't come back until late on Tuesday, and though I had heard news of events in Paris, I was stunned at what awaited me on my return. The city was a war zone. The university was closed, and nobody knew when, or in what form, it would reopen. Even the familiar smell of the city – its coffee, cheese and something slightly overripe aroma – had changed, and it now smelled of fire, burnt plastic and rubber. I could taste ashes in my mouth.

I wandered the Latin Quarter in a dream, remnants of the previous day's tear gas stinging my eyes, barricades improvised from torn-up paving stones all over the place. Everywhere I went I saw the CRS, looking like invaders from space in their gleaming black helmets, with chinstraps and visors, thick black uniforms, jackboots and heavy truncheons. They turned up out of nowhere in coaches with windows covered in wire mesh, clambered out and blocked off whole streets apparently at random. Everywhere they could, people gathered and talked politics. The mood was swinging: you could taste it in the air along with the gas and ashes. This wasn't just another student demonstration, another Communist or Anarchist protest; this was civil war. Even the bourgeoisie were appalled at the violence of the police attacks. There were reports of pregnant women being beaten, of young men being tortured, their genitals shredded.

This was the aftermath of what later came to be known as 'Bloody Monday', when the 'Nanterre Eight' had appeared at the Sorbonne, triumphantly singing the 'Internationale', and sparked off riots.

I had missed April terribly while I was in Brussels, and now I was worried that she might have been hurt or arrested. I immediately tried to seek her out, but it wasn't easy. She wasn't at her student residence, nor at Brad's hotel. I tried the Café de la Lune and various other watering holes in the area, but to no avail. Eventually I ran into someone I knew, who was able to tell me that he thought she was helping one of the student groups produce posters, but he didn't know where. I gave up and went back to my room, unable to sleep, expecting her gentle rap on the door at any moment. It never came.

I saw her again on Thursday, putting up posters on the Rue St Jacques.

'I was worried about you,' I told her.

She smiled and touched my arm. For a moment I let myself believe that my concern actually mattered to her. I could understand her dedication to what was happening; after all, she was young, and it was her country. I knew that all normal social activities were on hold, that the politics of revolution had little time or space for the personal, for such bourgeois indulgences as love, but still I selfishly wanted her, wanted to be with her.

My chance came at the weekend, when the shit really hit the fan.

•

All week negotiations had been going back and forth between the government and the students. The university stayed closed and the students threatened to 'liberate' it. De Gaulle huffed and puffed. The Latin Quarter remained an occupied zone. On Friday the workers threw in their lot with the students and called for a general strike the following Monday. The whole country was on its knees in a way it hadn't been since the German occupation.

Thus far I had been avoiding the demonstrations, not out of cowardice or lack of commitment, but because I was British subject not a French one. By the weekend that no longer mattered. It had become a world struggle: us against them. We were fighting for a new world order. I was in. I had a stake. Besides, the university was closed so I didn't even have a job to protect any more. And perhaps, somewhere deep down, I hoped that heroic deeds on the barricades might win the heart of a fair lady.

So confusing was everything, so long running and spread out the battle, that I can't remember now whether it was Friday or Saturday. Odd that, the most important night of my life, and I can't remember what night it was. No matter.

It all started with a march towards the Panthéon, red and black flags everywhere, the 'Internationale' bolstering our courage. I had found April and Brad earlier, along with Henri, Alain and Brigitte, in the university quadrangle looking at the improvised bookstalls, and we went to the march together. April had her arm linked through mine on one side, and Alain on the other.

It was about half-past nine when things started to happen. I'm not sure what came first, the sharp explosions of the gas grenades or the flash of a Molotov cocktail, but all of a sudden pandemonium broke out, and there was no longer an organized march, only a number of battle fronts.

In the melee, April and I split off, losing Brad and the rest, and we found ourselves among those defending the front on the Boulevard St Michel. Unfortunate drivers, caught in the chaos, pressed down hard on their accelerators, honked their horns and drove through red lights to get away, knocking pedestrians aside as they went. The explosions were all around us now and a blazing CRS van silhouetted figures throwing petrol bombs and pulling up paving stones for the barricades. The restaurants and cafes were all closing hurriedly, waiters ushering clients out into the street and putting up the shutters.

The CRS advanced on us, firing gas grenades continuously. One landed at my feet and I kicked it back at them. I saw one student fall to them, about ten burly police kicking him as he lay and beating him mercilessly with their truncheons. There was nothing we could do. Clouds of gas drifted from the canisters, obscuring our view. We could see distant flames, hear the explosions and the cries, see vague shadows bending to pick up stones to throw at the darkness. The CRS charged. Some of us had come armed with Molotov cocktails and stones, but neither April nor I had any weapons, any means to defend ourselves, so we ran.

We got separated from the others, just the two of us now, and we were both scared. This was the worst the fighting had been so far. The demonstrators weren't just taking what the CRS dished out, they were fighting back, and that made the police even more vicious. They would show no quarter, neither with a woman nor a foreign national. We could hardly see for the tears streaming from our eyes as we tried to get away from the advancing CRS, who seemed to have every side street blocked off.

'Come on,' I said, taking April's hand in mine. 'This way.'

We jumped the fence and edged through the pitch-dark Luxembourg Gardens, looking for an unguarded exit. When we found one, we dashed out and across to the street opposite. A group of CRS saw us and turned. Fortunately, the street was too narrow and the buildings were too high for the gas guns. The police fired high in the air and most of the canisters fell harmlessly onto the roofs above us. Nobody gave chase.

Hand in hand, we made our way through the dark back streets to my pension, which, though close to the fighting, seemed so far unscathed. We ran up to my tiny room and locked the door behind us. Our eyes were streaming, and both of us felt a little dizzy and sick from the tear gas, but we also felt elated from the night's battle. We could still hear the distant explosions and see flashes and flames, like Guy Fawkes Night back in England. Adrenalin buzzed in our veins.

Just as I can't say exactly what night it was, I can't say exactly who made the first move. All I remember is that suddenly the room seemed too small for the two of us, our bodies were pressed together and I was tasting those moist, pink lips for the first time, savouring her small, furtive tongue in my mouth. My legs were like jelly.

'You know when I came here the other morning and you were in bed?' April said as she unbuttoned my shirt.

'Yes,' I said, tugging at her jeans.

She slipped my shirt off my shoulders. 'I wanted to get into bed with you.'

I unhooked her bra. 'Why didn't you?'

'I didn't think you wanted me.'

We managed to get mostly undressed before falling onto the bed. I kissed her breasts and ran my hands down her naked thighs. I thought I would explode with ecstasy when she touched me. Then she was under me, and I buried myself in her, heard her sharp gasp of pleasure.

At last, April was mine.

•

I lived on the memory of April's body, naked beside me, the two of us joined in love, while the country went insane. I didn't see her for three days, and even then we were part of a group; we couldn't talk intimately. That was what things were like then; there was little place for the individual. Everything was chaos. Normal life was on hold, perhaps never to be resumed again.

The university was closed, the campus hardly recognizable. The pillars in the square were plastered with posters of Marx, Lenin, Trotsky and Che Guevara. There was a general strike. Everything ground to a halt: the Metro, buses, coal production, railways. Everywhere I walked I saw burned-out vans and cars, gutted news kiosks, piles of paving stones, groups of truncheon-swinging CRS. People eating in the cafes had tears streaming down their faces from the remnants of tear gas in the morning-after air.

And every morning was a morning after.

I spotted Brad alone in a side street one night not long after dark, and as I had been wanting to talk to him about April, I thought I might never get a better opportunity. He was on his way to a meeting, he said, but could spare a few minutes. We took the steps down to the Seine by the side of the Pont St Michel, where we were less likely to get hassled by the CRS. It was dark and quiet by the river, though we could hear the crack of gas guns and explosions of Molotovs not so far away.

'Have you talked to April recently?' I asked him.

'Yes,' he said. 'Why?'

'I was wondering if . . . you know . . . she'd told you . . . ?'

'Told me what?'

'Well . . .' I swallowed. 'About us.'

He stopped for a moment, then looked at me and laughed. 'Oh, yes,' he said. 'Yes, she did, as a matter of fact.'

I was puzzled by his attitude. 'Well,' I said, 'is that all you have to say?'

'What do you want me to say?'

'Aren't you angry?'

'Why should I be angry? It didn't mean anything.'

I felt an icy fear grip me. 'What do you mean, *it didn't mean anything*?'

'You know. It was just a quickie, a bit of a laugh. She said she got excited by the street fighting and you happened to be the nearest man. It's not the first time, you know. I don't expect April to be faithful or any of that bourgeois crap. She's her own woman.'

'What did you say?'

'I said it didn't mean anything. You don't think she could be serious about someone like you, do you? Come off it, Richard, with your tatty jeans and your little goatee beard. You think you're a real hip intellectual, but you're nothing but a joke. That's all you were to her. A quickie. A laugh. A joke. She came straight to me afterwards for a real—'

The blow came from deep inside me and my fist caught him on the side of his jaw. I heard a sharp crack, distinct from the sound of a distant gas gun, and he keeled over into the Seine. We were under a bridge and it was very dark. I stopped, listened and looked around, but I could see no one, hear only the sounds of battle in the distance. Quickly, my blood turning to ice, I climbed the nearest stairs and re-entered the fray.

•

I had never imagined that love could turn to hatred so quickly. Though I had fantasized about getting rid of Brad many times, I had never really intended to harm him, and certainly not in the way, or for the reason, that I did. I had never thought of myself as someone capable of killing another human being.

They pulled his body out of the Seine two days later, and the Anarchists claimed that he had been singled out and murdered by the CRS. Most of the students were inclined to believe this, and another bloody riot ensued.

As for me, I'd had it. Had it with April, had it with the revolution and had it with Paris. If I could have, I would have left for London immediately, but the cross-Channel ferries weren't operating and Skyways had no vacancies for some days. What few tourists remained trapped in Paris were queuing for buses to Brussels, Amsterdam or Geneva, anywhere as long as they got out of France.

Mostly, I felt numb in the aftermath of killing Brad, though this was perhaps more to do with what he had told me about April than about the act itself, which had been an accident, and for which I didn't blame myself.

April. How could she deceive me so? How could she be so cold, so cruel, so callous? I meant nothing to her, just the nearest man to scratch her itch.

A quickie. A joke.

I saw her only once more, near the Luxembourg Gardens, the same gardens we jumped into that marvellous night a million years ago, and as she made to come towards me I took off into a side street. I didn't want to talk to her again, didn't even want to see her. And it wasn't only April. I stayed away from all of them: Henri, Alain, Brigitte, Nadine, the lot of them. To me they had all become inextricably linked with April's humiliation of me, and I couldn't bear to be with them.

One day Henri managed to get me aside and told me that April had committed suicide. He seemed angry rather than sad. I stared at him in disbelief. When he started to say something more, I cut him off and fled. I don't think anyone knew that I had killed Brad, but clearly April lamented his loss so much that she no longer felt her life was worth living. He wasn't worth it, I wanted to say, remembering the things he had told me under the bridge that night. If anyone was the killer, it was Brad not me. He had killed my love for April, and now he had killed April.

I refused to allow myself to feel anything for her.

The people at Skyways said I might have some luck if I came out to the airport and waited for a vacancy on standby, which I did. Before I left, I glanced around my room one last and saw nothing I wanted to take with me, not even April's silk scarf, which I had kept. So, in the clothes I was wearing, with the 500 francs that was all the Bank of France allowed to me withdraw, I left the country and never went back.

•

Until now.

I think it must be the memory of tear gas that makes my eyes water so. I wipe them with the back of my hand and the waiter comes to ask me if I am all right. I tell him I am and order another *pichet*. I have nowhere else to go except the grave; I might as well stay here and drink myself to death. What is the point of another miserable six months on earth anyway?

The girl who reminds me of April crushes out her cigarette and twists a strand of hair. Her lover is late. I dream of consoling her, but what have I to offer?

'Professor Dodgson? Richard? Is that you?'

I look up slowly at the couple standing over me. The man is grey-haired, distinguished looking, and there is something about him . . . His wife, or companion, is rather stout with grey eyes and short salt and pepper hair. Both are well dressed, healthy looking, the epitome of the Parisian bourgeoisie.

'Yes,' I say. 'I'm afraid you have me at a disadvantage.'

'Henri Boulanger,' he says. 'I was once your student. My wife, Brigitte, was also a student.'

'Henri? Brigitte?' I stand to shake his hand. 'Is it really you?'

He smiles. 'Yes. I wasn't sure about you at first. You haven't changed all that much in the face, the eyes, but you . . . perhaps you have lost weight?'

'I'm ill, Henri. Dying, in fact. But please sit down. Be my guests. Let's share some wine. Waiter.'

Henri looks at Brigitte, who nods, and they sit. She seems a little embarrassed, uncomfortable, though I can't for the life of me imagine why. Perhaps it is because I told them I am dying. No doubt many people would feel uncomfortable sitting in a cafe drinking wine with death.

'Funnily enough,' I tell them, 'I was just thinking about you. What are you doing here?'

Henri beams. 'Now *I'm* the professor,' he says with great pride. 'I teach literature at the Sorbonne.'

'Good for you, Henri. I always believed you'd go far.'

'It's a pity you couldn't have stayed around.'

'They were difficult times, Henri. Interesting, as the Chinese say.'

'Still . . . It was a sad business about that girl. What was her name?'

'April?' I say, and I feel an echo of my old love as I say her name. *Ap-reel.*

'April. Yes. That was around the time you went away.'

'My time here was over,' I tell him. 'I had no job, the country was in a state of civil war. It wasn't my future.'

Henri frowns. 'Yes, I know. Nobody blames you for getting out . . . it's not that . . .'

'Blames me for what, Henri?'

He glances at Brigitte, who looks deep into her glass of wine. 'You remember,' he says. 'The suicide? I told you about it.'

'I remember. She killed herself over an American boy the CRS beat to death.'

'Brad? But that wasn't . . . I mean . . .' He stares at me, wide-eyed. 'You mean you don't *know*?'

'Don't know what?'

'I tried to tell you at the time, but you turned away.'

'Tell me what?'

Brigitte looks up slowly from her wine and speaks. 'Why did you desert her? Why did you turn your back on her?'

'What do you mean?'

'You rejected her. You broke her heart. The silly girl was in love you, and you spurned her. *That's* why she killed herself.'

'That's ridiculous. She killed herself because of the American.'

Brigitte shakes her head. 'No. Believe me, it was you. She told me. She could talk only about you in the days before . . .'

'But . . . Brad?'

'Brad was jealous. Don't you understand? She was never more than a casual girlfriend to him. He wanted more, but she fell for you.'

I shake my head slowly. I can't believe this. Can't *allow* myself to believe this. The world starts to become indistinct, all shadows and echoes. I can't breathe. My skin tingles with pins and needles. I feel a touch on my shoulder.

'Are you all right? Richard? Are you all right?'

It is Henri. I hear him call for a brandy and someone places a cool glass in my hand. I sip. It burns and seems to dispel the mist a little. Brigitte rests her hand on my arm and leans forward. 'You mean you really didn't know?'

I shake my head.

'Henri tried to tell you.'

'Brad,' I whisper. 'Brad told me she just used me, that she thought I was a joke. I believed him.'

Henri and Brigitte look at one another, then back at me, concern and pity in their eyes. A little more than that in Henri's, too: suspicion. Maybe everybody wasn't convinced that the CRS had killed Brad after all.

'He was jealous,' Brigitte repeats. 'He lied.'

Suddenly, I start to laugh, which horrifies them. But I can't help myself. People turn and look at us. Henri and Brigitte are embarrassed. When the laughter subsides, I am left feeling hollow. I sip more brandy. Henri has placed his cigarettes on the table. Gauloises, I notice.

'May I?' I ask, reaching for the packet, even though I haven't smoked in twenty years.

He nods.

I light a Gauloise. Cough a little. What does it matter if I get lung cancer now? I'm already as good as dead. After a few puffs, the cigarette even starts to taste good, brings back, as tastes and smells do so well, even more memories of the cafes and nights of 1968. I begin to wonder whatever happened to that silk scarf I left in the drawer at my pension. I wish I could smell her jasmine scent again.

Outside, the girl's lover arrives. He is young and handsome and he waves his arms as he apologizes for being late. She is sulky at first, but she brightens and kisses him. He runs his hand down her smooth, olive cheek and I can smell tear gas again.

THE GOOD PARTNER

AN INSPECTOR BANKS STORY

1

The louring sky was black as a tax inspector's heart when Detective Chief Inspector Alan Banks pulled up outside 17 Oakley Crescent at eight o'clock one mid-November evening. An icy wind whipped up the leaves and set them skittering around his feet as he walked up the path to the glass-panelled door.

Detective Constable Susan Gay was waiting for him inside, and Peter Darby, the police photographer, was busy with his new video recorder. Between the glass coffee table and the brick fireplace lay the woman's body, blood matting the hair around her left temple. Banks put on his latex gloves, then bent and picked up the object beside her. The bronze plaque read, 'Eastvale Golf Club, 1991 Tournament. Winner: David Fosse.' There was blood on the base of the trophy. The man Banks assumed to be David Fosse sat on the sofa staring into space.

A pile of photographs lay on the table. Banks picked them up and flipped through them. Each was dated 13/11/93 across the bottom. The first few showed group scenes – red-eyed people eating, drinking and dancing at a banquet of some kind – but the last ones told a different story. Two showed a handsome young man in a navy blue suit, white shirt and garish tie, smiling lecherously at the photographer from behind a glass of whisky. Then the scene shifted to a hotel room, where the man had loosened his tie. None of the other diners were to be seen. In the last picture, he had also taken off his jacket. The date had changed to 14/11/93.

Banks turned to the man on the sofa. 'Are you David Fosse?' he asked.

There was a pause while the man seemed to return from a great distance. 'Yes,' he said finally.

'Can you identify the victim?'

'It's my wife, Kim.'

'What happened?'

'I . . . I was out taking the dog for a walk. When I got back I found . . .' He gestured towards the floor.

'When did you go out?'

'Quarter to seven, as usual. I got back about half past and found her like this.'

'Was your wife in when you left?'

'Yes.'

'Was she expecting any visitors?'

He shook his head.

Banks held out the photos. 'Have you seen these?'

Fosse turned away and grunted.

'Who took them? What do they mean?'

Fosse stared at the Axminster.

'Mr Fosse?'

'I don't know.'

'This date, 13 November. Last Saturday. Is that significant?'

'My wife was at a business convention in London last weekend. I assume they're the pictures she took.'

'What kind of convention?'

'She's involved in servicing home offices and small businesses. *Servicing*,' he sneered. 'Now there's an apt term.'

Banks singled out the man in the gaudy tie. 'Do you know who this is?'

'No.' Fosse's face darkened and both his hands curled into fists. 'No, but if I ever get hold of him—'

'Mr Fosse, did you argue with your wife about the man in these photographs?'

Fosse's mouth dropped. 'They weren't here when I left.'

'How do you explain their presence now?'

'I don't know. She must have got them out while I was taking Jasper for a walk.'

Banks looked around the room and saw a camera on the sideboard, a Canon. It looked like an expensive autofocus model. He picked it up carefully and put it in a plastic bag. 'Is this yours?' he asked Fosse.

Fosse looked at the camera. 'It's my wife's. I bought it for her birthday. Why? What are you doing with it?'

'It may be evidence,' said Banks, pointing at the exposure indicator. 'Seven pictures have been taken on a new film. I have to ask you again, Mr Fosse, did you argue with your wife about the man in these photos?'

'And I'll tell you again. How could I? They weren't there when I went out, and she was dead when I got back.'

The dog barked from the kitchen. The front door opened and Dr Glendenning walked in, a tall, imposing figure with white hair and a nicotine-stained moustache.

Glendenning glanced sourly at Banks and Susan and complained about being dragged out on such a night. Banks apologized. Though Glendenning was a Home Office pathologist, and a lowly police surgeon could pronounce death, Banks knew that Glendenning would never have forgiven them had they not called him.

As the Scene-of-Crime team arrived, Banks turned to David Fosse and said, 'I think we'd better carry on with this down at headquarters.'

Fosse shrugged and stood up to get his coat. As they left, Banks heard Glendenning mutter, 'A golf trophy. A bloody golf trophy! Sacrilege.'

2

'**Do you think** he did it, sir?' Susan Gay asked Banks.

Banks swirled the inch of Theakston's XB at the bottom of his glass and watched the patterns it made. 'I don't know. He certainly had means, motive and opportunity. But something about it makes me uneasy.'

It was almost closing time, and Banks and Susan sat in the warm glow of the Queen's Arms having a late dinner of microwaved steak and kidney pud, courtesy of Cyril, the landlord, who was used to their unsociable hours. Outside, rain lashed against the red and amber window panes.

Banks pushed his plate away and lit a cigarette. He was tired. The Fosse call had come in just as he was about to go home after a long day of paperwork and boring meetings.

They had learned little more during a two-hour interrogation at the station. Kim Fosse had left for London on Friday and returned on Monday with her business partner, Norma Cheverel. The convention had been held at the Ludbridge Hotel in Kensington.

David Fosse maintained his innocence, but sexual jealousy made a strong motive, and now he was languishing in the cells under Eastvale Divisional Headquarters. *Languish* was perhaps too strong a word, as the cells were as comfortable as many bed and breakfasts, and the food and service much better. The only problem was that you couldn't open the door and go for a walk in the Yorkshire Dales when you felt like it.

They learned from the house-to-house that Fosse *did* walk the dog – several people had seen him – and not even Dr Glendenning could pinpoint time of death to within the forty-five minutes he was out of the house.

Fosse could have murdered his wife before he left or when he got home. He could also have nipped back around the rear, where a path ran by the river, got into the house unseen the back way, then resumed his walk.

'Time, ladies and gentlemen please,' called Cyril, ringing his bell behind the bar. 'And that includes coppers.'

Banks smiled and finished his beer. 'There's not a lot more we can do tonight, anyway,' he said. 'I think I'll go home and get some sleep.'

'I'll do the same.' Susan reached for her overcoat.

'First thing in the morning,' said Banks, 'we'll have a word with Norma Cheverel, see if she can throw any light on what happened in London last weekend.'

3

Norma Cheverel was an attractive woman in her early thirties with a tousled mane of red hair, a high freckled forehead and the greenest eyes Banks had ever seen. Contact lenses, he decided uncharitably, perhaps to diminish the sense of sexual energy he felt emanate from her.

She sat behind her desk in the large carpeted office, swivelling occasionally in her executive chair. After her assistant had brought coffee, Norma pulled out a long cigarette and lit up. 'One of the pleasures of being the boss,' she said. 'The buggers can't make you stop smoking.'

'You've heard about Kim Fosse, I take it?' Banks asked.

'On the local news last night. Poor Kim.' She shook her head.

'We're puzzled about a few things. Maybe you can help us?'

'I'll try.'

'Did you notice her taking many photographs at the convention?'

Norma Cheverel frowned. 'I can't say as I did, really, but there were quite a few people taking photographs there, especially at the banquet. You know how people get silly at conventions. I never could understand this mania for capturing the moment. Can you, Chief Inspector?'

Banks, whose wife, Sandra, was a photographer, could understand it only too well, though he would have quibbled with 'capturing the moment'. A good photographer, a *real* photographer, Sandra had often said, did much more than that; she transformed the moment. But he let the aesthetics lie.

Norma Cheverel was right about the photo mania, though.

Banks had also noticed that since the advent of cheap, idiot-proof cameras every Tom, Dick and Harry had started taking photos indoors. He had been half-blinded a number of times by a group of tourists 'capturing the moment' in some pub or restaurant. It was almost as bad as the mobile-phone craze, though not quite.

'Did Kim Fosse share this mania?' he asked.

'She had a fancy new camera. She took it with her. That's all I can say, really. Look, I don't—'

'Bear with me, Ms Cheverel.'

'Norma, please.'

Banks, who reserved the familiarity of first-name terms to exercise power over suspects, not to interview witnesses, went on. 'Do you know if she had affairs?'

This time Norma Cheverel let the silence stretch. Banks could hear the fan cooling the microchip in her computer. She stubbed out her long cigarette, careful to make sure it wasn't still smouldering, sipped some coffee, swivelled a little, and said, 'Yes. Yes, she did. Though I wouldn't really describe them as affairs.'

'How would you describe them?'

'Just little flings, really. Nothing that really *meant* anything to her.'

'Who with?'

'She didn't usually mention names.'

'Did she have a fling in London last weekend?'

'Yes. She told me about it on the way home. Look, Chief Inspector, Kim wasn't a bad person. She just needed something David couldn't give her.'

Banks took a photograph of the man in the navy blue suit from his briefcase and slid it across the desk. 'Know him?'

'It's Michael Bannister. He's with an office-furnishings company in Preston.'

'And did Kim Fosse have a fling with him that weekend?'

Norma swivelled and bit her lip. 'She didn't tell me it was him.'

'Surprised?'

She shrugged. 'He's married. Not that that means much these

days. I've heard he's very much in love with his wife, but she's not very strong. Heart condition, or something.' She sniffled, then sneezed and reached for a tissue.

'What did Kim tell you about last weekend?'

Norma Cheverel smiled an odd, twisted little smile from the corner of her lips. 'Oh, Chief Inspector, do you really want all the details? Girl talk about sex is so much *dirtier* than men's, you know.'

Though he felt himself reddening a little, Banks said, 'So I've been told. Did she ever express concern about her husband finding out?'

'Oh, yes. She told me under no circumstances to tell David. As if I would. He's very jealous and he has a temper.'

'Was he ever violent towards her?'

'Just once. It was the last time we went to a convention, as a matter of fact. Apparently he tried to phone her in her room after midnight – some emergency to do with the dog – and she wasn't there. When she got home he lost his temper, called her a whore and hit her.'

'How long had they been married?'

Norma sniffled again and blew her nose. 'Four years.'

'How long have you and Kim Fosse been in business together?'

'Six years. We started when she was still Kim Church. She'd just got her MBA.'

'How did the partnership work?'

'Very well. I'm on the financial side and Kim dealt with sales and marketing.'

'Are you married?'

'I don't see that it's any of your business, Chief Inspector, but no, I'm not. I guess Mr Right just hasn't turned up yet,' she said coldly, then looked at her gold wristwatch. 'Are there any more questions?'

Banks stood up. 'No, that's all for now. Thank you very much for your time.'

She stood up and walked around the desk to show him to the

door. Her handshake on leaving was a little brisker and cooler than it had been when he arrived.

4

'So Kim Fosse was discreet, but she took photographs,' said Susan when they met up in Banks's office later that morning. 'Kinky?'

'Could be. Or just careless. They're pretty harmless, really.' The seven photographs from the film they had found inside the camera showed the same man in the hotel room on the same date, 14/11/93.

'Michael Bannister,' Susan read from her notes. 'Sales director for Office Comforts Ltd, based in Preston, Lancashire. Lives in Blackpool with his wife, Lucy. No children. His wife suffers from a congenital heart condition, needs constant pills and medicines, lots of attention. His workmates tell me he's devoted to her.'

'A momentary lapse, then?' Banks suggested. He walked over to his broken Venetian blind and looked out on the rainswept market square. Only two cars were parked there today. The gold hands on the blue face of the church clock stood at eleven thirty-nine.

'It happens, sir. Maybe more often than we think.'

'I know. Reckon we'd better go easy approaching him?'

'No sense endangering the wife's health, is there?'

'You're right. See if you can arrange to see him at his office.' Banks looked out of the window and shivered. 'I don't much fancy a trip to the seaside in this miserable weather anyway.'

5

The drive across the Pennines was a nightmare. All the way along the A59 they seemed to be stuck behind one lorry or another churning up gallons of filthy spray. Around Clitheroe, visibility was so poor that traffic slowed to a crawl. The hulking whale-shapes of the hills that flanked the road were reduced to faint grey outlines in the rain-haze. Banks played his Miles Davis *Birth of the Cool* tape, which Susan seemed to enjoy. At least, she didn't complain.

The office building on Ribbleton Lane, just east of the city centre, was three-storey red-brick. The receptionist directed them to Bannister's office on the second floor.

In the anteroom, a woman sat clicking away at a computer keyboard. Curly-haired, plump, in her forties. She came over and welcomed them. 'Hello, I'm Carla Jacobs. I'm Mr Bannister's secretary. He's in with someone at the moment, but he won't be a minute. He knows you're coming.'

Banks and Susan looked at the framed photographs of company products and awards on the walls as they waited. All the time, Banks sensed Carla Jacobs staring at the back of his head. After a couple of minutes, he turned around just in time to see her avert her gaze.

'Is anything wrong?' he asked.

She blushed. 'No. Well, not really. I mean, don't think I'm being nosy, but is Mr Bannister in some kind of trouble?'

'Why do you ask?'

'It's just that I'm a good friend of Lucy's, that's Mr Bannister's wife, and I don't know if you know, but—'

'We know about her health problems, yes.'

'Good. Good. Well . . .'

'Have you any reason to think Mr Bannister might be in trouble?'

She raised her eyebrows. 'Oh, no. But it's not every day we get the police visiting.'

At that moment the inner door opened and a small ferret-faced man in an ill-fitting suit flashed a smile at Carla as he scurried out. In the doorway stood the man in the photographs. Michael Bannister. He beckoned Banks and Susan in.

It was a large office, with Bannister's work desk, files and bookcases taking up one half and a large oval table for meetings in the other. They sat at the table, so well polished Banks could see his reflection in it, and Susan took out her notebook.

'I understand you attended a business convention in London last weekend?' Banks started.

'Yes. Yes, I did.'

'Did you meet a woman there called Kim Fosse?'

Bannister averted his eyes. 'Yes.'

Banks showed him a photograph of the victim, as she had been in life. 'Is this her?'

'Yes.'

'Did you spend the night with her?'

'I don't see what that's got—'

'Did you?'

'Look, for Christ's sake. My wife . . .'

'It's not your wife we're asking.'

'What if I did?'

'Did she take these photographs of you?' Banks fanned the photos in front of him.

'Yes,' he said.

'So you slept with Kim Fosse and she took some photographs.'

'It was just a lark. I mean, we'd had a bit to drink, I—'

'I understand, sir,' said Banks. 'You don't have to justify yourself to me.'

Bannister licked his lips. 'What's this all about? Will it go any further?'

'I can't say,' said Banks, gesturing for Susan to stand up. 'It depends. We'll keep you informed.'

'Good Lord, man,' said Bannister. 'Please. Think of my wife.' He looked miserably after them, and Banks caught the look of concern on Carla Jacobs's face.

'That was a bit of a wasted journey, wasn't it, sir,' Susan said on the way back to Eastvale.

'Do you think so?' said Banks, smiling. 'I'm not at all sure, myself. I think our Mr Bannister was lying about something. And I'd like to know what Carla Jacobs had on her mind.'

6

Sandra was out. After Banks hung up his raincoat, he went straight into the living room of his south Eastvale semi and poured himself a stiff Laphroaig. He felt as if the day's rain had permeated right to his bone marrow. He made himself a cheese and onion sandwich, checked out all the television channels, found nothing worth watching, and put some Bessie Smith on the CD player.

But 'Woman's Trouble Blues' took a background role as the malt whisky warmed his bones and he thought about the Fosse case. Why did he feel so ill at ease? Because David Fosse sounded believable? Because he had felt Norma Cheverel's sexual power and resented it? Because Michael Bannister had lied about something? And was Carla Jacobs in love with her boss, or was she just protecting Lucy Bannister? Banks fanned out the photographs on the coffee table.

Before he could answer any of the questions, Sandra returned from the photography course she was teaching at the local college. When she had finished telling Banks how few people knew the difference between an aperture and a hole in the ground, which Banks argued was a poor metaphor because an aperture *was* a kind of a hole, she glanced at the photos on the coffee table.

'What are these, evidence?' she asked, stopping herself before she touched them.

'Go ahead,' said Banks. 'We've got all we need from them.'

Sandra picked up a couple of the group shots, six people in evening dress, each holding a champagne flute out towards the photographer, all with the red eyes characteristic of cheap automatic flash.

'Ugh,' said Sandra. 'What dreadful photos.'

'Snob,' said Banks. 'She doesn't have as good a camera as you.'

'Doesn't matter,' said Sandra. 'A child of five could do a better job with a Brownie than these. What kind of camera was it, anyway.'

'A Canon,' said Banks, adding the model number. The identification tag on the evidence bag was etched in his memory.

Sandra put the photos down and frowned. 'A what?'

Banks told her again.

'It can't be.'

'Why not?'

Sandra leaned forward, slipped her long blonde tresses behind her ears and spread out the photos. 'Well, they've all got red-eye,' she said. 'The camera you mentioned protects against red-eye.'

It was Banks's turn to look puzzled.

'Do you know what red-eye is?' Sandra asked.

'I don't know an aperture from a hole in the ground.'

She nudged him in the ribs. 'Be serious, Alan. Look, when you're in a dark room, your pupils dilate, the iris opens to let in more light so you can see properly, just like an aperture on a camera. Right? You know what it's like when you first walk into a dark place and your eyes slowly adjust?'

Banks nodded. 'Go on.'

'Well, when you're subjected to a sudden, direct flash of light, the iris doesn't have time to close. Red-eye is actually caused by the flash illuminating the blood vessels in the eye.'

'Why doesn't it happen with *all* flash photographs, then? Surely the whole point of flash is that you use it in the dark?'

'Mostly, yes, but red-eye only happens when the flash is pointed *directly* at your iris. It doesn't happen when the flash is held from *above* the camera. The angle's different. See what I mean?'

'Yes. But you don't usually see people with hand-held flashes using cameras like that.'

'That's right. That's because there's another way of getting rid of red-eye. The more expensive models, like the one you just mentioned to me, set off a series of quick flashes first, *before* the exposure, and that gives the iris a chance to close. Simple, really.'

'So you're saying that these photographs couldn't have been taken with that camera?'

'That's right.'

'Interesting,' said Banks. 'Very interesting.'

Sandra grinned. 'Have I solved your case?'

'Not exactly, no, but you've certainly confirmed some of the doubts I've been having.' Banks reached for the telephone. 'After what you've just told me, I think I can at least make sure that David Fosse sleeps in his own bed tonight.'

7

Norma Cheverel wasn't pleased to see Banks and Susan late the next morning. She welcomed them with all the patience and courtesy of a busy executive, tidying files on her desk as Banks talked, twice mentioning a luncheon appointment that was fast approaching. For a while, Banks ignored her rudeness, then he said, 'Will you stop your fidgeting and pay attention, Ms Cheverel?'

She gave him a challenging look. There was no 'Call me Norma' this time, and the sexual voltage was turned very low. But she sat as still as she could and rested her hands on the desk.

'Yes, *sir*,' she said. 'You know, you remind me of an old schoolteacher.'

'Do you own a camera, Ms Cheverel?'

'Yes.'

'What model?'

She shrugged. 'I don't know. Just one of those cheap things everybody uses these days.'

'Does it have an automatic flash?'

'Yes. They all do, don't they?'

'What about red-eye?'

'What's that? A late-night flight?'

Banks explained. She started playing with the files again. 'I'd appreciate it if you'd let us examine your camera, Ms Cheverel.'

'Why on earth—'

'Because the photographs we found on the coffee table at the scene couldn't possibly have been taken by Kim Fosse's camera. That's why.' Banks explained what Sandra had told him, and what the result of tests earlier that morning had confirmed.

Norma Cheverel spread her hands. 'So someone else took them. I still don't see what that's got to do with me.'

Banks glanced over to Susan, who said, 'Ms Cheverel. Is it true that you lost almost fifty thousand pounds on a land speculation deal earlier this year?'

Norma Cheverel looked daggers at her and said to Banks through clenched teeth, 'My business deals are no—'

'Oh, but they are,' said Banks. 'In fact, Susan and I have been doing quite a bit of digging this morning. It seems you've made a number of bad investments these past couple of years, haven't you? Where's the money come from?'

'The money was mine. All mine.'

Banks shook his head. 'I think it came from the partnership.' He leaned forward. 'Know what else I think?'

'What do I care?'

'I think your cocaine habit is costing you a fortune, too, isn't it?'

'How dare you!'

'I noticed how jittery you were, how you couldn't keep still. And then there's the sniffling. Funny how your cold seems better this morning. How much? Say ten, twenty thousand a year up your nose?'

'I want my solicitor.'

'I think you were cheating the partnership, Ms Cheverel. I think you knew you'd gone so far it was only a matter of time before Kim Fosse found out about it. You dealt with the accounting, you told us, and she was on the marketing side. What could have been better? It would take her a while to discover something was wrong, but you couldn't keep it from your partner for ever, could you? So you came up with a plot to get rid of her and blame it on her husband. We only have *your* word for it that Kim Fosse was promiscuous. We only have your word that her husband was jealous enough to be violent.'

'Ask anyone,' said Norma Cheverel. 'They'll tell you. Everyone saw her black eye after the last convention.'

'We know about that. David Fosse told us this morning. It was something he regretted very much. But the only person Kim confided in was *you*, which gave you every opportunity to build a mountain of lies and suspicion on a small foundation of truth.'

'This is absurd.' Norma swivelled and reached for the phone. 'I'm calling my solicitor.'

'Go ahead,' said Banks. 'But you haven't been charged with anything yet.'

She held the phone halfway between her mouth and its cradle and smiled. 'That's right,' she said. 'You can make all the accusations you want but you can't prove anything. That business about the camera doesn't mean a thing, and you know that as well as I do.'

'It proves that Kim Fosse *didn't* take those photographs. Therefore, someone must have planted them to make it *look* as if she had been foolish as well as indiscreet.'

She put the phone down. 'You can't prove it was me. I defy you.'

Banks stood up. He was loath to admit it, but she was right. Short of finding someone who had seen her or her car in the vicinity of the Fosse house around the time of the murder, there was no proof. And Norma Cheverel wasn't the kind to confess. The bluff was over. But at least Banks and Susan *knew* as they walked out of the office that Norma Cheverel had killed Kim Fosse. The rest was just a matter of time.

8

The break took two days to come, and it came from an unexpected source.

The first thing Banks did after his interview with Norma Cheverel was organize a second house-to-house of Fosse's neighbourhood, this time to find out if anyone had seen Norma Cheverel or her car that evening. Someone remembered seeing a grey foreign car of some kind, which was about the closest they got to a sighting of Norma's silver BMW.

Next, he got a list of all 150 conventioneers and set a team to phone and find out if anyone remembered Norma Cheverel taking photos on the evening of the banquet. They'd got through seventy-one with no luck so far, when Banks's phone rang.

'This is Carla Jacobs, Inspector Banks. I don't know if you remember me. I'm Mr Bannister's secretary.'

'I remember you,' said Banks. 'What is it?'

'Well, I was going to ask you the same thing. You see, I've been talking to Lucy, and she's so worried that Michael is in trouble it's damaging her health.'

'Mr Bannister is in no trouble as far as I know,' said Banks. 'He just committed an unfortunate indiscretion, that's all. No blame.'

'But that's just it,' said Carla Jacobs. 'You see, she said he's been acting strangely. He's depressed. He shuts himself away. He doesn't talk to her. Even when he's with her she says he's withdrawn. It's getting her down. I thought if you could talk to her . . . just set her at ease.'

Banks sighed. Playing nursemaid. 'All right,' he said. 'I'll call her.'

'Oh, will you? Thank you. Thank you ever so much.' She lowered her voice. 'Mr Bannister is in his office now. She'll be by the phone at home.'

Lucy Bannister answered on the first ring. 'Yes?'

Banks introduced himself.

'I'm so worried about Michael,' she said, in that gushing manner of someone who's been waiting all week to pour it all out. 'He's never like this. Never. Has he done something awful? Are you going to arrest him? Please, you can tell me the truth.'

'No,' said Banks. 'No, he hasn't, and no we're not. He's simply been helping us with our enquiries.'

'That could mean anything. Enquiries into what?'

Banks debated for a moment whether to tell her. It would do no harm, he thought. 'He was at a business convention in London last weekend. We're interested in the movements of someone else who was there, that's all.'

'Are you sure that's all?'

'Yes.'

'And it's nothing serious?'

'Not for your husband, no.'

'Thank you. You don't know what this means to me.' He could hear the relief in her voice. 'Because of my heart condition, you see, Michael is a bit over-protective. I don't deny I'm weak, but sometimes I think he just takes too much upon himself.' She paused and gave a small laugh. 'I don't know why I'm telling you all this. It must be because I'm so relieved. He's a normal man. He has needs like any other man. I know he goes with other women and I never mention it because I know it would upset him and embarrass him. He thinks he keeps it from me to protect me from distress, and it's just easier to let him think that.'

'I can appreciate that,' Banks said, only half listening. Why hadn't he realized before? Now he knew what Michael Bannister had lied about, and why. 'Look, Mrs Bannister,' he cut in, 'you might be able to help us. Do you think you could talk to your husband, let him know you know?'

'I don't know. I don't want to upset him.'

Banks felt a wave of annoyance. The Bannisters were so damn busy protecting one another's feelings that there was no room for the truth. He could almost hear her chewing her lip over the line. He tried to keep the irritation out of his voice. 'It could be very important,' he said. 'And I'm sure it won't do any harm. If that's what he's feeling guilty about, you can help him get over it, can't you?'

'I suppose so.' Hesitant, but warming to the idea.

'I'm sure you'd be helping him, helping your relationship.' Banks cringed to hear himself talk. First a nursemaid, now a bloody marriage guidance counsellor.

'Perhaps.'

'Then you'll do it? You'll talk to him?'

'Yes.' Determined now. 'Yes, I will, Mr Banks.'

'And will you do me one more favour?'

'If I can.'

'Will you give him these telephone numbers and tell him that if he thinks of anything else he can call me without fear of any charges being made against him?' He gave her his work and home phone numbers.

'Ye-es.' She clearly didn't know what he meant, but that didn't matter.

'It's very important that you tell him there'll be no action taken against him and that he should talk to *me* personally. Is that clear?'

'Yes. I don't know what all this is about, but I'll do as you say. And thank you.'

'Thank you.' Banks headed for a pub lunch in the Queen's Arms. It was too early to celebrate anything yet, but he kept his fingers crossed as he walked in the thin November sunshine across Market Street.

9

Norma Cheverel's luxury flat was every bit as elegant and expensively furnished as Banks had expected. Some of the paintings on her walls were originals, and her furniture was all hand-crafted, by the look of it. She even had an oak table from Robert Thompson's workshop in Kilburn. Banks recognized the trademark: a mouse carved on one of the legs.

When Banks and Susan turned up at seven-thirty that evening, Norma had just finished stacking her dinner dishes in the machine. She had changed from her work outfit and wore black leggings, showing off her shapely legs, and a green woollen sweater that barely covered her hips. She sat down and crossed her legs, cigarette poised over the ashtray beside her.

'Well,' she said. 'Do I need my solicitor yet?'

'I think you do,' said Banks. 'But I'd like you to answer a few questions first.'

'I'm not saying a word without my solicitor present.'

'Very well,' said Banks. 'That's your right. Let me do the talking, then.'

She sniffed and flicked a half-inch of ash into the ashtray beside her. Her crossed leg was swinging up and down as if some demented doctor were tapping the reflex.

'I might as well tell you first of all that we've got Michael Bannister's testimony,' Banks began.

'I don't know what you're talking about.'

'I think you do. It was *you* who took those photographs at the banquet and in the hotel room afterwards. It was *you* who spent the night with Michael Bannister, not Kim Fosse.'

'That's ridiculous.'

'No, it's not. You told him later that if anyone asked he'd better say it was Kim Fosse he slept with or you'd tell his wife what he'd done. You knew Lucy had a weak heart, and that he thought such a shock might kill her.'

Norma had turned a shade paler. Banks scratched the small scar beside his right eye. Often, when it itched, it was telling him he was on the right track. 'As it turns out,' he went on, 'Lucy Bannister was well aware that her husband occasionally slept with other women. It was just something they didn't talk about. He thought he was protecting her feelings; she thought she was protecting his. I suggested they talk about it.'

'Bastard,' Norma Cheverel hissed. Banks didn't know whether she meant him or Michael Bannister.

'You seduced Michael Bannister and you planted incriminating photographs on Kim Fosse's living-room table *after* you'd killed her in the hope that we would think her husband had done it in a jealous rage, a rage that you also helped set us up to believe. We've checked the processing services, too. I'm sure you chose Fotomat because it's busy, quick and impersonal, but the man behind the counter remembers *you* picking up a film on Wednesday, not Kim Fosse. Beauty has its drawbacks, Norma.'

Norma got up, tossed back her hair and went to pour herself a drink. She didn't offer Banks or Susan anything. 'You've got a nerve,' she said. 'And a hell of an imagination. You should work for television.'

'You knew that David Fosse walked the dog every evening, come rain or shine, between six forty-five and seven-thirty. It was easy for you to drive over to the house, park your car a little distance away, get the unsuspecting Kim to let you in, and then, still wearing gloves, hit her with the trophy and plant the photos. After that, all you had to do was convince us of her infidelity and her husband's violent jealousy. There was even a scrap of truth in it. Except you didn't bargain for Lucy Bannister, did you?'

'This is ridiculous,' Norma said. 'What about the film that was in the camera? You can't prove any of this.'

'I don't believe I mentioned that there was a film *in* the camera,' said Banks. 'I'm sure it seemed like a brilliant idea at the time, but *that* film couldn't possibly have been taken by Kim's camera, either, or Michael Bannister wouldn't have had red eyes.'

'This is just circumstantial.'

'Possibly. But it all adds up. Believe me, Norma, we've got a case and we've got a good chance of making it stick. The first film wasn't enough, was it? We might have suspected it was planted. But with a second film *in* the camera, one showing the same scene, the same person, then there was less chance we'd look closely at the photographic evidence. How did it happen? I imagine

Kim had perhaps had a bit too much to drink that night and you put her to bed. When you did, you also took her room key. At some point during the night, when you'd finished with Michael Bannister, you rewound your second film manually in the dark until there was only a small strip sticking out of the cassette, then you went to Kim Fosse's room and you put it in her camera, taking out whatever film she had taken herself and dumping it.'

'Oh, I see. I'm that clever, am I? I suppose you found my fingerprints on this film?'

'The prints were smudged, as you no doubt knew they would be, and you wiped the photographs and camera. When you'd loaded the film, you advanced it in the dark with the flash turned off and the lens cap on. That way the double exposure wouldn't affect the already-exposed film at all because no light was getting to it. When you'd wound it on so that the next exposure was set at number eight, you returned it to Kim Fosse's room.'

'I'm glad you think I'm so brilliant, Inspector, but I—'

'I don't think you're brilliant at all,' Banks said. 'You're as stupid as anyone else who thinks she can get away with the perfect crime.'

In a flash, Norma Cheverel picked up the ashtray and threw it at Banks. He dodged sideways and it whizzed past his ear and smashed into the front of the cocktail cabinet.

Banks stood up. 'Time to call that solicitor, Norma.'

But Norma Cheverel wasn't listening. She was banging her fists on her knees and chanting 'Bastard! Bastard!' over and over again.

SOME LAND IN FLORIDA

The morning they found Santa Claus floating face down in the pool, I had a hangover of gargantuan proportions. By midday I was starting to feel more human. By late afternoon, on my third Michelob at Chloe's, I was almost glad to be alive again. Almost. I was also coming to believe that Santa's death hadn't been quite the accident it appeared.

'Happy Hour' at Chloe's – a dim, horseshoe-shaped bar adjoining a restaurant – lasts from eleven a.m. to seven p.m., and by late afternoon the desperation usually starts to show through the cracks: the men tell the same joke for the third or fourth time; the women laugh just a little too loudly.

The afternoon after Santa's death I found myself sitting opposite his small coterie. They were an odd group, the three of them who formed the central core. There was a grey-haired man, about sixty, who always looked ill to me, despite his brick-red complexion; a size fourteen woman in her mid forties who wore size ten clothes; and a pretty blonde, no older than about twenty-five. Maybe I'm being sexist or ageist or whatever, but I could only wonder why she was hanging around with such a bunch of losers. Christ, didn't she know that if she played her cards right she could have me?

OK, so I'm no oil painting. But despite a bit of a beer gut, I'm reasonably well-preserved for a man of my age and drinking habits. I've still got a fine head of hair, even if it is grey. And I may be a bit grizzled and rough-edged, but I've been told I'm not without a certain cuddly quality.

Anyway, in my humble opinion, Santa – in reality Bud Schiller, a retired real estate agent from Kingston, Ontario – was a total asshole. Most people only needed to spend a couple of minutes in his company before heading for the hills. But not these three. Oh, no. They laughed at all his jokes; they hung on his every word. Of course, Schiller bought most of the drinks, but I thought his company was a hell of a price to pay for the occasional free beer.

'So, who do you think did it, then, Jack?'

Al French had slipped onto the empty stool beside me. Al was a cross between a loner and a social butterfly: he seemed to know everyone, but like a butterfly he never lit in any one place for long. He said he was a writer from Rochester, but I've never seen any of his books in the shops. If you ask him to be more specific, he just gets evasive.

Al tipped back his bottle and his Adam's apple bobbed as he swallowed. He was a skinny little guy with a long nose, slicked back hair and a perpetual five o'clock shadow. Today he was wearing a Hawaiian shirt and Bermuda shorts.

'It was an accident,' I said.

'Bullshit. And you know it.' Al put his bottle down and whispered in my ear. He sounded as if he'd had a few already. 'When a jerk like Bud Schiller dies, there has to be something more behind it than mere accident. Come on, buddy, you're supposed to be the private eye.'

'True. But I'm on vacation.'

'A real gumshoe never rests until he discovers the truth and sees that justice is done.'

I rolled my eyes. 'Where d'you read that, Al? An old *Black Mask* magazine?'

Al looked hurt. 'I didn't read it anywhere. I wrote it.'

'You write private eye stories?'

'We were talking about Bud Schiller's murder.'

See what I mean? Evasive. And persistent. I ordered another round of Michelob and offered Al a cigar.

'Cuban?' he asked.

'Uh-huh.'

Al shrugged and took the cigar. 'What they gonna do, huh? Arrest me for smoking?'

I laughed. 'Seriously, Al, the cop I talked to said it was an accident. She asked me if I'd seen or heard anything unusual, then she left.'

'Had you?'

'No.'

I wasn't going to tell Al, but I'd spent the evening sitting out in the lanai smoking a cigar, reading Robertson Davies and working my way through a bottle of Maker's Mark. I could hear the singalong in the distance, and I remember thinking there was something absurd about a bunch of adults singing 'Jingle Bells' and 'White Christmas' under the palms, especially with an asshole like Bud Schiller dressed as Santa leading them along. About nine-thirty, when the singalong ended, the print in my book was too blurred to read any more, and by ten o'clock or thereabouts, like most people in the Whispering Palms Condominium Estate, I was sawing logs.

'He'd been drinking,' I went on. 'Mary Pasquale, the girl in the office, she told me he was three sheets to the wind. He must have been carrying his piano away after the party when he tripped near the edge of the pool and pitched in, head first.'

Al just raised his eyebrows.

He had a point. Even as I repeated the official line, something nagged at the back of my mind. As an ex-cop turned PI, I've seen enough weird crime scenes in my time, like the guy they found dead on the subway tracks and couldn't find his head. But in this case, I had to ask myself two questions: first, wouldn't Schiller have dropped the piano as he flung his arms out to protect himself from the fall?

And second, perhaps more to the point, why on God's earth was Santa's electric piano *still plugged in*?

'I've noticed you talking to Schiller's cronies,' I said to Al quietly, so they wouldn't overhear. 'Do you know any of them well enough to think one of them killed him?'

Al shook his head. 'Not really. Just casting the nets, you know. Ed Brennan, the red-faced one, he's into the ponies. We went to the dog track at Naples once. But he's a sore loser. Too desperate. And I played golf with Schiller a couple of times a few years back. He cheats. Did you know that?'

I didn't rate cheating at golf as high on my list of motives for murder, but you never knew. 'What about the girl?'

Al raised his eyebrows. 'Ah-hah! *Cherchez la femme*, is it? Her name's Karen Lee. Kindergarten teacher, I think.'

'I wish my kindergarten teacher had looked like that.'

'You'd've been too young to appreciate it. Besides, if you've got any thoughts in that direction, Jack, forget them. I warn you, she's strictly an ice queen.'

I looked at Karen Lee. She was running her finger around the rim of a tall, frosted glass – abstractedly, rather than in any deliberately erotic way, but it still looked sexy as hell. She sure didn't look like an ice queen to me.

'How long has Schiller been coming here?' I asked.

'Longer than me, and I've been a regular for, what, nine, ten years now.'

'How did they all hook up with each other?'

'I don't know, except they're all from Canada. Every year Schiller would manage to gather a few luckless characters around him, but, like me, they didn't usually come back for more. Ed was the first one who did, about four years ago. The blonde was next, year after, I think, then Mama Cass showed up just last year.'

'What's her real name?'

'Ginny Fraser. Three time loser from Smith's Falls, far as I can gather. Single mother. Welfare.'

'How can she afford to come here?'

'Don't ask me.'

'What does Ed do?'

'Retired. Used to be a school caretaker in Waterloo.'

Kindergarten teacher; welfare case; retired caretaker. Not exactly high-paying jobs. And all Canadian. Still, that didn't mean much. Half of Canada rents condos in Florida in the winter - and Canada's a big country. I looked at them again, trying to read their faces for signs of guilt. Nothing. Karen was still running her finger around her glass rim. Ed was attempting to tell a joke, the kind, he said loudly, that he 'just knew old Bud would have appreciated'. Only Ginny was laughing, chins wobbling, tears in her eyes.

I finished my beer, said goodbye to Al and left. When I got back to the condo that evening with a bottle of Chilean wine and a pound of jumbo shrimp for the barbecue, I tried to put Al's suggestion of murder out of my mind.

But it wouldn't go away.

The problem was what, if anything, was I going to do about it? Back home, I'm a licensed private investigator, but down here I'm not even a citizen.

Still, that evening out on the lanai, after the wine and the shrimps, I decided to keep my bourbon intake down. A good night's sleep and no hangover would be the best bet for whatever tomorrow might bring.

•

The grass pricked my feet as I walked towards the pool the next morning for my pre-breakfast swim. Already the temperature was in the low seventies and the sky was robin's egg blue.

I stood for a moment on the bridge and looked down into the murky water for the huge turtles and catfish. Evenings, just before dark, I'd got in the habit of feeding them chunks of bread. But there was nobody around this morning.

A couple of hundred yards away, over the swathe of dry grass, the squat, brown condo units were strung out in a circle around the central island, connected to the mainland by a wooden bridge over the narrow moat. The pool, the office and the tennis courts were all on the island. And that was Whispering Palms. Someone had bought some land in Florida and got very rich.

An old man, fuzz of white body hair against leathery skin, was lying out on a lounge chair catching the early rays. The scent of coconut sun screen mingled with the whiff of chlorine. The pool was still marked off by yellow police tape.

I noticed that the office door was ajar, and when I popped my head inside, I saw Mary sitting at her desk, staring into space. I like Mary. She's about twenty-five, an athletic sort of girl with a swimmer's upper body and a runner's thighs. She has a shiny black pony tail and one of those open, friendly faces, the kind you trust on sight.

'Oh, Mr Erwin. You startled me. You weren't wanting to use the pool, were you?'

'I was. But I see it's still off-limits.'

A frown wrinkled Mary's smooth, tanned brow. 'Well, I mean, it's not on account of the cops or anything,' she said. 'It's just . . . well, I didn't think the residents would like it, you know, swimming in a dead man's water.' She turned her nose up. 'So I've called maintenance and they're gonna clean it out and refill it all fresh. Should be ready by this afternoon. Sorry.'

'No, you're right. It's a good idea,' I said.

Most people probably *would* be put off by swimming in the same water where an electrocuted Santa Claus had floated around all night alone in the dark, but it didn't bother me much. I had seen death close up more times than I cared to remember. Besides, people swam in the ocean all the time and thousands have died there over the centuries.

'Mary,' I asked, 'do you happen to know who the last people to see Mr Schiller alive were?'

'His friends. Mr Brennan, Miss Lee and Miss Fraser. They said he was fine when they left.'

Of course. The ubiquitous trio.

Mary shook her head. 'Never could understand what Miss Lee saw in that group, pretty girl like her.'

So I was vindicated for thinking exactly the same thing yesterday. And if a young woman like Mary could think it too, it couldn't be either ageist or sexist, could it?

'Mind if I ask *you* something?' Mary said with a frown.

'Go ahead.'

'Mr Schiller was a Canadian citizen, right?'

'As far as I know.'

'Well, I was worried, you know, like his relatives might come down and make some sort of lawsuit. What do you think?'

Aha, the great American paranoia raises its ugly head: lawsuits. 'I'm no legal expert,' I said.

'You hear about things like that all the time, don't you? I mean, they could sue for millions. I could be liable. It would ruin me.' She laughed. 'Even if they sued for hundreds it would bankrupt me. I could lose my job. I need this job, Mr Erwin. I need the money to go back to school.'

I smiled as reassuringly as I could and told her I didn't think that would happen. We didn't even know if Schiller had any next of kin, for a start. And she couldn't be responsible for his behaviour when he was drunk.

'But the cops said he must have tripped over that crack in the tiles.'

'What crack?'

'Come on, I'll show you.'

We went outside. The old guy in the lounge chair was still working on his skin cancer. Near the side of the pool, Mary pointed out the crack. It didn't look like much to me. I put my foot in front of it and slid forward slowly. My big toe slipped right over the crack and the rest of my foot followed. I could hardly even feel the rough edge of the tile. 'It's hardly enough to trip over,' I said to Mary.

'He was wearing flip-flops.'

'Santa Claus was wearing flip-flops?'

She nodded.

'I suppose that might make a difference. Even so . . . It's still a long way from the water. Maybe six feet. Schiller was a little guy, only around five-four, wasn't he?'

'Yeah. I thought about that, too. But he must have been walking fast, or running, then he tripped and skidded in. Those tiles can get pretty slippery, especially if they're wet.'

'But wouldn't the piano just rip out of the socket?'

Mary shrugged. 'It was one of those ultra-light things,' she said. 'And it had a long cord.'

Still, I couldn't help but wonder why the hell Santa Claus should be running *towards* the swimming pool in the dark with a live electric piano in his arms, no matter how tight he was or how light the piano.

A heron landed by the side of the moat. Just for a moment, I felt a slight shiver run up my spine to the hairs at the back of my neck. It was a sign I recognized. I was being watched. And not by the heron or the sunbather.

Mary turned and walked back to the office, sandals clip-clopping against the tiles. I followed her, admiring the way her thigh muscles rippled with each step. I felt strangely detached, though; I could admire the sculpted, athletic beauty of her body, but I didn't feel attracted to her sexually. But, then, it had been a long time since I *had* been attracted to anyone sexually, except maybe Karen Lee.

Mary sat down at her desk again.

'Look,' I said, leaning forward and resting my hands on the warm wood, 'I know this might sound strange to you, but I'd like you to do me a favour without telling anyone or asking too many questions. Do you think you could do that?'

Mary nodded slowly, tentatively. 'Depends,' she said, 'on what it is.'

•

When I got back to the condo, it was time for breakfast, but without the swim, my appetite wasn't up to much. I put on a pot of coffee, drank a glass of orange juice and ate a bowl of high-fibre bran. The healthy life.

Usually I took my second cup out to the lanai and worked on one of the cryptics from the *Sunday Times* book of crosswords. That was one thing always annoyed me about American newspapers: you couldn't find a cryptic in any of them I'd seen. This morning, though, I took the two sheets of paper that Mary had printed out for me.

OK, so Schiller was alone at the pool after the singalong, or so Ed, Karen and Ginny said. Anyone could have gone there in the dark, killed him and tried to make it look like an accident. And at least three people knew he was there: Ed, Karen and Ginny. Were they telling the truth?

There was some risk – there always is with murder – but it was minimal. Most of the residents are elderly and they're usually in bed by ten. This isn't like some of the places where you get kids drinking all night and skinny-dipping; there are no kids at Whispering Palms.

First, I looked over the list of condo owners I had persuaded Mary to print for me.

Schiller's unit was owned on paper by Gardiner Holdings, registered in Grand Cayman Island. If that didn't set alarm bells ringing in an old gumshoe's mind, what would? But I couldn't for the life of me figure out what it meant.

Ginny Fraser's unit was a timeshare, though Ginny herself wasn't listed as owning any time.

Ed Brennan's unit was registered to a Dr Joseph Brady in Waterloo, Canada, and Karen Lee's to a travel agency called *EscapeItAll*, based in Sarasota.

One way or another, these four had all ended up at Whispering Palms, Fort Myers, Florida, and I was damned if I could see any reason other than pure chance.

So which one of them did it? And why? Or was it someone else?

I pushed my glasses back up the bridge of my nose and reached for the telephone. Being a private investigator from Toronto has *some* advantages in Florida.

•

When I'd finished on the phone I felt the need to go out for a drive. Not far. Maybe over the skyway to Sanibel and Captiva. Lunch at the Mucky Duck. Seafood and Harp lager. After all, I was on vacation, whatever Al said about gumshoes and the search for truth and justice.

But when I walked out to the car, I saw Karen Lee bent over the front tyre of her red Honda rental just a few parking spots down, white cotton shorts stretched taut over her ass.

I stood and admired the view for a while then walked towards her and asked if she could use any help. Why not? She could only tell me to get lost, that she was perfectly capable of fixing the tyre herself. Or she could accept my offer graciously.

She did the latter.

Turning on her haunches and shielding her eyes from the sun, she smiled and said, 'Why, thanks, yes. I'd appreciate that.' She had dimples at each corner of her mouth. Cute.

Then she stood up and brushed the dust off her hands. She was wearing a pink tank top, and a little sweat had darkened the cotton between her breasts.

'Flat,' she said.

A facetious reply formed in my mind, but before I could voice it she went on, 'The tyre. I should have done something about it last night. I thought something was wrong, maybe a slow leak. But I couldn't be bothered. Then, when I came out just now I saw it was flat.'

'No problem,' I said, and in no time we took off the flat and put on the spare.

'Thanks a lot,' said Karen, smiling. 'It's not that I'm helpless or anything. I mean, I know how to change a tyre. But—'

'Forget it,' I told her, 'My pleasure.'

'What I was going to say was it was nice to have a bit of

company.' And she smiled again, giving me the full benefit of her dimples and baby blues. The front of her tank top was even damper now and I could see beads of moisture on the tops of her breasts, between the tiny hairs. She had her hair tied back and fixed with barrettes, but a few strands had come loose and stuck to her flushed face. Some ice queen.

'Hot, isn't it,' she said, waving her hand in front of her face. 'Look, why don't you come in and clean up? It's the least I can do.'

I could have gone to my own place, just a few buildings down, but I'm no fool. I followed her up the steps to her second-storey unit. Inside, it was pretty much the same layout as mine: open-plan kitchen and living room, two bedrooms – one with its own bathroom – guest bathroom, and the lanai out front.

'Sorry about the mess,' Karen said, picking up a few magazines scattered on the sofa. 'I wasn't expecting company. Please go ahead. Use the bathroom.'

The bathroom was full of the mysterious paraphernalia of feminine beauty – potions, eyebrow pencils, little sponges, cotton wool, Q-tips. I washed the sweat and grime off my hands and face and flushed the toilet, using the noise to cover up the sound as I went through the drawers and cupboards. There was nothing out of the ordinary: soap, deodorant, shampoo, talcum, tampons, Advil, Maalox. The only interesting item was a bottle of Prozac. These days it seems half the world's on Prozac.

When I got back to the living room, Karen had just finished tidying things into neat piles. She smiled. 'Cold drink?'

'A Coke would be great.'

'I'll just go freshen up.' She looked down at her body and spread her arms, then seemed embarrassed by the gesture. In fact, now we were inside, her manner had grown much more nervous and I didn't know how to put her at ease. Too many movies about the nice guy next door turning out to be a psycho, I suppose.

'I'll help myself,' I said. 'You go wash up.'

'OK . . . I'll . . . er . . . It's in the fridge. I won't be long. Are you sure you'll be OK?'

'I'll be fine. Don't worry.'

When she went into her bathroom, the lock clicked behind her. As soon as I heard the shower start up, I began a quick search, not knowing what the hell I was looking for. If Schiller had been murdered, Karen had to be a suspect. Much as I hoped she hadn't done it, she had been one of the three to know where he was after the singalong. And how drunk he was.

All I found out was that Karen was halfway through *The Concrete Blonde*; that she more than likely slept alone; that she favoured casual clothes but had a couple of expensive dresses; that she didn't seem to watch videos very much; and that her musical tastes extended from Mozart to Alanis Morissette.

When she came out, she was wearing red shorts and a white shirt. Her hair was still damp from the shower and it hung in long hanks, framing her pale oval face.

'There,' she said, hoisting herself onto a stool at the kitchen counter. 'That's better. What a start to the day.'

I poured her a Coke. 'I guess you must still be pretty upset about your friend dying?' I said.

'Bud. Yes. How did you . . . ? Of course. I've seen you in Chloe's, haven't I? Always alone. No wife? Girlfriend?'

A definite hint of flirtation there, I thought. 'My wife died three years ago. Auto accident.'

'Oh, I'm so sorry. That must be terrible.'

I shrugged. 'There's good days and bad. Were you very close to Mr Schiller?'

She looked away. 'Not really.'

'I don't mean pry or anything,' I said, 'but were you . . . I mean, what drew you to him?'

'I don't know. We weren't an item, if that's what you're getting at.' She blushed. 'I'd just been through a painful divorce. I was depressed. I suppose I came down here to escape . . . I don't know . . . I guess maybe I succeeded. Bud and the others, they were my escape. It was all fun. No demands. Bud was a laugh. He never took anything seriously.'

'You were one of the last people to see him alive, weren't you?'

Karen nodded. 'Yes. With Ed and Ginny.'

'What happened?'

'We'd all had a bit too much to drink. When everyone else left after the carols, we started joking around by the pool. I fell in. I wanted to go home and change out of my wet clothes, so the three of us came to my place. Bud said he had a couple of things to do, then he was going to turn in.'

'Did he say what he had to do?'

'No. Just a couple of things.'

'Do you think he could have been meeting someone?'

'I suppose so . . . I . . .' She looked me in the eye. 'Why?'

'Just curious. How did he seem?'

'He was very drunk.' She frowned, then went on. 'You know, I've thought time and time again that we should have done something, that I should have said something.'

'Like what?'

'Oh, made him come with us, something like that. Somehow I feel responsible.'

'Don't be silly. There's no way you could have known.'

'Even so . . . I can't help feeling guilty.' She held her hands up. 'Look, I don't know how we got into this, but it's a beautiful day out there and I don't want to get even more depressed.'

Interview over. 'You're right,' I said, getting up. 'I'd better be going myself.'

She walked me to the door. 'Thanks for the help. It was nice talking to you.'

'You too.' Before she could close the door on me, I turned. 'Don't think this too presumptuous of me,' I began, 'but how would you like to come out for dinner or a drink tonight?'

'Tonight?' Her face dropped. 'Oh, I can't. I'm busy.'

I started to turn away. 'It's OK. I understand. Believe me. My mistake, especially after what you said about the divorce and all. I'm sorry.'

But she rested her warm hand on my arm. 'It's nothing like

that,' she said. 'I don't want you to think I'm making an excuse. I'm not. I really *do* have something on tonight. The three of us are having a sort of wake. I couldn't miss it.'

Maybe this wasn't the brush off, then. Heart thumping, fear of rejection bringing me out in a sweat, I persevered. 'How about tomorrow night then?'

She smiled. 'I'd love to. Really, I would.'

'Great. Do you like seafood?'

'Sure.'

'How about the Big Fin?'

'Fine. Look, I'll meet you at the bar there at seven. I've got some running around to do first, and I'm not sure if I'll have time to get back here. OK?'

'Fine. Big Fin. Bar. Seven.' I walked off, grinning like an idiot.

•

The phone started ringing, the way they do, the minute I stuck my key in the door that afternoon. I put the groceries I'd bought at Publix on the kitchen counter and picked up the extension.

'Jack, it's Mike.'

My partner. 'You were quick.'

'Well, partly it's a slow week.'

'And . . . ?'

'And partly there's not a hell of a lot to report.'

'Go ahead anyway.'

'Nothing on any of the people on the list. Squeaky clean, every one of them.'

'What about Schiller?'

'That's the only interesting part. As far as I can make out, nobody knows him. I checked out the Kingston address you gave me. It's owned by a couple called Renard. They confirmed that a man called Bud Schiller rents it from them and the cheques come in regularly.'

'Where from?'

'That they wouldn't tell me. Anyway, I got the name of the guy next door to the Schiller place, and he said the house is empty most of the time.'

Now what the hell did that mean? 'Anything else?'

'That doctor in Waterloo, Joseph Brady, he checks out. He's Edward Brennan's family doctor, has been for years, and he rented the condo to Ed for the first time a few years back. Apparently the poor guy needed to recuperate from some illness - nothing specific, you know doctors - but I got the impression this Ed character had suffered various health problems on and off over—'

'Mental or physical?'

'Can't say. But Brady's a family doctor, Jack, not a shrink.'

'OK. Go on.'

'So it was a kind of convalescent holiday. He liked it and kept coming back.'

'How about *EscapeItAll*?'

'Perfectly legit. They own a few condos down the Gulf Coast and rent them through local agencies. Quite a lot of the Toronto travel agents do business with them, and the ones I talked to said they never had any problems.'

'And the timeshare?'

'Also legit. There is one thing, though. Virginia Fraser, one of the names you gave me?'

'Right.' Ginny Fraser.

'I talked to the woman she rented from, and it turns out that the dates Fraser got weren't available originally.'

'So?'

'So she paid over the odds.'

'Ah-ha. On welfare, too. Is that all?'

'Just about. Gardiner Holdings, that company in the Caymans? Looks like it's the front of a front of a front. I couldn't get even get a whiff of the real movers and shakers behind it.'

'OK,' I said. 'Thanks a lot Mike. You did good work.' Then I hung up and mulled over what I'd learned.

•

'Gee, I dunno, Mr Erwin. I really shouldn't be doing this,' Mary said when she found the right key.

'It'll have to be cleaned out, anyway,' I said.

'Yeah, I know. It's just . . . Still, you *are* a licensed private investigator, right?'

'Right. And maybe we can check on next of kin, make sure no one's gonna come down and file a lawsuit against you.' I hated pressuring her that way, but I had to get inside Schiller's condo if I was to get any further. I was now more or less convinced that someone – either one of his three pals or someone he had arranged to meet – had gone to the pool and murdered him. It would help if I could find out whether he had anything to hide.

Still biting her lip, Mary turned the key in the lock.

Schiller certainly travelled light. A quick search of the master bedroom revealed only warm-climate clothes and a tattered Tom Clancy paperback on the bedside table. No papers in the drawers, no photographs, nothing. The cops must have taken his passport. The bathroom held only what a single man's bathroom would, and the guest bedroom was empty except for the bed, stripped down to its mattress. Kitchen and fridge contained the usual – milk, bread, condiments, a couple of TV dinners, cutlery, booze. By the looks of it, Schiller ate out a lot.

In the living room, the stereo, TV and VCR took up one corner. A cabinet under the VCR held a stock of tapes. One of the movies was from a local rental store, and it was overdue by two days. The tape was still in the machine.

'I'll take this back tomorrow,' I said to Mary, casually slipping the tape back in the box.

Mary just nodded and glanced nervously at the door.

'I think that's about all,' I said, 'if you want to go now.'

Mary was out the front door like a shot. 'You didn't find anything about next of kin?'

'Nothing. No news is good news. Don't worry.'

She flashed an anxious smile. 'I'll try not to.'

And I hurried back to call the courier company. It was late, but with luck, they could get a package to Mike overnight.

•

'Jack?'

'Uh-huh.'

'Mike.'

'Hang on . . . Just a minute . . .' I sat up quickly. It felt like I had to drag myself a long way back from God knew where. I rubbed my eyes and checked my watch. Three-thirty in the afternoon. I must have dozed off after lunch. I opened the fridge and popped the tab on a can of Michelob, then picked up the phone again. 'Yeah, go ahead, Mike. Sorry about that.'

'No problem. I took video down to Ident first thing this morning. It was a bit of a mess – must have been a popular movie down there – but Harry found a match you might be interested in.'

'Schiller's got a record?'

'Not Schiller. The only prints we could find on file belong to a Sherman Smith.'

'That rings a bell.'

'It should do,' he went on. 'Remember that land scam twenty years ago? Smith defrauded hundreds of people out of their life savings.'

'What was it, some land in Florida turned out to be swamp?'

'Something like that. Smith disappeared with the money and was never seen or heard of again. In all there must've been over two or three million bucks.'

I whistled. 'What happened?'

'The Mounties followed the paper trail for a while, then they lost it. Smith never surfaced again.'

Except as Schiller, I thought. He probably split his time between Florida and the Cayman Islands, travelling on a phony Canadian passport but not staying in Canada for long. Too risky. 'Do we recognize any of the victims' names?' I asked Mike.

I could almost hear him grinning over the phone. 'I thought you'd never ask. As a matter of fact we do: a Mr Edward Brennan.'

•

Karen was sitting at a stool at the bar sipping something colourful and cluttered through a candy-striped straw. She was wearing a green silk off-the-shoulder number, one I had seen in her closet, with her legs crossed. I caught an eyeful of slim, tanned thigh as I walked towards her. She smiled and said hello. Her shiny blonde hair fell over her shoulder on one side, and she had tucked the other side behind her ear, fixing it there with a pink flower that matched her lipstick. Nice touch.

I must admit I'd been relieved to find out it was Ed who had the connection with Smith, not Karen. It didn't mean he was the killer, of course, but it sure gave him one hell of a motive. I still had a lot of questions for Karen, though, and I wasn't sure how, or if, I could mix business and pleasure.

I ordered a bourbon on the rocks and we walked through to the table. It was a tacky-looking kind of restaurant, with nets hanging from the ceilings and old barrels converted into chairs, but the food was always superb.

Karen examined the menu, then she said, 'I'd like to start with some oysters. How about you?'

'Fine by me.' Oysters! For an ice queen? Maybe Al French had an agenda of his own? So we ordered a dozen oysters and a bottle of Californian champagne, followed by swordfish steak for me and coquilles Saint-Jacques for Karen. She avoided my eyes as the waiter lit candles on the table.

We chatted about this and that. Karen seemed nervous, on edge, attention all over the place, so much so that she seemed skittish. But just when I thought I'd lost her, she'd look me in the eye and come back with the kind of remark that showed she was there all the time, maybe even a step or two ahead.

'Did you know Bud, Ed or Ginny back home?' I asked when the subject came around to last night's wake.

She shook her head. 'One rule about a world you escape to is that neither it nor any of its inhabitants can exist in the world you regularly live in.' She fingered the napkin ring on the table as she spoke, shadows flitting in the depths of her eyes.

'I can understand that,' I said, thinking it sounded like something out of a computer-game manual. The oysters arrived and we helped ourselves. 'I suppose it's an escape for me too.'

'Is it? In what way?'

'I used to come down here with my wife.'

Karen frowned. 'Then it's not an escape you're after,' she said. 'It's *catharsis*.'

'Maybe you're right. If so, it hasn't happened yet.'

She put her hand lightly on mine. 'Give it time, Jack. Give it time.'

We finished the oysters, and the main courses arrived. I tried to find a way to steer the conversation back to Bud Schiller. As usual, I couldn't find a subtle way, so halfway through my swordfish, during a temporary lull, I said, 'Remember when you told me the three of you went to your room and Bud stayed out by the pool?'

She nodded. 'And you thought he might be meeting someone?'

'That's right. Did any of the others leave your room at any time?'

'Not until later.' She blushed. 'Ed must have passed out there. I found him on the couch in the morning.'

'Did Ed ever mention knowing Bud from before?'

Karen looked down at her plate and speared a scallop. 'No.' Then she looked back at me and her eyes widened. 'What are you suggesting? That Ed murdered Bud? You can't be serious?'

'I don't know, Karen. I'm just curious, that's all.'

'But why? Why are you interested? Are you a cop?'

'I'm a private investigator,' I told her, 'but I'm not licensed to operate down here.' I shrugged. 'It just seemed suspicious to me, that's all.'

I paused for a moment, then I jumped right in and told her

about Schiller's true identity and the land scam, in which one Edward Brennan lost his life's savings. When I finished, Karen was pale. She excused herself to visit the washroom.

When she came back, she looked a lot better. She didn't wear much make-up, but she had given herself a fresh coat of the basics and looked good as new.

'I'm sorry for overreacting,' she said. 'Honestly, I'd never really considered that Bud's death could have been deliberate. I suppose I was too busy blaming myself. But Ed . . . ?'

'I can't be sure,' I said. 'But it doesn't look good. Are you certain he never left your condo?'

'He went over to his own unit to pick up some Scotch. I'd run out. But he wasn't gone for more than ten minutes.'

'Ten minutes was enough.'

'What are you going to do?'

'Tell the authorities, I suppose.'

She nodded slowly. 'That would be the right thing to do, of course. But poor Ed. I don't like the thought of him spending the rest of his life in jail. Can't you just . . . you know . . . let it go?'

'However much of an asshole Bud Schiller was, he didn't deserve to die like that.'

'You're right,' she whispered. 'I'd like to go home.'

As I followed Karen's Honda back to Whispering Palms, I was beginning to think that I'd blown my chances of a pleasant end to the evening. But she invited me up for a nightcap.

Once we were inside, she busied herself preparing the drinks, flitting nervously between fridge and cocktail cabinet, chattering brightly away. Ever since we got back, I'd sensed a certain tension between us and I thought it was sexual. When she walked past me to open the sliding glass door to the lanai, I put my hand out and touched her shoulder. She turned, gave me a swift peck on the cheek and said she had to go the bathroom.

I gazed out at the dark island beyond the lanai, the Christmas lights on the bridge, drink in hand, waiting for her. What did the peck on the cheek mean? Was it promise or consolation? You're an old fool, Jack Erwin, I told myself. You should stick to your bourbon and blues.

Then I heard a door open behind me. Thinking it was Karen coming back, I turned around.

Ed Brennan stood there, a baseball bat in his hands.

Before I had time to react, the front door opened and Ginny Fraser walked in carrying a long kitchen knife.

Karen came out of the bathroom. She wasn't carrying any weapon and she looked as if she had been crying. 'Oh, Jack,' she said, shaking her head. 'I'm so sorry.'

'What are you going to do?' I asked, trying to sound more confident than I felt. 'Hit me on the head with the baseball bat then stab me and pretend it was an accident? Just to protect Ed here? Come on, Karen, he's not worth it.'

'You don't understand,' Karen said. 'You think you know everything but you don't. You don't know anything.'

My breath caught in my throat. 'What the hell are you talking about?'

Then a strange thing happened. I saw Karen flash a quick, sad glance at Ed, and he just seemed to deflate right before my eyes. His baseball bat dropped to the floor. 'He's right, Karen,' he said. 'We can't do this. We're not killers.'

I looked at Ginny Fraser. She dropped the kitchen knife and flopped onto the sofa.

After I got my breath back, I turned to Karen and said, 'Right, now we've got that charade out of the way, will someone tell me what's going on here?'

•

'I'm sorry,' Ed said for the third time. 'I don't know what came over us. We were desperate. I still can't imagine what made us think we could kill an innocent man. When Karen phoned from the restaurant and told us you knew . . . we just panicked.'

'I'm sorry I deceived you,' Karen said. 'I admit I was trying to find out if you knew anything. After I saw you and the woman from the office looking at the pool yesterday, I thought you might be trouble. So I arranged the puncture.'

Well that makes two of us acting from impure motives, I thought. 'So you're all sorry,' I said. 'Whoop-a-de-doodah. Now would someone tell me why I shouldn't call the police right now?'

'We can't stop you,' Ed said. 'We *won't* stop you. In a way, it would be a relief.'

I poured three fingers of Karen's bourbon into my glass and settled down on the sofa beside Ginny. Karen and Ed sat opposite in matching easy chairs. 'Just tell me what it's all about,' I said. 'Who really did kill Schiller?'

'We all did,' Ed answered.

I looked at Karen and Ginny, who both nodded.

Jesus Christ, I thought, it's *Murder on the Orient Express* all over again.

'Ginny and I pushed him into the pool,' Ed went on. 'He thought we were playing games. Karen plugged in the piano, and we all lowered it in after him. After that all we had to was lie to the police and tell them he was still alive when we left him.'

'What I really don't understand,' I went on, 'is why. I know Smith cheated Ed out of his life's savings, but what did he ever do to you, Karen?'

'My father,' she said flatly. 'Vernon Connant. You'll find *his* name on your list. Lee's my married name. Smith swindled him out of every penny we had. When the news broke he killed my mother, then himself. With a shotgun. I was five at the time. Just before he put the gun in his mouth and pulled the trigger, he looked at me. He was going to kill me, too, but at the last moment, he couldn't do it. I'll never forget that look. I've spent my whole life trying, one shrink to another, pills, the lot. You can't tell me that Sherman Smith didn't deserve to die.'

I took a long sip of bourbon and let the fire fill my mouth before swallowing. 'What about you, Ginny? You weren't on the list, either.'

'My husband. Harvey Pellier. I went back to my maiden name.'

'What happened?'

Ginny gave a harsh laugh. 'Nothing quite so dramatic as Karen's story. Harvey lost everything, and it broke his spirit. He left us. Just walked out and never came back. We hadn't been really well off, but we'd been happy. When Harvey left, the family just fell apart. I couldn't hold it together. The kids did badly at school, started hanging with a bad crowd. You know the sort of thing. They drifted into drugs, street life. Will died of an overdose. Jane's still somewhere out on the streets. I haven't heard from her in years.'

After a few moments of silence, Ed ran his hands through his hair and said he wouldn't mind a drink. Karen got him a Scotch on the rocks. Then he began. 'I bumped into Smith about four years ago. Pure chance. Coincidence. I just couldn't believe it. I suppose, when you think about it, you never know who's going to be renting from who. Anyway, I saw him, after over fifteen years, and do you know what?'

I shook my head.

'He didn't recognize me. I mean, you ought to recognize people whose lives you ruined, don't you think? Because of him I had a nervous breakdown, I got hooked on the booze, lost job after job. You name it.' He thumped his chest with his fist. 'Then, when I began to relive what he'd done to me, I realized the anger was still there. Only now I had the advantage. But I couldn't kill him. Not alone.' He glanced at Karen and Ginny. 'When it first happened – I mean twenty years ago – lots of us had meetings with lawyers, and I became close to Karen's father and Ginny's husband. But Smith had never seen Karen or Ginny. So I got in touch with them, told them the situation and we planned what to do. We befriended him, one by one, pretended we didn't know each other, then we killed him.'

Ed fell silent and the others looked at me. It was hard to imagine the havoc Sherman Smith had wreaked on these lives, hard not to sympathize with the three of them, but who was I to judge?

'It's up to you now, Jack,' Karen said, seeming to sense my

dilemma. 'You know the whole story now. We're guilty of premeditated murder.' She glanced at Ed. 'If you want my honest opinion, I don't think it's helped any of us. I don't think it's going to make our lives any easier to bear – probably the opposite – but it's done and you're the only one who knows about it. We can't kill you, but we're not going to give ourselves up willingly, either. It's your decision.'

So whether I liked it or not, it *was* up to me. I finished my bourbon, then I nodded and went back to my condo.

•

Almost exactly one year to the day later, I found myself in Chloe's for 'Happy Hour'. There were one or two faces I recognized around the bar, but most of the people were strangers. I still didn't know why I kept coming back year after year. Especially this year. Maybe Karen had been right and I *was* looking for catharsis.

Or for Karen.

I looked across the bar at where I had first really noticed her last year, running her finger around the rim of a glass. Now a chain-smoking brunette with a hard face sat there instead.

'Hi, Shamus.'

Al French slipped onto the empty stool beside me.

'Beer?' I offered.

'My turn.' Al ordered two beers. 'Did you ever get to the bottom of that mysterious death?' he asked.

'Which one was that?'

'You know. Last year. That asshole Bud Schiller.'

'Oh, him.' I shook my head. 'I don't think there was anything mysterious about it at all. I think he was drunk, he tripped and he fell into pool.'

'Yeah, and he pulled the piano in after him just for good measure. Come on, Jack.'

I shrugged. 'You know, Al, sometimes the strangest of accidents *do* happen. Did I ever tell you about the guy they found dead on the subway tracks and couldn't find his head?'

THE WRONG HANDS

'Is everything in order?' the old man asked, his scrawny fingers clutching the comforter like talons.

'Seems to be,' said Mitch.

Drawing up the will had been a simple enough task. Mr Garibaldi and his wife had the dubious distinction of outliving both their children, and there wasn't much to leave.

'Would you like to sign it now?' he asked, holding out his Mont Blanc.

The old man clutched the pen the way a child holds a crayon and scribbled his illegible signature on the documents.

'There . . . that's done,' said Mitch. He placed the papers in his briefcase.

Mr Garibaldi nodded. The movement brought on a spasm and such a coughing fit that Mitch thought the old man was going to die right there and then.

But he recovered. 'Will you do me a favour?' he croaked when he'd got his breath back.

Mitch frowned. 'If I can.'

With one bent, shrivelled finger, Mr Garibaldi pointed to the floor under the window. 'Pull the carpet back,' he said.

Mitch stood up and looked.

'Please,' said Mr Garibaldi. 'The carpet.'

Mitch walked over to window and rolled back the carpet. Underneath was nothing but floorboards.

'One of the boards is loose,' said the old man. 'The one directly in line with the wall socket. Lift it up.'

Mitch felt and, sure enough, part of the floorboard was loose. He lifted it easily with his fingernails. Underneath, wedged between the joists, lay a package wrapped in old newspaper.

'That's it,' said the old man. 'Take it out.'

Mitch did. It was heavier than he had expected.

'Now put the board back and replace the carpet.'

After he had done as he was asked, Mitch carried the package over to the bed.

'Open it,' said Mr Garibaldi. 'Go on, it won't bite you.'

Slowly, Mitch unwrapped the newspaper. It was from 18 December 1947, he noticed, and the headline reported a blizzard dumping twenty-eight inches of snow on New York City the day before. Inside, he found a layer of oilcloth. When he had folded back that too, a gun gleamed up at him. It was old, he could tell that, but it looked in superb condition. He hefted it into his hand, felt its weight and balance, pointed it towards the wall as if to shoot.

'Be careful,' said the old man. 'It's loaded.'

Mitch looked at the gun again, then put it back on the oilcloth. His fingers were smudged with oil or grease, so he took a tissue from the bedside table and wiped them off as best he could.

'What the hell are you doing with a loaded gun?' he asked.

Mr Garibaldi sighed. 'It's a Luger,' he said. 'First World War, probably. Old, anyway. A friend gave it to me many years ago. A German friend. I've kept it ever since. Partly as a memento of him and partly for protection. You know what this city's been getting like these past few years. I've maintained it, cleaned it, kept it loaded. Now I'm gonna die I want to hand it in. I don't want it to fall into the wrong hands.'

Mitch set the Luger down on the bed. 'Why tell me?' he asked.

'Because it's unregistered and I'd like you to hand it over for me.' He shook his head and coughed again. 'I haven't got long left.

I don't want no cops coming round here and giving me a hard time.'

'They won't give you a hard time.' More like give you a medal for handing over an unregistered firearm, Mitch thought.

'Maybe not. But . . .' Mr Garibaldi grabbed Mitch's wrist with his talon. The fingers felt cold and dry, like a reptile's skin. Mitch tried to pull back a little, but the old man held on, pulled him closer and croaked, 'Sophie doesn't know. It would make her real angry to know we had a gun in the house the last fifty years and I kept it from her. I don't want to end my days with my wife mad at me. Please, Mr Mitchell. It's a small favour I ask.'

Mitch scratched the side of his eye. True enough, he thought, it *was* a small favour. And it might prove a profitable one, too. Old firearms were worth something to collectors, and Mitch knew a cop who had connections. All he had to say was that he had been entrusted this gun by a client, who had brought it to his office, that he had put it in the safe and called the police immediately. What could be wrong with that?

'OK,' he said, rewrapping the gun and slipping it in his brief-case along with the will. 'I'll do as you ask. Don't worry. You rest now. Everything will be OK.'

Mr Garibaldi smiled and seemed to sink into a deep sleep.

•

Mitch stood on the porch of the Garibaldi house and pulled on his sheepskin-lined gloves, glad to be out of the cloying atmosphere of the sickroom, even if it was minus ninety or something outside.

He was already wearing his heaviest overcoat over a suit and a wool scarf, but still he was freezing. It was one of those clear winter nights when the ice cracks underfoot and the breeze off the lake seems to numb you right to the bone. Reflected street lamps splintered in the broken mirror of the sidewalk, the colour of Mr Garibaldi's jaundiced eyes.

Mitch pulled his coat tighter around his scarf and set off, cracking the iced-over puddles as he went. Here and there, the remains of last week's snow had frozen into ruts, and he almost slipped and fell a couple of times on the uneven surface.

As he walked, he thought of old Garibaldi, with no more than a few weeks or days left to live. The old man must have been in pain sometimes, but he never complained. And he surely must be afraid of death? Maybe dying put things in perspective, Mitch thought. Maybe the mind, facing the eternal, icy darkness of death, had ways of dealing with its impending extinction, of discarding the dross, the petty and the useless.

Or perhaps not. Maybe the old man just lay there day after day running baseball statistics through his mind; or wishing he'd slept with his neighbour's wife when he had the chance.

As Mitch walked up the short hill, he cursed the fact that you could never get a decent parking spot in these residential streets. He'd had to park in the lot behind the drug store, the next street over, and the quickest way there was through a dirt alley just about wide enough for a garbage truck to pass through.

It happened as he cut through the alley. And it happened so fast that, afterwards, he couldn't be quite sure whether he felt the sharp blow to back of his head before his feet slipped out from under him, or after.

•

When Mitch opened his eyes again, the first thing he saw was the night sky. It looked like a black satin bed-sheet with some rich woman's diamonds spilled all over it. There was no moon.

He felt frozen to the marrow. He didn't know how long he had been lying there in the alley – long enough to die of exposure it felt like – but when he checked his watch, he saw he had only been out a little over five minutes. Not surprising no one had found him yet. Not here, on a night like this.

He lay on the frozen mud and took stock. Despite the cold, everything hurt – his elbow, which he had cracked trying to break his fall; his tailbone; his right shoulder; and, most of all, his head – and the pain was sharp and spiky, not at all numb like the rest of him. He reached around and touched the sore spot on the back of his head. His fingers came away sticky with blood.

He took a deep breath and tried to get to his feet, but he could only manage to slip and skitter around like a newborn deer, making himself even more dizzy. There was no purchase, nothing to grip. Snail-like, he slid himself along the ice towards the rickety fence. There, by reaching out and grabbing the wooden rails carefully, he was able to drag himself to his feet, picking up only a few splinters for his troubles.

At first, he wished he had stayed where he was. His head started to spin and he thought it was going to split open with pain. For a moment, he was sure he was going to fall again. He held onto the fence for dear life and vomited, the world swimming around his head. After that, he felt a little better. Maybe he wasn't going to die.

The only light shone from a street lamp at the end of the alley, not really enough to search by, so Mitch used the plastic penlight attached to his key-ring to look for his briefcase. But it wasn't there. Stepping carefully on the ribbed ice, still in pain and unsure of his balance, Mitch extended the area of his search in case the briefcase had skidded off somewhere on the ice when he fell. It was nowhere to be found.

Almost as an afterthought, as the horrible truth was beginning to dawn on him, he felt for his wallet. Gone. So he'd been mugged. The blow had come *before* the fall. And they'd taken his briefcase.

Then Mitch remembered the gun.

•

The next morning was a nightmare. Mitch had managed to get himself home from the alley without crashing the car, and after a long, hot bath, a tumbler of Scotch and four extra-strength Tylenol, he began to feel a little better. He seemed to remember his mother once saying you shouldn't go to sleep after a bump on the head – he didn't know why – but it didn't stop him that night.

In the morning, he awoke aching all over.

When he had showered, taken more Tylenol and forced himself to eat some bran flakes, he poured a second cup of strong black coffee and sat down to think things out. None of his thoughts brought any comfort.

He hadn't gone to the cops. How could he, given what he had been carrying? Whichever way you looked at it, he had been in possession of an illegal, unregistered firearm when he was mugged. Even if the cops had been lenient, there was the Law Society to reckon with, and like most lawyers, Mitch feared the Law Society far more than he feared the police.

Maybe he could have sort of skipped over the gun in his account of the mugging. After all, he was pretty sure that it couldn't be traced either to him or to Garibaldi. But what if the cops found the briefcase and the gun was still inside it? How could he explain that?

Would that be worse than if the briefcase turned up and the gun was gone? If the muggers took it, then chances were someone might get shot with it. Either way, it was a bad scenario for Mitch, and it was all his fault. Well, maybe *fault* was too strong a word – he couldn't help getting mugged – but he still felt somehow responsible.

All he could do was hope that whoever took the gun would get rid of it, throw it in the lake, before anyone came to any harm.

Some hope.

•

Later that morning, Mitch remembered Garibaldi's will. That had gone, too, along with the briefcase and the gun. And it would have to be replaced.

There's only one true will – copies have no legal standing – and if you lose it you could have a hell of a mess on your hands. Luckily, he had Garibaldi's will on his computer. All he had to do was print it out again and hope to hell the old guy hadn't died during the night.

He hadn't. Puzzled, but accepting Mitch's excuse of a minor

error he'd come across when proof-reading the document, Garibaldi signed again with a shaking hand.

'Is the gun safe?' he asked afterwards. 'You've got it locked away in your safe?'

'Yes,' Mitch lied. 'Yes, don't worry, the gun's perfectly safe.'

•

Every day Mitch scanned the paper from cover to cover for news of a shooting or a gun found abandoned somewhere. He even took to buying the *Sun* – which he normally wouldn't even use as toilet paper up at the cottage – because it covered more lurid local crime than the *Globe* or the *Star*. Anything to do with firearms was certain to make it into the *Sun*.

But it wasn't until three weeks and three days after the mugging – and two weeks after Mr Garibaldi's death 'peacefully, at home' – that the item appeared. And it was big enough news to make the *Globe and Mail*.

> Mr Charles McVie was shot dead in his home last night during the course of an apparent burglary. A police spokesperson says Mr McVie was shot twice, once in the chest and once in the groin, while interrupting a burglar at his Beaches mansion shortly after midnight last night. He died of his wounds three hours later at East General Hospital. Detective Greg Hollins, who has been assigned the case, declined to comment on whether the police are following any significant leads at the moment, but he did inform our reporter that preliminary tests indicate the bullet was most likely fired from an old 9mm semi-automatic weapon, such as a Luger, unusual and fairly rare these days. As yet, police have not been able to locate the gun. Mr McVie, 62, made his fortune in the construction business. His wife, Laura, who was staying overnight with friends in Windsor when the shooting occurred, had no comment when she was reached early this morning.

The newspaper shook in Mitch's hands. It had happened. Somebody had died because of him. But while he felt guilt, he also felt fear. Was there really no way the police could tie the gun to him or Mr Garibaldi? Thank God the old man was dead, or he might hear about the shooting and his conscience might oblige him to come forward. Luckily, his widow, Sophie, knew nothing.

With luck, the Luger was in the deepest part of the lake for sure by now. Whether anyone else had touched it or not, Mitch knew damn well that *he* had, and that his greasy fingerprints weren't only all over the grip and the barrel, but on the wrapping paper, too. The muggers had probably been wearing gloves when they robbed him – it was a cold night – and maybe they'd had the sense to keep them on when they saw what was in the briefcase.

Calm down, he told himself. Even if the cops did find his fingerprints on the gun, they had no way of knowing *whose* prints they were. Mitch had never been fingerprinted in his life, and the cops would have no reason to subject him to it now.

And they couldn't connect Charles McVie to either Mr Garibaldi or to Mitch.

Except for one thing.

Mitch had drawn up McVie's will two years ago, after his marriage to Laura, his second wife.

•

Mitch had known that Laura McVie was younger than her husband, but even that knowledge hadn't prepared him for the woman who opened the door to him three days after Charles McVie's funeral.

Black became her. Really became her, the way it set off her creamy complexion, long blonde hair, Kim Basinger lips and eyes the colour of a bluejay's wing.

'Yes?' she said, frowning slightly.

Mitch had put on his very best, most expensive suit, and he knew he looked sharp. He didn't want her to think he was some ambulance-chaser come after her husband's money.

As executor, Laura McVie was under no obligation to use the same lawyer who had prepared her husband's will to handle his estate. Laura might have a lawyer of her own in mind. But Mitch *did* have the will, so there was every chance that if he presented himself well she would choose him to handle the estate too.

And there was much more money in estates – especially those as big as McVie's – than there was in wills.

At least, Mitch thought, he wasn't so hypocritical as to deny that he had mixed motives for visiting the widow. Didn't everyone have mixed motives? He felt partly responsible for McVie's death, of course, and a part of him genuinely wanted to offer the widow help.

After Mitch had introduced himself, Laura looked him over, plump lower lip fetchingly nipped between two sharp, white teeth, then she flashed him a smile and said, 'Please come in, Mr Mitchell. I was wondering what to do about all that stuff. I really could use some help.' Her voice was husky and low-pitched, with just a subtle hint of that submissive tone that can drive certain men wild.

Mitch followed her into the high-ceilinged hallway, watching the way her hips swayed under the mourning dress.

He was in. All right! He almost executed a little jig on the parquet floor.

•

The house was an enormous heap of stone overlooking the ravine. It had always reminded Mitch of an English vicarage, or what he assumed an English vicarage looked like from watching PBS. Inside, though, it was bright and spacious and filled with modern furniture – not an antimacassar in sight. The paintings that hung on the white walls were all contemporary abstracts and geometric designs, no doubt originals and worth a small fortune in themselves. The stereo equipment was state-of-the art, as were the large screen TV, VCR and DVD player.

Laura McVie sat on a white sofa and crossed her legs. The

dress she wore was rather short for mourning, Mitch thought, though he wasn't likely to complain about the four or five inches of smooth thigh it revealed. Especially as the lower part was sheathed in black silk stockings and the upper was bare and white.

She took a cigarette from a carved wooden box on the coffee table and lit it with a lighter that looked like a baseball. Mitch declined the offer to join her.

'I hope you don't mind,' she said, lowering her eyes. 'It's my only vice.'

'Of course not.' Mitch cleared his throat. 'I just wanted to come and tell you how sorry I was to hear about the . . . the tragic accident. Your husband was—'

'It wasn't an accident, Mr Mitchell,' she said calmly. 'My husband was murdered. I believe we should face the truth clearly and not hide behind euphemisms, don't you?'

'Well, if you put it like that . . .'

She nodded. 'You were saying about my husband?'

'Well, I didn't know him well, but I *have* done some legal work for him – specifically his will – and I am aware of his circumstances.'

'My husband was very rich, Mr Mitchell.'

'Exactly. I thought . . . well . . . there are some unscrupulous people out there, Mrs McVie.'

'Please, call me Laura.'

'Laura. There are some unscrupulous people out there, and I thought if there was anything I could do to help, perhaps give advice, take the burden off your hands . . .?'

'What burden would that be, Mr Mitchell?'

Mitch sat forward and clasped his hands on his knees. 'When someone dies, Mrs – Laura – there are always problems, legal wrangling and the like. Your husband's affairs seem to be in good order, judging from his will, but that was made two years ago. I'd hate to see someone come and take advantage of you.'

'Thank you,' Laura said. 'You're so sweet. And why shouldn't you handle the estate? Someone has to do it. I can't.'

Mitch had the strangest feeling that something was going awry here. Laura McVie didn't seem at all the person to be taken advantage of, yet she seemed to be swallowing his line of patter. That could only be, he decided, because it suited her, too. And why not? It *would* take a load off her mind.

'That wasn't the main reason I came, though,' Mitch pressed on, feeling an irrational desire to explain himself. 'I genuinely wanted to see if I could help in any way.'

'Why?' she asked, blue eyes open wide. 'Why should you? Mr Mitchell, I've come to learn that people do things for selfish motives. Self-interest rules. Always. I don't believe in altruism. Nor did my husband. At least we were agreed on that.' She turned aside, flicked some ash at the ashtray and missed. In contrast to everything else in the place, the tin ashtray looked as if it had been stolen from a lowlife bar. 'So you want to help me?' she said. 'For a fee, of course.'

Mitch felt embarrassed and uncomfortable. The part of him that had desperately wanted to make amends for his part in Charles McVie's death was being thwarted by the frankness and openness of the widow. Yes, he could use the money – of course he could – but that really *wasn't* his only reason for being there, and he wanted her to know that. How could he explain that he really wasn't such a bad guy?

'There are expenses involved in settling an estate,' Mitch went on. 'Disbursements. Of course, there are. But I'm not here to cheat you.'

She smiled at him indulgently. 'Of course not.'

Which definitely came across as, '*As if you could.*'

'But if you'll allow me to—'

She shifted her legs, showing more thigh. 'Mr Mitchell,' she said. 'I'm getting the feeling that you really do have another reason for coming to see me. If it's not that you're after my husband's money, then what are you after?'

Mitch swallowed. 'I . . . I feel. You see, I—'

'Come on, Mr Mitchell. You can tell me. You'll feel better.'

The voice that had seemed so submissive when Mitch first heard it now became hypnotic, so warm, so trustworthy, so easy to answer. And he had to tell someone.

'I feel partly responsible for your husband's death,' he said, looking into her eyes. 'Oh, I'm not the burglar, I'm not the killer. But I think I inadvertently supplied the gun.'

Laura McVie looked puzzled. Now he had begun, Mitch saw no point in stopping. If he could only tell this woman the full story, he thought, then she would understand. Perhaps she would even be sympathetic towards him. Forgive him. So he told her.

When he had finished, Laura stood up abruptly and walked over to the picture-window with its view of a back garden as big as Central Park. Mitch sat where he was and looked at her from behind. Her legs were close together and her arms were crossed. She seemed to be turned in on herself. He couldn't tell whether she was crying or not, but her shoulders seemed to be moving.

'Well?' he asked, after a while. 'What do you think?'

She let the silence stretch a moment, then dropped her arms and turned around slowly. Her eyes did look moist with tears. 'What do I think?' she said. 'I don't know. I don't know what to think. I think that maybe if you'd reported the gun stolen the police would have searched for it and my husband wouldn't have been murdered.'

'But I would have been charged, disbarred.'

'Mr Mitchell, surely that's a small price to pay for someone's life? I'm sorry. I think you'd better go. I can't think straight right now.'

'But I—'

'Please, Mr Mitchell. Leave.' She turned back to the window again and folded her arms, shaking.

Mitch got up off the sofa and headed for the door. He felt defeated, as if he had left something important unfinished, but there was nothing he could do about it. Only slink off with his tail between his legs feeling worse than when he had come. Why hadn't he just told her he was after handling McVie's estate. Money, pure and simple. Self-interest like that she would have understood.

•

Two days later, and still no developments reported in the McVie investigation, Laura phoned.

'Mr Mitchell?'

'Yes.'

'I'm sorry about my behaviour the other day. I was upset, as you can imagine.'

'I can understand that,' Mitch said. 'I don't blame you. I don't even know why I told you.'

'I'm glad you did. I've had time to think about it since then, and I'm beginning to realize how terrible you must feel. I want you to understand that I don't blame you. It's not the gun that commits the crime, after all, is it? It's the person who pulls the trigger. I'm sure if the burglar hadn't got that one, he'd have got one somewhere else. Look, this is very awkward over the telephone, do you think you could come to the house?'

'When?'

'How about this evening. For dinner?'

'Fine,' said Mitch. 'I'm really glad you can find it in your heart to forgive me.'

'Eight o'clock?'

'Eight it is.'

When he put down the phone, Mitch jumped to his feet, punched the air, shouted, 'Yes!'

•

'Dinner' was catered by a local Italian restaurant, Laura McVie not being, in her own words, 'much of a cook'. Two waiters delivered the food, served it discreetly, and took away the dirty dishes.

Mostly, Mitch and Laura made small talk in the candlelight over the pasta and wine, and it wasn't until the waiters had left and they were alone, relaxing on the sofa, each cradling a snifter of Courvoisier XO cognac, with mellow jazz playing in the background, that the conversation became more intimate.

Laura was still funereally clad, but tonight her dress, made of semi-transparent layers of black chiffon – more than enough for decency – fell well below knee height. There was still no disguising the curves, and the rustling sounds as she crossed her legs made Mitch more than a little hot under the collar.

Laura puckered her lips to light a cigarette. When she had blown the smoke out, she asked, 'Are you married?'

Mitch shook his head.

'Ever been?'

'Nope.'

'Just didn't meet the right girl, is that it?'

'Something like that.'

'You're not gay are you?'

He laughed. 'What on earth made you think that?'

She rested her free hand on his and smiled. 'Don't worry. Nothing made me think it. Nothing in particular. Just checking, that's all.'

'No,' Mitch said. 'I'm not gay.'

'More cognac?'

'Sure.' Mitch was already feeling a little tipsy, but he didn't want to spoil the mood.

She fetched the bottle and poured them each a generous measure. 'I didn't really *love* Charles, you know,' she said when she had settled down and smoothed her dress again. 'I mean, I respected him, I even liked him, I just didn't love him.'

'Why did you marry him?'

Laura shrugged. 'I don't know really. He asked me. He was rich and seemed to live an exciting life. Travel. Parties. I got to meet all kinds of celebrities. We'd only been married two years, you know. And we'd only known one another a few weeks before we got married. We hadn't even . . . you know. Anyway, I'm sorry he's dead . . . in a way.'

'What do you mean?'

Laura leaned forward and stubbed out her cigarette. Then she brushed back a long blonde tress and took another sip of cognac before answering. 'Well,' she said, 'now that he's dead, it's all mine, isn't it? I'd be a hypocrite and a fool if I said that didn't appeal to me. All this wealth and no strings attached. No responsibilities.'

'What responsibilities were there before?'

The left corner of her lips twitched in a smile. 'Oh, you know. The usual wifely kind. Charles was never, well . . . let's say he wasn't a very passionate lover. He wanted me more as a showpiece than anything else. A trophy. Something to hang on his arm that looked good. Don't get me wrong, I didn't mind. It was a small price to pay. And then we were forever having to entertain the most boring people. Business acquaintances. You know the sort of thing. Well now that Charles is gone, I won't have to do that any more, will I? I'll be able to do what I want. Exactly what I want.'

Almost without Mitch knowing it, Laura had edged nearer towards him as she was speaking, and now she was so close he could smell the warm, acrid smoke and the cognac on her breath. He found it curiously intoxicating. Soon she was close enough to kiss.

She took hold of his hand and rested it on her breast. 'It's been a week since the funeral,' she said. 'Don't you think it's time I took off my widow's weeds?'

•

When Mitch left Laura McVie's house the following morning, he was beginning to think he might be onto a good thing. Why stop at being estate executor? he asked himself. He already knew that, under the terms of the will, Laura got everything – McVie had no children or other living relatives – and *everything* was somewhere in the region of five million dollars.

Even if he didn't love her – and how could you tell if you loved someone after just one night? – he certainly felt passionately drawn to her. They got on well together, thought alike, and she was a wonderful lover. Mitch was no slouch, either. He could certainly make up for her late husband in that department.

He mustn't rush it, though. Take things easy, see what develops . . . Maybe they could go away together for a while. Somewhere warm. And then . . . well . . . five million dollars.

Such were his thoughts as he turned the corner, just before the heavy hand settled on his shoulder and a deep voice whispered in his ear, 'Detective Greg Hollins, Mr Mitchell. Homicide. I think it's about time you and I had a long talk.'

•

Relieved to be let off with little more than a warning in exchange for cooperating with the police, Mitch turned up at Laura's the next evening as arranged. This time they skipped the dinner and drinks preliminaries and headed straight for her bedroom.

Afterwards she lay with her head resting on his shoulder, smoking a cigarette.

'My God,' she said. 'I missed this when I was married to Charles.'

'Didn't you have any lovers?' Mitch asked.

'Of course I didn't.'

'Oh, come on. I won't be jealous. I promise. Tell me.'

She jerked away, stubbed out the cigarette on the bedside ashtray, and said, 'You're just like the police. Do you know that? You've got a filthy mind.'

'Hey,' said Mitch. 'It's me. Mitch. OK?'

'Still . . . They think I did it, you know.'

'Did what?'

'Killed Charles.'

'I thought you had an alibi.'

'I do, idiot. They think the burglary was just a cover. They think I hired someone to kill him.'

'Did you?'

'See what I mean? Just like the cops, with your filthy, suspicious mind.'

'What makes you think they suspect you?'

'The way they talked, the way they questioned me. I think they're watching me.'

'You're just being paranoid, Laura. You're upset. They always suspect someone in the family at first. It's routine. Most killings are family affairs. You'll see, pretty soon they'll drop it.'

'Do you really think so?'

'Sure I do. Just you wait and see.'

And moments later they were making love again.

•

Laura seemed a little distracted when she let him in the next night. At first he thought she had something on the stove, but then he remembered she didn't cook.

She was on the telephone, as it turned out. And she hung up the receiver just as he walked into the living room.

'Who was that?' he asked. 'Not reporters, I hope?'

'No,' she said, arms crossed, facing him, an unreadable expression on her face.

'Who, then?'

Laura just stood there. 'They've found the gun,' she said finally.

'They've what? Where?'

'In your garage, under an old tarpaulin.'

'I don't understand. What are you talking about? When?'

She looked at her watch. 'About now.'

'How?'

Laura shrugged. 'Anonymous tip. You'd better sit down, Mitch.'

Mitch collapsed on the sofa.

'Drink?'

'A large one.'

Laura brought him a large tumbler of Scotch and sat in the armchair opposite him.

'What's all this about?' he asked, after the whisky had warmed his insides. 'I don't understand what you're saying. How could they find the gun in my garage? I told you what happened to it.'

'I know you did,' said Laura. 'And I'm telling you where it ended up. You're really not very bright, are you, Mitch? How do *you* think it got there?'

'Someone must have put it there.'

'Right.'

'One of the muggers? But . . .?'

'What does it matter? What matters is that it will probably have your fingerprints on it. Or the wrapping will. All those greasy smudges. And even if it doesn't, how are you going to explain its presence in your garage?'

'But why would the cops think *I* killed Charles?'

'We had a relationship. We were lovers. Like I told you, I'm certain they've been watching me, and they can't fail to have noticed that you've stayed overnight on more than one occasion.'

'But that's absurd. I hadn't even met you before your husband's death.'

'Hadn't you?' She raised her eyebrows. 'Don't you remember, honey, all those times we met in secret, made love cramped in the back of your car because we didn't even dare be seen signing in under false names in the Have-a-Nap Motel or wherever? We had to keep our relationship very, very secret. Don't you remember?'

'You'd tell them that?'

'The way they'll see it is that the relationship was more important to you than to me. You became obsessed by jealousy because I was married to someone else. You couldn't stand it any more. And you thought by killing my husband you could get both me and my money. After all, you did prepare his will, didn't you? You knew all about his finances.'

Mitch shook his head.

'I *would* like to thank you, though,' Laura went on. 'Without you, we had a good plan – a very good one – but *with* you we've got a perfect one.'

'What do you mean?'

'I mean you were right when you suggested I had a lover. I do. Oh, not you, not the one I'm handing over to the police, the one who became so obsessed with me that it unhinged him and he murdered my husband. No. I've been very careful with Jake. I met him on the Yucatan peninsula when Charles and I were on holiday there six months ago and Charles went down with Montezuma's revenge. I know it sounds like a romantic cliché, but it was love at first sight. We hatched the plan very quickly and we knew we had to keep our relationship a total secret. Nobody must suspect a thing. So we never met after that vacation. There were no letters or postcards. The only contact we had was through public telephones.'

'And what happens now?'

'After a decent interval – after you've been tried and convicted of my husband's murder – Jake and I will meet and eventually get married. We'll sell up here, of course, and live abroad. Live in luxury. Oh, please don't look so crestfallen, Mitch. Believe me, I *am* sorry. I didn't know you were going to walk into my life with that irresistible little confession, now, did I? I figured I'd just ride it out, the cops' suspicions and all. I mean they might suspect me, but they couldn't prove anything. I *was* in Windsor staying with friends. They've checked. And now they've got you into the bargain . . .' She shrugged. 'Why would they bother with little old me? I just couldn't look a gift horse in the mouth. You'll make a wonderful fall guy. But because I like you, Mitch, I'm at least giving you a little advance warning, aren't I? The police will be looking for you, but you've still got time to make a break, leave town.'

'What if I go to them, tell them everything you've told me?'

'They'll think you're crazy. Which you are. Obsession does that to people. Makes them crazy.'

Mitch licked his lips. 'Look, I'd have to leave everything behind. I don't even have any cash on me. Laura, you don't think you could—'

She shook her head. 'Sorry, honey. No can do. Nothing personal.'

Mitch slumped back in the chair. 'At least tell me one more thing. The gun. I still don't understand how it came to be the one that killed your husband.'

She laughed, showing the sharp, white teeth. 'Pure coincidence. It was beautiful. Jake happens to be . . .

•

. . . a burglar by profession, and a very good one. He has worked all over the States and Canada, and he's never been caught. We thought that if I told him about the security system at the house, he could get around it cleverly and . . . Of course, he couldn't bring his own gun here from Mexico, not by air, so he had to get one. He said that's not too difficult when you move in the circles he does. The kind of bars where you can buy guns and other stolen goods are much the same anywhere, in much the same sort of neighbourhoods. And he's done jobs up here before.

'As luck would have it, he bought an old Luger off two inexperienced muggers. For a hundred bucks. I just couldn't believe it when you came around with your story. There couldn't be two old Lugers kicking around the neighbourhood at the same time, could there? I had to turn away from you and hold my sides, I was laughing so much. It made my eyes water. What unbelievable luck!'

'I'm so glad you think so,' said Mitch.

'Anyway, when I told Jake, he agreed it was too good an opportunity to miss, so he came back up here, dug the gun up from where he had buried it, safe in its wrapping, and planted it in your garage. He hadn't handled it without gloves on, and he thought the two young punks he bought it from had been too scared to touch it, so the odds were, after you told me your story, that your fingerprints would still be on it. As I said, even if they aren't . . . It's still perfect.'

Only tape hiss followed, and Detective Greg Hollins switched off the machine. 'That it?' he asked.

Mitch nodded. 'I left. I thought I'd got enough.'

'You did a good job. Jesus, you got more than enough. I was hoping she'd let something slip, but I didn't expect a full confession and her accomplice's name in the bargain.'

'Thanks. I didn't have a lot of choice, did I?'

The last two times Mitch had been to see Laura, he had been wearing a tiny but powerful voice-activated tape recorder sewn into the lining of his suit jacket. It had lain on the chair beside the bed when they made love, and he had tried to get her to admit she had a boyfriend, as Hollins had suspected. He had also been wearing it the night she told him the police were about to find the Luger in his garage.

The recorder was part of the deal. Why he got off with only a warning for not reporting the theft of an unregistered firearm.

'What'll happen to her now?' he asked Hollins.

'With any luck, both she and her boyfriend will do life,' said Hollins. 'But what do you care? After the way she treated you. She's a user. She chewed you up and spat you out.'

Mitch sighed. 'Yeah, I know . . .' he said. 'But it could have been worse, couldn't it?'

'How?'

'I could've ended up married to her.'

Hollins stared at him for a moment, then he burst out laughing. 'I'm glad you've got a sense of humour, Mitchell. You'll need it, what's coming your way next.'

Mitch shifted uneasily in his chair. 'Hey, just a minute! We made a deal. You assured me there'd be no charges over the gun.'

Hollins nodded. 'That's right. We did make a deal. And I never go back on my word.'

Mitch shook his head. 'Then I don't understand. What are you talking about?'

'Well, there's this lady from the Law Society waiting outside, Mitchell. And she'd *really* like to talk to you.'

THE TWO LADIES OF ROSE COTTAGE

In our village, they were always known as the 'Two Ladies of Rose Cottage': Miss Eunice with the white hair, and Miss Teresa with the grey. Nobody really knew where they came from, or exactly how old they were, but the consensus held that they had met in India, America or South Africa and decided to return to the homeland to live out their days together. And in 1939 they were generally believed to be in or approaching their nineties.

Imagine our surprise, then, one fine day in September, when the police car pulled up outside Rose Cottage, and when, in a matter of hours, rumours began to spread throughout the village: rumours of human bones dug up in a distant garden; rumours of mutilation and dismemberment; rumours of murder.

•

Lyndgarth is the name of our village. It is situated in one of the most remote Yorkshire Dales, about twenty miles from Eastvale, the nearest large town. The village is no more than a group of limestone houses with slate roofs clustered around a bumpy, slanted green that always reminded me of a handkerchief flapping in the breeze. We have the usual amenities – grocer's shop, butcher's, newsagent's, post office, school, a church, a chapel, three public houses – and proximity to some of the most beautiful countryside in the world.

I was fifteen in 1939, and Miss Eunice and Miss Teresa had been living in the village for twenty years, yet still they remained strangers to us. It is often said that you have to 'winter out' at least two years before being accepted into village life, and in the case of a remote place like Lyndgarth, in those days, it was more like ten.

As far as the locals were concerned, then, the two ladies had served their apprenticeship and were more than fit to be accepted as fully paid up members of the community, yet there was about them a certain detached quality that kept them ever at arm's length.

They did all their shopping in the village and were always polite to people they met in the street; they regularly attended church services at St Oswald's and helped with charity events; and they never set foot in any of the public houses. But still there was that sense of distance, of not quite being - or not *wanting* to be - a part of things.

•

The summer of 1939 had been unusually beautiful despite the political tensions. Or am I indulging in nostalgia for childhood? Our dale can be one of the most grim and desolate landscapes on the face of the earth, even in August, but I remember the summers of my youth as days of dazzling sunshine and blue skies. In 1939 every day was a new symphony of colour - golden buttercups, pink clover, mauve cranesbill - ever changing and recombining in fresh palettes. While the tense negotiations went on in Europe, while Ribbentrop and Molotov signed the Nazi-Soviet pact, and while there was talk of conscription and rationing at home, very little changed in Lyndgarth.

Summer in the dale was always a season for odd-jobs - peat-cutting, wall-mending, sheep-clipping - and for entertainments, such as the dialect plays, the circus, fairs and brass bands. Even after war was declared on 3 September, we still found ourselves rather guiltily having fun, scratching our heads, shifting from foot to foot, and wondering when something really warlike was going to happen.

Of course, we had our gas masks in their cardboard boxes,

which we had to carry everywhere; street lighting was banned, and motor cars were not allowed to use their headlights. This latter rule was the cause of numerous accidents in the dale, usually involving wandering sheep on the unfenced roads.

Some evacuees also arrived from the cities. Uncouth urchins for the most part, often verminous and ill-equipped for country life, they seemed like an alien race to us. Most of them didn't seem to have any warm clothing or Wellington boots, as if they had never seen mud in the city. Looking back, I realize they were far from home, separated from their parents, and they must have been scared to death. I am ashamed to admit, though, that at the time I didn't go out of my way to give them a warm welcome.

This is partly because I was always lost in my own world. I was a bookish child and had recently discovered the stories of Thomas Hardy, who seemed to understand and sympathize with a lonely village lad and his dreams of becoming a writer. I also remember how much he thrilled and scared me with some of the stories. After 'The Withered Arm' I wouldn't let anyone touch me for a week, and I didn't dare go to sleep after 'Barbara of the House of Grebe' for fear that there was a horribly disfigured statue in the wardrobe, that the door would slowly creak open and . . .

I think I was reading *Far from the Madding Crowd* that hot July day, and, as was my wont, I read as I walked across the village green, not looking where I was going. It was Miss Teresa I bumped into, and I remember thinking that she seemed remarkably resilient for such an old lady.

'Do mind where you're going, young man!' she admonished me, though when she heard my effusive apologies, she softened her tone somewhat. She asked me what I was reading, and when I showed her the book, she closed her eyes for a moment and a strange expression crossed her wrinkled features.

'Ah, Mr Hardy,' she said, after a short silence. 'I knew him once, you know, in his youth. I grew up in Dorset.'

I could hardly hold back my enthusiasm. Someone actually *knew* Hardy! I told her that he was my favourite writer of all time, even better than Shakespeare, and that when I grew up I wanted to be a writer, just like him.

Miss Teresa smiled indulgently. 'Do calm down,' she said, then she paused. 'I suppose,' she continued, with a glance towards Miss Eunice. 'that if you are really interested in Mr Hardy, perhaps you might like to come to tea some day?'

When I assured her I would be delighted, we made an arrangement that I was to call at Rose Cottage the following Tuesday at four o'clock, after securing my mother's permission, of course.

•

That Tuesday visit was the first of many. Inside, Rose Cottage belied its name. It seemed dark and gloomy, unlike ours, which was always full of sunlight and bright flowers. The furnishings were antique, even a little shabby. I recollect no family photographs of the kind that embellished most mantelpieces, but there was a huge gilt-framed painting of a young girl working alone in a field hanging on one wall. If the place sometimes smelled a little musty and neglected, the aroma of Miss Teresa's fresh-baked scones more often than not made up for it.

'Mr Hardy was full of contradictions,' Miss Teresa told me on one occasion. 'He was a dreamer, of course, and never happier than when wandering the countryside alone with his thoughts. But he was also a fine musician. He played the fiddle on many social occasions, such as dances and weddings, and he was often far more gregarious and cheerful than many of his critics would have imagined. He was also a scholar, head forever buried in a book, always studying Latin or Greek. I was no dullard, either, you know, and I like to think I held my own in our conversations, though I had little Latin and less Greek.' She chuckled, then turned serious again. 'Anyway, one never felt one really *knew* him. One was always looking at a mask. Do you understand me, young man?'

I nodded. 'I think so, Miss Teresa.'

'Yes, well,' she said, staring into space as she sometimes did while speaking of Hardy. 'At least that was *my* impression. Though he was a good ten years older than me, I like to believe I got glimpses of the man behind the mask. But because the other villagers thought him a bit odd, and because he was difficult to know, he also attracted a lot of idle gossip. I remember there was talk about him and that Sparks girl from Puddletown. What was her first name, Eunice?'

'Tryphena.'

'That's right.' She curled her lip and seemed to spit out the name. 'Tryphena Sparks. A singularly dull girl, I always thought. We were about the same age, you know, she and I. Anyway, there was talk of a child. Utter rubbish, of course.' She gazed out of the window at the green, where a group of children were playing a makeshift game of cricket. Her eyes seemed to film over. 'Many's the time I used to walk through the woodland past the house, and I would see him sitting there at his upstairs window seat, writing or gazing out on the garden. Sometimes he would wave and come down to talk.' Suddenly she stopped, then her eyes glittered, and she went on, 'He used to go and watch hangings in Dorchester. Did you know that?'

I had to confess that I didn't, my acquaintance with Hardy being recent and restricted only to his published works of fiction, but it never occurred to me to doubt Miss Teresa's word.

'Of course, executions were public back then.' Again she paused, and I thought I saw, or rather *sensed* a little shiver run through her. Then she said that was enough for today, that it was time for scones and tea.

I think she enjoyed shocking me like that at the end of her little narratives, as if we needed to be brought back to reality with a jolt. I remember on another occasion she looked me in the eye and said, 'Of course, the doctor tossed him aside as dead at birth, you know. If it hadn't been for the nurse he would never have survived. That must do something to a man, don't you think?'

We talked of many other aspects of Hardy and his work, and, for the most part, Miss Eunice remained silent, nodding from time to time. Occasionally, when Miss Teresa's memory seemed to fail her on some point, such as a name or what novel Hardy might have been writing in a certain year, she would supply the information.

I remember one visit particularly vividly. Miss Teresa stood up rather more quickly than I thought her able to, and left the room for a few moments. I sat politely, sipping my tea, aware of Miss Eunice's silence and the ticking of the grandfather clock out in the hall. When Miss Teresa returned, she was carrying an old book, or rather two books, which she handed to me.

It was a two-volume edition of *Far from the Madding Crowd*, and, though I didn't know it at the time, it was the first edition, from 1874, and was probably worth a small fortune. But what fascinated me even more than Helen Paterson's illustrations was the brief inscription on the flyleaf: *To Tess, With Affection*, Tom.

I knew that Tess was the diminutive of Teresa because I had an Aunt Teresa in Harrogate, and it never occurred to me to question that the 'Tess' in the inscription was the person sitting opposite me, or that the 'Tom' was none other than Thomas Hardy himself.

'He called you Tess,' I remember saying. 'Perhaps he had you in mind when he wrote *Tess of the d'Urbervilles*?'

Miss Teresa's face drained of colour so quickly I feared for her life, and it seemed that a palpable chill entered the room. 'Don't be absurd, boy,' she whispered. 'Tess Durbeyfield was hanged for murder.'

•

We had been officially at war for about a week, I think, when the police called. There were three men, one in uniform and two in plain clothes. They spent almost two hours in Rose Cottage, then came out alone, got in their car and drove away. We never saw them again.

The day after the visit, though, I happened to overhear our local constable talking with the vicar in St Oswald's churchyard.

By a great stroke of fortune, several yews stood between us and I was able to remain unseen while I took in every word.

'Murdered, that's what they say,' said PC Walker. 'Bashed his 'ead in with a poker, then chopped 'im up in little pieces and buried 'em in t'garden. Near Dorchester, it were. Village called 'igher Bockhampton. People who lived there were digging an air-raid shelter when they found t'bones. 'Eck of a shock for t'bairns.'

Could they possibly mean Miss Teresa? That sweet old lady who made such delightful scones and had known the young Thomas Hardy? Could she really have bashed someone on the head, chopped him up into little pieces and buried them in the garden? I shivered at the thought, despite the heat.

But nothing more was heard of the murder charge. The police never returned, people found new things to talk about, and after a couple of weeks Miss Eunice and Miss Teresa reappeared in village life much as they had been before. The only difference was that my mother would no longer allow me to visit Rose Cottage. I put up token resistance, but by then my mind was full of Spitfires, secret codes and aircraft carriers anyway.

Events seemed to move quickly in the days after the police visit, though I cannot be certain of the actual time period involved. Four things, however, conspired to put the murder out of my mind for some time: Miss Teresa died, I think in the November of that same year; Miss Eunice retreated into an even deeper silence than before; the war escalated; and I was called up to military service.

•

The next time I gave any thought to the two ladies of Rose Cottage was in Egypt, of all places, in September 1942. I was on night watch with the Eighth Army, not far from Alamein. Desert nights have an eerie beauty I have never found anywhere else since. After the heat of the day, the cold surprises one, for a start, as does the sense of endless space, but even more surprising is the desertscape of wrecked tanks, jeeps and lorries in the cold moonlight, metal wrenched and twisted into impossible patterns like some petrified forest or exposed coral reef.

To spoil our sleep and shatter our nerves, Rommel's Afrika Korps had got into the routine of setting up huge amplified speakers and blaring out 'Lili Marlene' over and over all night long. It was on a night such as this, while I was trying to stay warm and awake and trying to shut my ears to the music, that I struck up a conversation with a soldier called Sidney Ferris from one of the Dorset regiments.

When Sid told me he had grown up in Piddlehinton, I suddenly thought of the two ladies of Rose Cottage.

'Did you ever hear any stories of a murder around there?' I asked, offering Sid a cigarette. 'A place called Higher Bockhampton?'

'Lots of murder stories going around when I was a lad,' he said, lighting up, careful to hide the flame with his cupped hand. 'Better than the wireless.'

'This would be a wife murdering her husband.'

He nodded. 'Plenty of that and all. And husbands murdering their wives. Makes you wonder whether it's worth getting married, doesn't it? Higher Bockhampton, you say?'

'Yes. Teresa Morgan, I believe the woman's name was.'

He frowned. 'Name don't ring no bell,' he said, 'but I do recall a tale about some woman who was supposed to have killed her husband, cut him up in pieces and buried them in the garden. A couple of young lads found some bones when they was digging an air-raid shelter a few years back. Animal bones, if you ask me.'

'But did the villagers believe the tale?'

He shrugged. 'Don't know about anyone else, but I can't say as I did. So many stories like that going around, they can't all be true, or damn near all of us would be murderers or corpses. Stands to reason, doesn't it?' And he took a long drag on his cigarette, holding it in his cupped hand, like most soldiers, so the enemy wouldn't see the pinpoint of light.

'Did anyone say what became of the woman?' I asked.

'She went away some years later. There was talk of someone else seen running away from the farmhouse, too, the night they said the murder must have taken place.'

'Could it have been him? The husband?'

Sid shook his head. 'Too slight a figure. Her husband was a big man, apparently. Anyway, that led to more talk of an illicit lover. There's always a lover, isn't there? Have you noticed? You know what kind of minds these country gossips have.'

'Did anyone say who the other person might have been?'

'Nobody knew. Just rumours of a vague shape seen running away. These are old wives' tales we're talking about.'

'But perhaps there's some tru—'

But at that point I was relieved of my watch, and the next weeks turned out to be so chaotic that I never even saw Sid again. I heard later that he was killed at the Battle of Alamein just over a month after our conversation.

•

I didn't come across the mystery of Rose Cottage again until the early 1950s. At that time I was living in Eastvale, in a small flat overlooking the cobbled market square. The town was much smaller and quieter than it is today, though little about the square has changed, from the ancient market cross, the Queen's Arms on the corner, the Norman church and the Tudor-fronted police station.

I had recently published my first novel and was still basking in that exquisite sensation that comes only once in a writer's career: the day he holds the first bound and printed copy of his very first work. Of course, there was no money in writing, so I worked part-time in a bookshop on North Market Street, and on one of my mornings off, a market day as I remember, I was absorbed in polishing the third chapter of what was to be my second novel when I heard a faint tap at my door. This was enough to startle me, as I rarely had any visitors.

Puzzled and curious, I left my typewriter and went to open the door. There stood a wizened old lady, hunch-shouldered, white-haired, carrying a stick with a brass lion's head handle and a small package wrapped in brown paper, tied with string.

She must have noticed my confused expression because, with a faint smile, she said, 'Don't you recognize me, Mr Riley? Dear, dear, have I aged that much?'

Then I knew her, knew the voice.

'Miss Eunice!' I cried, throwing my door open. 'Please forgive me. I was lost in my own world. Do come in. And you must call me Christopher.'

Once we were settled, with a pot of tea mashing beside us – though, alas, none of Miss Teresa's scones – I noticed the dark circles under Miss Eunice's eyes, the yellow around the pupils, the parchment-like quality of her skin, and I knew she was seriously ill.

'How did you find me?' I asked.

'It didn't take a Sherlock Holmes. Everyone knows where the famous writer lives in a small town like Eastvale.'

'Hardly famous,' I demurred. 'But thank you anyway. I never knew you took the trouble to follow my fortunes.'

'Teresa would have wished it. She was very fond of you, you know. Apart from ourselves and the police, you were the only person in Lyndgarth who ever entered Rose Cottage. Did you know that? You might remember that we kept ourselves very much to ourselves.'

'Yes, I remember that,' I told her.

'I came to give you this.'

She handed me the package and I untied it carefully. Inside was the Smith, Elder & Co first edition of *Far from the Madding Crowd*, complete with Hardy's inscription to 'Tess'.

'But you shouldn't,' I said. 'This must be very valuable. It's a fir—'

She waved aside my objections. 'Please take it. It is what Teresa would have wished. And I wish it, too. Now listen,' she went on. 'That isn't the only reason I came. I have something very important to tell you, to do with why the police came to visit all those years ago. The thought of going to my grave without telling someone troubles me deeply.'

'But why me? And why now?'

'I told you. Teresa was especially fond of you. And you're a writer,' she added mysteriously. 'You'll understand. Should you wish to make use of the story, please do so. Neither Teresa nor I have any living relatives to offend. All I ask is that you wait a suitable number of years after my death before publishing any account. And that death is expected to occur at some point over the next few months. Does that answer your second question?'

I nodded. 'Yes. I'm sorry.'

'You needn't be. As you may well be aware, I have long since exceeded my three score and ten, though I can hardly say the extra years have been a blessing. But that is God's will. Do you agree to my terms?'

'Of course. I take it this is about the alleged murder?'

Miss Eunice raised her eyebrows. 'So you've heard the rumours?' she said. 'Well, there was a murder all right. Teresa Morgan murdered her husband, Jacob, and buried his body in the garden.' She held out her teacup and I poured. I noticed her hand was shaking slightly. Mine was, too. The shouts of the market vendors came in through my open windows.

'When did she do this?' was all I could manage.

Miss Eunice closed her eyes and pursed her cracked lips. 'I don't remember the exact year,' she said. 'But it really doesn't matter. You could look it up, if you wanted. It was the year the Queen was proclaimed Empress of India.'

I happened to know that was in 1877. I have always had a good memory for historical dates. If my calculations were correct, Miss Teresa would have been about twenty-seven at the time. 'Will you tell me what happened?' I asked.

'That's why I'm here,' Miss Eunice said rather sharply. 'Teresa's husband was a brute, a bully and a drunkard. She wouldn't have married him, had *she* had any choice in the matter. But her parents approved the match. He had his own small farm, you see, and they were only tenants. Teresa was a very intelligent girl, but that counted for nothing in those days. In fact, it was a positive disadvantage. As was her wilfulness. Anyway, he used to beat her to within an inch of her life – where the bruises wouldn't show, of course. One day she'd had enough of it, so she killed him.'

'What did she do?'

'She hit him with the poker from the fireplace and, after darkness had fallen, she buried him deep in the garden. She was afraid that if the matter went to court the authorities wouldn't believe her and she would be hanged. She had no evidence, you see. And Jacob was a popular man among the other fellows of the village, as is so often the case with drunken brutes. And Teresa was terrified of being publicly hanged.'

'But did no one suspect her?'

Miss Eunice shook her head. 'Jacob was constantly talking about leaving his wife and heading for the New World. He used to berate her for not bearing him any children – specifically sons – and threatened that one day she would wake up and he would be gone. Gone to another country to find a woman who could give him the children he wanted. He repeated these threats in the ale house so often that no one in the entire county of Dorset could fail to know about them.'

'So when he disappeared, everyone assumed he had followed through on his threats to leave her?'

'Exactly. Oh, there were rumours that his wife had murdered him, of course. There always are when such mysteries occur.'

Yes, I thought, remembering my conversation with Sid Ferris one cold desert night ten years ago: rumours and fancies, the stuff of fiction. And something about a third person seen fleeing from the scene. Well, that could wait.

'Teresa stayed on at the farm for another ten years,' Miss Eunice went on. 'Then she sold up and went to America. It was a brave move, but Teresa no more lacked for courage than she did for beauty. She was in her late thirties then, and even after a hard life, she could still turn heads. In New York, she landed on her feet and eventually married a financier. Sam Cotter. A good man. She also took a companion.'

'You?' I asked.

Miss Eunice nodded. 'Yes. Some years later Sam died of a stroke. We stayed on in New York for a while, but we grew increasingly homesick. We came back finally in 1919, just after the Great War. For obvious reasons, Teresa didn't want to live anywhere near Dorset, so we settled in Yorkshire.'

'A remarkable tale,' I said.

'But that's not all,' Miss Eunice went on, pausing only to sip some tea. 'There was a child.'

'I thought you said—'

She took one hand off her stick and held it up, palm out. 'Christopher, please let me tell the story in my own way. Then it will be yours to do with as you wish. You have no idea how difficult this is for me.' She paused and stared down at the brass lion's head for so long I feared she had fallen asleep, or died. Outside in the market square a butcher was loudly trying to sell a leg of mutton. Just as I was about to go over to Miss Eunice, she stirred. 'There was a child,' she repeated. 'When Teresa was fifteen, she gave birth to a child. It was a difficult birth. She was never able to bear any other children.'

'What happened to this child?'

'Teresa had a sister called Alice, living in Dorchester. Alice was five years older and already married with two children. Just before the pregnancy started to show, both Teresa and Alice went to stay with relatives in Cornwall for a few months, after it had been falsely announced that Alice was with child again. You would be surprised how often such things happened. When they came back, Alice had a fine baby girl.'

'Who was the father?'

'Teresa would never say. The one thing she did make clear was that no one had forced unwanted attentions on her, that the child was the result of a love match, an infatuation. It certainly wasn't Jacob Morgan.'

'Did she ever see the child again?'

'Oh, certainly. What could be more natural than visiting one's sister and seeing one's niece grow up? When the girl was a little older, she began to pay visits to the farm, too.' Miss Eunice stopped here and frowned so hard I thought her brow would crack like dry paper. 'That was when the problems began,' she said quietly.

'What problems?'

Miss Eunice put her stick aside and held out her teacup. I refilled it. Her hands steady now, she held the cup against her scrawny chest as if its heat were the only thing keeping her alive. 'This is the most difficult part,' she said in a faint voice. 'The part I didn't know whether I could ever tell anyone.'

'If you don't wish—'

She waved my objection aside. 'It's all right, Christopher, I didn't know how much I could tell you before I came here, but I know now. I've come this far. I can't go back now. Just give me a few moments to collect myself.'

Outside, the market was in full swing and during the ensuing silence I could hear the clamour of voices selling and buying, arguing over prices.

'Did I ever tell you that Teresa was an extremely beautiful young girl?' Miss Eunice asked after a while.

'I believe you mentioned it, yes.'

She nodded. 'Well, she was. And so was her daughter. When she began coming by herself to the house, she was about twelve or thirteen years of age. Jacob didn't fail to notice her, how well she was "filling out" as he used to say. One day Teresa had gone into the village for firewood and the child arrived in her absence. Jacob, just home from the ale house, was there alone to greet her. Need I say more, Mr Riley?'

I shook my head. 'I don't mean to excuse him in any way, but I'm assuming he didn't know the girl was his stepdaughter?'

'That is correct. He never knew. Nor did *she* know Teresa was her mother. Not until much later.'

'What happened next?'

'Teresa came in before her husband could have his way with the struggling, half-naked child. Everything else was as I said. She picked up the poker and hit him on the head. Not once, but six times. Then they cleaned up and waited until after dark and buried him deep in the garden. She sent her daughter back to her sister's and carried on as if her husband had simply left her, just as he had threatened to do.'

So the daughter was the mysterious third person seen leaving the farm in Sid Ferris's account. 'What became of the poor child?' I asked.

Miss Eunice paused again and seemed to struggle for breath. She turned terribly pale. I got up and moved towards her, but she stretched out her hand. 'No, no. I'm all right, Christopher. Please sit.'

A motor car honked outside and one of the street vendors yelled a curse. Miss Eunice patted her chest. 'That's better. I'm fine now, really I am. Just a minor spasm. But I do feel ashamed. I'm afraid I haven't been entirely truthful with you. It's so difficult. You see, I was, I *am*, that child.'

For a moment my mouth just seemed to flap open and shut and I couldn't speak. Finally, I managed to stammer, 'You? *You* are Miss Teresa's daughter? But you can't be. That's not possible.'

'I didn't mean to shock you,' she went on softly, 'but, really, you only have yourself to blame. When people see two old ladies together, all they see is two old ladies. When you first began calling on us at Rose Cottage fifteen years ago, Teresa was ninety and I was seventy-six. I doubt a fifteen-year-old boy could tell the difference. Nor could most people. And Teresa was always remarkably robust and well preserved.'

When I had regained my composure, I asked her to continue.

'There is very little left to say. I helped my mother kill Jacob Morgan and bury him. And we didn't cut him up into little pieces. That part is pure fiction invented by scurrilous gossip-mongers. My foster parents died within a short time of one another, around the turn of the century, and Teresa wired me the money to come and live with her in New York. I had never married, so I had no ties to break. I think that experience with Jacob Morgan, brief and inconclusive as it was, must have given me a lifelong aversion to marital relations. Anyway, it was in New York that Teresa told me she was really my mother. She couldn't tell Sam, of course, so I remained there as her companion, and we always lived more as friends than as mother and daughter.' She smiled. 'When we came back to England, we chose to live as two spinsters, the kind of relationship nobody really questions in a village because it would be in bad taste to do so.'

'How did the police find you after so long?'

'We never hid our identities. Nor did we hide our whereabouts. We bought Rose Cottage through a local solicitor before we returned from America, so it was listed as our address on the all the official papers we filled in.' She shrugged. 'The police soon recognized that Teresa was far too frail to question, let alone put on trial, so they let the matter drop. And to be quite honest, they didn't really have enough evidence, you know. You didn't know it – and Teresa would never have told you – but she already knew she was dying before the police came. Just as I know I am dying now.'

'And did she really die without telling you who your father was?'

Miss Eunice nodded. 'I wasn't lying about that. But I always had my suspicions.' Her eyes sparkled for a moment, the way a fizzy drink does when you pour it. 'You know, Teresa was always unreasonably jealous of that Tryphena Sparks, and Mr Hardy did have an eye for the young girls.'

•

Forty years have passed since Miss Eunice's death, and I have lived in many towns and villages in many countries of the world. Though I have often thought of the tale she told me, I have never been moved to commit it to paper until today.

Two weeks ago, I moved back to Lyndgarth, and as I was unpacking I came across that first edition of *Far from the Madding Crowd*. 1874: the year Hardy married Emma Gifford. As I puzzled again over the inscription, words suddenly began to form themselves effortlessly in front of my eyes, and all I had to do was copy them down.

Now that I have finished, I suddenly feel very tired. It is a hot day, and the heat haze has muted the greens, greys and browns of the steep hillsides. Looking out of my window, I can see the tourists lounging on the village green. The young men are stripped to the waist, some bearing tattoos of butterflies and angels across their shoulder blades; the girls sit with them in shorts and T-shirts, laughing, eating sandwiches, drinking from pop or beer bottles.

One young girl notices me watching and waves cheekily, probably thinking I'm an old pervert, and as I wave back I think of another writer – a far, far greater writer than I could ever be – sitting at his window seat writing. He looks out of the window and sees the beautiful young girl passing through the woods at the bottom of the garden. He waves. She waves back. And she lingers, picking wild flowers, as he puts aside his novel and walks out into the warm summer air to meet her.

LAWN SALE

When Frank walked through to the kitchen, glass crunched under his feet, and he sent knives, forks and spoons skittering across the linoleum. He turned on the light. Someone had broken in while he had been at the Legion. They had cut the wire screen and smashed the glass in the kitchen door. They must have emptied the drawers looking for silverware because the cutlery was all over the place.

Someone had also been in the front room. Whoever it was had knocked or pushed over the tailor's dummy and the little table beside his armchair where he kept his reading glasses, book and coffee mug.

Suddenly afraid in case they were still in the house, Frank climbed on a stool to reach the high cupboard above the sink. There, at the back, where nobody would look beyond Joan's unused baking dishes, cake tins and cookie cutters shaped like hearts and lions, lay his old service revolver wrapped in an oily cloth. He had smuggled it back from the war and kept it all these years. Kept it loaded, too.

With the gun in his hand, he felt safer as he checked the rest of the house. Slowly, with all the lights on, he climbed the stairs. They had broken the padlock on Joan's room. Heart thumping, he turned on the light. When he saw the mess, he slumped against the wall.

They had emptied out all her dresser drawers, scattering underwear and trinkets all over the shiny pink coverlet on the bed. And it looked as if someone had swept off the lotions and perfumes from the dressing table right onto the floor. One of the caps must have come loose because he could smell Joan's sharp, musky perfume.

The lacquered jewellery case, the one he had bought her in New York with the ballet dancer that spun to the 'Dance of the Sugar-Plum Fairy' when you opened it, lay silent and empty on the bed. Frank sat down, gun hanging between his legs. They'd taken all Joan's jewellery. Why? The stuff obviously wasn't valuable. Just trinkets, really. None of it could possibly be worth anything to them. They had even taken her wedding ring.

Frank remembered the day he bought it all those years ago: the fairground across the street from the small jeweller's; the air filled with the smells of candyfloss and fried onions and the sounds of children laughing and squealing with delight. A little girl in a white frock with pink smocking had smiled at him as she passed by, one arm hugging a huge teddy bear and the other hand holding her mother's. How light his heart had been. Inside, the ring was inscribed, 'FRANK AND JOAN. 21 JULY 1946. NO GREATER LOVE.' The bastards. It could mean nothing to them.

Listlessly, he checked his own room. Drawers pulled out, socks and underwear scattered on the bedclothes. Nothing worth stealing except the spare change he kept on his bedside table. Sure enough, it was gone, the $3.37 he had piled neatly into columns of quarters, dimes, nickels and pennies last night.

They didn't seem to have got far in the spare room, where he kept his war mementos. Maybe they got disturbed, scared by a sound, before they could open the lock on the cabinet. Anyway, everything was intact: his medals; the antique silver cigarette lighter that had never let him down; the bayonet; the Nazi armband; the tattered edition of Mein Kampf; the German dagger with the mother-of-pearl swastika inlaid in its handle.

Frank went downstairs and considered what to do. He knew he should put the gun back in its hiding place and call the police. But that would mean intrusion, questions. He valued his privacy and he knew that the neighbours thought he was a bit of an oddball.

What would the police think of him, a man who kept the torso of a tailor's dummy in his living-room, along with yards of moth-eaten material and tissue-paper patterns? What if they found his gun?

No, he couldn't call the police; he couldn't have them trampling all over his house. They never caught burglars, anyway; everyone knew that. Weary, and still a little frightened, Frank nailed a piece of plywood over the broken glass, then carried his gun upstairs with him to bed.

•

The following morning was one of those light, airy days of early June, the kind that brings the whole city to the Beaches. The sky was robin's-egg blue, the sun shone like a pale yolk, and a light breeze blew off the lake to keep the temperature comfortable. In the gardens, apple and cherry blossom clung to the trees and the tulips were still in full bloom. It was a day for sprinklers, swimsuits, barbecues, bicycle rides, volleyball and lawn sales.

Normally, Frank would have gone down to the boardwalk, about the only exercise he got these days. Today, however, a change had come over him; a shadow had crept into his life and chilled him to the bone, despite the fine weather. He felt a deep lassitude and malaise. So much so that he delayed getting out of bed.

Maybe it was the dream made him feel that way. Though perhaps it wasn't right to call it a dream when it was so close to something that had really happened. It recurred every few months, and he had come to accept it now, much as one accepts the chronic pain of an old wound, as a kind of cross to bear.

Separated from his unit once in rural France during the Second World War, he had dragged himself out of a muddy stream, cigarettes tied up safely in army-issue condoms to keep them dry, and entered a forest. A few yards in, he had come face to face with a young German soldier, who looked as if he had also probably lost his comrades. They stared open-mouthed at each other for the split second before Frank, operating purely on survival instinct, aimed his revolver first and fired. The boy simply looked surprised and disappointed at the red patch that spread over his chest, then his face emptied of all expression for ever. Light-headed and numb, Frank moved on, looking for his unit.

It wasn't the first German he had killed, but it was the first he had looked in the eye. The incident haunted him all the way back to his unit, but a few hours later he had convinced himself that he had done the right thing and put it behind him.

After the war the memory surfaced from time to time in dreams. Details changed, of course. Each time the soldier had a different face, for example. Once, Frank even reached forward and put his finger into the bullet hole. The soft, warm flesh felt like half-set jelly. He was sure he had never touched it in real life.

Another time, the boy spoke to him. He spoke in English and Frank couldn't remember what he said, though he was sure it was a poem, and the words 'I knew you in this dark' stuck in his mind. But Frank knew nothing of poetry.

This time the bullet had gone straight through, leaving a clean circle the size of a ring, and Frank had seen a winter landscape, all flat white and grey, through the hole.

He still had the gun he had used that day. It was the same one he had got down from the high cupboard last night when he thought the burglars might still be in the house. It was the one he felt for now under the pillow beside him.

•

Had he got up that day? He couldn't remember. He sat propped against pillows on his bed that night watching television as usual. He felt agitated, and whatever the figures on the screen were doing or saying didn't register. For some reason, he couldn't get the wedding ring out of his mind, the senselessness of its theft and the unimaginable value it had for him. He hadn't realized it fully until the ring was gone.

Then he thought he heard some noise outside. He turned the

sound off with the remote and listened. Sure enough, he could hear voices. Beyond his back garden was a narrow alleyway, then came the backs of the stores and low-rise apartment buildings on Queen Street. Sometimes in this warm weather, when everyone had their windows open, you could hear arguments, television programmes and loud music. These were real voices, Frank could tell. Television voices sounded different. There were two of them, a woman's and a man's, hers getting louder.

'No, Daryl, it won't do!' he heard the woman shout. 'Haven't I told you before it's wrong to steal? Haven't I brought you up to respect other people's property? Haven't I?'

Frank couldn't hear the muffled answer, no matter how much he strained. He dragged himself up from the bed and went to the window.

'So if Marvin Johnson stuck his finger in a fire, you'd do that as well, would you? Christ, give me a break. How stupid can you get?'

Another inaudible reply.

'Right. So how do you think *they* feel, eh? The people whose house you broke into. Come on. What did you do with it?'

Frank couldn't hear the reply, though he held his breath.

'Don't lie to me. What do think this is? It's a gold chain, isn't it? And what about these? Don't tell me you've suddenly started wearing earrings? I found these hidden in your room. You stole them, didn't you?'

Frank's heart knocked against his ribs. Joan had a gold chain and earrings, and they were among the items that had been stolen. But what about the ring? The ring?

'Shut up!' the woman yelled. 'I don't want to hear it. I want you to put together everything you stole and take it back, or so help me I'll call the police. I don't care if you are my son. Do you understand me?'

There came another inaudible reply followed by a sharp smack, then the sound of a door slamming. After that Frank heard a sound he didn't recognize at first. A cat in the garden, maybe? Then he realized it was the woman crying.

About five of the apartments in the building had lights on at the back, and Frank hadn't been able to tell from which one the argument came. Now, though, he could see the silhouette of the woman with her head bowed and her hands held to her face. He thought he knew who she was. He had seen both her and her son on the street.

•

Frank sat in the coffee shop across from the apartment building early the next morning and watched people come and go. The building was one of those old places with a heavy wood and glass door, so warped by heat and time that it wouldn't shut properly. He knew who he was looking for, all right. It was that peroxide blonde, the one who looked like a hooker.

At about eight-thirty, her son, the thief, came out. He had a spotty face, especially around the nose and mouth, and he obviously had a skinhead haircut, or a completely shaved head, under the baseball hat he wore the wrong way around. He also wore a shiny silver jacket with a stylized black eagle on the back under some red writing. Below his baggy trousers, crotch right down to the knees, the laces of his sneakers trailed loose. At the corner, he hooked up with a couple of similarly dressed kids and they shuffled off, shoving each other, spitting and generally glaring down at the sidewalk as they went.

At about ten o'clock Frank had to move to the next coffee shop, a bit more up market, as he kept getting nasty looks from the owner. He ordered a cappuccino and a doughnut and sat by the window, watching.

At about a quarter to eleven, *she* came out, the boy's mother. She struggled with a shop cart of laundry through the front door and set off down the street.

Old though he was, Frank could still appreciate a good figure when he saw one. She wore a white tube-top, tight over her heavy breasts, revealing a flat tummy, and even tighter white shorts cut sharp and high over long, tanned thighs. But she wore too much make-up and he could see the dark roots in her hair. Common as muck, Joan would have said, in the Lancashire accent that had never left her, no matter how long she'd been here. A real tart, a piece of white trash. No wonder her kid was a burglar, a ring thief, a robber of memories, defiler of all things decent and wholesome.

Frank watched her totter down the street on her ridiculous high heels and go into the laundromat. It took about half an hour for the wash cycle and about as long again to get things dry. That gave Frank an hour. He paid his bill, crossed the street and entered the apartment building.

•

He hadn't really formed a plan, even during the hours he had spent watching the building that morning. He knew from last night that the apartment was on the third floor at the back, right in the centre, which made it easy to find. The corridor smelled of soiled diapers and Pine-Sol. When he stood outside the door, he listened for a while. All he could hear was a baby crying on the next floor up and the bass boom of a stereo deep in the basement.

Frank had never broken the law in his life, and he was intelligent enough to recognize the irony of what he was about to do. But he was going to do it anyway because the absence of the ring was beginning to make his life hell. Nothing else really mattered.

For three days he had waited for the boy to return Joan's jewellery, as his mother had told him to do. Three days of nail-biting memories: dreaming about the German soldier he had killed again; reliving Joan's long illness and death; watching again, as if it were yesterday, the woman he had loved and lived with for nearly fifty years waste away in agony in front of his eyes. So thin did she become that one day the ring simply slipped off her finger onto the shiny pink quilt.

And now that he was on the brink of remembering the final horror, her death, the ring had assumed the potency of a talisman.

He must have it back to keep his sanity, to keep the last memories at bay.

He had watched people on television open doors with credit cards, so he took out his seniors' discount card and tried to push it between the door and the lock. It wouldn't fit. He could get it part of the way in, then something blocked it; he waggled it back and forth, but still nothing happened. He cursed. This didn't happen on television. What was he going to do now? It looked as if he was destined to fail. He rested his head against the wood and tried to think.

'What the hell do you think you're doing?'

His heart jumped and he turned as quickly as he could.

'I said what do you think you're doing?'

It was her, the slut, standing there with her hands on her hips. It was disgusting, that bare midriff. He could see her belly button. He looked away.

'No, please.' He found his voice. 'Don't. I won't harm you.'

She laughed. 'You harm me!' she said. 'That's a laugh. Now go on, get out of here before I really *do* call the police. *Old* man.'

Frank had to admit she certainly didn't look scared. 'No, you don't understand,' he said. There was nothing for it now but to trust her. 'The robbery. I overheard. You see, it was *my* house your son broke into.'

She stared at him for a moment, her expression slowly softening, turning sad. She was quite pretty, really; he thought. She had a nice mouth, though her eyes looked a bit hard.

'You'd better come in, hadn't you?' she said, pushing past him and opening the door. 'I came back for more quarters. Just as well I did, isn't it, or who knows what might have happened?' She had a husky voice, probably from smoking too much.

The room was sparsely furnished, mostly from the Salvation Army or Goodwill, by the looks of it, but it was clean and the only unpleasant smell Frank noticed was stale tobacco. The woman pulled a packet of Rothmans from her bag, sat down on the wing of an armchair and lit up. She blew out a plume of smoke, crossed her legs and looked at Frank. 'Sit down, it'll hold your weight,' she said, nodding towards the threadbare armchair opposite her. He sat. 'Now what do you want? Is it money?'

'I just want what's mine,' Frank said. 'Your son stole my wife's jewellery. It's very important to me, especially the wedding ring. I'd like it back.'

She frowned. 'Wedding ring? There wasn't no wedding ring.'

'What?'

'I told you. There wasn't no wedding ring.' Sighing, she got up and went into another room. She came back with a handful of jewellery. 'That's all I found.'

Frank looked through it. The only pieces he recognized were the gold chain and the pair of cheap earrings. The rest, he supposed, must have been stolen from another house. 'I don't understand,' he said. 'What happened to the ring?'

'How should I know?' she stubbed her half-smoked cigarette out viciously. 'Maybe he sold it already, or threw it away. Look, I gotta go before someone steals the laundry. That's *all* need.'

He grabbed her arm. 'No, wait. Can I talk to him? Maybe he'll tell me. I have to find that ring. I'm sorry . . . I . . .' He let her go, and before he knew it, he was crying.

She rubbed her arm. 'Oh, come on,' she said. 'There's no need for that. Shit. Listen, Daryl's a bit non-communicative these days. It's his age, just a phase he's going through. You know what teenagers are like. Basically, he's a good kid, it's just . . . well, with his father gone . . . Look, I'll talk to him again, OK? I promise. But I don't want you coming round here bothering us no more, you understand? I know he's done wrong, and he'll pay for it. Just leave it to me, huh? Take the chain and the earrings for now. For Christ's sake, take it all.'

'I only want the ring,' Frank said. 'He can keep the rest.'

'I told you, I'll talk to him. I'll ask him about it. OK? Here.'

Frank looked up to see her thrusting a handful of tissues towards him at arm's length. Her eyes had softened a little but still remained wary. He took the tissues and rubbed his face. 'I'm sorry,' he said. 'It's been such an ordeal. My wife died three years ago. Cancer. I keep a few of her things, for memories, you understand, and the ring's very important. I know it's sentimental of me, but we were happy all those years. I don't know how I've survived without her.'

'Yeah, tell me about it,' she said. 'Ain't life a bitch. Look, I'm sorry, mister, really I am. But please, don't go to the police, OK? That's trouble I could do without right now. I promise I'll do what I can. All right? Give me your number. I'll call you.'

Frank watched the broken cigarette still smouldering in the ashtray. He couldn't think of anything else to say. He nodded, gave the woman his telephone number and shuffled out of the apartment. Only when he found himself holding the revolver in his hand at home in the early evening did he realize he didn't even know the woman's name.

•

A day passed. Nothing. Another day. Nothing. Long gaps between the memories, when nothing seemed to be happening at all. Most of the time Frank sat at his bedroom window, lights out, watching the apartment. He cleaned his gun. There were no more rows. Mostly the place was dark and empty at night.

At first, he thought they'd moved, but on the second night he saw the light come on at about midnight and glimpsed the boy cross by the window. Then it went dark again until about two, when he saw the woman. She must work in a bar or something, he thought. It figured. The next thing he knew it was morning and he couldn't remember why he had been sitting by the window all night. The sun was up, the birds were singing, and his joints were so stiff he could hardly stand up.

Still he heard nothing from the mother. He had been a fool to trust her.

After three days he decided to confront her again. Rather, he found himself walking into her building, for that was the way things seemed to be happening more and more these days. He could never remember the point at which he decided to do something; he just found himself doing it.

Halfway up the stairs to her apartment, he suddenly had no idea where he was or why he was there. He stopped, heart heavy and chest tight with panic. Then the memory flooded back in the image of the ring, burnished gold, bright as fire in his mind's eye, slightly tilted so he could read the inscription clearly: 'NO GREATER LOVE.' He walked on.

He hammered on the door so hard that people came out of other apartments to see what was going on, but nobody answered.

'My ring!' he shouted at the door. 'I want my ring.'

'Get out before I call the police,' one of the neighbours said. Frank turned and glared. The frightened woman backed into her apartment and slammed the door. He felt the sweat bead on his wrinkled forehead and ran his hand over his sparse grey hair. Slowly, he walked away.

•

Finally his telephone rang. He snatched up the receiver. 'Yes? Hello,' he said.

'It's me.' It was the woman's voice, husky and low. He heard her blow out smoke before she went on. 'I heard you come over here again. You shouldn't of done that. Look, I've talked to Daryl and I'm sorry. He said he threw the ring away because it had writing on it and he didn't think he'd be able to sell it. I know how important it was to you, but—'

'Where did he throw it?'

'He says he doesn't remember. Look, mister, give us a break here, please. Things are tough enough as it is. He's not a real criminal, otherwise he'd of known he could sell it to someone who'd melt it down, wouldn't he? He won't do anything like that again, honest.'

'That won't bring my ring back, will it?'

'I'm sorry. If I could bring it back, I would. What can I do? I'll save up. I'll give you some money.' He heard her inhale the smoke again and blow it out, then he thought he heard her sniffle. 'Look, maybe we can even come to some . . . arrangement . . . if you know what I mean. You must be lonely, aren't you? I saw the way you were looking at me when I found you outside my door. Just give Daryl a chance. Don't go to the police. Please, I'm beg—'

Frank slammed the phone down. If only he could think clearly. Things had gone too far. This whore and her evil offspring had conspired to ruin what little peace he had left in his life: his memories of Joan. What did they know about his marriage, about the happy years, the shock of Joan's illness and the agony of her death, the agony he suffered with her? How could a woman like that know how much the ring meant to him? She probably hadn't even *tried* to find it.

The next thing he knew, he was walking along the boardwalk. When he took stock of his surroundings and saw the ruffled blue of the lake and the tilted white sails of boats, heard the seagulls screech and the children play, he felt as if he were in one of those jump-frame videos he had seen on television once, with no idea how he got from one frame to the next, and with seconds, minutes, hours missing in between.

•

It was dark. That much he knew. Dark and the boy was at home. She was at work. He knew because he had followed her to the bar where she worked, watched her put on her apron and start serving drinks. He didn't know where he had been or what he had done or dreamed all day, but now it was dark, the boy was at home and the gun lay heavy and warm in his pocket.

The boy, Daryl, simply opened the door and let him in. Such arrogance. Such cockiness. Frank could hardly believe it. The music was deafening.

'Turn it off,' he said.

Daryl shrugged and did so. 'What do you want?' he asked. 'My mother told me you've been pestering her. We should call the law on you. I'll bet you're one of those dirty old men, aren't you? Are you trying to get in my mother's pants? Or are you a pervert? Is it young boys you like?' He struck a parody of a sexy pose.

Out of the window, Frank could see the upstairs light he had left on in his house over the laneway. Daryl was smoking, his free hand slapping against his baggies in time to some imaginary music. He wouldn't keep still, kept walking up and down the room. Frank just stood there, by the door.

'How old are you?' Frank asked.

'What's it to you, pervert?'

'Have you been taking drugs?'

'What if I have? What are you going to do about it?'

'Where's my ring?'

He curled his upper lip back and laughed. 'Bottom of the lake. Or maybe in the garbage. I don't remember.'

'Please,' said Frank. 'Where is it? It's all I have left of her.'

'Tough shit. Get a life, old man.'

'You don't understand.'

Daryl stopped pacing and thrust his chin out towards Frank. The tendons in his neck stood out like cables. 'Yes, I do. You think I'm a fucking retard, don't you, just like the teachers do? Well, fuck the lot of you. It was your wife's ring. It's all you've got to remember her by. Read my lips. *I don't fucking care!*'

Blinking back the tears, Frank stuck his hand in his pocket for the gun. He actually felt his hand tighten around the handle and his finger slip into the trigger guard before he relaxed his grip and let go. At the time he didn't know why he was doing it, but the next thing he knew he was walking down the stairs.

'And stay away from us!' he heard Daryl shout after him.

Out in the street, with no memory of going out the door, he found himself on the boardwalk again. It was dark and there was nobody else around except a man walking his dog. Frank went and sat out on the rocks. The lake stretched like black satin ahead of him, smudged with thin white moonlight. Water slopped around the rock at his feet and splashed over his ankles. He thought he could see lights over on the American side.

The next thing Frank knew he was at home and something like a thunderbolt cracked inside his head, filling it with light. It was all so clear now. It was time to let go. He laughed. So simple. From his window, he could see Daryl light another cigarette, hear the loud music. What did his feelings matter to Daryl or his mother? They didn't. And why should they? Nothing really mattered now, but at least he knew what he had to do. He had known the moment he got close enough to Daryl to see the tattoo of a swastika on his cheek below his left eye.

•

Even though it was dark, Frank managed to arrange the stuff on his lawn. He was thinking clearly now. His life had regained its sense of continuity. No more jump-frame reality. The memory he had tried so hard to deny had forced itself on him now the ring was gone, the talisman that had protected him for so long. It wasn't such a bad thing. In a way, he was free. It was all over.

It was a warm night. A raccoon snuffled around the neighbour's garbage. It stopped and looked at Frank with its calm, black-ringed eyes. He moved forward and stamped his foot on the sidewalk to make it go away. It simply stared at him until it was ready to go, then it waddled arrogantly along the street. Far in the distance, a car engine revved. Other shapes detached themselves from the darkness and proved even more difficult to chase away than the raccoon, but Frank held his ground.

Carefully, he arranged the objects around him on the dark lawn. By the time he had finished, the sun was coming up, promising a perfect day for a lawn sale. Now that everything was neatly laid out, the memory was complete; he could keep nothing at bay.

What a death Joan's had been. She had spent ten years doing it, in and out of hospital, one useless operation after another, night after sleepless night of agony despite the pills. He remembered now the times she had begged him to finish her, saying she would do it herself if she had the strength, if she could move without making the knives twist and cut up her insides.

And every time he let her down. He couldn't do it, and he didn't really know why. Surely if he really loved her, he told himself, he would have killed her to stop her suffering? But that argument didn't work. He knew that he loved her, but he still couldn't kill her.

Once, he stood over her for ten minutes holding a pillow in his hands, and he felt her willing him to push it down over her face. Her tongue was swollen, her gums had receded and her teeth were falling out. Every time he smoothed her head with his hand, tufts of dry hair stuck to his palm.

But he had thrown the cushion aside and run out of the house. Why couldn't he do it? Because he couldn't imagine life without her, no matter how much pain and anguish she suffered to stay with him, no matter how little she now resembled the wife he had married? Perhaps. Selfishness? Certainly. Cowardice? Yes.

At last she had gone. Not with a quiet whisper like a candle flame snuffed out, not gently, but with convulsions and loud screams as if fish hooks had ripped a bloody path through her insides.

And he remembered her last look at him, the bulging eyes, the blood trickling from her nose and mouth. How could he forget that look? Through all the final agony, through the knowledge that the release of death was only seconds away, the hard glint of accusation in her eyes was unmistakable.

Frank wiped the tears from his stubbly cheeks and held the gun on his lap as the sun grew warmer and the city came to life around him. Soon he would find the courage to do to himself what he hadn't been able to do for the wife he loved, what he had only been able to do to some nameless German soldier who haunted his dreams. Soon.

By the time the tourists got here all they would see was an old man asleep amid the detritus of his life: the torso of a tailor's dummy; yards of moth-eaten fabrics and folded patterns made of tissue paper; baking dishes; cake tins; cookie cutters shaped like hearts and lions; a silver cigarette lighter; a Nazi armband; a tattered copy of *Mein Kampf*; medals; a bayonet; a German dagger with a mother-of-pearl swastika inlaid in its handle.

GONE TO THE DAWGS

It was the penultimate week of the NFL football pool and Charlie Firth was ahead by ten points. Nothing could stop the smug bastard from winning again now. Nothing short of murder.

Such was the uncharitable thought that crossed the mind of Calvin Bly as he sat with the usual crowd in the local bar watching the Monday night game, St Louis at Tampa Bay. Outside, in the east end of Toronto, the wind was howling, piling up snow in the side streets and swirling it in surreal patterns across the main roads, but inside it was warm, and the occasional single malt between pints of Guinness helped make it even warmer.

There were six of them at the table, the usual crowd, all in the pool. Calvin was second, having come up with a complicated system of mathematical checks and balances that had earned him solid eights and nines all season, plus the occasional eleven. Behind him by six points was Marge, the only girl in the group. Well, woman really, he supposed, seeing as she was in her fifties. The other three, Chris, Jeff and Brad, weren't even in the running.

'How's your mother, Calvin?' Charlie's loud voice boomed across the table. Calvin looked away from his conversation with Marge and saw the sneer on Charlie's face, the baiting grin, the arrogant, disdaining eyes.

'She's fine, thank you,' he said.

Charlie looked at his watch. 'Only it's getting late. I'm surprised she lets you stay out this long.'

He laughed and some of the others joined in, but more because it was the thing to do than because they had any heart for it. Truth be told, nobody really found Charlie's sense of humour funny. Vicious, yes. Cutting and hurtful, yes. But funny, no way.

Perhaps it wasn't worth murdering someone for two thousand dollars, Calvin thought, but it might be worth it just to clear the world of the loud-mouthed fucker. People would probably thank him for it. Three years in a row Charlie Firth had won that NFL pool, and he hadn't let a soul forget it. Twice Calvin had come in second, and Charlie wasn't about to let him forget that either. The teasing would go on well into the baseball season.

Yes, if he got rid of Charlie, he would be doing the world a favour.

The Buccs threw a touchdown pass to take the lead in the dying seconds of the game, and Calvin shook himself free of his dark thoughts. Of course he wouldn't murder Charlie. He'd never harmed a soul in his life, didn't have the guts for it. It was nothing but a pleasant, harmless fantasy.

Got that one, thought Calvin when the game was over, and Charlie had picked the Rams. He was still nine points ahead of the field, though, pretty much impossible to catch, and Marge was still six behind as they went into the final week. It had been a weekend of upsets – the Seahawks beat the Raiders, the Chiefs beat the Broncos and the Lions beat the Jets – but Calvin had come away with nine points.

'Say hi to your mom from me,' Charlie called out as Calvin bundled up and headed out to clear the snow off his car. He didn't bother answering.

•

Calvin hadn't been home five minutes, was watching the news quietly on TV, when the banging started. Mother had a walking stick which she didn't use to walk with as she rarely bothered to walk, but to bang on the floor of her bedroom to summon her son, calling out his name. With a sigh, Calvin hauled himself out of the La-Z-Boy and climbed up the stairs.

He hated Mother's sick room, the unpleasant smells – she never opened the window and didn't bathe very often – the way she lay there looking frail, hands like talons clutching the sheet tight around her neck as if he were going to rape her or something, when the very idea of her nakedness disgusted him.

'Yes, Mother?'

'You were out late.'

'It was a long game.'

'Anything could have happened to me. I could have had a seizure. What would I have done, then?'

'Mother, you're not going to have a seizure. The doctor told you yesterday your health's just fine.'

'Doctor, schmoctor. What does that quack know?' Her tone became wheedling, flirtatious. 'Calvin, baby, I can't sleep. I'm having one of my bad nights. Make Mommy some hot milk and bring my pills, Little Calvin. Pullleeeease.'

Calvin went back downstairs and poured some milk into a saucepan, enough for two, as he decided he might as well treat himself to some hot chocolate if he was heating up milk anyway. While he listened to the hiss of the gas flame and watched the milk's surface change as it heated, he thought again how pleasant it would be if he had the guts to do something about Charlie Firth.

The man was insufferable. For a start, he was well off and always made a point of letting you know how much his possessions cost, from the Porsche to his leather Italian loafers. Women, of course, just wouldn't leave him alone. He had a big house on Kingswood, prime Beach property – all to himself, as he had never married, probably because no woman in her right mind could stand his company for more than a night – and as well as winning the NFL pool, he had been his company's real-estate agent of the year more than once. A success. And Calvin, what had he got? Nothing. Unemployment benefits. A savings account that was thinning out as quickly as his hair, a pot belly that seemed to be getting bigger, a hypochondriac mother who would probably live to torment him for ever, a small, gloomy, draughty row house on the wrong side of Victoria Park. Nothing. Sweet fuck all.

Bubbles started to surface on the milk. Time to turn down the heat. Mother hated it when he burnt the milk. Before he had even got the mugs out of the cupboard he heard the banging on the ceiling again. As if the silly old cow thought banging with that stick of hers would make milk boil any faster. He burned himself as he slopped the hot milk into the cup, forgot about his hot chocolate and hurried upstairs.

•

In the light of the next day, killing Charlie didn't seem like such a good idea. Given Calvin's luck, he was bound to get caught for a start. And, technically, Charlie would still be the winner. If you didn't phone your picks in on time, the administrator assigned you the underdogs, and even with the DAWGS, as they were called, Charlie would still beat the field. He would be too dead to collect his winnings, of course, and Calvin supposed they would go to whoever came second.

The way the pool worked was every Wednesday before five o'clock you phoned in your picks, based on that day's point spread, to the administrator, who ran the whole thing from his desk at one of the major newspapers downtown. You always got his answering machine with its curt message: 'I'm away from my desk right now. Please leave your message after the beep.' There were over a hundred people in the pool, at a hundred bucks each for the season, and in addition to the grand prize of $2000, there were also smaller weekly prizes. Calvin had actually covered this year's entry fee on one weekly win. Usually by Friday evening a photocopy of everyone's picks, along with the weekly and accumulated scores, was faxed to Jeff, who made copies and distributed them in the bar.

Calvin liked to see which teams everyone else had chosen – especially Charlie – but this week he would miss it. On Thursday he had to accompany Mother down to Fort Myers, where they would spend Christmas with their only living relatives, his Aunt Vicky and Uncle Frank, who had retired there seven years ago and were generous enough to help out with the airfare.

The Florida trip used to be the highlight of Calvin's year. Not because he liked the place. Three or four days was about all he could stand. It was too hot and too full of old people, or people who didn't speak English, as if Toronto wasn't bad enough that way. No, what Florida used to mean to him was freedom, glorious freedom! Mother used to stay down there for at least six weeks, and as soon as she was 'settled' Calvin was allowed to go home alone. God only knew how Vicky and Frank put up with the old bat, Calvin thought, but they did. Now she was too worried about getting sick and not being able to afford US medical bills, so they were both returning on the following Wednesday.

That Tuesday morning at breakfast Calvin checked the sports section to see if the spreads had changed since Monday. He liked to do that, factor it into his calculations. Sometimes you could guess a lot just by the ways the spreads were changing. After that, his day followed its usual dull routine. He cleared the driveway of snow, did household chores, did some food shopping and took care of Mother. But on Tuesday evening Calvin had a date.

This was one thing nobody knew about him – at least, so he believed. Calvin had a secret girlfriend. Heidi. Probably no one would believe it if he told them that a pudgy, balding, boring fifty-one-year-old man like him could have an attractive blonde forty-year-old woman as a girlfriend. Sometimes he could hardly believe it himself. They had met six months ago in HMV downtown, both looking at the selection of show tunes. A common interest in film musicals led them to venture to a local coffee shop together, where they found they enjoyed one another's company immensely. A loner by nature – apart from the easy and informal gregariousness of the bar – Calvin found it hard to talk to her at first, but Heidi had a way of drawing him out of his shell. There was, of course, a big problem.

Heidi was married.

Slowly, piece by piece, it emerged over furtive meetings in the city centre, first just for coffees, then regular lunches at Red Lobster, that Heidi was not exactly happy with her marriage. Her children had both left home, one for Winnipeg, poor sod, and the other for southern California, so it was only a matter of time, she told Calvin, before the separation occurred. Until then, they had to be very careful and keep their relationship a secret. Her husband worked shifts for a security company, and this week he was working evenings. Calvin would go over to the west end, where Heidi lived, not far from High Park, and they would talk and make love until midnight, at which time he would dress and sneak out of the back door to where he had parked his car several blocks away.

That Tuesday Heidi did not seem to be in her usual good spirits.

'What's wrong?' Calvin asked, after he had suspected her of counting cracks in the ceiling while they made love.

'Nothing,' she said.

'Come on. I can tell there's something bothering you.'

'I told you, it's nothing. Leave it.'

'Maybe I can help.'

Heidi turned, propped herself on her elbow and looked at him. 'I don't think I can go on,' she said after a pause.

Calvin felt his chest tighten, his heart race. 'What do you mean?'

'This. You and me. I don't think I can go on.'

'But why?'

'It's not that I don't like you, Calvin.' She stroked his cheek. 'It's just . . . oh, everything, the lies, the guilt. Joe and I had a really long talk the other night.'

'For God's sake, Heidi, you didn't tell him . . . ?'

'No. No, of course not. What sort of a fool do you think I am? No, we just . . . well, he realized he'd been neglecting me, and I realized I missed him more than I thought. We decided . . . you know . . . to try to make a go of things.'

'Make a go of things?'

'Yes.' She smiled. 'We're going to start with a trip to Mexico. A sort of second honeymoon. We're going for New Year.'

'B-but . . .'

'Oh, Calvin. Don't be upset. Please don't be upset. You had fun while it lasted, didn't you?'

'Yes, but . . . but I thought . . .'

'You thought what?'

'I mean, just now, even when you knew this, you . . . we . . .' He shook his head.

'Was that so unfair of me, Calvin? Just to have you one last time? Was that too selfish of me?'

'It's not that.'

'Then what?'

'It just seems so sudden, so abrupt, that's all.' Calvin sat on the edge of the bed and reached for his clothes.

'But you knew it had to end one day.'

'I sort of hoped that when you and Joe split up, we might . . . you know . . .'

'Oh, Calvin, that's sweet. That's *too* sweet.'

'I gather you didn't?'

Heidi lay back on the pillow. 'I never thought, really, not beyond the next time. I've hurt you, haven't I?'

'It's all right. I'll mend.'

'I'm sorry, Calvin.'

'Don't worry about it. I'll go now.'

'You'll be careful? Make sure no one sees you?'

'I'll be careful.'

Calvin bent over to give her a goodnight kiss, as he always did. She turned her head and offered him her cheek. He kissed it lightly and found it surprisingly cool, then he went downstairs and sneaked out of the back door. He thought of making a lot of noise, but Calvin wasn't the type to draw too much attention to himself.

•

He was OK to drive, he told himself as he headed out of the nearest bar – to which he had gone as soon as he'd left Heidi's – he'd only had two pints and a shot of whisky, and he felt in control. Sad, hurt, but in control.

The city crews had been through the neighbourhood and the roads were pretty clear. He headed down Roncesvalles towards Lakeshore and the Gardiner, noting how quiet the roads were. Hardly surprising, as it was going on for half past one on a cold, miserable Tuesday evening.

It was all over with Heidi. He couldn't believe it, couldn't believe the callous way she had treated him. How could she? He had even fantasized a real life for them: restaurants, theatres, musicals, weekends together. Now this.

Almost home. He stopped at a red light. Nobody around. Lights from TV sets in a couple of windows. Christmas trees. lights.

As he neared the next set of traffic lights, he saw someone come out of a bar alone and start to cross just as the lights were changing. It was Charlie. There was no mistaking that expensive leather jacket, the hand-tooled cowboy boots. He was clearly a bit pissed, not falling down drunk, but definitely unsteady. And unobservant. Calvin was driving slowly enough to stop, but something, he couldn't say what, some demon, some inner compulsion, seemed to take control of him. A quick glance to make sure there were no other cars visible ahead or behind, nobody on the street in seeing distance, and almost unbidden his foot pressed down on the gas pedal as if it was made of lead.

Charlie knew something was wrong, saw it coming at the last moment, but was too late to do anything about it. Calvin saw the horrified expression on his face, even fancied he saw recognition there, too, then the car hit him with a satisfying, meaty smack and threw him away from the car. Calvin felt the shuddering bump and crunch as he ran over the body. No stopping now. He sped off and turned the first corner, heading into the maze of residential streets that would eventually take him home, heart in his mouth, blood pulsing hard through his veins, but alive, alive at last.

•

Calvin didn't sleep at all that night and spent the next day in terror of the knock upon his door. The newspaper reported Charlie's death and asked anyone who might have seen anything to contact them. Calvin was almost certain that no one had seen him, but there was still room for doubt, and that doubt bred fear. If the police came to check out his car, they would see the damage Charlie's body had caused to radiator and the headlight. They could probably even match paint chips from the body to his car; he had seen them do it on TV.

So terrified was he that he almost forgot to phone in his picks. Almost. At four-thirty he picked up the phone with trembling hands and dialled the administrator's number. Just as the answering machine cut in, Mother's stick banged on the floor above. He automatically held the phone at arm's length and put his hand over the mouthpiece, even though there wasn't a real person on the other end, and shouted up that he was busy and would be with her in a few moments. When he got back to the phone, he was just in time to hear the familiar beep. He began: 'Giants, Broncos, Bills, Jets, Rams, Bears . . .'

•

The journey to Fort Myers on Thursday morning was a nightmare for Calvin. Not because of the weather, though the flight was delayed more than an hour and the wings had to be de-iced. Not even because of Mother, despite the fact that she never stopped complaining for one moment until the plane took off, when she immediately fell asleep. No, it was because he expected to be arrested at every stage of the journey. At the check in he noticed two airline officials huddled to one side talking, and occasionally they seemed to be looking in his direction. Sweat beaded on his forehead. But nothing happened. Next, at US Immigration, just when he expected the firm hand on his shoulder, the hushed 'Please step this way, Mr Bly,' the immigration officer wished him and Mother happy holidays after barely a glance at their passports.

Could getting away with murder really be that easy? Calvin wondered when he disembarked at Fort Myers and found no policemen waiting for him, only Frank and Vicky in the crowd waving, ready to drive him and Mother back to the condo. Nothing had happened. Nobody had come for him. He must have got away with it.

Though the locals thought the weather cold and farmers were worried about the citrus crop, Calvin found it comfortable enough to sit out on the deck. As he poured himself a Jack Daniels and looked out over the long strip of beach to the blue-green sea, Charlie's murder began to seem distant and unreal. After a few hours and three or four bourbons, he could almost believe it hadn't happened, that it had merely been a bad dream, and the following morning he imagined that when he got back to Toronto and walked into the bar they would all be waiting there, as usual, including Charlie, flashing his winnings.

In the late afternoon Florida sun, how easy it was to believe that snowy Tuesday night in Toronto had never happened.

•

By Christmas Eve, Calvin was already two games up, having picked the Bills to beat a three-point spread against the Seahawks and the Broncos to win plus seven over the 49ers on Saturday. He'd lost the Giants – Jaguars game, but even with his system he could never expect to win them all.

He was sipping a Jack Daniels on the rocks and watching Miami against New England, hoping the Pats would beat the spread, when during the halftime break came a brief interview with a convicted killer called Leroy Cody, scheduled to be electrocuted early in the New Year. Instead of pushing the mute button, Calvin turned the sound up a notch or two and leaned forward in his chair. He'd read about Cody in *USA Today* and found his curiosity piqued by the man's nonchalant, laconic manner and his total lack of remorse.

The interview was a special from death row, Leroy in his cell in drab prison clothes, hair cropped close to his skull, no emotion in his eyes, his face all sharp angles.

'You shot a liquor store clerk for fifteen dollars, is that right?' the interviewer asked.

'I didn't know he'd only got a lousy fifteen dollars when I shot him, now, did I?' Leroy answered in his slow, surprisingly high-pitched drawl.

'But you shot him, and fifteen dollars is all you got?'

'Yessir. Sure was a disappointment, let me tell you.'

'And then you shot a pregnant woman and dragged her out of her car to make your escape.'

'I didn't know she was pregnant.'

'But you shot the woman and stole her car?'

Leroy spat on the floor of his cell. 'Hell, I had to make a fast getaway. I don't have no car of my own. I had to take a goddamn cab to the store, but I was damned if I was gonna hang around and try to flag one after I done robbed the place.'

'And you feel no remorse for any of this?'

'Remorse?'

'Regrets.'

'Regrets? Nope. No regrets. I'm a killer. That's what I am.'

'You regret nothing at all?'

Leroy smiled; it looked like an eclipse of the sun moving slowly across his features. 'Only getting caught,' he said.

Calvin's attention wandered as the presenter started to comment, and then they were back at the half-time show, catching up on scores. But even as he checked the numbers, part of Calvin's mind stayed with Leroy Cody. 'I'm a killer. That's what I am.' He liked that. It was honest, direct, had a ring to it.

Calvin tried it out loud: 'I'm a killer. That's what I am.' It sounded good. He let the fantasy wander, trying on his new self and finding it a perfect fit. 'I'm a killer. That's what I am. Me and

Leroy. Yeah, man.' And if he was a killer, he could kill again. Why stop at Charlie? He could kill Heidi's husband. Could even kill that bitch Heidi herself, maybe make her beg a little first. He could kill . . .

There was no upstairs in the condo, but he heard the click-click of Mother's walking stick on the tile floor before he heard her voice. 'Leroy,' she said (he was sure she called him Leroy), 'are you going to just sit here and watch this garbage all Christmas? Why don't you come and play cribbage with the old folks for a while?' Calvin sighed, picked up the remote, turned off the game and muttered, 'Coming, Mother.'

•

There were no cops waiting at the airport when Calvin and Mother got back to Toronto on Wednesday. It was over a week since Charlie's death, and still nothing to fear.

After settling Mother at home, against her protests, Calvin decided to drop in at the bar. As he had suspected, the usual crowd was there. Minus Charlie.

'Calvin,' said Marge, patting his arm when he sat down beside her. 'Welcome home. You've heard the news?'

Calvin nodded sadly. 'Heard just before we left for Florida. It's tragic, isn't it?'

'I still can't believe it,' said Marge. 'He always seemed so . . .'

'Alive?' Calvin suggested.

'Yes. Alive. That's it. Alive.'

'Is there any progress?' he asked the table in general.

'No,' Jeff answered. 'You know the cops. They've put it down as a hit and run, asked for the public's co-operation, and that's the last you'll hear of it.'

'Unless someone comes forward,' Calvin said.

'Yes,' Jeff agreed. 'Unless someone comes forward. By the way,' he went on, 'here's the final scores on the pool.' He handed Calvin the sheets of paper.

Kelly, the waitress with the walk out of a forties' *noir* movie, finally came over with his drink. Calvin desperately wanted to see the final scores, but he didn't want to appear too anxious. After all, Charlie *was* dead. So he sipped some beer, talked a little about his Christmas, and then, casually, glanced down at the sheets.

The first thing that caught his eye was his weekend's score: 5. That had to be wrong. Calvin had checked the game scores after the cribbage game and found he had nine. He had also won the evening game, the Raiders over the Panthers, *and* the Monday evening game, when the Titans had creamed the Cowboys. So how could he end up with *five*? He had *eleven*.

He turned to the column of picks and noticed scrawled across the line where his should be, the word 'DAWGS.' Charlie, of course, had got the same. It meant they hadn't got their picks in on time.

But Calvin *had* got his picks in; he remembered phoning them. It was late in the afternoon, four-thirty to be precise, but definitely *before* the five o'clock deadline. So what was going on?

'Calvin?'

The voice came as if from a long way. 'Huh? Sorry. What?'

'Just that you've gone pale. Are you OK?' It was Marge, and her hand was on his arm.

'I'm fine,' he said. 'Must be . . . you know . . . Charlie . . . delayed shock.'

Marge nodded. 'I don't suppose it seemed real until you got back here, did it?' she said.

'Something like that. What's happening with the pool?'

Marge frowned. 'Well,' she said, 'with Charlie gone and you forgetting to phone in . . . er . . . I won.'

'You?'

Marge laughed nervously. 'Well, don't look so surprised, Calvin. I've been up there with the best of you all season.'

'I know. It's not that . . .'

'What, then?'

'Never mind. Congratulations, Marge.' Calvin knew he couldn't complain. Whatever had gone wrong here, however he had gone from eleven to five, there was nothing he could do about it, and getting upset about the result would only look suspicious.

'Thanks,' said Marge. 'I know it must be a disappointment, you being so close and all.' She managed a weak smile. 'I only beat you by one, if that means anything at all. It was my best week of the whole season. Twelve.'

Calvin laughed. He couldn't help himself. 'So what are you going to do with your winnings?'

Marge looked at the others, then said. 'I decided – well, we all decided, really – that I'd use the money for a wake, you know, to pay for a wake here. For Charlie. He would have liked that.'

'Yes,' said Calvin, still quaking with laughter inside while he tried to keep a straight face. 'Yes, I think he would.'

•

When Calvin got home he poured himself a large whisky and tried to figure out what had gone wrong. *Five*. The *DAWGS*. It was an insult, a slap in the face.

He cast his mind back to that Wednesday afternoon and remembered first that his hand had been shaking as he dialled. He had, after all, just killed Charlie the previous evening. Could he have misdialled? The first three numbers were all the same, and connected him to the newspaper the administrator worked for. The last four were 4697. It would have been easy, say, to transpose the six and the nine, or even to dial seven first rather than four, given that he was upset at the time. He tried both and got the same message: 'I'm away from my desk right now. Please leave a message after the beep.' The only difference was that 7694 was a woman's voice and 4967 was a man's. So that was what had happened. In his disturbed state of mind, Calvin had dialled the wrong number. Why had it happened like that? Why hadn't he listened to the message, noticed the difference in voice and realized what he had done?

Then he remembered. Just as he had got through, Mother had knocked on the bedroom floor for him. He had held the phone at arm's length and covered the mouthpiece, as you do, and yelled up that he was coming in a minute. He *hadn't heard* the administrator's message, only vaguely recognized it was a man's voice on the answering machine, heard the usual beep and left his picks with someone else at the paper.

Someone who hadn't a clue what he was talking about.

Calvin held his head in his hands. *The wrong number*. All for nothing. He drank some more whisky. Well, maybe not *all* for nothing, he thought after a while. Hadn't he already decided that, nice as it would have been, he hadn't killed Charlie only for the money? Wasn't $2000 a paltry sum to murder for? More than $15, but still . . . he knew he had had more reason than the money. Winning the pool was a part of it, of course, but that wasn't to be. So what was left? What could he salvage from this disaster?

'I'm a killer. That's what I am.'

The voice seemed to come into his head from nowhere, and slowly as the whisky warmed his insides, understanding dawned on Calvin.

'I'm a killer. That's what I am.'

The sound of a heavy stick hammering on the ceiling above broke into his thoughts. He could hear her muffled yelling. 'Leroy! Leroy! I need my hot milk, Leroy!'

Calvin put his glass down, looked up at the ceiling and got to his feet. 'Coming, Mother,' he said softly.

IN FLANDERS FIELDS

I considered it the absolute epitome of irony that, with bombs falling around us, someone went and bludgeoned Mad Maggie to death.

To add insult to injury, she lay undiscovered for several days before Harry Fletcher, the milkman, found her. Because milk was rationed to one or two pints a week, depending on how much the children and expectant mothers needed, he didn't leave it on her doorstep the way he used to do before the war. Even in a close community like ours, a bottle of milk left unguarded on a doorstep wouldn't have lasted five minutes.

These days, Harry walked around with his float, and people came out to buy. It was convenient, as we were some way from the nearest shops, and we could always be sure we were getting fresh milk. However mad Maggie might have been, it wasn't like her to miss her milk ration. Thinking she might have slept in, or perhaps have fallen ill with no one to look after her, Harry knocked on her door and called her name. When he heard no answer, he told me, he made a tentative try at the handle and found that the door was unlocked.

There she lay on her living-room floor in a pool of dried blood dotted with flies. Poor Harry lost his breakfast before he could dash outside for air.

Why Harry came straight to me when he found Mad Maggie's body I can't say. We were friends of a kind, I suppose, of much the same age, and we occasionally passed a pleasurable evening together playing dominoes and drinking watery beer in the Prince Albert. Other than that, we didn't have a lot in common: I was a schoolteacher – English and history – and Harry had left school at fourteen; Harry had missed the first war through a heart ailment, whereas I had been gassed at Ypres in 1917; I was a bachelor, and Harry was married with a stepson, Thomas, who had just come back home on convalescent leave after being severely wounded during the Dunkirk evacuation. Thomas also happened to be my godson, which I suppose was the main thing Harry and I had in common.

Perhaps Harry also came to me because I was a Special Constable. I know it sounds impressive, but it isn't really. The services were so mixed up that you'd have the police putting out fires, the Home Guard doing police work, and anyone with two arms carrying the stretchers. A Special Constable was simply a part-time policeman, without any real qualifications for the job except his willingness to take it on. The rest of the time I taught what few pupils remained at Silverhill Grammar School.

As it turned out, I was glad that Harry did call on me because it gave me a stake in the matter. The regular police were far more concerned with lighting offences and the black market than they were with their regular duties, and one thing nobody had time to do in the war was investigate the murder of a mad, mysterious, cantankerous old woman.

Nobody except me, that is.

Though my position didn't grant me any special powers, I pride myself on being an intelligent and perceptive sort of fellow, not to mention nosy, and it wasn't the first time I'd done a spot of detective work on the side. But first, let me tell you a little about Mad Maggie . . .

•

I say *old* woman, but Maggie was probably only in her mid-forties, about the same age as me, when she was killed. Everyone just called her *old*; it seemed to go with *mad*. With a certain kind of woman, it's not so much a matter of years, anyway, but of demeanour, and Maggie's demeanour was old.

Take the clothes she wore, for a start: most women were trying to look like one of the popular film stars like Vivien Leigh or Deanna Durbin, with her bolero dresses, but even for a woman of her age, Maggie wore clothes that could best be described as old-fashioned, even antique: high, buttoned boots, long dresses with high collars, ground-sweeping cloaks and broad-brimmed hats with feathers.

Needless to say, the local kids – at least those whose parents hadn't packed them off to the countryside already – used to follow her down the street in gangs and chant, 'Mad Maggie, Mad Maggie, she's so mad, her brain's all claggy . . .' Children can be so cruel. Most of the time she ignored them, or seemed oblivious to their taunts, but once in a while she wheeled on them, eyes blazing, and started waving her arms around and yelling curses, usually in French. The children would squeal with exaggerated horror, then turn tail and run away.

Maggie never had any visitors; none of us had ever been inside her house; nobody in the community even knew what her real name was, where she had come from, or how she had got to be the way she was. We simply accepted her. There were rumours of course. Some gossip-mongers had it that she was an heiress cut off by her family because she went mad; others said she had never recovered from a tragic love affair; still others said she was a rich eccentric and kept thousands of pounds stuffed in her mattress.

Whoever and whatever Mad Maggie was, she managed to take care of life's minutiae somehow; she paid her rent, she bought newspapers, and she handled her ration coupons just like the rest of us. She also kept herself clean, despite the restriction to only five inches of bath water. Perhaps her eccentricity was just an act, then, calculated to put people off befriending her for some reason? Perhaps she was shy or anti-social? All in all, she was known as Mad Maggie only because she never talked to anyone except herself, because of the old clothes she wore, because of her strange outbursts in French and because, as everyone knew, she never went to the shelters during air-raids, but would either stay indoors alone or walk the blacked-out streets muttering and arguing with herself, waving her arms at the skies as if inviting the bombs to come and get her.

•

When Harry called that Monday morning, I was lying in bed grappling with one of my frequent bouts of insomnia, waiting for the birds to sing me back to sleep. I couldn't even tell if it was daylight or not because of the heavy blackout curtains. I had been dreaming, I remembered, and had woken at about half-past four, gasping for air, from my recurring nightmare about being sucked down into a quicksand.

I heard Harry banging at my door and calling my name, so I threw on some clothes and hurried downstairs. I thought at first that it might be something to do with Tommy, but when I saw his pale face, his wide eyes and the thin trickle of vomit at the corner of his mouth, I worried that he was having the heart attack he had been expecting daily for over twenty years.

He turned and pointed down the street. 'Frank, please!' he said. 'You've got to come with me.'

I could hear the fear in his voice, so I followed him as quickly as I could to Maggie's house. It was a fine October morning, with a hint of autumn's nip in the air. He had left the door ajar. Slowly, I pushed it open and went inside. My first impression was more surprise at how clean and tidy the place was than shock at the bloody figure on the carpet. In my defence, lest I sound callous, I had fought in the first war and, by some miracle, survived the mustard gas with only a few blisters and a nasty coughing fit every now and then. But I had seen men blown apart; I had been spattered with the brains of my friends; I had crawled though trenches and not known whether the soft, warm, gelatinous stuff I was putting my hands in was mud or the entrails of my comrades. More recently, I had also helped dig more than one mangled or dismembered body from the ruins, so a little blood, a little death, never bothered me much. Besides, despite the pool of dried blood around her head, Mad Maggie looked relatively peaceful. More peaceful than I had ever seen her in life.

Funny, but it reminded me of that old Dracula film I saw at the Crown, the one with Bela Lugosi. The count's victims always became serene after they had wooden stakes plunged through their hearts. Mad Maggie hadn't been a vampire, and she didn't have a stake through her heart, but a bloodstained posser lay by her side, the concave copper head and wooden handle both covered in blood. A quick glance in the kitchen showed only one puzzling item: an unopened bottle of milk. As far as I knew, Harry's last round had been the morning of the air raid, last Wednesday. I doubted that Maggie would have been able to get more than her rations; besides, the bottle top bore the unmistakable mark of the dairy where Harry worked.

Harry waited outside, unwilling to come in and face the scene again. Once I had taken in what had happened, I told him to fetch the police, the real police this time.

They came.

•

And they went.

One was a plainclothes officer, Detective Sergeant Longbottom, a dull-looking bruiser with a pronounced limp, who looked most annoyed at being called from his bed. He asked a few questions, sniffed around a bit, then got the ambulance men to take Maggie away on a stretcher.

One of the questions Sergeant Longbottom asked was the victim's name. I told him that, apart from 'Mad Maggie', I had no idea. With a grunt, he rummaged around in the sideboard drawer and found her rent book. I was surprised to discover that she was called Rose Faversham, which I thought was actually quite a pretty name. Prettier than Mad Maggie, anyway. Sergeant Longbottom also asked if we'd had any strangers in the area. Apart from an army unit billeted near the park where they were carrying out training exercises, and the gypsy encampment in Silverhill Woods, we hadn't.

'Ah, gypsies,' he said, and wrote something in his little black notebook. 'Is anything missing?'

I told him I didn't know, as I had no idea what *might* have been here in the first place. That seemed to confuse him. For all I knew, I went on, the rumour might have been right, and she could have had a mattress stuffed with banknotes. Sergeant Longbottom checked upstairs and came back scratching his head. 'Everything *looks* normal,' he said, then he poked around a bit more, noting the canteen of sterling silver cutlery, and guessed that Mad Maggie had probably interrupted the thief, who had killed her and fled the scene – probably back to the gypsy encampment. I was on the point of telling him that I thought the Nazis were supposed to be persecuting gypsies, not us, but I held my tongue. I knew it would do no good.

Of course, I told him how everyone in the neighbourhood knew Mad Maggie paid no attention to air raids, how she even seemed to enjoy them the way some people love thunderstorms, and how Tom Sellers, the ARP man, had remonstrated with her on many occasions, only to get a dismissive wave and the sight of her ramrod-stiff back walking away down the street. Maggie had also been fined more than once for blackout infringements, until she solved that one by keeping her heavy black curtains closed night *and* day.

I also told Longbottom that, in the blackout, anyone could have come and gone easily without being seen. I think that was what finally did it. He hummed and hawed, muttered 'Gypsies' again, made noises about a continuing investigation, then put his little black notebook away, said he had pressing duties to attend to and left.

•

And there things would have remained had I not become curious. No doubt Mad Maggie would have been fast forgotten and some poor, innocent gypsy would have been strung up from the gallows.

But there was something about the serenity of Mad Maggie's features in death that haunted me. She looked almost saintlike, as if she had sloughed off the skin of despair and madness that she had inhabited for so long and reverted to the loving, compassionate Christian woman she must have once been. She had a real name now, too: *Rose Faversham.* I was also provoked by Detective Sergeant Longbottom's gruff manner and his obvious impatience with the whole matter. No doubt he had more important duties to get back to, such as the increased traffic in black market onion substitutes.

I would like to say that the police searched Maggie's house thoroughly, locked it up fast and put a guard on the door, but they did nothing of the kind. They did lock the front door behind us, of course, but that was it. I imagined that, as soon as he found out, old Grasper, the landlord, would slither around, rubbing his hands and trying to rent the place out quickly again, for twice as much, before the army requisitioned it as a billet.

One thing I had neglected to tell Detective Sergeant Longbottom, I realized as I watched his car disappear around a pile of rubble at the street corner, was about Fingers Finnegan, our local black marketeer and petty thief. Human nature is boundlessly selfish and greedy, even in wartime, and air raids provided the perfect cover for burglary and black market deals. The only unofficial people on the streets during air raids were either mad, like Maggie, or up to no good, like Fingers. We'd had a spate of burglaries when most decent, law-abiding people were in St Mary's church crypt, or at least in their damp and smelly backyard Anderson shelters, and Fingers was my chief suspect. He could be elusive when he wanted to be, though, and I hadn't seen him in a number of days.

Not since last Wednesday's air raid, in fact.

•

After the police had gone, Harry and I adjourned to my house, where, despite the early hour, I poured him a stiff brandy and offered him a Woodbine. I didn't smoke, myself, because of that little bit of gas that had leaked through my mask at Ypres, but I had soon discovered that it was wise to keep cigarettes around when they were becoming scarce. Like all the rationed items, they became a kind of currency. I also put the kettle on, for I hadn't had my morning tea yet, and I'm never at my best before my morning tea. Perhaps that may be one reason I have never married; most of the women I have met chatter far too much in the morning.

'What a turn up,' Harry said, after taking a swig and coughing. 'Mad Maggie, murdered. Who'd imagine it?'

'Her killer, I should think,' I said.

'Gypsies.'

I shook my head. 'I doubt it. Oh, there's no doubt they're a shifty lot. I wouldn't trust one of them as far as I could throw him. But killers? A defenceless woman like Maggie? I don't think so. Besides, you saw her house. It hadn't been touched.'

'But Sergeant Longbottom said she might have interrupted a burglar.'

I sniffed. 'Sergeant Longbottom's an idiot. There was no evidence at all that her killer was attempting to burgle the place.'

'Maybe she was one of them once – a gypsy – and they came to take her back?'

I laughed. 'I must say, Harry, you certainly don't lack imagination, I'll grant you that. But no, I rather fancy this is a different sort of matter altogether.'

Harry frowned. 'You're not off on one of your Sherlock Holmes kicks again, are you, Frank? Leave it be. Let the professionals deal with it. It's what they're paid for.'

'*Professionals*! Hmph. You saw for yourself how interested our Detective Sergeant Longbottom was. Interested in crawling back in his bed, more like it. No, Harry, I think that's the last we've seen of them. If we want to find out who killed poor Maggie, we'll have to find out for ourselves.'

'Why not just let it be, Frank?' Harry pleaded. 'We're at war. People are getting killed every minute of the day and night.'

I gave him a hard look, and he cringed a little. 'Because this is different, Harry. While I can't say I approve of war as a solution to man's problems, at least it's socially sanctioned murder. If the government, in all its wisdom, decides that we're at war with Germany and we should kill as many Germans as we can, then so be it. But nobody sanctioned the killing of Mad Maggie. When an individual kills someone like Maggie, he takes something he has no right to. Something he can't even give back or replace, the way he could a diamond necklace. It's an affront to us all, Harry, an insult to the community. And it's up to us to see that retribution is made.' I'll admit I sounded a little pompous, but Harry could be extremely obtuse on occasion, and his using the war as an excuse for so outrageous a deed as Rose's murder brought out the worst in me.

Harry seemed suitably cowed by my tirade, and when he'd finished his brandy he shuffled off to finish his deliveries. I never did ask him whether there were was any milk left on his unattended float.

•

I had another hour in which to enjoy my morning tea before I had to leave for school, but first I had to complete my ritual and drop by the newsagent's for a paper. While I was there, I asked Mrs Hope behind the counter when she had last seen Mad Maggie. Last Wednesday, she told me, walking down the street towards her house just before the warning siren went off, muttering to herself. That information, along with the unopened milk and the general state of the body, was enough to confirm for me that Rose had probably been killed under cover of the air raid.

That morning, I found I could neither concentrate on *Othello*, which I was supposed to be teaching the fifth form, nor could I be bothered to read about the bombing raids, evacuation procedures and government pronouncements that passed for news in these days of propaganda and censorship.

Instead, I thought about Mad Maggie, or Rose Faversham, as

she had now become for me. When I tried to visualize her as she was alive, I realized that had I looked closely enough, had I got beyond the grim expressions and the muttered curses, I might have seen her for the handsome woman she was. *Handsome*, I say, not pretty or beautiful, but I would hazard a guess that twenty years ago she would have turned a head or two. Then I remembered that it was about twenty years ago when she first arrived in the neighbourhood, and she had been Mad Maggie right from the start. So perhaps I was inventing a life for her, a life she had never had, but certainly when death brought repose to her features, it possessed her of a beauty I had not noticed before.

When I set off for school, I saw Tommy Markham, Harry's stepson, going for his morning constitutional. Tommy's real dad, Lawrence Markham, had been my best friend. We had grown up together and had both fought in the Third Battle of Ypres, between August and November 1917. Lawrence had been killed at Passchendaele, about nine miles away from my unit, while I had only been mildly gassed. Tommy was in his mid twenties now. He never knew his real dad, but worshipped him in a way you can worship only a dead hero. Tommy joined up early and served with the Green Howards as part of the ill-fated British Expeditionary Force in France. He had seemed rather twitchy and sullen since he got back from the hospital last week, but I put that down to shattered nerves. The doctors had told Polly, his mother, something about nervous exhaustion and about being patient with him.

'Morning, Tommy,' I greeted him.

He hadn't noticed me at first – his eyes had been glued to the pavement as he walked – but when he looked up, startled, I noticed the almost pellucid paleness of his skin and the dark bruises under his eyes.

'Oh, good morning, Mr Bascombe,' he said. 'How are you?'

'I'm fine, but you don't look so good. What is it?'

'My nerves,' he said, moving away as he spoke. 'The doc said I'd be all right after a bit of rest, though.'

'I'm glad to hear it. By the way, did your fath—, sorry, did

Harry tell you about Mad Maggie?' I knew Tommy was sensitive about Harry not being his real father.

'He said she was dead, that's all. Says someone clobbered her.'

'When did you last see her, Tommy?'

'I don't know.'

'Since the raid?'

'That was the day after I got back. No, come to think of it, I don't think I have seen her since then. Terrible business, in'it?'

'Yes, it is.'

'Anyway, sorry, must dash. Bye, Mr Bascombe.'

'Bye, Tommy.'

I stood frowning and watched him scurry off, almost crabwise, down the street.

•

There was another air raid that night, and I decided to look for Fingers Finnegan. By then I had talked to enough people on the street to be certain that no one had seen Rose since the evening of the last raid.

We lived down by the railway, the canal and the power station, so we were always copping it. The Luftwaffe could never aim accurately, though, because the power station sent up clouds of appalling smoke as soon as they heard there were enemy planes approaching. If the bombs hit anything of strategic value, it was more by good luck than good management.

The siren would go off, wailing up and down the scale for two minutes, and it soon became an eerie fugue as you heard the sirens from neighbouring boroughs join in, one after another. The noise frightened the dogs and cats and they struck up, wailing and howling, too. At first, you could hardly see a thing outside, only hear the droning of the bombers high above and the swishing and whistling sound of the bombs as they fell in the distance. Then came the explosions, the hailstone of incendiaries on roofs like a rain of fire, the flames crackling, blazing through the smoke. Even the sounds seemed muffled, the distant explosions no more than dull, flat thuds, like a heavy book falling on the floor, the crackle of anti-aircraft fire like fat spitting on a griddle. Sometimes you could even hear someone scream or shout out a warning. Once I heard a terrible shrieking that still haunts my nightmares.

But the city had an eldritch beauty during an air raid. In the distance, through the smoke haze, the skyline seemed lit by a dozen suns, each a slightly different shade of red, orange or yellow. Searchlights criss-crossed one another, making intricate cat's cradles in the air, and ack-ack fire arced into the sky like strings of Christmas lights. Soon, the bells of the fire engines became part of the symphony of sound and colour. The smoke from the power station got in my eyes and up my nose, and with my lungs, it brought on a coughing fit that seemed to shake my ribs free of their moorings. I held a handkerchief to my face, and that seemed to help a little.

It wasn't too difficult to get around, despite the blackout and the smoke. There were white stripes painted on the lampposts and along the kerbside, and many people had put little dots of luminous paint on their doorbells, so you could tell where you were if you knew the neighbourhood well enough.

I walked along Lansdowne Street to the junction with Cardigan Road. Nobody was abroad. The bombs were distant but getting closer, and the smell from a broken sewage pipe was terrible, despite my handkerchief. Once, I fancied I saw a figure steal out of one of the houses, look this way and that, then disappear into the smoky darkness. I ran, calling out after him, but when I got there he had vanished. It was probably Fingers, I told myself. I'd have a devil of a time catching him now I had scared him off. My best chance was to run him down in one of the back-street cafes where he sold his stolen goods the next day.

So instead of pursuing my futile task, and because it was getting more and more difficult to breathe, I decided that my investigation might next benefit best from a good look around Rose's empty house.

It was easy enough to gain access via the kitchen window at

the back, which wasn't even latched, and after an undignified and painful fall from the sink to the floor, I managed to regain my equilibrium and set about my business. It occurred to me that if I had such an easy time getting in, then her killer would have had an easy time, too. Rose had been killed with the posser, which would most likely have been placed near the sink or tub in which she did her washing.

Because of the blackout curtains, I didn't have to worry about my torch giving me away; nor did I have to cover it with tissue paper, as I would outside, so I had plenty of light to see by. I stood for a few moments, adjusting to the room. I could hear fire-engine bells not too far away.

I found little of interest downstairs. Apart from necessities, such as cutlery, pans, plates and dishes, Rose seemed to own nothing. There were no framed photographs on the mantelpiece, no paintings on the drab walls. There wasn't even a wireless. A search of the sideboard revealed only the rent book that Longbottom had already discovered, a National Identity Card, also in the name of Rose Faversham, her ration book, various coupons, old bills and about twenty pounds in banknotes. I did find two bottles of gin, one almost empty, in the lower half of the china cabinet. There were no letters, no address books, nothing of a personal nature. Rose Faversham's nest was clean and tidy, but it was also quite sterile.

Wondering whether it was worth bothering, I finally decided to go upstairs to finish my search. The first of the two bedrooms was completely bare. Most people use a spare room to store things they no longer use but can't bear to throw out just yet; there was nothing like this in Rose's spare bedroom, just some rather austere wallpaper and bare floorboards.

I felt a tremor of apprehension on entering Rose's bedroom. After all, she had lived such a private, self-contained life that any encroachment on her most intimate domain seemed a violation. Nonetheless, I went inside.

Apart from the ruffled bedclothes, which I assumed were

the result of Detective Sergeant Longbottom's cursory search, the bedroom was every bit as neat, clean and empty as the rest of the house. The one humanizing detail was a library book on her bedside table: Samuel Butler's *The Way of All Flesh*. So Rose Faversham had been an educated woman. Butler's savage and ironic attack on Victorian values was hardly common bedtime reading on our street.

I looked under the mattress and under the bed, and found nothing. The dressing table held those few items deemed essential for a woman's appearance and hygiene, and the chest of drawers revealed only stacks of carefully folded undergarments, corsets and the like, among which I had no desire to go probing. The long dresses hung in the wardrobe beside the high-buttoned blouses.

About to give up and head home to bed, I tried one last place – the top of the wardrobe, where I used to keep my secret diaries when I was a boy – and there I found the shoebox. Even a brief glance inside told me it was the repository of whatever past and personal memories Rose Faversham might have wanted to hang onto. Instead of sitting on the bedspread to read by torchlight, I went back downstairs and slipped out of the house like a thief in the night, which I suppose I was, with Rose's shoebox under my arm. A bomb exploded about half a mile away as I sidled down the street.

•

I should have gone to one of the shelters, I know, but I was feeling devil-may-care that night, and I certainly didn't want anyone to know I had broken into Rose's house and stolen her only private possessions. Back in my own humble abode, I made sure my curtains were shut tight, poured a large tumbler of brandy – perhaps, apart from nosiness and an inability to suffer fools gladly, my only vice – then turned on the standard lamp beside my armchair and settled down to examine my haul. There was a certain excitement in having pilfered it, as they say, and for a moment I imagined I had an inkling of that illicit thrill Fingers Finnegan must get every time *he* burgles someone's house. Of course, this was different; I hadn't broken into Rose's house for my own benefit, to line my own pockets, but to solve the mystery of her murder.

The first thing the shoebox yielded was a photograph of three smiling young women standing in front of an old van with a cross on its side. I could tell by their uniforms that they were nurses from the First World War. On the back, in slightly smudged ink, someone had written 'Midge, Rose and Margaret – Flanders, 30 July 1917. Friends Inseparable For Ever!'

I stared hard at the photograph and, though my imagination may have been playing tricks on me, I thought I recognized Rose as the one in the middle. She had perfect dimples at the edges of her smile, and her eyes gazed, pure and clear, directly into the lens. She bore little resemblance to the Rose I had known as Mad Maggie, or indeed to the body of Rose Faversham as I had seen it. But I think it was her.

I put the photograph aside and pulled out the next item. It was a book of poetry: *Severn and Somme* by Ivor Gurney. One of my favourite poets, Gurney was gassed at St Julien, near Passchendaele, and sent to a war hospital near Edinburgh. I heard he later became mentally disturbed and suicidal, and he died just two or three years ago, after nearly twenty years of suffering. I have always regretted that we never met.

I opened the book. On the title page, someone had written, 'To My Darling Rose on her 21st Birthday, 20 March 1918. Love, Nicholas.' So Rose was even younger than I had thought.

I set the book aside for a moment and rubbed my eyes. Sometimes I fancied the residual effects of the gas made them water, though my doctor assured me that it was a foolish notion, as mustard gas wasn't a lachrymator.

I hadn't been in the war as late as March 1918. The injury that sent me to a hospital in Manchester, my 'Blighty', took place the year before. Blistered and blinded, I had lain in bed there for months, unwilling to get up. The blindness passed, but the scarring remained, both inside and out. In the small hours, when I can't sleep, I relive those early days of August 1917 in Flanders: the driving rain, the mud, the lice, the rats, the deafening explosions. It was madness. We were doomed from the start by incompetent leaders, and as we struggled waist deep through mud, with shells and bullets flying all around us, we could only watch in hopeless acceptance as our own artillery sank in the mud, and our tanks followed it down.

Judging by the words on the back of the photograph, Rose had been there, too: *Rose*, one of the angels of mercy who tended the wounded and the dying in the trenches of Flanders' fields.

I opened the book. Nicholas, or Rose, had underlined the first few lines of the first poem, 'To the Poet Before Battle':

> *Now, youth, the hour of thy dread passion comes;*
> *Thy lovely things must all be laid away;*
> *And thou, as others, must face the riven day*
> *Unstirred by rattle of the rolling drums*
> *Or bugles' strident cry.*

Perhaps Nicholas had been a poet, and Gurney's call for courage in the face of impending battle applied to him, too? And if Nicholas had been a poet, was Rose one of the 'lovely things' he had to set aside?

Outside, the all-clear sounded and brought me back to earth. I breathed a sigh of relief. Spared again. Still, I had been so absorbed in Rose's treasures that I probably wouldn't have heard a bomb if one fell next door. They say you never hear the one with your name on.

I set the book down beside the photograph and dug around deeper in the shoebox. I found a medal of some sort – I think for valour in wartime nursing – and a number of official papers and certificates. Unfortunately, there were no personal letters. Even so, I managed to compile a list of names to seek out and one or two official addresses where I might pursue my enquiries into Rose

Faversham's past. No time like the present, I thought, going over to my escritoire and taking out pen and paper.

•

I posted my letters early the following morning, when I went to fetch my newspaper. I had the day off from school, as the pupils were collecting aluminium pots and pans for the Spitfire Fund, so I thought I might slip into Special Constable mode and spend an hour or two scouring Fingers Finnegan's usual haunts.

I started at Frinton's, on the High Street, where I also treated myself to two rashers of bacon and an egg. By mid-morning, I had made my way around most of the neighbouring cafes, and it was lunchtime when I arrived at Lyon's in the city centre. I didn't eat out very often, and twice a day was almost unheard of. Even so, I decided to spend one and threepence on roast beef and Yorkshire pudding. There was a lot of meat around then because the powers that be were slaughtering most of the farm animals to turn the land over to crops. I almost felt that I was doing my national duty by helping eat some before it went rotten.

As I waited, I noticed Finnegan slip in through the door in his usual manner, licking his lips, head half-bowed, eyes flicking nervously around the room trying to seek out anyone who might be after him, or to whom he might have owed money. I wasn't in uniform, and I was pretending to be absorbed in my newspaper, so his eyes slid over me. When he decided it was safe, he sat down three tables away from me.

My meal came, and I tucked in with great enthusiasm, managing to keep Finnegan in my peripheral vision. Shortly, another man came in – dark-haired, red-faced – and sat with Finnegan. The two of them put their heads together, all the time Finnegan's eyes flicking here and there, looking for danger signs. I pretended to pay no attention but was annoyed that I couldn't overhear a word. Something exchanged hands under the table, and the other man left: Finnegan fencing his stolen goods again.

I waited, lingering over my tea and rice pudding, and when

Finnegan left, I followed him. I hadn't wanted to confront him in the restaurant and cause a scene, so I waited until we came near a ginnel not far from my own street, then I speeded up, grabbed him by the shoulders and dragged him into it.

Finnegan was not very strong – in fact, he was a scrawny, sickly sort of fellow, which is why he wasn't fit for service – but he was slippery as an eel, and it took all my energy to hang onto him until I got him where I wanted him, with his back to the wall and my fists gripping his lapels. I slammed him against the wall a couple of times to take any remaining wind out of his sails, then when he went limp, I was ready to start.

'Bloody hell, Constable Bascombe!' he said when he'd got his breath back. 'I didn't recognize you at first. You didn't have to do that, you know. If there's owt you want to know why don't you just ask me? Let's be civilians about it.'

'The word is *civilized*. With you? Come off it, Fingers.'

'My name's Michael.'

'Listen, Michael, I want some answers and I want them now.'

'Answers to what?'

'During last night's air raid I saw you coming out of a house on Cardigan Road.'

'I never.'

'Don't lie to me. I know it was you.'

'So what? I might've been at my cousin's. He lives on Cardigan Road.'

'You were carrying something.'

'He gave me a couple of kippers.'

'You're lying to me, Fingers, but we'll let that pass for the moment. I'm interested in the raid before that one.'

'When was that, then?'

'Last Wednesday.'

'How d'you expect me to remember what I was doing that long ago?'

'Because murder can be quite a memorable experience, Fingers.'

He turned pale and slithered in my grip. My palms were

sweaty. 'Murder? Me? You've got to be joking! I've never killed nobody.'

I didn't bother pointing out that that meant he must have killed *somebody* – linguistic niceties such as that being as pointless with someone of Finnegan's intelligence as speaking loudly to a foreigner and hoping to be understood – so I pressed on. 'Did you break into Rose Faversham's house on Aston Place last Wednesday during the raid?'

'Rose Faversham. Who the bloody hell's she when she's at home? Never heard of her.'

'You might have known her as Mad Maggie.'

'*Mad Maggie*. Now why would a bloke like me want to break into *her* house? That's assuming he did things like that in the first place, hypnotically, like.'

Hypnotically? Did he mean *hypothetically*? I didn't even ask. 'To rob her, perhaps?'

'Nah. You reckon a woman who went around looking like she did would have anything worth stealing? Hypnotically, again, of course.'

'Of course, Fingers. This entire conversation is *hypnotic*. I understand that.'

'Mad Maggie hardly draws attention to herself as a person worth robbing. Not unless you're into antiques.'

'And you're not?'

'Wouldn't know a Chippendale from a Gainsborough.'

'Know anybody who is?'

'Nah.'

'What about the thousands of pounds they say she had hidden in her mattress?'

'And pigs can fly, Constable Bascombe.'

'What about silverware?'

'There's a bob or two in a nice canteen of cutlery. Hypnotically, of course.'

The one thing that might have been of value to someone other than herself was Rose's silverware, and that had been left alone.

Even if Fingers had been surprised by her and killed her, he would hardly have left his sole prize behind when he ran off. On the other hand, with a murder charge hanging over it, the silverware might have turned out to be more of a liability than an asset. I looked at his face, into his eyes, trying to decide whether he was telling the truth. You couldn't tell anything from Finnegan's face, though; it was like a ferret mask.

'Look,' he said, licking his lips, 'I might be able to help you.'

'Help me?'

'Yeah. But . . . you know . . . not standing here, like this . . .'

I realized I was still holding him by the lapels, and I had hoisted him so high he had to stand on his tiptoes. I relaxed my grip. 'What do you have in mind?'

'We could go to the Prince Albert, have a nice quiet drink. They'll still be open.'

I thought for a moment. The hard way hadn't got me very far. Maybe a little diplomacy was in order. Though it galled me to be going for a drink with a thieving illiterate like Fingers Finnegan, there were larger things at stake. I swallowed my pride and said, 'Why not.'

•

Nobody paid us a second glance, which was all right by me. I bought us both a pint, and we took a quiet table by the empty fireplace. Fingers brought a packet of Woodbines out of his pocket and lit up. His smoke burned my lungs and caused me a minor coughing fit, but he didn't seem concerned by it.

'What makes you think you can help me?' I asked him when I'd recovered.

'I'll bet you're after Mad Maggie's murderer, aren't you?'

'How do you know that?'

'Word gets around. The *real* police think it was gypsies, you know. They've got one of them in the cells right now. Found some silver candlesticks in his possession.'

'How did they know whether Rose had any silver candlesticks?'

He curled his lip and looked at me as if I were stupid. 'They don't, but they don't know that she didn't, do they? All they need's a confession, and he's a brute in the interrogation room is that short-arse bastard.'

'Who?'

'Longbottom. It's what we call him. Longbottom. Short-arse. Get it?'

'I'm falling off my chair with laughter. Have you got anything interesting to tell me or haven't you?'

'I might have seen someone, mightn't I?'

'Seen someone? Who? Where?'

He rattled his empty glass on the table. 'That'd be telling, wouldn't it?'

I sighed, pushed back the disgust I felt rising like vomit in my craw and bought him another pint. He was smirking all over his ferret face when I got back.

'Ta very much, Constable Bascombe. You're a true gentleman, you are.'

The bugger was *enjoying* this. 'Fingers,' I said, 'you don't know how much your praise means to me. Now, to get back to what you were saying.'

'It's Michael. I told you. And none of your Micks or Mikes. My name's Michael.'

'Right, Michael. You know, I'm a patient man, but I'm beginning to feel just a wee bit let down here. I'm thinking that perhaps it might not be a bad idea for me to take you to Detective Sergeant Longbottom and see if he can't persuade you to tell him what you know.'

Fingers jerked upright. 'Hang on a minute. There's no need for anything drastic like that. I'm just having my little bit of fun, that's all. You wouldn't deny a fellow his little bit of fun, would you?'

'Heaven forbid,' I muttered. 'So now you've had your fun, Fin — er . . . Michael, perhaps we can get back to business?'

'Right . . . well . . . theatrically speaking, of course, I might have been in Aston Place on the night you're talking about.'

Theatrically? Let it go, Frank. 'Last Wednesday, during the air raid?'

'Right. Well I might have been, just, you know, being a concerned citizen and all, going round checking up all the women and kids was in the shelters, like.'

'And the old people. Don't forget the old people.'

'Especially the old people. Anyway, like I said, I just *might* have been passing down Aston Place during the air raid, seeing that everyone was all right, like, and I *might* just have seen someone coming out of Mad Maggie's house.'

'Did you?'

'Well, it was dark, and that bloody smoke from the power station doesn't make things any better. Like a real pea-souper, that is. Anyway, I might just have seen this figure, like, a quick glimpse.'

'I understand. Any idea who it was?'

'Not at first I hadn't, but now I've an idea. I just hadn't seen him for a long time.'

'Where were you?'

'Coming out of— Can't have been more than two or three houses away. When I saw him he gave me a real fright, so I pressed myself back in the doorway, like, so he couldn't see me.'

'But you got a look at him?'

'Not a good one. First thing I noticed, though, is he was wearing a uniform.'

'What kind of uniform?'

'I don't know, do I? Soldier's, I suppose.'

'Anything else?'

'Well, he moved off sort of sideways, like.'

'Crabwise?'

'Come again?'

'Like a crab?'

'If you say so, Constable Bascombe.'

Something about all this was beginning to make sense, but I wasn't sure I liked the sense it made. 'Did you notice anything else?'

'I saw him go into a house across the street.'

'Which one?' I asked, half of me not wanting to know the answer.

'The milkman's,' he said.

•

I didn't want to, but I had to see this through. *Tommy Fletcher*. My own godson. All afternoon I thought about it, and I could see no way out of confronting Harry and Tommy. No matter how much thinking I did, I couldn't come up with an explanation, and if Tommy *had* murdered Rose Faversham, I wanted to know why. He had certainly been acting oddly since he came back from the army hospital, but I had acted rather strangely myself after they released me from the hospital in Manchester in 1918. I knew better than to judge a man by the way he reacts to war.

I consoled myself with the fact that Tommy might not have killed Rose, that she was already dead when he went to see her, but I knew in my heart that didn't make sense. Nobody just dropped in on Mad Maggie to see how she was doing, and the idea of two people going to see her in one night was absurd. No, I knew that the person Fingers had seen coming out of Rose's house had to be her killer, and he swore that person was Tommy Fletcher.

Fingers could have been lying, but that didn't make sense, either. For a start, he wasn't that clever. He must also know that I would confront Tommy and that, one way or another, I'd find out the truth. No, if Fingers had killed Mad Maggie and wanted to escape blame, all he had to do was deny that he had been anywhere near her house and let the gypsy take the fall.

I steeled myself with a quick brandy, then I went around to Harry's house just after eight o'clock. They were all listening to a variety programme on the Home Service, and someone was torturing 'A Nightingale Sang in Berkeley Square'. As usual, Tommy was wearing his army uniform, even though he was on extended leave. He still looked ill, pale and thin. His mother, Polly, a stout, silent woman I had known ever since she was a little girl, offered to make tea and disappeared into the kitchen.

'What brings you out at this time of night, then?' Harry asked. 'Want some company down at the Prince Albert?'

I shook my head. 'Actually, it's your Tommy I came to see.'

A shadow of fear crossed Harry's face. 'Tommy? Well, you'd better ask him yourself, then. Best of luck.'

Tommy hadn't moved yet, but when I addressed him, he slowly turned to face me. There was a look of great disappointment in his eyes, as if he knew he had had something valuable in his grasp only to have it taken from him at the last minute. Harry turned off the radio.

'Tommy,' I said, speaking as gently as I could, 'did you go to visit Mad Maggie last Wednesday night, the night of the air raid?'

Harry was staring at me, disbelief written all over his face. 'For God's sake, Frank!' he began, but I waved him down.

'Did you, Tommy? Did you visit Mad Maggie?'

Slowly, Tommy nodded.

'You don't have to say any more,' Harry said, getting to his feet. He turned to me as if I were his betrayer. 'I've considered you a good friend for many years, Frank, but you're pushing me too far.'

Polly came back with the teapot and took in the scene at a glance. 'What's up? What's going on?'

'Sit down, Polly,' I said. 'I'm asking your Tommy a few questions, that's all.'

Polly sat. Harry remained standing, fists clenched at his sides, then Tommy's voice broke the deadlock. 'It's all right, Mum,' he said to Polly. 'I want to tell him. I want to get it off my chest.'

'I don't know what you're talking about, son,' she said.

Tommy pointed at Harry. 'He does. He's not as daft as he looks.'

I looked at Harry, who sat down again and shook his head.

Tommy turned back to me. 'Did I go visit Mad Maggie? Yes I did. Did I kill her? Yes, I did. I got in through the back window. It wasn't locked. I picked up the posser and went through into the living room. She was sitting in the dark. Didn't even have a wireless. She must have heard me, but she didn't move. She looked at me just once before I hit her, and I could swear she knew why I was doing it. She understood and she knew it was right. It was *just*.'

As Tommy spoke, he became more animated and his eyes started to glow with life again, as if his prize were once more within his grasp.

'Why did you do it, Tommy?' I asked. 'What did she ever do to harm you?'

He looked at Harry. 'She killed my dad.'

'She what?'

'I told you. She killed my dad. My real dad.'

Polly flopped back in her armchair, tea forgotten, and put her hand to her heart. 'Tommy, what are you saying?'

'He knew,' he said, looking at Harry again. 'Or at least he suspected. I told him about the field, about the villagers, the madwoman.'

Harry shook his head. 'I *didn't* know,' he said. 'You never told me it was *her*. All I knew was that you were upset, you were saying crazy things and acting strange. Especially when you came in from the raid that night. I was worried, that's all. If I ever suspected you, that's the only reason, son, I swear it. When I found her body, I thought if there was the remotest possibility . . . That's why I went for Frank. I told him to lay off it, to let the gyppos take the blame. But he wouldn't.' Harry pointed his finger at me, red in the face. 'If you want to blame anyone, blame him.'

'Calm down, Harry,' I told him. 'You'll give yourself a heart attack.'

'It's not a matter of blame,' Tommy said. 'It's about justice. And justice has been served.'

'Better tell me about it, Tommy,' I said. The air-raid siren went off, wailing up and down the scale. We all ignored it.

Tommy paused and ran his hand through his closely cropped

hair. He looked at me. 'You should understand, Mr Bascombe. You were there. He was your best friend.'

I frowned. 'Tell me, Tommy.'

'Before Dunkirk, a group of us got cut off and we were in this village near Ypres for a few days, before the Germans got too close. We almost didn't make it to the coast in time for the evacuation. The people were frightened about what the Germans might do if they found out we were there, but they were kind to us. I became quite friendly with one old fellow who spoke very good English, and I told him my father had been killed somewhere near here in the first war. Passchendaele. I said I'd never seen his grave. One day, the old man took me out in his horse and cart and showed me some fields. It was late May, and the early poppies were just coming out among the rows of crosses. It looked beautiful. I knew my father was there somewhere.' Tommy choked for a moment, looked away and wiped his eyes.

'Then the old man told me a story,' he went on. 'He said there was a woman living in the village who used to you . . . you know . . . with the British soldiers. But she was in love with a German officer, and she passed on any information she could pick up from the British directly to him. One soldier let something slip about some new trench positions they were preparing for a surprise attack, and before anyone knew what had hit them, the trenches were shelled and the Germans swarmed into them. They killed every British soldier in their path. It came to hand to hand combat in the end. Bayonets. And the woman's German lover was one of the last to die.'

Tommy paused, glanced at his mother and went on, 'He told me she never recovered. She went mad, and for a while after the armies had moved on she could be heard wailing for her dead German lover in the poppy fields at night. Then nothing more was heard of her. The rumour was that she had gone to England, where they had plenty of other madwomen to keep her company. I thought of Mad Maggie right from the start, of course, and I remembered the way she used to burst into French every now and then. I asked him if he had a photograph, and he said he thought he had an old one. We went back to his house, and he rummaged through his attic and came down with an old album. There she was. The same sort of clothes. That same look about her. Much younger and very beautiful, but it was *her*. It was Mad Maggie. And she had killed my father. He was in one of those trenches.'

'What happened next, Tommy?'

'I don't remember much of the next couple of months. The Germans got too close and we had to make a hasty departure. That's when I was wounded. I was lucky to make it to Dunkirk. If it hadn't been for my mates . . . They carried me most of the way. Anyway, for a while I didn't know where I was. In and out of consciousness. To be honest, half the time I preferred to be out of it. I had dreams, nightmares, visions, and I saw myself coming back and avenging my father's death.'

His eyes shone with pride and righteousness as he spoke. Outside, the bombs were starting to sound alarmingly close. 'Let's get down to the shelter,' Harry suggested.

'No,' said Tommy, holding up his hand. 'Hear me out now. Wait till I'm done.' He turned to me. 'You should understand, Mr Bascombe. She killed my dad. He was your best friend. You should understand. I only did what was right.'

I shook my head. 'There's no avenging deaths during wartime, Tommy. It's every man for himself. Some German bullet or bayonet had Larry's name on it, and that was that. Wrong place, wrong time. It could just as easily have been me.'

Tommy stared at me in disbelief.

'Besides,' I went on, getting a little concerned at the explosions outside, 'are you sure it was her, Tommy? It seems an awful coincidence that she should end up living on our street, don't you think?'

'I'm sure. I saw the photograph. I've still got it.'

'Can I have a look?'

Tommy opened his top pocket and handed me a creased photograph. There was no doubt about the superficial resemblance between the woman depicted there, leaning against a farmer's fence, wearing high buttoned-boots, smiling and holding her hand to her forehead to keep the sun out of her eyes. But it wasn't the same woman whose photograph I had found in Rose Faversham's shoebox. In fact, it wasn't any of the three – Midge, Rose or Margaret. There were no dimples, for a start, and the eyes were different. We all have our ways of identifying people, and with me it's always the eyes. Show me someone at six, sixteen and sixty and I'll know if it's the same person or not by the eyes.

Another bomb landed far too close for comfort, and the whole house shook. Then a split second later came a tremendous explosion. Plaster fell off the ceiling. The lights and radio went off. I could hear the drone of the bombers slowly disappearing to the south-east, on their way home again. We were all shaken, but I pulled myself to my feet first and suggested we go outside to see if anyone needed help.

I didn't really think he'd make a run for it, but I stuck close to Tommy as we all went outside. The smell was awful; the bitter, fiery smell of the explosive and a whiff of gas from a fractured pipe mixed with dust from broken masonry. The sky was lit up like Guy Fawkes night. It was a terrible sight that met our eyes, and the four of us could only stand and stare.

A bomb had taken out about three houses on the other side of the street. The middle one, now nothing but a pile of burning rubble, was Mad Maggie's.

•

When the answers to my letters started trickling in a couple of weeks after Tommy's arrest, I picked up some more leads, one of which eventually led me to Midge Livesey, now a mother of two boys – both in the RAF – who was living only thirty miles away, in the country. I telephoned her, and she seemed pleased to hear from someone who had known Rose, though she was saddened by the news of Rose's death, and she suggested I be her guest for the weekend.

Though it was late October, the weather was fine when I got off the train at the tiny station. It was a wonderful feeling to be out in the country again. I had been away for so long I had almost forgotten what the autumn leaves looked like and how many different varieties of birdsong there are. The sweet, acrid scent of burning leaves from someone's garden made a fine change from the stink of the air raids.

Midge and her husband, Arthur, welcomed me at the door of their cottage and told me they had already prepared the spare room. After I had laid out my things on the bed, I opened the window. Directly outside stood an apple tree, and beyond that I could see the landscape undulating to the north, where the large anvil shapes of peaks and fells were visible in the distance. I took in a deep breath of fresh air – as deep as I could manage with my poor lungs – and for once it didn't make me cough. Perhaps it was time I left the city, I thought. But no, there were police duties to attend to, and I loved my teaching job. After the war, perhaps, I would think of about it again, see if I could get a job in a village school.

When I showed Midge the photograph of the three of them over dinner that evening, a sad smile played across her features, and she touched the surface with her fingers, as if it could send out some sort of message to her.

'Yes,' she said, 'that was Rose. And that was Margaret. Poor Margaret, she died in childbirth ten years ago. The war wasn't all bad for us. We did have some good times. But I think the day that photograph was taken marked the beginning of the end. It was the day before the third Ypres battle started, and we were field nurses. We used to go onto the fields and into the trenches to clean up after the battles.' She shook her head and looked at Arthur, who tenderly put his hand on top of hers. 'You've never . . . well, I suppose you have.' She looked at her husband. 'Arthur understands, too. He was wounded at Arras. I worry about my boys. Just remembering, just thinking about it, makes me fear for them terribly. Does that make sense?'

'Yes,' I said.

She paused for a moment and poured us all tea. 'Anyway, Rose was especially sensitive,' she went on. 'She wrote poetry and wanted to go to university to study English literature when it was all over. French, too. She spoke French very well and spent a lot of time talking to the poor wounded French soldiers. Often they were with the English, you know, and there was nobody could talk to them. Rose did. She fell in love with a handsome young English lieutenant. Nicholas, his name was.' She smiled. 'But we were young. We were always falling in love back then.'

'What happened to her?' I asked.

'Rose? She broke under the strain. Shell shock, I suppose you'd call it. You hear a lot about the poor boys, the breakdowns, the self-inflicted wounds, but you never hear much about the women, do you? Where are we in the history books? We might not have been shooting at the Germans and only in minimal danger of getting shot at ourselves – though there were times – but we were *there*. We saw the slaughter first hand. We were up to our elbows in blood and guts. Some people just couldn't take it, the way some of the boys couldn't take combat. I'll say this, though, I think it was Nicholas's death that finally sent Rose over the edge. It was the following year, 1918, the end of March, near a little village on the Somme called St Quentin. She found him, you know, on the field. It was pure chance. Half his head had been blown away. She was never the same. She used to mutter to herself in French and go into long silences. Eventually, she tried to commit suicide by taking an overdose of morphine, but a doctor found her in time. She was invalided out in the end.'

'Do you know what happened next?'

'I visited her as soon as the war was over. She'd just come out of the hospital and was living with her parents. They were wealthy landowners – very posh, you might say – and they hadn't a clue what to do with her. She was an embarrassment to them. In the end they set up a small fund for her, so she would never have to go without, and left her to her own devices.'

After a moment or two's silence, I showed Midge the book of

poetry. Again, she fingered it like a blind person looking for meaning. 'Oh, yes. Ivor Gurney. She was always reading this.' She turned the pages. 'This was her favourite.' She read us a short poem called 'Bach and the Sentry', in which the poet on sentry duty hears his favourite Bach prelude in his imagination and wonders how he will feel later, when he actually plays the piece again in peacetime. Then she shook her head. 'Poor mad Rose. Nobody knew what to do with her. Do tell me what became of her.'

I told her what I knew, which wasn't much, though for some reason I held back the part about Tommy and his mistake. I didn't want Midge to know that my godson had mistaken her friend for a traitor. It seemed enough to lay the blame at the feet of a gypsy thief and hope that Midge wasn't one of those women who followed criminal trials closely in the newspapers.

Nor did I tell her that Rose's house had been destroyed by a bomb almost a week after the murder and that she would almost certainly have been killed anyway. Midge didn't need that kind of cruel irony. She had suffered enough; she had enough bad memories to fuel her nightmares, and enough to worry about in the shape of her two boys.

I simply told her that Rose was a very private person, certainly eccentric in her dress and her mannerisms, and that none of us really knew her very well. She was a part of the community, though, and we all mourned her loss.

So Mad Maggie was another of war's victims, I thought, as I breathed in the scent of the apple tree before getting into bed that night. One of the uncelebrated ones. She came to our community to live out her days in anonymous grief and whatever inner peace she could scrounge for herself, her sole valuable possessions a book of poetry, an old photograph and a nursing medal.

And so she would have remained, a figure to be mocked by the children and ignored by the adults, had it not been for another damn war, another damaged soul and the same poppy field in Flanders.

Requiescat in pace, Rose, though I am not a religious man. *Requiescat in pace.*

•

It should never have happened, but they hanged Tommy Fletcher for the murder of Rose Faversham at Wandsworth Prison on 25 May 1941, at eight o'clock in the morning.

Everyone said Tommy should have got off for psychiatric reasons, but his barrister had a permanent hangover, and the judge had an irritable bowel. In addition, the *expert* psychiatrist hired to evaluate him didn't know shell shock from an Oedipus complex.

The only thing we could console ourselves with was that Tommy went to the gallows proud and at peace with himself for having avenged his father's death.

I hadn't the heart to tell him that he was wrong about Mad Maggie, that she wasn't the woman he thought she was.

THE DUKE'S WIFE

I was absolutely speechless. After everything that had happened, there he stood, bold as brass, telling all the world we were going to be married. *Married!* You would have been speechless, too.

Let me give you a little background. My name is Isabella, and until that moment I had been all set to enter a convent. I fear I have a wayward and impulsive nature that needs to be kept in check, and the convent I had in mind, the votarists of St Clare, was one of strict restraint. Imagine my feelings when, head swimming from the twists and turns of recent events, I heard I was to be married to the duke!

But there's more, much more.

A short while ago the duke realized that he had become lax in his duties, being of too mild and gentle a nature to enforce the laws of the land to their fullest. Of special concern to him, because it ate away at the very institution of marriage itself, was the law that forbade, on pain of death, a man to live with a woman to whom he was not married.

Fearing that the people would revolt if he were suddenly to change course and start enforcing the law rigorously himself, the duke thought it better to slip away for a while and leave his deputy, Angelo, in charge. Thus, Angelo was invested with all the duke's powers and charged with cleaning up Vienna.

Mistake. Big mistake.

Where do I come into all this? you might be wondering. Well, it so happens that my brother Claudio had plighted his troth to his fiancée Juliet, and they were sleeping together. The problem was that they had kept their marriage contract a secret in the hope that Juliet's family would in time come to favour their union and provide a dowry, and this brought them within the scope of the law against fornication.

Now, Angelo *could* have exercised mercy, realizing that this was a very minor infringement indeed, and that the two were, in all but the outward ceremony itself, legally married, but Angelo is a cold fish and a sadistic, ruthless dictator. He likes to hurt people and make them squirm; it gives him pleasure. Believe me, I *know*.

Finding himself so suddenly and inexplicably condemned to death, Claudio asked me to intercede with Angelo on his behalf and see if I could secure a pardon. This I did, with disastrous results: Angelo told me he was in love with *me*, and he would only let Claudio go if I slept with *him*.

Now, while I do realize that in many people's eyes to give up one's virginity for one's brother's life might not seem too much to ask, you must bear in mind that I was to join the votarists of St Clare. I was to be married to God. This was my life, my destiny, and all of that – my very *soul* itself – would be sacrificed if I gave in to Angelo's base demands.

And don't think I didn't care about Claudio. Don't think for a moment that the thought of complying didn't cross my mind, but I wasn't going to give in to that kind of blackmail. I didn't trust Angelo anyway. For all I knew, he might take my virginity *and* have Claudio executed as well – which, as it turned out, was exactly what he had in mind.

The whole process was degrading, me pleading passionately for my brother's life, going down on my knees on the cold stone to beg, Angelo making it clear that only by yielding up my body to his will could I save Claudio. Humiliating.

When I told him my decision, Claudio wasn't at all understanding. Of everyone, he should have been the one to see how important my virginity was, but no. He even had the effrontery to suggest that I should reconsider and commit this vile sin to save his life. Claudio was afraid of death, and all he could talk about was his fear of dying when *I* was facing a much greater enemy than death.

I told him he would find his comfort in the bosom of the Lord. He didn't seem to agree.

Where was the wily duke during all this? You may well ask. As it turns out he was secretly directing events, disguised as a friar, and he was the one who came up with a cunning plan. He may be of a tender and mild disposition, but he has a devious mind and he likes to play games. Nor does he always stop to think who might get hurt by them.

Angelo had once been betrothed to a woman called Mariana, but her dowry went down on the same ship as her brother Frederick, and Angelo left her in tears, pretending he had discovered some stain on her honour when it was, in fact, the loss of the dowry that turned him against her. If you needed any more evidence of his worthlessness, that's the kind of person he is.

Now, if I were to go back to Angelo and pretend to agree to his demands, the friar suggested, we could arrange things so that Mariana went to his chamber in my stead, breaking no laws and saving both my virginity and Claudio's life.

It seemed a very good plan, and it worked, though the friar did have to do a little juggling with severed heads later on to convince Angelo that Claudio had indeed been beheaded. Then, for reasons of his own, the friar let me go on believing that Claudio had been executed – I did say he likes to play games, didn't I? – until the final scenes had been played out.

He had Mariana beg for Angelo's life, and the poor woman importuned *me* to beg with her! Thus, I found myself on my knees for a second time, this time pleading for the life of a man I hated, the man who, I thought, had killed my brother even though, he thought, he had enjoyed the treasures of my body.

So is it any wonder I was speechless when in walked Claudio, as alive as you or I, and the duke announced that I was to be his duchess?

•

I could have said no, I suppose, but at the time I was too stunned to say anything, and the next thing I knew we were married.

Though it took me many months, I got over the shock of it all and adapted myself as best I could to my new life. I hadn't actually taken my vows, so there was no legal problem with the marriage. The duke took over Vienna again and enforced the law himself, tempered with mercy and charity, and things were back on an even keel. I'm not saying that fornication ceased. That could never happen here. We Viennese are an odd lot, our lives full of secret vices and lies, and anyone with an interest in the human mind and perverse behaviour would have a field day studying us.

Being the duke's wife had many advantages, I soon found, though I did have some trouble adjusting to his husbandly demands. He wasn't a young man, but he was certainly vigorous, though he needed certain props to help him perform those functions he liked so much. In particular, he liked to dress as a friar and intone Latin vespers when he took me from behind, as was his wont. That, I could deal with, but I drew the line when he asked *me* to dress as a nun. That would have been far too much of a travesty for me to take, given everything that had happened.

So time passed, and on the whole I quite enjoyed the life of idleness and luxury. I loved my horses, enjoyed the theatre and the frequent grand balls, and I came to rely on the kind attentions of my maids and the delicious concoctions of my cooks. As I say, the sacrifices were bearable. Once in a while, I had a wistful thought for the life I might have led, but I must confess that when I hosted a magnificent banquet or walked the grounds and gardens of our wonderful palace, the thought of a bare, cold, tiny cloister lost much of its appeal. Mind you, I still attended church regularly and prayed every night, and we gave generously to the votarists of St Clare.

•

You might be interested in knowing what happened to the others. Claudio and Juliet were married, after which they moved to the country. By all accounts they are happy enough, though we don't see them very often. Angelo and Mariana were also married – it was *her* wish, the duke's dictate, and in accord with the law – but their story didn't end happily at all. Well, how could it with an evil, sadistic pervert like Angelo for a husband? Mariana is very sweet, but she is *such* a naif when it comes to men. Even back when I was headed for the convent I had more idea than she did.

So I wasn't at all surprised when she came to me in tears about six months after her marriage.

'Dry your, eyes, dear,' I said to her, 'and let's walk in the garden.' It was a beautiful spring day, with a warm gentle breeze wafting the scents of flowers through the mild air.

'I can't go on,' she said.

'What's wrong?'

'It's Angelo.'

'What about him?'

'He doesn't love me any more.'

He never did love her, I could have said, but I held my tongue. I doubted that was what she wanted to hear at the moment. 'What makes you think that?' I asked.

She looked around, then leaned in towards me and lowered her voice. 'He has other women.'

I could have laughed out loud. Just about every husband in Vienna has other women. I suspect even my own duke has one from time to time, but if it spares me the friar's costume and the Latin vespers for a night, who am I to complain? But Mariana, I could see, was really upset. 'It's just men, Mariana,' I told her. 'They're like that. They can't help themselves. It's their nature. Every time they see an attractive woman they just have to conquer her.'

'But am *I* not attractive?'

'That's neither here nor there. You're his *wife*. That's all that counts.'

'Yes, I am his wife, so why does he have to sleep with other women? I'll sleep with him any time he wants. I'll do *anything* he wants me to, even if it hurts me, even that disgusting thing with the—'

'Mariana! I told you, it's just their nature. You'll have to learn to live with it or your life will be a very unhappy one.'

'But I *am* unhappy already. I can't live with it. I want to die.'

I took her arm. 'Don't be so histrionic, Mariana,' I said. 'You'll get used to it.'

She broke away. 'I won't! Never! I want to die. I'm going to kill myself.'

I sighed. 'Over a man? There must be better reasons. Look, who is this woman he's been seeing?'

Mariana looked at me. Her eyes were so full of pain that my heart cried for her, even though I thought she was being foolish. 'It's not just *one* woman.'

'How many?'

'I don't know.'

'Two, three?'

'I told you. I don't know.'

'You must have some idea. Is it three, four, or five?'

'About three. I think that's about right.'

'So he's sleeping with three other women?'

'Three a week. Yes.'

'*What?*'

'He has them sent to him. There's a man called Pandarus, a Greek I think, a despicable human being, and Angelo pays him to procure young women. Usually young virgins from the provinces who are new in town and haven't settled into employment. They're so young. They don't . . . I mean they don't all know what to expect.'

'He forces them?'

Marian nodded. 'I've heard cries. Screams, sometimes, and he swears they will die terribly if they ever speak of what happened.'

Mariana's story was starting to interest me. I had heard of this Pandarus, though I had never met him, and I knew that he affected a respectable enough surface and was able to move among varying levels of society. Procuring wasn't new to Vienna, even among the higher echelons – nothing to do with sex is new to Vienna – but this Pandarus intrigued me all the same. 'How do you know all this?' I asked.

'A dear friend told me. She had conversation with one . . . with one of the girls.'

'And you're certain it's true?'

Mariana nodded. 'One night I lay in wait, hiding in the bushes, and watched. We have always had separate quarters, and Angelo maintains the same chamber he used . . . do you remember, that night when I went to him in your stead?'

I nodded. It wasn't a memory I cared to dwell on. Not one of my finest moments.

'They come in the darkest of night, and he burns no candles. Everything is just as it was that night.'

'I see,' I said. I had hated Angelo long and deeply enough for what he had inflicted on me that, even as we spoke, the beginnings of a plan began to form itself effortlessly in my mind.

'What can I do, dear Isabel? Pray, tell me, what can I do?'

I took her hand. 'Do nothing,' I said. 'At least not for the moment. I know it pains you, but bear with it. I'm certain there's a solution and I promise that your suffering will come an end ere long.'

Her eyes widened and lit up at that little sliver of hope. 'Really? You promise? Oh, Isabel, is it possible I can be happy again?'

'We'll see,' I said, busy thinking. 'We'll see.'

•

I was finally satisfied enough with my changed appearance and the peasant clothes I had painstakingly made to venture out into the city streets in the guise of a country girl seeking employment. Through further, cautious questioning of Mariana, I had already determined that Pandarus tended to prey on his victims in the busy public square near the coach station, often approaching them the very moment they arrived in the city. He had, I imagined, a skilled eye and knew exactly who was vulnerable to his approach and who best to leave alone. I affected to look lost and weak, and on my second visit, a man came up to me. His clothes and his bearing signified a certain level of wealth and influence in society, and his general manner was that of a gentleman.

'Are you new here?' he asked.

'Me?' I responded shyly, keeping my head down. 'Yes, sir.'

'Where are you from?'

I named a distant village I had once heard one of my husband's ministers mention.

'And what, may I ask, brings you to Vienna?'

'I seek employment, sir.'

'You do, do you? And what skills do you possess?'

'I can cook, sir, and wash, and mend clothes.'

'Valuable skills, indeed. Come, walk with me.'

I couldn't just go with him, not that easily. I had to play the shy country girl. 'I cannot, sir.'

'Cannot? Why not?'

'I don't know, sir. It just seems so . . . forward. I don't know you.'

'Forward? Walking alongside a perfect gentlemen in a public place?' He smiled. He really did have a warm smile, the kind that leads you to trust a person. 'Come, come, don't be silly.'

So I walked beside him. He offered his arm, but I didn't take it. That didn't seem to upset him too much. 'You know, I think I might be able to help you,' he said, stroking his moustache.

'Help me, sir? You mean *you* require my services?'

He laughed. 'Me? Oh, no. Not me. A friend of mine. And I will speak for you.'

'But you don't know me, sir. How can you speak for me? You don't even know my name.'

He stopped walking and put his fingers under my chin, lifting my face. He was taller than I, so I had to look up, though I tried to keep my eyes down under my fluttering lashes. I felt myself blush. 'I am an excellent judge of character,' he said. 'I believe you to be an honest country maiden, and I believe you are exactly what he has in mind.' He let me go and carried on walking. This time I picked up my pace to keep up with him, showing interest. 'He does, however, have one peculiarity I must mention,' he went on.

'What might that be, sir?'

'He prefers to conduct his business at night.'

'That is strange, indeed, sir.'

He shrugged. 'It is a mere trifle.'

'If you say so, sir.' As a country girl, I could, of course, have no idea of the ways of city folk.

'So, should you be interested – and he is a most kind, considerate and bountiful master – you must go to him through his garden at night and he will acquaint you with his needs. You need have no fears. He is an honourable man, and I shall be close by.'

Again, I had to remind myself that I was playing the role of a simple country girl. 'If you think so, sir.'

'Tonight, then?'

I hesitated for just as long as necessary. 'Tonight,' I whispered finally.

'Meet me here,' he said, then he melted into the crowds.

•

My plan was simple enough. I intended to gain entry to Angelo's chamber under cover of darkness and . . . Well, I hadn't really thought much past that, except that I planned to confront him and expose him for what he was. If necessary, I would claim that I went to visit my friend Mariana and that he attempted to ravage me, but I doubted it would come to that. One of the many advantages of being the duke's wife is that subjects tend to fear my husband's power, and I had no doubt that Angelo would give up his nightly escapades if faced with their possible political consequences. A wife's railing is easy enough to ignore, but the power of the duke is another matter entirely.

I could not help but feel restless all evening as I waited for the appointed hour. After the usual antics with cassock and vespers, I slipped a sleeping draught into the duke's nightcap, and he went out like a snuffed candle. When the servants were all in bed, I donned my disguise and slipped out of the house.

The dark streets frightened me, as I had not gone out alone at night before, and I feared lest some drunken peasant or soldier should molest me. In case of just such an incident, I carried a dagger concealed about my person, a present to the Duke from a visiting diplomat. But either the denizens of the night are better behaved than I had imagined, or I was blessed by fortune, for I made my way to the square without any hindrance whatsoever. When I got there, I was surprised at how many people were still out and about at such a late hour, lounging by the fountain, talking and laughing by the light of braziers and flaming torches. I had no idea that such a world of shadows existed, and I found that the discovery oddly excited me.

Pandarus appeared at my side as if by magic, wrapped in dark robes, his head hooded, as was mine.

'Are you ready?' he asked.

I nodded.

'Then come with me.'

I followed him through the narrow alleys and across the broad cobbled courtyards to Angelo's quarters, where we paused at a gate in the high wall surrounding the garden.

'This gate is unlocked,' said Pandarus. 'Cross the garden directly to the chamber before you, where you will find the door also unlocked. Enter, and all will be explained.'

I managed to summon up one last show of nerves. 'I'm not certain, sir. I mean . . . I do not . . .'

'There's nothing to fear,' he said softly.

'Will you accompany me, sir?'

'I cannot. My friend prefers to conduct his business in private.'

He stood there while I gathered together all my strength, took a deep breath and opened the gate. There were no lights showing beyond the garden, so I had to walk carefully to make sure I didn't trip and fall. Finally, I reached the door of Angelo's chamber, and it opened when I pushed it gently, hinges creaking a little. By this time I could make out the varying degrees of shadows, so I was aware of the large canopied bed and of the silhouette standing before me: Angelo.

'Come in, my little pretty one,' he said. 'Make yourself comfortable. Has my friend Pandarus told you what you must do?'

I curtsied. 'Yes, sir. He told me you might have a position for me, but that you only conduct interviews at night.'

Angelo laughed. 'He's a fine dissembler, my Pandarus. But in that, he is not all wrong. I do, indeed, have a *position* for you.'

With this he moved towards me, and I felt his lizard-like hand caress my cheek. I should have drawn back, I know, and at that moment told him who I was and why I was there, but something in me, some innate curiosity compelled me to continue my deception.

Angelo led me slowly to the bed and bade me sit, then he sat beside me and began his caresses again, this time venturing into more private territory than before. I took hold of his hand and moved it away, but he was persistent, growing rougher. Before I knew it, he had me on my back on the bed and his hand was groping under my skirts, rough fingers probing me. I struggled and tried to tell him who I was, but he put his other hand over my mouth to silence me.

All the time he manhandled me thus, he was calling out my name. 'Isabella . . . Oh, my beautiful Isabella! Do it for me, Isabella. Please do it for me!' At first this confused me, for I was certain he hadn't recognized me. Then I realized with a shock that he *didn't* know who I was, but that this must be what he said to all his night-time visitors. He called them *all* Isabella.

And then I understood.

The whole thing, the recreation of the exact same conditions as the night I was to visit him in exchange for Claudio's life – the hour, the insistence on absolute darkness. Though Mariana had gone to him in my stead, Angelo either refused to believe this, or thought that by duplicating the trappings he could enjoy the treasures of my body time after time in the darkness of his vile imagination.

As we struggled there on the bed, disgust and outrage overcame any simple desire I harboured for justice, and I knew then what I had been planning to do all along. Angelo's behaviour just made it all that much easier.

I slipped out my dagger and plunged it into his back with as much force as I could muster. He stiffened, as if stung by a wasp, and reared back, hand behind him trying to staunch the flow of blood.

Then I plunged the dagger into his chest and said, 'This for Mariana!'

He croaked my name: 'Isabella . . . my Isabella . . .'

'Yes, it's me,' I said, 'but I'm *not* yours.' And I plunged the dagger in again. 'This is for me!' I said, and he rolled to the floor, pleading for his life. I knelt over him and plunged the dagger in one more time, into his black heart. 'And this is for not being able to tell us apart in the dark!'

After that he lay still. I didn't move for several minutes, but knelt there over Angelo's body catching my breath until I was sure that no one had heard. The house remained silent.

Knowing that Pandarus was probably still lurking by the garden gate, I left by the front door and hurried home through the dark streets. Nobody accosted me; I saw not a soul. When I got home, in the light of a candle in my chamber, I saw that my clothing was bloodstained. No matter. I would burn it. As soon as that was done and I was washed clean of Angelo's blood, all would be well. Mariana might shed a tear or two for her miserable, faithless husband, but she would get over him in time and he would never hurt her or anyone else again.

And as for me, as I believe I have already told you, there are many advantages to be gained from being the duke's wife, not the least of which is the unlikelihood of being suspected of murder.

GOING BACK

AN INSPECTOR BANKS NOVELLA

1

Banks pulled up outside his parents' council house and parked his Renault by the side of the road. He wondered if it would be safe left out overnight. The estate had had a bad reputation even when he grew up there in the sixties, and it had only got worse over recent years. Not that there was any alternative, he realized, as he made sure it was locked and the security system was working; his parents didn't own a garage.

He couldn't very well remove the CD player for the weekend, but to be on the safe side he stuffed the CDs themselves into his overnight bag. He didn't think any young joyriders would want to steal Thelonious Monk, Cecilia Bartoli or the Grateful Dead, but you couldn't be too careful. Besides, he had a portable disc player now, and he liked to listen to music in bed as he drifted off to sleep.

Banks's parents' house stood near the western edge of the estate, close to the arterial road, across from an abandoned factory and a row of shops. Banks paused for a moment and took in the red-brick terrace houses – rows of five, each with a little garden, low wall and privet hedge. His family had moved here from the tiny, grim back-to-back when he was twelve, when the houses were new.

It was a Friday afternoon near the end of October, and Banks was home for the weekend of his parents' golden wedding anniversary that Sunday, only his second overnight stay since he had left home at the age of eighteen to study business at London

Polytechnic. When that didn't work out, and when the sixties lost their allure in the early seventies, he joined the police. Since then, long hours, hard work, and his parents' overt disapproval of his career choice had kept him away. Visiting home was always a bit of a trial, but they *were* his mother and father, Banks reminded himself; he owed them more than he could ever repay, he had certainly neglected them over the years, and he knew they loved him in their way. They weren't getting any younger either.

He took a deep breath, opened the gate, walked up the path and knocked on the scratched red door, a little surprised by the loud music coming from the next house. He saw his mother approach through the frosted-glass pane. She opened the door, rubbed her hands together as if drying them and said, 'Alan, lovely to see you. Come on in, love, come in.'

Banks dropped his overnight bag in the hall and followed his mother through to the living room. It stretched from the front of the house to the back, and the back area, next to the kitchen, was permanently laid out as a dining room. The wallpaper was a wispy brown autumn leaves pattern, the three-piece suite a matching brown velveteen, and a sentimental autumn landscape hung over the electric fire.

His father was sitting in his usual armchair, the one with the best straight-on view of the television. He didn't get up, just grunted, 'Son, nice of you to come.'

'Hello, Dad. How are you doing?'

'Mustn't complain.' Arthur Banks had been suffering from mild angina for years, ever since he'd been made redundant from the sheet-metal factory, and it seemed to get neither better nor worse as time went on. He took pills for the pain and didn't even need an inhaler. Other than that, and the damage booze and fags had wreaked on his liver and lungs over the years, he had always been as fit as a fiddle. Hollow-chested and skinny, he still sported a head of thick dark hair with hardly a trace of grey. He wore it slicked back with lashings of Brylcreem.

Banks's mother, Ida, plump and nervy, fussed a little more

about how thin Banks was looking, then the kitchen door opened and a stranger walked into the room.

'Kettle's on, Mrs B. Now, who have we got here? Let me guess.'

'This is our son, Geoff. We told you he was coming. For the party, like.'

'So this is the lad who's done so well for himself, is it? The Porsche and the mews house in South Kensington?'

'No, that's Roy, the other one. He's not coming till Sunday afternoon. He's got important business. No, this is our eldest, Alan. I'm sure I told you about him. The one in that picture.'

The photograph she pointed to, half-hidden by a pile of women's magazines on one of the cabinet shelves showed Banks at the age of sixteen, when he captained the school rugby team for a season. There he stood in his purple and yellow strip, holding the ball, looking proud. It was the only photograph of him they had ever put on display.

'This is Geoff Salisbury,' said Ida Banks. 'Geoff lives up the street at number fifty-five.'

Geoff moved forward, hand stretched out like a weapon. He was a small, compact man, with lively, slightly watery eyes and cropped grey hair, about Banks's age. His smile revealed what looked to Banks like a set of perfect false teeth. His handshake was firm, and his hands calloused and ingrained with oil or grease from manual labour.

'Please to meet you, Alan,' he said. 'I'd love to stay and chat, but I can't just now.' He turned to Banks's mother. 'Have you got that shopping list, Mrs B? I'll be off to Asda now.'

'Only if you're sure it's no trouble.'

'Nothing's too much trouble for you, you know that. Besides, I have to go there myself.'

Banks's mother picked up her handbag, took out her purse and gave Geoffrey a handwritten list and a twenty-pound note. 'Will that cover it?'

'Easily, Mrs B. Easily. I'll be back in a tick. Coach and Horses tonight, Arthur?'

'Maybe. We'll see how I feel,' said Banks's father. On closer examination, he did look tired and drawn, Banks thought. More than when he had last seen him in the summer. His eyes had the look of milky marbles and his skin was the colour of porridge. It could be the strain of preparing for the upcoming party – Arthur Banks, while gregarious enough in the pub, had never liked a house full of relatives – but most of the organization, Banks guessed, would have fallen to his mother. Perhaps it was simple old age catching up fast.

Geoff Salisbury left, and Banks saw him go up to the red Fiesta with the rusted chassis, parked behind Banks's Renault. Geoff paused and looked Banks's car over before getting into his own and driving off.

'Who's that?' Banks asked his mother.

'I told you. Geoff Salisbury. He's a neighbour.'

'He seems at home here.'

'I don't know what we'd do without him,' said Mrs Banks. 'He's just like a son to us. Anyway, sit yourself down. Have a cuppa.'

Banks sat and his mother poured. 'So Roy's not coming till Sunday, then?' he said.

'No. He rang us last night, didn't he, Arthur?' She said it as if it were some momentous event. Arthur Banks nodded. 'He's got an important business meeting all day Saturday,' she went on. 'Something to do with some Yanks flying in, and they have to be back in New York by evening . . . I don't know. Anyway, he says he should be here by Sunday lunchtime.'

'Good of him to bother,' Banks muttered.

His mother cast him a long-suffering glance. Banks knew she had been used to the brothers' bickering when they both lived at home, and it was no surprise whose side she usually took. 'What time are you planning on starting the party?' Banks asked.

'We told everyone to come about six o'clock. That'll give us time to clear up and get things ready after lunch. By the way, I don't suppose you've heard yet, but Mrs Summerville passed away.' She announced it in the sort of soft and solemn tones generally reserved for those who had *passed away*.

'I'm sorry to hear it,' said Banks. Mrs Summerville was the mother of the first girl he had ever slept with, though he had always believed that neither the late Mrs Summerville nor his own mother knew that. 'What did she die of?'

'It wasn't anything suspicious, if that's what you're thinking.'

'Perish the thought.'

His mother studied him, frowning. 'Yes . . . well, it was a blessing really. She'd been very poorly. Died in her sleep, according to Alice Green.'

'Still—' said Banks, uncertain what to say. He sipped some tea. As usual, it was milky and sweet, though he had stopped taking milk and sugar twenty years ago.

'And how are the Marshalls?' he asked. The Marshalls were the parents of Banks's school friend Graham, who had disappeared at the age of fourteen and whose body had been discovered the previous summer. Banks had come down to help the locals work on the case and the solution hadn't pleased anyone. It was during that time he had met Detective Inspector Michelle Hart, whom he had been seeing on and off ever since. Pity she wasn't around this weekend, he thought.

'Same as ever, I suppose,' said Mrs Banks. 'We don't see much of them, do we, Arthur?'

Arthur Banks shook his head.

'It's as if they've shut themselves away since you were last down.' Banks's mother cast him an accusing glance, as if their becoming recluses were his fault. And maybe it was, in a way. The truth is rarely as liberating as people would have us believe; it often binds more than it frees.

'I'm sorry to hear that,' he said.

'You know,' his mother went on, 'while you're here, you ought to go and see Mrs Green. She keeps asking about you, and she was very put out you didn't drop by and see her in the summer. She still thinks very fondly of you, though I can't see why, the noise you lot used to make at her house.'

Banks smiled. He remembered Mrs Green fondly, too. She was the mother of an old school friend, Tony Green, whom Banks hadn't seen since he left home. Tony hadn't been one of the real in-crowd, but he had been on the rugby team with Banks, and Banks had always liked Mrs Green. Most of the kids did. She didn't stop them from smoking in her house, and she didn't mind them playing the sort of music – the Beatles and the Rolling Stones mostly – that most adults hated. Once or twice she had given Banks and Tony half a crown apiece and sent them off to the pictures out of her way. She had also been very pretty, with the kind of bosom young boys dream about, and she certainly had a mouth on her. Mrs Green had a reputation for speaking her mind, nobody ruffled her feathers and got away with it. Tony had gone off to Canada, Banks remembered. And Mr Green had died of emphysema about nine months ago. His mother had told him over the telephone, and he had sent a sympathy card. Yes, he would pay Mrs Green a visit.

2

So Banks sipped tea with his mother and father, catching up on the local gossip. The usual stuff: another school friend had emigrated to Australia, an old neighbour, who had moved into a home a year ago, had died, and the Venables lad from number sixty-six had been sent to Borstal for mugging a pensioner. Banks didn't bother telling his mother that it wasn't called 'Borstal' any more but 'detention centre' or 'youth custody centre'. They weren't much interested in what he'd been doing, outside of the divorce from Sandra. They were more interested in Brian and Tracy, and they expressed regret that neither could come to the party on Sunday: Brian's band was playing an important series of gigs in Germany, and Tracy had flu. Not entirely convinced this wasn't some excuse, Banks had dropped by and offered to drive her from her university residence in Leeds, but when he saw her, he took pity and said he'd look in again on his way back. Fortunately, she had friends there who would feed her chicken noodle soup and Lemsip in the meantime.

'Have you seen who's moved in next door?' Mrs Banks asked.

'No,' said Banks, 'but I heard them.'

'Not that side. The other. A Paki family, that's who. I must say, though,' she went on, 'they seem really nice. Very quiet they are, even the kids, aren't they, Arthur? And polite. Always say good morning and ask how you're doing. Talk just like us, they do. Makes a change from that lot on the other side.'

'Who are they?' Banks asked.

She shook her head. 'I don't even know their name. They moved in about two weeks ago. They're not very friendly neighbours. Don't know how many of them live there, either. Shifty-looking lot. Comings and goings all hours of the day and night. Noise. And the place is a pigsty.'

It sounded like a drug house. Banks made a mental note to keep his eyes open. If he noticed anything suspicious, he'd get onto the local police.

Banks's father picked up the remote control and turned the television on at half-past five, as Banks remembered he did every weekday. 'Is that the time?' said Ida Banks. 'I'd better get the tea on. Pork chops, peas and chips all right?'

'Fine,' said Banks, his stomach sinking. As if there was a choice.

'And a nice bit of steamed pudding and custard for sweet.'

'I'll help.' Banks followed her into the kitchen.

True to his word, Geoff Salisbury came back from Asda with a bag of groceries. He dumped it on the kitchen table and handed Ida Banks two pound coins in change, then they went through to the living room. Banks, peeling potatoes at the time, started to unload the groceries. As he did so, he came across the printed receipt stuck by condensation to the side of a bottle of chilled apple juice.

The print was a little blurred, but even so he could see that the total came to £16.08, which left a discrepancy of £1.92 between that and the £2 Geoff had handed his mother. Holding the receipt, Banks went into the living room.

'I think you've got the change wrong,' he said, holding out the receipt for Geoff both to see.

Banks mother frowned. 'Alan! Must you?' Then she turned to Geoff. 'I'm so sorry. Our Alan's in the police and he can't seem to let us forget it,' she said with a dismissive sniff.

'One of the boys in blue, eh?'

'CID, actually,' said Banks.

'Ah. All that Sherlock Holmes stuff.'

'Something like that.'

'Let's see, then.' Geoff took a pair of bifocals from his shirt pocket and squinted at the list. 'Bloody hell, you're right,' he admitted, blushing. He showed the receipt to Ida Banks. 'It's a fair cop. See there, Mrs B? It looks like an eight to me but it's really a six. That's what comes of being too vain to wear my glasses in the supermarket.'

Ida Banks laughed and slapped him on the arm playfully. 'Oh, get away with you, Geoff. Anyone could make a mistake like that.'

Geoff counted out the rest of the change into her hand. He glanced sideways at Banks, still slightly red with embarrassment. 'I can see I'll have to watch myself now there's a copper around,' he joked.

'Yes,' said Banks, not laughing. 'I think you better had.'

3

'There was no need for that, Alan,' Banks's mother said after Geoff Salisbury had left. 'Embarrassing us all.'

'I wasn't embarrassed,' Banks said. 'Besides, he tried to cheat you.'

'Don't be silly. It's like he said, he couldn't see the figures properly.'

'Does he do this often?'

'Do what?'

'Go shopping for you.'

'Yes. We can't get around like we used to, you know, what with your dad's angina and my legs and feet.'

'Legs and feet?'

'My varicose veins and bunions. Getting old is no treat, Alan, I can tell you that much. You'll find out yourself one day. Anyway, he's been good to us, has Geoff, and now you've gone and upset him.'

'I don't think he's upset at all.'

'Only here five minutes, and there's trouble already.'

'Mum, I really don't think I upset him. Maybe he'll just be more careful in future.'

'And maybe we'll have to find *someone else* who'll do our shopping for us and give the place a good dust and a vacuum every now and then. Fat chance of that.'

'I'm sure he'll be fine.'

'Well, I just hope you'll apologize next time you see him.'

'Apologize?'

'Yes. You as good as called the man a thief.'

'Fine,' said Banks, raising his hands in surrender. 'I'll apologize.'

His mother gave another disapproving little sniff. 'I'd better see to those pork chops.' Then she strode off into the kitchen and shut the door behind her.

4

The Coach and Horses, about a hundred yards away on the main road, was one of those pubs that had hardly changed at all in the past forty years or so. True, they'd got in a jukebox and a few video machines, and the brewery had forked out for a minor facelift sometime in the eighties, hoping to pull in a younger, freer-spending crowd. But it didn't take. The people who drank at the Coach and Horses had, for the most part, been drinking there most of their lives. And their fathers had supped there before them.

Though there were few young people to be seen, it still managed to be a warm and lively pub, Banks noticed as he walked in with his father just after eight o'clock that night, the steamed pudding and custard still weighing heavy in his stomach. His father had managed the walk without too much puffing and wheezing, which he put down to having stopped smoking two years ago. Banks, who had only stopped that summer, still felt frequent and powerful urges.

'Arthur! Arthur! Come on, lad, come on over.'

It was Geoff Salisbury. He was sitting at a table with an elderly couple Banks didn't recognize and two other men in their sixties he remembered from his previous visit. They cleared a little space when Banks and his father walked over to join them.

'My shout,' said Geoff. 'Name your poison.'

'No,' said Banks, still standing. 'I'm the visitor. Let me buy the first round.'

That got no argument, so Banks wandered off to the bar. He hardly had to fight his way through the crowds of impatient drinkers. The bartender, the same one Banks remembered when he had last been in the Coach that summer, nodded a curt greeting and proceeded to pull the pints. When Banks carried the tray back to the table, his father was already talking football with one of his old pals, Harry Finnegan. Harry looked up and said hello to Banks, asked him how he was doing.

'Fine,' said Banks. 'You're looking well yourself.'

'Fair to middling. Sorry to hear about you and that young lass of yours splitting up.'

Sandra. No secrets here. He wondered if they also knew about Sean and the imminent baby. 'Well,' said Banks, 'these things happen.' More to his generation than theirs, he realized. Theirs tended to stick at marriage even when all the love had gone out of it. He didn't know if that was better or worse than changing wives every decade. Probably best not to get married at all, he suspected.

But his mother and father still loved one another, or so he believed. Fifty years together meant they probably didn't have much new to say to one another any more, and the passion might have disappeared from their relationship years ago, but they were comfortable together. Besides, passion is transitory and infinitely transferable, anyway, Banks believed. What his parents had was stronger, deeper, more permanent; it was what he would never get to experience with Sandra: growing old together. He was used to the loss by now, but every now and then he still felt a pang of regret for what might have been and a lump came to his throat.

Harry introduced Banks to the couple at the table, Dick and Mavis Conroy. The other man, Jock McFall, said hello and shook hands.

'I hear you're a Leeds United supporter these days, Alan,' said Harry, a twinkle in his eye.

Banks nodded. 'For my sins. Not that I get the chance to go to Elland Road very often. *Match of the Day* is usually the closest I get.'

'*Elland Road*,' his father said. 'You'd not be able to bloody afford it on what a copper earns, son.' They all laughed.

Banks laughed with them. 'Too true.'

As the conversations went on in that vein, people started to pair off: Dick and Mavis talking to Jock McFall about the latest supermarket price wars; Harry and Arthur Banks discussing Peterborough United's miserable performance that season. Banks edged his chair closer to Geoff Salisbury's.

'Sorry about that business with the change,' said Geoff. 'My eyesight's not what it used to be. Honest mistake.'

Banks nodded. 'Honest mistake. No offence,' he said, though he still wasn't convinced. It was the closest he was willing to get to an apology, so it would just have to do. There was certainly no point in antagonizing Geoff and upsetting his mother even more.

After all, he was only down for the weekend; these people had to live close to one another day in day out. And if Banks couldn't be around to help his parents with their shopping and house-cleaning, then it was a good thing Geoff Salisbury was.

'How long have you lived on the estate, Geoff?' Banks asked.

'About a year.'

'Where did you live before?'

'Oh, here and there. Bit of a wanderer, really.'

'What made you settle down?'

Geoff laughed and shrugged. 'My age, I suppose. I don't know. Wandering lost its appeal.'

'Well, there's something to be said for knowing you've always got a roof over your head.'

'There is that.' Geoff took a stick of chewing gum from his pocket. When he had unwrapped it and put it in his mouth, he folded the silver paper time and time again until it was just a tiny square, which he set down in the ashtray. He noticed Banks watching him and laughed. 'Habit,' he said. 'Stopped smoking five years ago and got addicted to this bloody stuff. Wish I'd stuck with cigarettes sometimes.'

'You're probably better off as you are,' Banks said. 'What line of work are you in?'

'Odd jobs, mostly.'

'What? Fixing things? Carpentry?'

'Cars, mostly. Tinkering with engines. I used to be a mechanic.'

'Not any more?'

'Got made redundant from the last garage I worked at, and I just couldn't seem to get taken on anywhere else. My age, I suppose. Again. They can get young kids still wet behind the ears and pay them bugger all to do the same job.'

'I suppose so,' Banks said. 'So you work for yourself now?'

'I don't need much, just enough to keep the wolf from the door.'

'And you help out Mum and Dad?'

'Grand folk, Arthur and Ida,' Geoff said. 'Been like a mother and father to me, they have.'

If there was any irony intended in the remark, Geoff didn't seem aware of it.

'How long have you known them?' Banks asked.

'Since not long after you'd left this summer. They told me about that business with the missing lad. Terrible. Anyway, they always said hello right from the start, you know, like, when they saw me in the street. Invited me in for a cup of tea. That sort of thing. And with them not being . . . well, you know what I mean, not as able to get around as well as they used to do, I started doing them little favours. Just washing, cleaning, shopping and the like, helping them out with their finances. I like to help people.'

'Finances?'

'Paying bills on time, that sort of thing. They do get a bit forgetful sometimes, just between you and me. And taking the rent down to the council office. It's an awful bother for them.'

'I'm sure they appreciate it, Geoff.'

'I think they do.' He nodded. 'Another?'

Banks looked at his empty glass. 'Yes,' he said. 'Go on, then. One more.' He looked over at his father. 'All right, Dad?'

Arthur Banks nodded and went back to his conversation with Harry Finnegan. The pub had filled up in the last half hour or so, and Banks thought he recognized some of the faces. One or two people looked at him as if they knew him, then decided perhaps they didn't, or didn't want to. Banks watched Geoff Salisbury at the bar. He seemed to know everyone; he was shaking more hands and patting more backs than a politician on election day. Popular fellow.

Geoff came back with the drinks and excused himself to talk to someone else. Banks chatted with Dick and Mavis for a while – they wanted to know if he'd helped catch the Yorkshire Ripper – then, after his second drink, his father said he was tired and would like to go home. 'You can stay if you like,' he said to Banks.

'No, I'll walk back with you. I'm feeling a bit tired myself.'

'Suit yourself.'

They said their goodbyes and walked out into the cool autumn night. It was mild for the time of year, Banks thought: light jacket weather rather than overcoats, but the leaves were changing colour, winter was in the air and the weather forecast said they had a shower or two in store. Neither Banks nor his father had anything to say on the way home, but then Arthur Banks needed all his breath for walking.

5

Banks's bedroom, he had been amazed to discover that summer, was almost exactly as it had been when he first left home. Only the wallpaper, curtains and bedding had been changed. The bed itself was also the same one he had had since he was about twelve.

As he squeezed himself between the tightly tucked sheets on his narrow bed, he remembered how he used to hold the old transistor radio to his ear under the sheets, listening to Radio Luxembourg amidst the whistles and crackles. First, Jimmy Saville playing the latest top-ten hit from 'member number 11321', Elvis Presley. Then, a few years later, came the pirate stations, with even more static and interference: John Peel playing the Mothers of Invention, Jefferson Airplane and Country Joe and the Fish, names from another world, music so startling and raw it transcended even the poor radio reception.

Banks's eyes were too tired and scratchy from the smoky pub to read his Graham Greene, so he put on the Cecilia Bartoli CD of Gluck arias and listened as he drifted towards sleep.

As he lay there, he couldn't help but think about Geoff Salisbury. Something about the man put Banks on his guard. It wasn't just the wrong change – that *could* have been an honest mistake – but the manner in which he seemed to have insinuated himself into the lives of Banks's parents, the ease with which he breezed in and out of the house. Banks wouldn't be surprised if Geoff had a key. He switched off the CD and turned on his side, trying to shake off the uneasy feeling, telling himself he was being too mistrusting, and that he probably only felt this way because he felt guilty he wasn't taking care of his ageing parents himself. He knew he ought to be glad that *someone* was doing the job; he only wished that someone wasn't Geoff Salisbury.

6

Banks awoke with a start the following morning and experienced a moment of absolute panic when he had no idea who or where he was. It was as if he had woken from a coma after many years, all memory gone and the world around him totally changed, or as if he had been abducted and had woken up in an alien spaceship.

But it only lasted a second or two, thank God, and after that he managed to orient himself and his heartbeat slowed to normal. He was in his old bedroom, of course, the room he had slept in between the ages of twelve and eighteen. It was at the back of the house and looked over back yards, an alleyway and a stretch of waste ground to the north, where he and his friends used to play. When Banks looked out of his window, he noticed that the builders had moved in since his last visit and laid the foundations for yet more houses. As if Peterborough needed to grow any more. Since the mid-sixties, when the developers decided to make it a catchment area for London's overcrowded suburbs, it had done nothing but grow, swamping outlying villages with housing estates and business parks. The planners and promoters said it blended old and new in unique and interesting ways. Even so, Banks thought, King Paeda, who had founded the city, would turn in his grave.

On a Saturday morning, the building site was deserted; concrete mixers sat idle and quiet, and the thick sheets of polythene covering pallets of bricks or boards flapped in the wind. It was another grand autumn morning: sunshine, bright blue sky and a cool wind to make everything look and feel fresh. Banks checked his watch. It was after nine o'clock, and he was surprised he had slept so long and so deeply; he couldn't remember having any dreams at all. He listened for sounds of life from downstairs and thought he could hear talking on the radio and dishes rattling in the sink. They were up.

Desperate for tea or coffee, Banks dressed quickly and made his way downstairs. In the living room, his father looked up from his paper and grunted, 'Morning, son.'

'Morning, Dad,' Banks replied, glancing out of the window to make sure his car was still there. It was. His father's newspaper rustled back into position, and the local radio station, according to the DJ, was about to play a request for 'Memories Are Made of This' by Val Doonican, for Mrs Patricia Gaitskell, of 43 Wisteria Drive, Stamford. Jesus, thought Banks, he could have been caught in a time warp while he slept, back to the B-side of 1967. Perhaps that was why he had felt so disorientated the minute he awoke.

He walked through to the kitchen, where his mother, washing the breakfast dishes, gave him a cursory glance and said, 'Well, you've decided to get up at last, have you?' It was exactly what she used to say when he was a teenager and liked to lie in bed most of the morning. The only thing that saved him from seriously doubting his sanity was the little television on the kitchen table showing a breakfast programme. That hadn't been there all those years ago; nor had breakfast television.

Banks made some comment about having had a long drive and put on the kettle. 'Want a cup of tea?' he asked his mother.

'No, thanks. We had ours ages ago.'

'Well, you could have another.'

She gave him a withering look, and he busied himself looking for the tea bags, telling himself that his parents really weren't being especially nasty to him. They had their routine; it just took a little getting used to.

'They're where they've always been,' his mother told him.

That didn't help much, as he couldn't remember where they'd

always been. A terracotta jar in the cupboard with TEA engraved on the front looked promising, but it turned out to be empty. Beside it, however, Banks found a jar of instant coffee. Might as well, he thought. As long as you convince yourself it's a different drink, not really coffee at all, then it doesn't taste too bad. The kettle boiled and Banks made himself a cup of instant coffee. Specks of undissolved powder floated on the surface no matter how much he stirred it.

'Don't you want any breakfast?' his mother asked, drying her hands on her pinafore. 'We got some Sugar Puffs in for you specially. You always used to like Sugar Puffs.'

When I was about twelve, thought Banks. 'I'll give them a miss this morning,' he said. 'Maybe tomorrow.'

He wandered into the living room again, his mother not far behind. Val Doonican had given way to the Searchers singing 'Some Day We're Gonna Love Again'. An improvement, Banks thought. Funny how the Searchers were exactly the kind of 'pop rubbish' his parents dismissed thirty-five years ago, but now they were as acceptable as Val Doonican.

Banks needed a newspaper to complete his morning ritual. His father was still buried deep in the *Daily Mail*, which, being a Labour man, he only read so he could find things to complain about. The *Mail* wasn't Banks's kind of paper anyway. No real meat on its bones. Especially at the weekend. He needed something with a bit more writing and fewer pictures, like the *Independent* or the *Guardian*.

'I'm off to the newsagent's for a paper,' he announced. 'Anything I can get for you?'

'You'll be lucky if they've got any left at this time,' his mother said. His father just grunted.

Banks took their responses as a 'no' and set off. In the house next door the upstairs windows were all open and music thudded out. It definitely wasn't Val Doonican or the Searchers; more like Nine Inch Nails or Metallica. Banks studied the house. There were no curtains on the windows, and the front door was wide open. As he was looking, a scruffy couple walked out onto the overgrown path. They looked like Fred and Rosemary West on acid. The man's eyes, in particular, reminded Banks of the opening of *Vertigo*.

'Morning,' said Banks. 'Lovely day, isn't it?'

They looked at him as if he were from Mars – or as if they were *on* it – so he shrugged and walked down to the newsagent's across the main road. The short strip of shops there, set back from the road by a stretch of tarmac, had gone through dozens of changes over the years. When he first moved to the estate, Banks remembered, there had been a fish and chip shop, a ladies' hairdresser, a butcher's, a greengrocer's and a launderette; now there was a video-rental shop, a takeaway pizza and tandoori place called Caesar's Taj Mahal, a minimart and a unisex hair salon. The only constants were the fish and chip shop, which now sold takeaway Chinese food, too, Banks noticed, and Walker's, the newsagent's.

Banks waited to cross the busy road. On the other side, lower down from the shops, stood the remains of the old ball-bearing factory. The gates were chained and padlocked shut and it was surrounded by high wire-mesh fencing with barbed wire on top, the windows beyond covered by rusty grilles. Despite these security precautions, most of them were broken anyway, and the front of the blackened brick building was covered in colourful graffiti.

Banks remembered when the place was in production, lorries coming and going, factory whistle blowing and crowds of workers waiting at the bus stop. A lot of them were young women, or girls scarcely out of school, and he had a crush on one of them. Called Mandy by her friends, she used to stand at the bus stop smoking, a faraway look in her eyes, scarf done up like a turban on her head. She had pale smooth skin and lips like Julie Christie, whom Banks had gone to see in *Darling* with a couple of school friends because she did a nude scene in it. They had only been fourteen or fifteen at the time, but the bored woman in the ticket office at the local fleapit hardly even looked at them before issuing their one and threepennies. The nude scene was terrific, but he didn't understand much of the rest of the film; it didn't make the same sense as *Billy Liar* did for him when he saw it only a few months later. Escaping a boring environment was something he could easily relate to.

One day Mandy started wearing an engagement ring, and a few weeks later she no longer stood at the bus stop with the others, and he never saw her again. He spent ages in his room moping, and even a few years later, when he bought *Beggars Banquet* and listened to 'Factory Girl', he thought of her.

Banks went into the newsagent's. Mrs Walker moved much more slowly now, and the joints on her left hand were swollen. Arthritis by the look of it. There was still a small pile of *Independents* under the magazine rack, so Banks picked one up and took it to the counter.

'You're the Banks lad back again, aren't you?' she said.

'That's me,' said Banks.

'I thought so. My body might be falling to pieces but my mind's still all right. Haven't seen you since that business in the summer. How are you doing?'

'Fine, thanks. I see you're still soldiering on.'

'I'll be here till I drop.'

'I'm surprised you can manage all by yourself.'

'Oh, I've got help. Some local lads help with the papers, and there's Geoff helps with going to wholesalers, stocktaking and whatnot.'

'Geoff?'

'Geoff Salisbury. Nice lad. Well, I say "lad", but he's probably your age or older. Always there when you need him is Geoff. And with a smile on his face, too. There's not too many folk you can say that about these days.'

'True enough,' Banks agreed. So the ubiquitous Geoff Salisbury had his feet under Mrs Walker's table, too. Still, he did say he did odd jobs, and Banks assumed Mrs Walker paid him for his 'help'. He had to make a living somehow. It didn't seem that one could go far around the estate, though, without finding some traces of its patron saint, Geoff bloody Salisbury.

The bell jangled and someone else walked into the shop. Banks half-expected it to be Salisbury himself, but when he turned he was gobsmacked by who he saw. It was Kay Summerville. And looking hardly a day older than when he had last seen her thirty years ago. That was an exaggeration, of course – her eyes had gathered a few crow's feet, and the long blonde hair that still cascaded over her shoulders now showed evidence of dark roots – but she still had her figure and her looks.

A hoarse 'Kay' was about all he could manage.

She seemed equally stunned. 'Alan.'

'Are you two going to stand there gawping at one another all afternoon or are you going to step aside, young man, and let the lady get what she's come for?' said Mrs Walker.

'Of course.' Banks moved aside.

Kay smiled. She was wearing a thin white T-shirt under a blue denim jacket, and hip-hugging blue jeans. The hips looked as if they were worth hugging. She caught him looking at her and gave him a shy smile.

'Packet of Polo mints, please, Mrs Walker, and –' she turned to the magazine rack and picked out a copy of *Marie Claire* – 'and I'll take this, too.'

Banks stood by the door and loitered, pretending to be looking at a display of anniversary cards. When Kay had finished, she walked towards him.

'Walk back with you?' he said.

She did a little curtsy. 'Why, thank you, kind sir.'

Banks laughed. He had been sixteen when he had first met Kay, and just about to go into the lower sixth. Kay had been fifteen, about to enter her O level year. Her family had just moved up from north London, and Banks had seen her walking along the street in her blue jeans and orange jacket, or in her school uniform – white blouse, maroon jacket, grey skirt probably just a couple of inches too short for the principal's liking – pouty lips, pale skin, head in the air, and her long blonde hair trailing halfway down her back.

She had seemed unobtainable, ethereal, like Mandy from the factory and, if truth be told, like most of the women or girls Banks lusted after, but one day they met in the newsagent's, just like today, both wanting the latest issue of *New Musical Express*. There was only one copy left, so Banks, being the gentleman, let Kay take it. They walked back to the estate together, chatting about pop music. Both were Cream fans, upset about the band splitting up that summer. Both loved Canned Heat's 'On the Road Again' and hated Mary Hopkins's 'Those Were the Days'. Kay said she would lend her *NME* to Banks when she had finished with it. He asked her when that would be, and she said probably Saturday. Emboldened, he went on and asked if she'd like to go to the pictures with him on Saturday night. He could have dropped in his tracks when she said yes.

They went to see *Here We Go Round the Mulberry Bush*, on a double bill with *I'll Never Forget Whatshisname*, and that was it, the start of Banks's first serious relationship.

'I heard about your mother,' Banks said, holding the door for her. 'I'm sorry.'

Kay pushed a stray tress of hair from her forehead. 'Thank you. She'd been ill for a long time. She was riddled with cancer and her heart wasn't strong. I know it's a cliché, but in this case it really was a blessing.'

'Is that why you're up here?'

'Yes. I've got to deal with the house before the council relets it. The rent paid up till the end of the month, so I thought I'd take a few days and get it all sorted. You?'

'It's Mum and Dad's golden wedding tomorrow.'

'That's marvellous.'

'It is pretty remarkable, isn't it? Fifty years. What kind of work do you do?'

'Investment banking.'

'Oh.'

Kay laughed. 'Yes, that's usually the reaction. Quite a conversation stopper.'

'I'm sorry, it's just . . . I don't . . .'

She smiled at him. 'It's OK. Most people don't. Even the ones who *do* it. What about you? I seem to remember Mum saying you had something to do with the police.'

'True. Detective Chief Inspector, CID, Major Crimes.'

'Well, well, well. I *am* impressed. Just like Morse.'

It was Banks's turn to laugh. 'Except I'm not on telly. I'm real. And I'm still alive. Like your job, it's usually a conversation stopper. You must be the first person who hasn't jumped a mile when I told them what I do for a living. No skeletons in your closet?'

She wiggled her eyebrows. 'That's for me to know and you to find out.'

They reached Banks's parents' house and stopped on the pavement, both a little awkward, embarrassed. It was one of those moments, Banks felt, like the one thirty years ago when he had asked her out for the first time. 'Look,' he said, 'seeing as we're both up here this weekend, would you like to go out tonight, maybe find a country pub, have a bite to eat or a drink, do a bit of catching up? I mean, bring your husband, by all means, you know—'

Kay smiled at his discomfort. 'Sorry, there's only me,' she said. 'And yes, I'd love to. Pick me up at half past seven?'

'Good. Great, I mean.' Banks grinned. 'OK, then, see you this evening.'

Banks watched Kay walk away, and he could have sworn she had a bit of a spring in her step. He definitely had one in his, which couldn't be dampened even by the sight of Geoff Salisbury talking to his mother in the hall when he opened the front door.

'Morning, Alan,' Geoff said. 'Have a good time last night?'

'Fine,' said Banks.

'That the Summerville girl you were talking to?'

'Yes,' said Banks. 'We're old friends.'

Geoff frowned. 'I was sorry to hear about her poor mother.

Anyway, must dash. Just a passing visit.' He turned back to Ida Banks. 'Right, then, Mrs B, don't you fret. I'll pick up everything we need for tomorrow, and I'll pop around in the morning and do a bit of tidying and vacuuming for you. How's that?'

'It's all right,' said Banks. 'I can do that.'

'Don't be silly,' his mother chided him. 'You don't know one end of a vacuum cleaner from the other.' Which might have been true at one time but certainly wasn't any more. 'That'll be just dandy, Geoff,' she said, handing him a plastic card, which he put quickly in his pocket. 'I know we can always rely on you.'

It was too late to argue. With a smile and a wave, Geoff Salisbury was halfway down the path, whistling 'Colonel Bogey' as he went.

'I mean it,' said Banks. 'Anything needs doing, just ask me.'

His mother patted his arm. 'I know, son,' she said. 'You mean well. But Geoff's . . . well we're *used* to having him around. He knows where everything is.'

Does he, indeed? thought Banks. 'By the way,' he asked, 'what was that you just gave him?'

'What?'

'You know. The card.'

'Oh, yes. That's the Abbeylink card. He'll need some cash, won't he, if he's going to get the food and drink in for tomorrow?'

Banks almost choked. 'You mean he knows your PIN number?'

'Well, of course he does, silly. A fat lot of use the card would be to him without it.' Shaking her head, she edged past Banks towards the living room. 'And what's this about you and Kay Summerville?' she asked, turning. 'Didn't you two used to go out together?'

'That was a long time ago. Actually, we're going to have dinner together tonight.'

His mother's face dropped. 'But I was going to make us toad-in-the-hole. Your favourite.'

True, Banks had once expressed an enthusiasm for toad-in-the-hole when he was about fourteen. 'I'm sorry,' he said, 'but it's the only chance we'll get to catch up.'

'Well,' his mother said, that familiar, hurt, hard-done-by tone in her voice. 'I suppose if that's really what you want to do. I must say, she always seemed like a nice lass. Her mother and me weren't close at all, just to say hello to in passing, like, but you tell her she's welcome to drop by tomorrow, for the party. I'd like to offer her my condolences.'

'I'll ask her,' said Banks, then he hurried upstairs.

7

With his bedroom window open, Banks could hear the polythene from the building site flapping in the breeze and the cars whooshing by on the main road. He could also hear a dull, bass rumbling from next door along with the occasional shout and bang. Their back garden, he noticed, was full of rubbish like a tip: broken furniture, rocks, a dismantled bicycle. Maybe there was even a body or two buried there.

His knees cracked as he squatted to read the spines of the books in the old glass-fronted bookcase. There they were, a cross-section of his early years' reading, starting with the large, illustrated *Black Beauty*, which his mother had read to him when he was small, old *Beano*, *Dandy* and *Rupert* annuals, and Noddy books – the originals, where Noddy and Big Ears slept together, hung out with Golliwog, and 'gay' meant 'cheerful'. He must have kept Enid Blyton in luxury almost single-handed, he thought, as he had moved on to the Famous Five and the Secret Seven.

Then came his high school reading: Billy Bunter, Jennings and William, followed by war stories such as Biggles, *The Wooden Horse, The Guns of Navarone* and *Camp on Blood Island.* Next to these were several editions of the *Pan Book of Horror Stories*, from a phase he went through in his teens, along with some H. P. Lovecraft and M. R. James. There wasn't much crime fiction, but he did still have a few dog-eared old Saint paperbacks, the Father Brown stories and a complete Sherlock Holmes. The James Bond books were all there, too, of course, and a few Sexton Blakes.

There were also history books, the kind with lots of illustrations, some Oxford and Penguin anthologies of poetry and those children's illustrated encyclopedias that came out with a letter a week, none of which he'd got beyond C or D.

In addition, on the bottom shelf, there were books about his many hobbies, including photography, coins, birds, stamps and astronomy, and several Observer books of cars, aircraft, geology, trees, music and pond life. He'd seen these old editions in second-hand book shops and some of them were worth a bit now. Maybe he should take them back up to Yorkshire with him, he thought. Would that upset his parents? Were his books and his room some sort of virtual umbilical cord that was all that tied him to them now? It was a depressing thought.

One book stood out. Sitting between Enid Blyton's *The River of Adventure* and *The Mountain of Adventure* was a used, orange-spined Penguin edition of *Lady Chatterley's Lover*, a 1966 reprint with Richard Hoggart's introduction. Curious, Banks picked it out. He didn't remember buying it and was surprised when he opened it up and saw written on the flyleaf: 'Kay Summerville, London, June 7th, 1969'. Banks remembered that day well. Smiling, he put it aside. He would give it back to her tonight.

The more he thought about his 'date' with Kay the more he looked forward to it. Not only was she an extremely attractive woman, she was also intelligent and she shared some of his past with him. He didn't imagine the date would lead to anything of a sexual nature – he certainly wasn't out to seduce her – but you never knew. He wondered how he would feel about that. Michelle Hart was on holiday in Tuscany. Besides, they had made no commitments, and Michelle always seemed to be holding back, on the verge of ending the tenuous relationship they did have. Banks didn't know why, but he sensed she had deep and painful secrets she didn't want to share. It seemed that all the women he had met since parting with Sandra – including Annie Cabbot back up in Yorkshire – shied away from intimacy.

Banks stood up and looked down at the books. Well, there they all were, for what they were worth, like those strata of different coloured rock or the layers of antiquities at an archaeological dig. His mother called up: 'Alan, are you coming down? Lunch is on the table. It's potted meat sandwiches.'

Banks sighed. 'Coming,' he shouted. 'I just have to wash my hands. I'll be right there.' True, he had once loved potted meat, the same way he had liked Sugar Puffs and toad-in-the-hole, when he was a teenager, but he hadn't touched the stuff in years.

8

The people next door were out in force, Banks noticed, on his way to see Mrs Green after lunch. There was an unmarked delivery van outside their house, and two strapping young lads were carrying what looked like a fifty-inch television set up the path. It hardly looked as if it would fit through the door. Fred and Rosemary stood on the lawn, rubbing their hands together in glee, practically salivating at the sight, and their various children, aged between about five and fifteen, milled about beside them. Banks hadn't seen so many shaved heads since the nit nurse had visited his school. He tried wishing them good morning again, but everyone was far too intent on the imminent television even to notice him. He would have bet a pound to a penny it was stolen.

The wind had picked up even more, Banks noticed, bringing a few fast-flying clouds and a chill with it, and there was a smell of rain in the air. Banks zipped his leather jacket all the way up and walked the short distance to the close, where Mrs Green lived. She answered Banks's knock and expressed delight at seeing him again. She had certainly aged – thickened at the waist, drooped at the bosom – but she had lost none of her sprightliness, and she fussed around making tea and bringing out a plate of scones. Her living room was sparsely decorated – plain cream wallpaper, no prints or paintings – and a few framed family photographs stood on the mantelpiece.

'How's Tony doing?' Banks asked. 'I've always regretted we didn't manage to stay in touch.'

'These things happen,' said Mrs Green. 'People drift apart over the years. It's only natural. It doesn't mean they don't share good memories, though.'

'I suppose not.'

'Anyway, Tony's doing fine. He lives in Vancouver now, you know. He's a tax lawyer. This is him about two years ago.' She picked up one of the photographs and handed it to Banks. It showed the smile he remembered, the mischief in the eyes, surrounded by a bald head on a pudgy body in brightly coloured shorts and a red T-shirt. Tony stood with a relaxed, smiling woman Banks took to be his wife, and two bored and /or cool-looking teenage children. They were on a beach and there were cloud-topped mountains in the background. 'I'll let him know you were asking about him,' Mrs Green said.

'Please do.' Banks replaced the photo on the mantelpiece. 'I've been to Toronto, but never Vancouver.'

'You should go if you get a chance. Bill and I visited him there five years ago. It's a lovely city. I'm sure Tony and Carol would be happy to have you stop with them. They've got a big house.'

'Maybe I will,' said Banks.

'We don't see you down here very often, do we?'

'Well,' said Banks, feeling guilty he hadn't made time for Mrs Green on his previous visit, 'I keep pretty busy up north. You know how it is.' He sipped some tea.

'Your parents are really very proud of you, you know.'

Banks almost choked on his tea. Where had that come from?

Mrs Green considered him through her tortoiseshell glasses. 'You might not think so,' she said, 'and they might not admit it, but they are. Especially since that business last summer.'

'What makes you say that?'

'Oh, don't think I don't know about your differences. They never did approve of what you chose to do with your life, did they? Your dad thought you'd joined the enemy and your mother thought you'd let her down. That was clear enough to anyone who knew them.'

'Was it?'

'Oh, yes. And I knew where they were coming from, of course.'

'What do you mean?'

She smiled. 'Oh, don't be so obtuse, Alan. You always did have that infuriating habit of pretending not to see the obvious. You wouldn't have got far in your chosen career if you couldn't even add together the basics. You had all the opportunities; they had none. They had to settle for their lot in life. And the Thatcher years were pretty tough around here. How do you think your dad felt when he saw coppers laying into workers on the news? Miners, whatever they were, they were still working men, like himself. How do you think he felt when he saw the police in riot gear waving their overtime pay in the faces of men who'd lost everything? Do you think he actually enjoyed working at that factory every day of his life? I'd say it was a cause for celebration when they made him redundant, but for him it was a blow to his pride. And your mother, cleaning up other folk's messes? They made a lot of sacrifices for you, so you could do better than they had. And what did you do? You joined the police force. You must have known how people around here felt about the police.'

'I'd say they expect us to make sure their cars are safe and keep the muggings and gang fights to a minimum.'

'You always were a cheeky young beggar, Alan Banks. Perhaps now they do. But not back then.'

'I know what you mean,' said Banks.

'But what I'm telling you is they know you've done well for yourself now. Every time you got a promotion they told me, and you should have heard the pride in their voices. "Our Alan's a detective *sergeant* now," they'd say. Or "They've made Alan detective *chief* inspector now!" I got sick of hearing about you. It just took them a long time to work it out, and they don't find it easy to express. It also helped that you came down on the right side last time you were here. Of course, they always did dote on that useless brother of yours.'

'Roy.'

'Yes. I'm sorry, but you know I've always spoken my mind, and I can't say I ever took to him. Sly, he seemed to me, two-faced, always up to something behind your back. You were no angel, mind, but you weren't sly.'

Banks smiled as he buttered his scone, thinking about the time he had orchestrated going to bed with Kay while his parents were visiting his granny, and the time he and Tony Green had drunk some of Mr Green's whisky and topped the bottle up with water. Whether he spotted it or not they never knew. Sly? All kids are sly, Banks thought; they have to be in their constant struggle with the inexplicable and unreasonable rules and regulations imposed on them by adults. But Banks knew how to take a compliment when he was offered one, even at the expense of his brother.

'Thanks,' he said. 'Roy could be a bit of a handful.'

'To say the least. Anyway, I don't see much of your mum and dad any more, except when I bump into Ida on the street,' Mrs Green went on. 'That's how I knew about the golden wedding. She invited me. It's sad, though. People seem to isolate themselves when they get old. They don't get out as much, and I don't go to the Coach and Horses. How are they?'

'Same as ever,' said Banks. 'Mum's complaining about varicose veins and her bunions, but she doesn't seem to do too badly. Dad's still got his angina, but it doesn't seem any worse. There's a neighbour helps out. Bloke called Geoff Salisbury. Know him?'

Banks couldn't swear to it, but he thought Mrs Green's expression darkened for a moment. Her lips certainly tightened.

'I know him,' she said.

Banks leaned forward in his armchair. 'You don't sound so thrilled about it.'

'Can't say as I am. Oh, he's a charmer all right is Geoff Salisbury. Bit too much of one for my liking.'

'How did you meet him?'

'He seems to have some sort of radar for all the old folks in trouble on the estate. He turns up everywhere at one time or another. Usually when you need help.'

'What do you mean?'

'More tea?'

'Please.' Banks held out his cup.

'You know, you can smoke if you like.' She smiled. 'If I let you do it when you were fifteen, I can hardly stop you now you're . . . what would it be?'

'A lot older.' Banks put his hand to his left temple. 'Can't you tell by the grey?'

Mrs Green laughed and touched her own head. 'You call *that* grey?' It was true, she had an entire head of fluffy grey hair.

'Anyway,' Banks said, remembering what Mr Green had died of, 'thanks, but I've stopped.'

'I won't say that's not good news. If only we'd all known all along what it was doing to us.'

'You were saying? About Geoff Salisbury.'

'I was, wasn't I?' She sat back in her chair, tea and saucer resting on her lap. 'Oh, you know me. I tend to go off half-cocked on things.'

'I'd still be interested to hear your thoughts,' said Banks. 'To be honest, I haven't really taken to him myself, and he seems to be spending an awful lot of time around Mum and Dad.'

She waved a hand. 'It's nothing, really. He started coming around when Bill was sick. It was near the end and Bill was in a wheelchair, breathing from that horrible oxygen tank.'

'What did he want?'

'Want? Nothing. He never asked for a thing. Only to help. Give him his due, he's a hard and willing worker, and he was certainly useful at the time. He fixed a few things around the house, ran errands.'

'So what was the problem?'

'You'll think I was imagining things.'

'Not necessarily.'

'Well, it wasn't any one thing, really. Just little things. The wrong change, or one of Bill's tools would go missing. Nothing you could really put your finger on.'

Banks remembered the short change Geoff Salisbury had handed his mother yesterday evening. 'Anything else?'

'Ooh, just listen to us,' said Mrs Green, refilling her teacup. 'I'm being questioned by a policeman.'

Banks smiled. 'I'm sorry, I didn't mean it to seem like that. Comes with the territory, I suppose.'

She laughed. 'It's all right, Alan. I was only teasing. But it's hard to talk about. It was only a feeling.'

'What feeling?'

She clasped the collar of her frock. 'That he was . . . hovering . . . like the Angel of Death or something. Listen to me now. What a fool I sound.'

'You don't think Geoff Salisbury had anything to do with your husband's death, do you?'

'Of course not. No, it's nothing like that. It was a faulty valve, they said, on the oxygen tank.' She gave a harsh laugh. 'Someone told me if we'd been living in America I'd have got millions of dollars in compensation.'

'That's probably true.'

'Yes, well, if we'd been living in America we probably wouldn't have been able to afford the medical treatment in the first place, and Bill would have died a lot sooner.'

'Also true,' said Banks. 'Can you explain a bit more clearly? About this feeling you had.'

'I'm not sure. I felt as if he were, you know, waiting, waiting in the wings until Bill died.'

'For what?'

'I don't know. So he could take over more, maybe, manipulate me more.'

Banks smiled at her. 'He obviously didn't know who he was dealing with.'

She didn't smile back. 'You'd be surprised how easy it is to take advantage when people are vulnerable.' She looked at him. 'Or maybe you wouldn't. You probably see a lot of it in your job. Anyway, I felt as if he was hovering, waiting for Bill to die so that he could be more in control.'

'But what could possibly have been in it for him?'

'I don't know. Like I said, I was probably imagining things anyway.'

'I don't suppose you won the lottery recently?'

'Never bought a ticket.'

'And you don't have a million pounds hidden in the mattress or anything?'

She laughed. 'Wish I had. No, there's nothing, really. Bill's insurance policy. Old-age pension. I'm not complaining, mind you. It's enough to get by on.'

'What happened?'

'After Bill died, I gave Geoff Salisbury his marching orders. I was nice about it. I thanked him for his help, but said I was perfectly capable of managing by myself and I'd prefer it if he didn't come around any more. It wasn't that I couldn't still have used the sort of help he had to offer, but I just didn't feel comfortable having him around. Maybe I was being oversensitive as well as ungrateful.'

'I don't know,' said Banks. 'As I said, I haven't taken to him myself and I'm not sure why.'

'You'll be feeling guilty because he's looking after your parents while you're not there to do it.'

'Perhaps. Partly, yes. But there's more. I don't trust him. I don't know what he's up to, but I don't trust him. Maybe it's copper's instinct.'

'Well, I can tell you one thing for a start: you'll get no thanks around these parts for going after Geoff Salisbury.'

'Popular, is he?'

'To hear some talk, you'd think the sun shone out of his . . . well, you know what.'

Banks smiled. 'I think I can guess. How did he take your rejection?'

Mrs Green shrugged. 'Well enough, I suppose. At least he didn't bother me after that. Oh, I see him around now and then, and he always smiles and says hello as if nothing ever happened. It's just that—'

'What?'

'Oh, probably me being silly again. But it feels just skin deep, as if underneath it all, if you were just to strip off the surface that, well, you'd find something else entirely under there. Something very nasty indeed.'

9

Banks decided to pay a quick visit to the city centre that afternoon. He needed to pick up a couple of things from the shops for tomorrow, such as a nice anniversary card and some candles. He asked his parents if they needed anything, but they said no (implying, Banks thought, that Geoff Salisbury was taking care of everything), so off he went. Rather than search the side streets for a vacant parking space, he parked in the short stay behind the town hall and walked through to Bridge Street.

Of course, the city centre had changed quite a lot since his schooldays. Most cities *had* changed a lot in the past thirty years, but Peterborough more so than many others. Gone were the small record shop in the back alley, where he used to buy a new single nearly every week and LPs whenever he could afford them – usually only Christmas and birthdays – and the musty used book shop, where he used to browse for hours among the dog-eared paperbacks, the one where the sour-faced woman behind the counter used to watch him like a hawk the entire time he was in there. The open-air market had closed; some of the pubs he used to drink in when he was sixteen and seventeen had disappeared and new ones had sprung up; an old cinema, after several years as a bingo hall, was now a nightclub; department stores had disappeared, moved or been given facelifts; Cathedral Square was now a pedestrian precinct.

Only yards from the Queensgate Centre stood the ancient cathedral itself. Throughout Banks's childhood, the majestic structure had simply *been there.* It didn't dominate the city the way York Minster did, and like most of the other local kids he had paid it scant attention unless school projects and organized visits demanded otherwise. After all, what kid was interested in a boring old cathedral where boring old farts had gone to pray and where even more boring ones were buried? But now he found himself admiring the west front, with its three soaring Gothic arches flanked by twin-pinnacled towers, the stone cream-coloured in the autumn sunshine.

In the Queensgate Centre, Banks bought an expensive golden anniversary card and some gold candles, then he browsed around for a while and picked up a CD he thought Kay would enjoy listening to on their way to dinner. It was one oldie he didn't have, and he had been aware of the gap in his collection for some time.

He looked at his watch. Four o'clock. He thought he just had time for a quick walk by the river before driving back to his parents' house.

As he walked down Bridge Street past the Magistrates' Court and the police station, he realized that he hadn't been able to put Geoff Salisbury out of his thoughts completely. Something about the man was still nagging away at him. Mrs Green had been partly right; of course he felt guilty that Geoff was doing all the things for his ageing parents that a good and dutiful son ought to be doing. But also, as the astute Mrs Green had realized, there was more to it than that. If nothing worse, he certainly got the impression that Geoff Salisbury was a petty thief.

He glanced towards the old Customs House with its light on top to guide the ships navigating the River Nene, then he made his way down to the footpath that ran along the Nene Way. There he found a bench and, away from the crowds, took out his mobile and phoned the detectives' room back at Eastvale. DI Annie Cabbot and DC Winsome Jackman were on weekends at Western Area HQ, and it was Annie who answered.

'DCI Banks, what a pleasant surprise. Can't leave us alone for a minute, can you, sir?'

'I take it you're not alone in the office?'

'That's right, sir. Just Winsome and I, as per the duty roster.'

'Everything all right?'

'Fine. Business as usual. Couple of fights after closing time last night and a sexual assault on the East Side Estate. We've got a man in for questioning.'

'Is that all?'

'Honestly, we're on top of it. Relax. Enjoy yourself.'

'I'm trying, Annie, I'm trying. Actually, I wasn't calling to check up on you. I'm sure everything's under control. I need you to do a little detective work for me.'

'Detective work?'

'Yes. I want you to check on a name for me. See if you come up with anything.'

'I don't believe it. Even at your parents' golden wedding anniversary you're still on the job?'

'You know the rules, Annie, we can't ignore wrongdoing whether we're on or off duty.'

'Oh, what a load of bollocks. OK. Go ahead.'

Banks gave her Geoff Salisbury's name and address, along with the number of his Fiesta, which he had memorized, for good measure.

'What's it about?' Annie asked.

'I don't know yet,' said Banks. 'Probably nothing. Just a suspicious character in the neighbourhood. I want to know if he's got form, first of all, then anything else you can dig up on him.'

'Will do. Where can I get in touch with you?'

'Call my mobile number. I'll leave it switched on.' Banks didn't want the call arriving at his parents' house. 'If there's no answer, don't worry. Leave a message and I'll get back to you.'

'OK. Will do.'

Feeling vaguely guilty, though he had done nothing to feel in the least bit guilty about, Banks put the phone in his pocket and walked back towards his car.

10

Bath water was always at a premium, even now they had a house with a real bathroom, and Banks had to be careful not to use all the hot water. After a short soak and a shave, he was ready. Not expecting to be going out on a date, he hadn't brought a great selection of clothes with him, so he had to settle for some casual grey cotton trousers and a blue button-down Oxford shirt. He first checked the pockets of his sports jacket for car keys, and wallet, then slipped in the copy of *Lady Chatterley's Lover* he had found in his bookcase before he went downstairs.

Annie hadn't rung back yet, and given that it was past seven on a Saturday evening, Banks guessed she probably wouldn't until tomorrow. He certainly didn't want his mobile ringing in the restaurant, so he turned it off for the evening. There was no real urgency about the matter, anyway; he just wanted to know if Geoff Salisbury had form.

'Here,' his mother said, 'you'd better take a key. You'll probably be late back.'

'I shouldn't think so,' said Banks.

'Take one anyway. I don't want you hammering on the door waking us up at some ungodly hour in the morning.'

Banks pocketed the key. 'We're only going out for dinner.'

'And be quiet when you do come in,' his mother went on. 'You know your father's a light sleeper.'

The only thing Banks knew was this his *mother* had always

complained of being a light sleeper, but he said nothing except goodnight and that he wouldn't be late.

11

Kay came to the door in a long, dark, loose skirt, white blouse tucked in the waistband, soft suede jacket on top. Banks complimented her on her appearance, feeling for all the world like that awkward teenager taking her to the ABC to see *Here We Go Round the Mulberry Bush.* The film had only exacerbated his teenage angst about living in a provincial town – and a 'New Town' at that – but the music, mostly by Traffic and the Spencer Davis Group, was as good as it got and, what's more, a young and lovely Judy Geeson starred in it.

The main attraction of the evening, of course, had been Kay Summerville.

There, on the back row with the other would-be lovers, Banks had somehow found the bottle to put his arm around Kay, and she hadn't seemed to mind. After a while, though, his arm had started to ache like hell, then he had felt it going numb, but he was damned if he was going to remove it after all the courage it had taken to put it there in the first place. Some of his school friends had told him that they had unbuttoned their girlfriends' blouses and felt their breasts in that very cinema, but Banks hadn't the nerve to try that. Not on their first time out together.

On their way home, they had held hands and necked for a while in the bus shelter, and that was as far as things had gone that night. Banks remembered it all vividly as Kay arranged herself next to him in the car: the warm, slightly hazy evening smearing the city lights; noise from a nearby pub; the fruity, chemical taste of her lipstick; the softness of her neck just below her ear; the way it made him tingle and turn hard as he touched her; the warmth of her small breasts crushed against him.

'Any ideas?' Kay asked.

'Ideas? What ideas?'

'About where to go. I'm almost as much a stranger to these parts as you are.'

'Oh, that. I thought I'd just drive out Fotheringhay way. It's not too far, and we ought to be able to find somewhere decent to eat.'

Kay laughed. 'It'll probably be called the Mary Queen of Scots or something.'

'She certainly did get around, that woman.'

'Didn't have much choice, did she? What a miserable existence.'

'Never wanted to be royalty?'

Kay shook her head. 'Not me. I'm happy being a commoner.'

Banks slipped the Blind Faith CD he had bought that afternoon into the stereo and Stevie Winwood's 'Had to Cry Today' came out as crisp and heart-rending as the day it was cut.

'That's not—' Kay began, then she put her head back. 'My God, I haven't heard that in decades. You still listen to this sort of stuff?'

'A lot of old sixties and early seventies stuff, yes,' said Banks. 'I reckon those eight or nine years or so between "Love Me Do" and the time everyone died produced about the best rock we'll ever hear.'

'That's a very sweeping statement. What about punk?'

'Too much noise and not enough talent. The Clash were all right, though.'

'Roxy Music? Bowie? REM? The Pretenders?'

'There are exceptions to every rule.'

Kay laughed. 'And what else, these days?'

'I'm a hip-hop fan, myself. What about you?'

Kay nudged him in the ribs. 'Seriously.'

'Mostly jazz and classical. But I still listen to a fair bit of rock and folk: Sheryl Crow, Lucinda Williams, Beth Orton.'

'I'm afraid I don't listen to much at all these days,' said Kay. 'Don't have the time. I have the radio on sometimes while I'm in the bath, but I hardly notice what's being played. I suppose if I had to pick something I'd choose a string quartet or some sort of chamber music. Schubert, perhaps.'

'Nothing wrong with old Franz. What about this place?'

By the time the band had got to 'Can't Find My Way Home', one of Banks's favourites, he had wandered off the main road, and they were passing through a small village of grey-stone, thatched cottages clustered around a broad green. Lights shone behind curtains, and here and there a television set flickered. The pub was not called the Mary Queen of Scots but a far more lowly Fox and Hounds. Banks parked the car out front and turned off the music.

Banks and Kay ducked as they walked under the low beam of the door. Already the place was busy, emanating that rosy glow of a village pub popular with the city crowd. They went up to the bar, where Banks ordered a pint of bitter and Kay a vodka and tonic, then a young girl, who looked no more than about sixteen, seated them in the dining area and pointed out that the evening's menu was written on the blackboard by the window. Just one glance told Banks they'd come to the right sort of place: a wide selection of real ale and good food beyond basic pub fare, but nothing too ambitious. The noise level was perfect, only the buzz of conversation from other tables, the thud of darts in the board at the opposite end, sometimes accompanied by a mild oath or a cheer, and the sounds of the cash register.

'Cheers,' said Banks when they'd sat down and had a good look at the blackboard. 'To – to—'

'To times gone by,' said Kay.

'To times gone by.'

They clinked glasses and each took a sip. Banks felt the need for a cigarette, partly from nerves and partly from habit – he *was* in a pub, after all – but he rode out the craving and soon forgot about it.

'Do you remember that concert?' he asked.

Kay's eyes sparkled. 'Of course I do. Well, not so much the music . . . I mean, if you asked me I couldn't tell you what they played or who else was on . . . but the occasion . . . yes, how could

I forget? My mother wouldn't let me out of the door for a week afterwards, except to go to school.'

Banks laughed. 'Mine, too.'

On 7 June 1969, earlier on the day Kay had bought *Lady Chatterley's Lover* at a second-hand book shop on Charing Cross Road, Banks and Kay had taken the train to London for the free Blind Faith concert in Hyde Park. Through a combination of circumstances – partly to do with going off to smoke dope in a flat in Chelsea with some people they met – they had missed their train back and ended up getting home very early the following morning. Needless to say, parental recriminations had been severe.

'So,' said Kay, 'tell me about the last thirty years. I suppose you're married? Children?'

'Two children: one girl at university, and one boy in a rock band. And don't say it serves me right.'

Kay laughed. 'Heaven forbid. Maybe he'll make enough money to keep you in your old age.'

'That's what I'm banking on.'

'What about your wife?'

The waitress came over, notepad in hand. 'Have you decided yet?'

Banks glanced at Kay, who nodded and ordered the sole and salad. Banks went for venison medallions in port and mushroom sauce.

'More drinks?'

Banks looked at his half-full glass and shook his head. Kay asked for a glass of white wine with her meal.

'You were saying?' Kay went on when the waitress had gone away. 'About your wife.'

Banks paused. 'I'm divorced.'

'How long?'

'Two years. She's already remarried.'

Kay whistled. 'That's pretty fast. Usually you'd expect some sort of . . . well . . . I don't know . . .'

'Period of mourning?'

'That's not the term I was looking for, but I suppose it'll do.'

'It took me by surprise too. I can't say I'm in any hurry to get married again.'

'Is there someone?'

Banks thought of Michelle and Annie, and experienced another pang of guilt as he said, 'No one serious. It's too soon for that.'

'Uh-huh.'

'You?'

'Me? What?'

'Are you still married?'

'Not for the past five years.'

'I'm sorry.'

'You needn't be. He ran away with his secretary.'

'That must have been tough.'

'At the time, yes, I'd say it was a bit of a blow to the old self-esteem. She was much younger than me, of course. But I'm over it now.'

'Someone new?'

'No one special.' Kay smiled and gave a slight blush as she picked up her glass and sipped. It was the same smile and blush Banks remembered from all those years ago when he had first asked her out. What had happened to them? he asked himself. Why had they split up? But he knew the answer: it had been his fault.

Their meals arrived and Kay's glass of wine soon followed. Banks stuck with his one pint, as he had to drive. 'How are you coping about your mother?' he asked, after they had both eaten a couple of mouthfuls.

'Not bad. I think. I've got most of it done except the cleaning.' She smiled. 'Never was my strong suit, not even in my own home. I'll probably do it tomorrow. Anyway, a local dealer's coming to take away the furniture on Monday morning. Didn't offer much for it, but what the hell . . . The rest is already packed and ready to go to my house.' She shook her head. 'It was difficult going through someone's life like that. Your own mother's memories. Do you know, I found letters to her from a young man – this was before she and Dad met, of course – but they were love letters. Quite spicy, too, one or two of them.'

'It *is* hard to imagine your parents having lives of their own, isn't it?'

Kay nodded. 'There was lots of other stuff, too. Old photos. Me when I was a kid at the seaside. Letters from me, too, when I was at university. Full of energy and ambition.' Tears glistened in her eyes.

'And now?'

Kay wiped away the tears. 'Oh, I suppose I'm still ambitious enough. I work practically all the hours God sends. I know I neglected Mum, especially after Dad died.' Banks remembered hearing that Kay's father had been killed ten years ago in a car accident, an accident her mother survived. It had been the talk of the estate for weeks, so his mother had told him. Kay laughed and made a dismissive gesture. 'I don't know, maybe there's something Freudian about it – I always was Daddy's little girl – but my career really started to take off around then, too. Life was exciting at last: lots of travel, parties, financial success. I hardly ever made time to come home and help Mum, even when she was ill. For crying out loud, I was in Zurich when she died. I barely managed to get back in time for the funeral. Some daughter. Some mother, too. Even my kids say they never see me.'

'Kids?'

'Three girls. All married. I'm a grandmother, Alan. Can you believe it? A bloody grandmother.'

'It's hard to believe, looking at you.'

She blushed and smiled again. 'Why, thank you. I'll tell you, though, it takes a lot of hard work and a lot of investment in potions and salves these days. Remember when we were kids? We thought we were immortal, that we'd be young for ever.'

'True enough,' Banks agreed. 'I'm still waiting for the wisdom that's supposed to come with age.'

'Me, too.'

They paused to eat in comfortable silence. Banks watched Kay break off flakes of moist sole with the edge of her fork. His venison was good, tender and tasty. He decided he could risk one more drink and asked the waitress to bring him a glass of red wine.

'How are *your* parents?' Kay asked.

'Fine. Oh, that reminds me: Mum asked me to invite you to drop by tomorrow, if you want.'

Kay nodded slowly. 'Yes. All right, that would be nice.'

'About six, OK?'

'Fine. Just for half an hour or so.' Kay frowned. 'You know, there is one thing that puzzles me a bit about Mum,' she said.

'Oh?'

'It's nothing, really, but I was going through her finances yesterday, and I noticed she'd withdrawn a hundred pounds from the cash machine the day she died, but I can't find it. There's only about six or seven pounds in her purse, and she wasn't the type to hide her money under the mattress.'

The little scar beside Banks's right eye began to itch. 'Maybe she had bills to pay, or she owed it to someone?'

'Neither a lender nor a borrower be. That was Mum's motto. And all her bills had been paid. No, it's a mystery. What do you have to say, O great detective?'

'I still think there's probably a logical explanation.'

'Probably. The other thing that puzzles me, though, is how did she get it?'

'What do you mean?'

'Well, she was bedridden for the last few days. There was a nurse on call twenty-four hours a day, of course, and Dr Grenville dropped by quite often, but . . . I just don't see how she could even have *got* to the cash machine.'

The itch got stronger. Banks scratched the side of his eye. 'Have you ever heard of a fellow called Geoff Salisbury?' he asked her.

Kay frowned. 'The name sounds vaguely familiar. I think he introduced himself to me at the funeral. A neighbour. Why?'

'Oh, nothing,' said Banks. 'Nothing important. Dessert?'

12

'Would you like some music on?' Kay asked. They were back at her parents' house, and Banks had accepted her invitation to come in for a nightcap – a half-bottle of 'medicinal' brandy that Kay had found while tidying out the kitchen cupboards. They drank it out of cracked teacups that she had been about to put in the dustbin.

'Sure,' said Banks.

Kay walked over to the old stereo system. 'Let's see,' she said, flipping though a box of LPs. 'I packed these last night but I didn't really pay much attention. There's probably not a lot of choice. Dad only liked the stuff he used to listen to in the war, and Mum wasn't much interested in music at all. As you can see, they don't own a CD player. I think the last LP they bought was in 1960.'

Banks went over and joined her, looking at the old-fashioned covers. At least he could read what was written on the backs of them, unlike the tiny print on CDs. 'That's after 1960,' he said, pointing to *Beatles for Sale.*

'That must be one of mine,' Kay said. 'I didn't even notice it.'

Banks flipped open the cover. Written inside, in tiny blue ballpoint over the photograph, were some words. They were hard to make out, but he thought they said, 'Kay Summerville loves Alan Banks'. Banks passed it to Kay, who blushed and put it away. 'I lent it to Susan Fish,' she said. 'The sneaky devil. I didn't know she'd done that.' She pulled out another LP. 'Ah, this will do fine.'

The needle crackled as it hit the groove, a sound that gave Banks an unexpected frisson of delight and nostalgia, and then Billie Holiday started singing 'Solitude'.

'Couldn't do much better,' he said.

'Dance?' Kay asked.

'I don't know,' said Banks. 'Remember the vicar wouldn't allow dancing at the youth club because he said it led to sex?'

Kay laughed. 'Yes, I remember.'

Then she was in his arms, Billie was singing about solitude, and they were doing what passed for dancing.

13

'A wise man, that vicar,' said Banks about an hour later, as he lay back on the sofa, Billie Holiday long finished, a naked Kay half on top of him, her head resting on his chest, fingertips trailing languorously over his skin. It had been good – no doubt much better than their youthful fumblings, which he could scarcely remember now – though there had been something a little melancholy and desperate about it, as if both had been straining to capture something that eluded them.

'What happened to us?' Kay asked. 'All those years ago.'

'We were just kids. What did we know?'

'I suppose so. But have you ever wondered what would have happened? You know, if we hadn't—'

'Of course I have.'

'And?'

'I don't know. It's hard for me to imagine a life without Sandra and the kids.'

'I know that. I mean, even though it ended badly, me and Keith had some good times. And the kids are marvellous. It's just a game. Imagining. You know, sometimes I've been places or experienced things and thought I'd have liked you there to share it.'

'You have?'

'Yes. Haven't you ever felt the same?'

'I can't say I have,' said Banks, who had.

She nudged him in the ribs. 'Bastard.'

'There's something I never told you before,' Banks said, stroking her silky blonde hair and touching the soft skin on her neck, just below her ear.

'And you want to tell me now?'

'Yes.'

'Are you sure that's a good idea?'

'The timing seems right.'

'Why?'

'No particular reason.'

Kay shifted position. 'OK. Go ahead.'

'You know that first time when my parents were out and you came over to the house? The day we'd decided we were finally going to do it?'

'How could I forget? I was about to lose my virginity. I was scared silly.'

'Me too. On both counts. Nervous as hell.'

Banks remembered that, as the months went on, he and Kay had graduated from kissing in the bus shelter to touching above the waist, first with clothing intact, then under her jumper, with only the thin bra between his hands and her bare, swollen flesh. After a few weeks of that, and much trouble fumbling with the clasp that held the thing on, he got beyond the bra to the unimaginably firm and tender mounds beneath.

They had been going out nearly a year before the subject of moving to below the waist came up, and both were understandably a bit nervous about it. This might have been the swinging sixties, when kids were making love openly at Woodstock, but Banks and Kay were young, unsophisticated, provincial kids, and the antics of drug-taking pop stars and free-loving hippies seemed as fantastic as Hollywood films.

But they had done it.

'Well,' Banks went on. 'I had to go and get some . . . you know . . . Durex.'

'Rubber Johnnies? Yes, I suppose you did. Do you know, I never really thought about that.'

'Well, I couldn't very well go to the local chemist's or the barber's, could I? They knew me there. Someone would have been bound to tell my parents.'

Kay propped herself on one elbow and leaned over him, her nipple hard against his chest. He could smell white wine and cheap brandy on her breath, see sparks of light dancing in her dark blue eyes. 'So what did you do? Where did you go?' she asked.

'I walked miles and miles to the other side of town and found a barber's where I was certain no one would recognize me.'

Kay giggled. 'Oh, how sweet.'

'I'm not finished yet.'

'Go on.'

'Do you know how the old barbers' shops had a sort of hallway with a counter between the outer and inner door, nice and private, where you could buy shampoo and razor blades and stuff?'

'And rubber Johnnies?'

'And rubber Johnnies.'

'I remember. My dad used to take me to the barber's with him sometimes when I was a little girl.'

'Right,' Banks went on. 'Well, as I said, I'd walked halfway to Cambridge and there I was, bold as brass, outside a barber's on a street where not a soul could possibly know who I was.'

Kay smiled. 'What happened?' She moved her head and her hair tickled his chest.

'Well, wouldn't you know it, but this particular establishment didn't have a discreet sales area. Oh no. I opened the front door and I found myself standing right by the barber's chair. He was giving a bloke a shave, I remember, and the place was full of grown men. I mean, every chair in the waiting area was taken, and I swear that the minute I walked in there they all looked up from their newspapers and every eye was on me.'

'My God! What did you do?'

'What could I do? I'd gone too far to turn back. I stood my ground and I said, in as deep a voice as I could manage, "Packet of three, please."'

Kay put her hand to her mouth to hold back the laughter. 'Oh, no!' she said. 'You're joking?'

'No word of a lie.'

'What did he say? The barber.'

'Not a word. He stopped mid-shave, straight-blade razor in his hand, and he went to his cabinet and got them for me. But you should have heard the other buggers laugh and cheer. You'd think Peterborough United had won a game. I went red as a beet.'

Kay burst into a fit of laughter and couldn't stop. Banks started laughing with her, holding her against his chest, and after a while laughter turned to lust.

14

It was after two o'clock when Banks slipped the key into the door of his parents' house and turned the lock as quietly as he could. He shut the door slowly behind him, without making much noise, and made sure the chain and bolt were on. The stairs creaked a little as he tiptoed up to bed. He couldn't very well go and brush his teeth as he would have to put the bathroom light on and the tap would make a noise. He thought he could just about manage to undress and crawl into bed in the dark. The bed would creak too, but that couldn't be helped. Fortunately, he'd had the foresight to use the toilet before leaving Kay's.

The minute he got to the landing he heard his mother muttering something to his father, who muttered something back. He couldn't catch the words but knew they were about him, how late he was. He felt himself blushing. Christ, it really didn't matter how quiet he had tried to be; she'd been lying awake until he came home, just like she used to do when he was a teenager.

15

Despite his late night, Banks woke early on Sunday morning to the sound of rain blowing in sharp gusts against his bedroom window. The rest of the house was quiet, and he didn't think his parents were awake yet. His first thought on finding consciousness was to wonder what the hell he and Kay had thought they were up to last night, but the more he remembered the less he regretted. Blame it on Billie Holiday, if you will, on dancing, the old estate and the romance of the past, but whatever it was, it was something special and he refused to feel guilty.

He only hoped Kay felt the same way in the damp grey of dawn.

Two memories assailed him almost simultaneously as he got out of bed and went over to the wardrobe for his overnight bag: that he had forgotten to give Kay her old copy of *Lady Chatterley's Lover* and that he was certain he had seen a tiny, neatly folded square of silver paper in the bathroom waste bin. Perhaps Mrs Summerville had taken to chewing gum in her final days, though he doubted it, or maybe Kay did, though he had seen no evidence of it last night, and he remembered that she had bought mints at the newsagent's, not gum. Which left him with the strongest suspicion that Geoff Salisbury had been there some time over the past few weeks, leaving Banks little doubt as to where the hundred pounds had gone.

What to do about him, that was the question.

Banks stretched as he pulled out his bag and decided to start the day dressed simply, in jeans and a polo-neck sweater. He would change for the party later. Today was his parents' big day, and Roy was due to come up from London. Banks resolved to be nice to Roy for his parents' sake.

As Banks put his bag back in the wardrobe, he noticed some cardboard boxes on the far side. On his previous visit he had found some old records and diaries, which were still there, but now it looked as if there was more. Curious, he opened the other door and lifted a box out. The flaps were shut, but not sealed, and written across the top, in his mother's inimitable scrawl was his name: *Alan*. More childhood stuff, then.

On top he found yet more old school reports, from the grammar school this time, most of them urging him to try harder and assuring him he could do better if he only put his shoulder to the wheel etc. The reports were handwritten in black ink, and Banks occasionally had difficulty reading the comments. He remembered some of the teachers' names – Mr Newman, Mr Phelps, Mr Hawtry – but most of them were a blur.

Along with the reports was a class photograph dated 14 May 1967. There they all were, three rows of teenage boys in their school uniforms. Banks remembered several of the faces: Steve Hill, Paul Major, Dave Grenfell, his best friends, then Tony Green, John McLeod, the school bully, and Ian Marston, who, so Banks's mother had told him, committed suicide seven or eight years ago after his courier business failed. The rest of them he hardly remembered except for the odd feature here and there, such as a long, freckled face, a big nose, or prominent ears, but he couldn't put a name to them. He had met up with Dave Grenfell and Paul Major on his previous visit, and he had found out then that Steve Hill had died of lung cancer, but what had become of everyone else he had no idea. Others would be dead, some would be dying, some would be successful, some would be failures, some would be criminals, many would be divorced. There was one angry-looking kid glaring into the camera with a cocky expression on his face, black hair just a little bit too long, tie slightly askew, top button undone against school regulations. Himself. Even more of a mystery than all the rest.

Next came a few school exercise books full of sums and compositions. One of them contained some poems Banks had written when he went through that stage of adolescence in which poetry was an acceptable means of expression as long as you kept it to yourself. It was with excruciating embarrassment that he looked over them again now, with the autumn rain starting to spatter against his bedroom window.

There were lines about the awkwardness of being an adolescent, love poems to Julie Christie and Judy Geeson, poems about how phony the world was. None of them rhymed, of course, nor were any overly concerned with metrics; the lines simply ended where he had decided to end them, for no other reason than that it looked like poetry on the page. There were no capital letters, either. Still, Banks reflected, from what he had seen that wasn't a hell of a lot different from the sort of thing most published poets did today. Awful lines and images jumped out at him, such as 'I feel like a corpse / in the coffin of your mind.' What on earth had prompted him to write that? About what? He couldn't even remember whose mind was supposed to be the coffin. And then there was a poem marked, 'For Kay', in which these immortal lines appeared:

i skimmed across
your life
like a pebble
on the water's surface

i sank

quickly
the tide went out

What had he been thinking of? There was another image about her being 'naked / on a sheepskin / by the crackling fire', but as far as Banks could remember, they had never lain on a sheepskin rug, and electric fires, which everyone on the estate had, didn't crackle. Poetic licence?

He remembered that first time up in this same room while his parents were out. The event was awkward and far less momentous for both of them than his imagination had convinced him it would be, but it went well enough in the end and they decided they liked it and would certainly try again. They got better and better over the next few months, stealing an hour or two here and there while parents were absent. Once they almost got caught when Kay's mother came home sooner than expected from a dental appointment. They just managed to get their clothes on and tidy up the bed in time to tell her they'd been listening to records, though judging by the expression on Mrs Summerville's face when she saw her daughter's dishevelled hair, Banks didn't think she was convinced. Kay told him later that that very evening she had got a lecture about the dangers of teenage pregnancy and what men think of women who haven't 'saved themselves' for marriage, though no overt mention was made of Banks or that afternoon's events, and nobody tried to stop them seeing one another.

Smiling at the memory, Banks slipped the exercise book of poetry into his overnight bag, determined to remember to feed it to the fire when he got back to his Gratly cottage. As he moved it, a newspaper cutting slipped out from between some of the unfilled pages. It was a report in the local paper on the disappearance of Graham Marshall, a school friend of Banks's, and the reason for his visit home in the summer. Alongside the article was a photograph of Graham with his fair hair, melancholy expression and pale face, like some fin de siècle poet.

Banks moved on to the bottom of the box, where he found more old forty-fives, ones he had forgotten he had: Procol Harum's 'A Whiter Shade of Pale', 'Juliet' by the Four Pennies, 'Hippy Hippy Shake' by the Swinging Blue Jeans, the Lovin' Spoonful's 'Summer in the City', 'Devil in Disguise' by Elvis Presley and 'Still I'm Sad' by the Yardbirds.

Banks put the box back on top of one marked *Roy* and tiptoed downstairs into the kitchen for a cup of tea. His heart almost stopped when he saw Geoff Salisbury sitting at the kitchen table eating buttered toast.

'Morning, Alan,' Geoff said. 'I've come to do some cleaning up. Already took your em and pee a cup of tea up, bless 'em. It's a big day for them, you know. Like a cuppa yourself?'

Banks felt like saying he would make his own tea, but he remembered he hadn't been able to find the tea bags. Instead, he got himself a mug. 'Thanks,' he grunted.

'Not much of a morning person?' Geoff asked. 'Still, I imagine after a late night like you had you must be feeling even more tired. Your poor old mum was lying awake worrying where you'd got to.'

Salisbury winked. 'Having a good time with that Summerville girl, were you?'

So Banks's mother had already told Geoff that her son had been out with Kay Summerville and had not returned home until the early hours of the morning. He knew all this, and it wasn't even nine o'clock yet. Geoff Salisbury was starting to get *really* annoying. Even though Banks hadn't had a chance to call Annie back about criminal records, he decided that now would be as good a time as any to go on the offensive and make a couple of things clear to him.

'I'm glad you're here, actually,' Banks said. 'I've been wanting to have a quiet word with you.'

'Oh? What about?'

'Your sticky fingers.'

'Come again?'

'You know what I'm talking about. Don't come the innocent. It doesn't work with me.'

'I understand that your job must make you cynical, but why are you picking on me? What have I done?'

'You know what you've done.'

'Look, if it's that business about the change, I thought I'd already made it clear to you it was a genuine mistake. I thought we'd put it behind us.'

'I might have done if it hadn't been for a few other interesting titbits I've heard since I've been down here.'

'It's that Summerville girl, isn't it? If she's been saying things, she's lying. She doesn't like me.'

'Well,' said Banks, 'that at least shows good taste on her part. It doesn't matter who's been saying what. The point is that I've been hearing from a number of independent sources about things sort of disappearing when you're in the vicinity. Money, for example.'

Salisbury turned red. 'I resent that.'

'I should imagine you do. But is it true?'

'Of course it isn't. I don't know who's—'

'I told you, it doesn't matter who.'

Salisbury stood up. 'Well, it does to me. You might not believe it, but there are people who have it in for me. Not everybody appreciates what I do for the decent folk around here, you know.'

'What do you mean?'

'Never you mind. Now, if you've finished with your groundless accusations, I've got work to do. Your parents' golden wedding might not be important to you, but it is to me. Arthur and Ida mean a lot to me.'

Before Banks could say another word, Salisbury had gone into the front room and started up the vacuum. Irritated both by Salisbury's reaction and his own fumbling accusation, Banks went across to the newsagent's to see if he could pick up a *Sunday Times*.

16

Banks went to the Bricklayer's Inn by himself for a quiet pint on Sunday lunchtime, taking the newspaper with him and promising to be back by two o'clock for lunch. It felt like his first real break that weekend, and he made the most of it, even getting the crossword three-quarters done, which was good for him without Annie's help. On his way home he took cover in the rain-lashed bus shelter by the gates of the derelict factory to call Annie in Eastvale. Though the shelter hadn't been there all those years ago, Banks still couldn't help but think of Mandy, with her Julie Christie lips and the faraway look in her eyes. He wondered what had happened to her, whether she had ever found that distant thing she had seemed to be dreaming of. Probably not; most people didn't. Though it seemed like another age, she would only be in her early fifties, after all, and that no longer sounded very old to Banks.

DC Winsome Jackman answered his ring. 'Is DI Cabbot not in?' Banks asked.

'I'm afraid not, sir,' said Winsome. 'She's out on the East Side Estate interviewing neighbours about that sexual assault.'

'Do you know when she'll be back?'

'No, sir. Sorry, but you'll just have to make do with me.'

Banks could hear teasing humour in her voice, the way it tinged her lilting Jamaican speech. Did she know that Annie and he used to have a thing? He wouldn't be surprised. No matter how much you try to keep something like that a secret, there are always people who seem able to pick up on it intuitively.

'DI Cabbot did leave a message for you, though, sir,' Winsome went on.

'Yes?'

'That man you were asking about, Geoffrey Salisbury.'

'Right. Any form?'

'Yes, sir. One conviction. Six years ago. Served eighteen months.'

'What for?'

'Fraud, sir. To put it in a nutshell, he tried to swindle a little old lady out of her life savings, but she was a lot smarter than he reckoned on.'

'Did he indeed?' Banks said. 'What a surprise.'

'Sir?'

'Nothing. Where did this happen?'

'Loughborough, sir.'

That wasn't very far away, Banks thought. 'Thanks a lot,' he said. 'And thank DI Cabbot. That's a great help.'

'There's more, sir. DI Cabbot said she's going to try to talk to the local police, the ones who handled the case. She said it looks like there might be more to it than meets the eye.'

'What did she mean by that?'

'Don't know, sir. Shall I ask her to ring you when she's been in touch with Loughborough police?'

'If you would, Winsome. And thanks again.'

'No problem, sir. Enjoy the party.'

17

Roy didn't turn up in time for Sunday lunch, which was pretty much what Banks had expected. They ate without him, Ida Banks fretting and worrying the whole time, unable to enjoy her food. Arthur tried to calm her, assuring her that nothing terrible had happened and that Roy wasn't trapped in a burning car wreck somewhere on the M1. Banks said nothing. He knew his mother well enough to realize that anything he said regarding Roy would only succeed in adding fuel to the fire. Instead, he ate his roast beef and Yorkshires like a good boy – and a fine lunch it was, too, especially if you liked your meat and vegetables overcooked – and counted his blessings. In the first place his mother was far too distracted to go on at him for being late home last night, and in the second place Geoff bloody Salisbury had buggered off home and wasn't eating with them, though he had promised to come back early to help set up for the party.

The phone finally rang at about half past two, just as they were starting their jam roly-poly, and Banks's mother leapt up and dashed into the hall to answer it. When she came back she was much calmer, and she informed Banks and his father that poor Roy had had a devil of a job getting away on time and the rain had caused some terrible delays. There was also a pile-up on the M25, so he was stuck in traffic there at the moment and would arrive as soon as he could.

'There you are, you see,' Arthur said. 'All that fretting for nothing. I told you he was all right.'

'But you never know, do you?' she said.

Banks offered to do the dishes and his offer was, to his surprise, accepted. His father had a nap with the open newspaper unread on his lap, and his mother went for a short lie-down to calm her nerves. When Banks had finished the dishes, he sneaked a couple of fingers of his father's Johnnie Walker to calm *his* nerves. He had no sooner downed it than the explosion went off.

At least that was what it sounded like at first. Eventually, Banks's ears adjusted enough to discern that it was music coming from next door. Heavy-metal gangsta rap, music only if you used the term very loosely indeed. Banks's father stirred in his armchair. 'At it again,' he grumbled. 'Never get a moment's peace.'

Banks sat by him on the arm. 'Does this happen a lot?' he asked.

His father nodded. 'Too often for me. Oh, I've tried having a word, but he's an ignorant bugger. If I were twenty or thirty years younger—'

Banks heard his mother's footsteps on the landing. 'At it again, I hear,' she called down.

'It's bad for her nerves,' Arthur Banks said.

'Have you talked to the council?'

'We've tried, but they say, apart from issuing a warning, they can't do anything.'

'What about Geoff Salisbury?'

'Geoff's got his strengths, but he's not got a lot of bottle. Proper tough guy him next door.'

'Right,' said Banks, standing up. 'Give me a few minutes.'

'Where are you going, Alan?' his mother asked, coming down the stairs as he got to the front door.

'Just off to have a quiet word with next door, that's all.'

'Don't you go causing any trouble. Do you hear? You just be careful. And remember we have to live here after you've gone, you know.'

Banks patted his mother's arm. 'Don't worry, Mum,' he said. 'I know what I'm doing. I'll make sure I don't cause you any trouble.'

It was still raining outside. Banks knocked on the door, but got no answer. Hardly surprising, as he supposed nobody could hear him over the music. The windows were all open and the angry heavy-metal rap spilled out into the street, someone bragging about raping a bitch and offing a pig.

Banks tried the front door. It was open. He found himself in a small hallway, where the stairs led up to the bedrooms. The wallpaper was peeling and something that looked like a sleeping bag lay on the staircase. Banks nudged it with his foot. It was empty.

He didn't like just walking in unannounced, but it seemed the only option. He called out a few times while he stood still in the hallway but he could hardly even hear his own shouts.

Finally, he went through into the living room. Now he knew why they kept the windows open; the smell was overwhelming. It was a mixture of things – human smells, definitely, such as sweat and urine, but also rotten vegetables, burnt plastic and marijuana. There were piles of old newspapers and other rubbish on the floor and it looked as though a dog had chewed up the furniture, though there wasn't one in evidence. Thankful for small mercies, Banks thought; they probably had a pit bull. Three people were slumped on sofas and armchairs, and one of them stood up when Banks walked in.

'Who the fuck do you think you are?' he shouted.

'I'm not a lip-reader,' Banks said, stepping over to the mound of stereo equipment and turning the volume down. 'That's better.'

It was the man of the house – Fred West to a T, eyebrows and all. The woman Banks assumed was his wife watched from one of the chairs. A girl Banks guessed to be about thirteen or fourteen sat in the other chair staring blankly at him.

The man squared up to Banks and gestured to the door with his thumb. 'Right, mate,' he said. 'I'm done being polite. On your bike.'

'I came to ask you to turn down the music,' Banks said. 'We can hardly hear ourselves think next door.'

'What's it to you? You're not from around here.'

'I was here a long time before you came on the scene. I grew up here. It's my parents' house and today's their wedding anniversary.'

'Well, bully for you. Sorry we forgot to buy them a present. Now just fuck off before I do you some real damage.'

'You don't understand,' said Banks, slipping his warrant card out. 'I'm a police officer and I'm asking you nicely to keep the noise down.'

The man actually leaned forward and scrutinized the card. 'North Yorkshire!' he said. 'You've got no powers down here. You're out of your jurisdiction, mate.'

'Big word that. I'm surprised you didn't choke on it.'

'I'm not scared of you. Now fuck off!'

'You should be,' said Banks.

The man walked over to the stereo and cranked up the volume again. The girl and the woman hadn't moved. They were just watching. Banks guessed they were stoned on something or other. He thought he could see a crack pipe half-hidden under a newspaper on the floor, but it wasn't crack they were on. These two weren't jerky or manic; they were practically comatose. Downers or smack, most likely.

With a sigh, Banks walked over to the stereo, picked up the CD player, ripped out the wires and dropped it on the floor. The music stopped. The women still didn't move, but Fred came right at him. He was a couple of inches taller than Banks, and thickset, muscular in the upper body. But Banks had his wiry and deceptive strength and speed going for him. He grabbed the man's wrist and twisted it so that he soon had him on his knees, arm up his back, foot placed solidly on his left kidney. By exerting just a little more pressure on the arm, Banks could make the pain excruciating. Even more pressure and the arm would snap or the shoulder joint would pop. The women just looked on, goggle-eyed. They'd never seen anything like this before.

'I'll do you for this!' the man yelled. 'I'll see you bloody locked up, copper or no. You've got no right going around destroying a man's private property.'

'Oh, give it a rest, Fred,' said Banks. 'It was probably nicked, anyway.'

'My name's Lenny. You've got the wrong bloke.'

'My mistake. Sorry, Lenny. Are you listening?'

'I'm still not scared of—'

Banks gave a little twist and Lenny screamed. Banks let him relax a moment and then repeated his question.

'All right,' said Lenny. 'All right, I'm listening. Let go.'

Banks didn't. 'I'm sorry about your CD player,' he said. 'I'm a music lover, myself, so it hurt me almost as it hurt you. I'm sure it'll be OK; it's just had rather a nasty shock, that's all. If it's not, then I'm sure you'll have no problem lifting another. But first I'd like a promise out of you.'

'What promise?'

Banks gave another little twist. Lenny screamed, his face red with pain. The woman Banks assumed was his wife lit a cigarette and contemplated the scene before her with great interest, as if she was watching a television programme. The girl started buffing her nails. Banks listened in the silence after the CD player's sudden demise, but he could hear no other sounds coming from anywhere in the house. A good sign. No ambush imminent.

'I'd like you to promise me that you won't ever, ever, play your music so loud again that it disturbs my mum and dad next door. Do you think you can do that, Lenny?'

'It's my house. I'll do what I like in my own fucking house.'

Twist. Scream.

'Lenny, you're not listening. If you really mean what you just said, you ought to consider moving to a detached house, you know, miles away from your nearest neighbours. Besides, it's not your house. It's the council's house. You just rent it.'

'You're a bastard, you are,' Lenny said, gasping. 'You're worse than the fucking criminals you put away. Filth!' He spat on the floor.

'Yeah, yeah. It's all been said before. But we're not talking about me, we're talking about your promise.'

'What promise? I haven't made any fucking promise.'

'But you're going to, aren't you?'

Lenny said nothing. The woman frowned as she looked at him. Banks could tell the suspense was killing her. *Will he or won't he*? The young girl got up and made to leave the room.

'Where are you going?' Banks asked her.

'Bog,' she said, making a squatting gesture.

Banks was a little concerned that she might reappear with a weapon. 'Hold on a minute, love,' he said. 'Wait till I'm finished here.'

'I'll piss myself.'

'I said hold on. You'll live with it.'

'These are me new jeans.'

Banks turned back to Lenny. The girl slumped against the door-post, legs crossed. Banks kept a close eye on her. She chewed on her lower lip and looked sulky.

'Right, Lenny, the quicker you give me your promise, the quicker your lass here will get to go to the toilet.'

'She's not *my* lass. Let her piss herself. I don't care. Won't be the first time.'

Banks gave a harder twist and Lenny cursed. 'What I want you to promise,' Banks said slowly, 'is that you won't play your music so loud that it upsets my mum and dad, remember?'

'I remember.'

'And if you do,' Banks said, 'I'll have the local drugs squad over here before you can flush a tab of E down the toilet. Is that clear?'

'It's clear.'

'Is it a promise?'

'I—'

Banks twisted again. 'Is it a promise?'

'All right, all right! Jesus Christ, yes, it's a fucking promise!'

'And if you do anything – anything at all – to harm or intimidate them in any way, I'll consider that promise broken. And I deal with broken promises myself. North Yorkshire's not that far away. Got it?'

'Got it. Let me go.'

Banks let go and Lenny squirmed on the floor for a while, rubbing his arm and his shoulder before subsiding into his armchair and lighting a cigarette with shaking hands.

'You're a nutter, you are,' he said. 'You ought to be locked up.'

'You've got that right.'

'Is it over?' the girl by the door asked. 'Are you done? Are you? 'Cos I'm bleeding bursting here.'

'It's over, love,' said Banks. 'Off you go.'

'About fucking time.' She dashed upstairs. The woman on the sofa looked at Lenny with contempt, but still said nothing.

'You in charge here, Lenny?' Banks asked, catching her look. 'Because there's no point my talking to the monkey, if you catch my drift.'

'I'm in fucking charge,' he said, glaring at the woman. 'They know that.'

She sniffed, but Banks could see fear in her eyes, the first emotion he had noticed in her. Lenny was in charge all right, and he probably used the same tactics Banks had just used to rule his roost. That didn't make Banks feel particularly good, but needs must. He wondered what other sorts of abuse went on in this house, in addition to drugs. The young girl, for example, or the other kids, wherever they were. Nothing would have surprised him. Maybe he'd call in the drugs squad, anyway, and the social. Someone ought to keep a close eye on this lot, that was for certain.

He heard the toilet flush as he left.

18

Roy's arrival at about four o'clock broke the tension for Banks. Until then he had been helping Geoff set up the bar and buffet on tables in the kitchen, keeping a tight rein on his temper for his parents' sake, even though Geoff treated him like an employee. 'Now, Alan, if you wouldn't mind just moving that over there . . . That's a good lad . . . If you could nip over to the shops and pick up . . .' And so on. He had also been wanting to get Geoff alone and have another go at him in the light of Winsome's information, but his mother was always around issuing instructions too. Wisely, his father had gone upstairs to 'rest'.

When the doorbell rang, Ida Banks practically ran to the front door, and Banks heard her shouts of glee as she greeted Roy. After divesting himself of his raincoat, the man himself came through to the living room, clutching a bottle-shaped bag, and with a young woman in tow. She looked about twenty, Banks thought, with short, shaggy hair, black streaked with blonde, a pale, pretty face, with beautiful eyes the colour and gleam of chestnuts in September. She also had a silver stud just below her lower lip. She was wearing jeans and a short woolly jumper, exposing a couple of inches of bare, flat midriff and a navel with a ring in it.

'This is Corinne,' said Roy. 'Say hello to my brother, Alan, Corinne.'

Corinne shook Banks's hand and said hello. She gave him a shy smile and averted her eyes.

Roy looked at Geoff, free hand stretched out, smiling like a salesman. 'And you are—?'

'Geoff. Geoff Salisbury.'

'Geoff. Of course! Pleased to meet you, Geoff. I've heard a lot about you. Mum and Dad say they'd be lost without you.'

Geoff beamed and shifted from foot to foot. 'Well . . . that's probably a bit of an exaggeration.'

Very 'umble, Banks thought.

'Not at all,' said Roy. 'Not at all.' He gave Geoff a firm handshake and clapped him on the shoulder. 'Good to meet you at last.'

Geoff basked in the glow of Roy's charm like a child in his mother's embrace.

All this time, Ida Banks had stood by, smiling on. Roy turned to her again and gave her a hug. Then he handed over the package he'd been carrying. Ida Banks opened it. It was a bottle of Veuve Clicquot champagne. Vintage.

She turned to her husband. 'Ooh, look at this, Arthur! Champagne.'

'It's the real stuff, too,' Roy said, with a wink at Banks. 'None of your Spanish *cava* or New World sparklers.'

Arthur Banks grunted. Banks happened to know that his father hated champagne, as much because it was a symbol of the upper classes as for its taste.

'I'd better put it away for a special occasion,' said his mother, taking it through the kitchen and placing it into the dark depths of the larder, where it would probably remain. Banks thought to mention that today was as special an occasion as they were likely to have in a while, but he knew it was best to keep quiet when Roy was in full benevolent swing. He'd bought a few cans of beer and lager, himself, and he knew that *they* would be emptied that very evening, without a doubt.

'Now, then,' said Ida Banks, rubbing her hands together and reaching out to touch Corinne's shoulder, 'what about a drink for everyone? Corinne, love, what'll you have?'

'Lager and lime?'

'Right you are, love. And you, Roy?'

'Just a Perrier for me, Mum,' said Roy. 'Driving.'

'Of course.' Ida Banks frowned. 'What did you say? Perrier? I don't think we have any of that, do we, Alan?'

Banks shook his head. 'Only tap water.'

'Well that won't do, will it?' his mother said scornfully.

'It's all right, Mrs B,' chimed in Geoff, 'I'll just nip over the road. Old Ali's bound to have some. He sells everything.' And before anyone could stop him he was off.

Ida Banks turned to Roy again. 'You won't be driving for ages yet, I hope, son. Won't you have a glass of something a bit stronger first?'

'Oh, go on, then,' said Roy. 'You've twisted my arm. I'll have a glass of white wine.'

Banks's mother gave him a questioning glance. 'We've got that, Mum,' he said, then looked at his brother. 'Screw top OK, Roy?'

'Whatever,' said Roy, his lip curling.

Banks and his father both opted for beer.

'Come on, then, Corinne, love,' said Ida Banks, taking Corinne by the arm. 'You can keep me company and help me pour.'

Banks couldn't believe it. His mother was fawning all over Roy's twenty-something bit of fluff, the sort of girl who'd have been granted no more than a sniff of distaste if Banks had brought her home. Still, he should have expected it. Roy was Banks's younger brother by five years. He had grown up watching Banks do everything wrong and getting caught for it – staying out too late as a teenager, listening to the radio under the bedsheets when he should have been asleep, smoking, leaving home to go to college in London, joining the police – and Roy had keenly observed his parents' reactions. Roy had learned well from his brother's mistakes, and he had done everything right. Now, in his mother's eyes, Roy could no wrong, and even Arthur Banks, not given to expressions of any kind, didn't seem to disapprove of Roy as much as he did of Banks. Which was odd, indeed, Banks thought, as Roy was the consummate capitalist.

Roy sat down, first pulling at the razor-sharp crease of his black suit trousers. 'So how's life at the cop shop?' he asked, looking away even before he'd got the words out, indicating to Banks that he didn't have the slightest iota of interest.

'Fine,' said Banks.

'Is that your Renault out there?'

'Yes. Why?'

'Not bad. Only it looks new. Been on the take?'

'Oh, you know me, Roy. A few thousand here, a few thousand there.'

Roy laughed. Corinne and Ida Banks, best friends now, came through with the drinks on a tray at the same time Geoff came back from the shop. 'Sorry, they didn't have any Perrier,' he said. 'I got this other stuff Ali recommended. St . . . something or other . . . I can't pronounce it. OK?'

'It'll do,' said Roy. 'Be a good bloke and pop it in the fridge, would you, Geoff?'

Geoff seemed only too pleased to oblige.

'Isn't this lovely?' said Ida Banks, handing out the drinks. 'We can have our own little family party before the rest of our guests arrive. Corinne tells me she's an accountant, Roy.'

'That's right, Mum. Saved me a fortune in taxes.'

Corinne sat on the floor near his feet and rested her head against his thigh. He stroked her hair the way one would a faithful dog. 'She's very good with figures, aren't you, Corinne?'

Corinne blushed. 'If you say so, Roy.'

She really did seem like a 'nice' girl to Banks, and that made him wonder all the more what she was doing with Roy. Not that Roy wasn't handsome or charming. In fact he possessed both of those attributes in spades. Under his suit, he wore a pale blue silk polo-neck. His hair, not quite so black as Banks's, was long, over his ears and collar, expensively cut, and he had a small shaving nick near the cleft of his chin. His energetic blue eyes resembled Banks's, except that they were predatory and calculating, whereas Banks's were curious and intense.

Banks had thought more than once that his brother Roy fitted the classic definition of the psychopath: he was glib and superficial, egocentric, manipulative, shallow and completely lacking in any feelings of remorse, empathy or guilt. Certainly all his behaviour and his emotional responses were learned, assumed through close observation of others as the best way to get on in the world. Underneath it all, Banks guessed, the only things that mattered to him were his needs, and how he could meet them, and his success, measured, of course, by money and power. Perhaps that was why he had already gone through three wives.

'Oops, mustn't forget,' Roy said, putting his glass down and getting suddenly to his feet. Corinne almost fell over sideways. 'Sorry, love.' He patted her shoulder. 'Just got to nip down to the Porsche. Forgot something. Wouldn't want to leave it out there too long. You never know on an estate like this. Give us a hand, will you, Geoff?'

Geoff, returned from the kitchen, beer in hand, stated that he was only too willing to do anything for Roy, and set his glass down on the table. Corinne smiled shyly as the two of them went out. Banks hadn't heard her speak yet and wondered what her voice was like, her accent. 'Where are you from?' he asked, just to find out.

'Canterbury,' she said. 'Well, I grew up there. After that I went to Manchester University.'

She didn't have much of a regional accent, Banks learned. She was well spoken, clearly educated, and her voice was pleasant, soft and musical, a little reedy.

'How long have you known Roy?'

'About three months.'

'They're getting engaged,' Ida Banks said. 'So now we've *really* got something to celebrate.'

Corinne blushed.

'That true?' Banks asked.

She smiled and nodded. He felt like warning her off. Roy had been married three times and two of his wives had ended up confiding in Banks about what an unfaithful, cruel bastard Roy was. He had never actually hit either of them – so they both swore – but he curtailed their freedom and terrorized them psychologically. The second, a particularly bright neurosurgeon called Maria, ended up seeing a psychiatrist for years after they split up, trying to splice together the frayed strands of her self-esteem. Banks had seen her change – albeit at infrequent intervals – from a secure, confident young doctor into an apologetic, tongue-tied wreck whose hands shook so much she couldn't thread a needle. The third wife, thank God, had seen the signs before it got too late and left Roy in time.

Roy and Geoff came back carrying large cardboard boxes, which they set down on the living-room floor. 'Happy anniversary,' Roy said. 'Go on. Open them.'

Banks's parents looked at one another, then his mother got some scissors from the kitchen drawer and came back and knelt by the largest box. Roy and Geoff helped, and soon between them had managed to drag out the computer monitor, processor unit and keyboard.

'It's a computer,' said Ida Banks, clearly at a loss.

'Now you'll be able to go on the Internet,' said Roy. 'We'll be able to send each other email.'

'Will we?'

'Yes.'

'But it's so . . . so expensive.'

'Oh, it's nothing. Everyone should have a computer these days. They're the future.'

Ida Banks reached out and touched it gingerly, as if it might bite. 'The future—'

'We'd better get it out of the way for the time being,' said Arthur Banks. 'Our guests will be arriving soon.'

'Right.'

Between them, Geoff, Roy and Banks took the computer upstairs and set it up on the desk in the spare room.

'That'll be nice for them,' said Geoff.

Banks thought it was the stupidest present he could think of. His parents were in their seventies; they weren't going to learn how to use a computer. His own present, a particularly moody Yorkshire landscape painting he had found in an antique shop in Richmond, had met with polite praise, but he felt it was probably destined for the back of the wardrobe. The computer, he suspected, would sit at this desk, not even plugged in, just gathering dust. Unless Geoff Salisbury decided to use it.

Just as the three of them started downstairs, the front doorbell rang.

'Here come the first guests,' said Geoff. 'It's started.'

19

First to arrive were Uncle Frank and Aunt Harriet, and after that Banks began to lose track. Here came relatives he hadn't seen for years, cousins he never even knew existed. It was only to be expected with both his mother and father coming from large families – six and four respectively – but it was a shock nonetheless.

Geoff took to bartending duties like a fish to water, and Roy worked the room like a politician, all hail-fellow-well-met, as if these people he had probably never seen before meant more to him than his own life. If the truth were known, he had been home even less often than Banks and hardly ever in touch with the more distant relatives.

Arthur Banks seemed bewildered by it all, tired, sticking to his armchair, glass of beer at hand, though Ida got into the party spirit and Banks fancied she even became a little tipsy. Music played quietly in the background, mostly crooners and big bands, though pop entered the mix when someone found an old compilation album. It was pretty much the same stuff as Banks had found in his room, or at least softer stuff from the same period – Cliff Richard, Eden Kane, Frank Ifield, Billy Fury, the Bachelors and the ubiquitous Val Doonican – but it was only for background, wall-paper music.

In a lull after the first few guests had arrived, Banks managed to get Roy alone for a few minutes while a couple of young cousins, similarly bedecked, admired Corinne's body-piercing,

'I've been wanting a word in your ear,' Banks said. 'It's about that Geoff Salisbury.'

'What about him? Seems like a decent chap. Takes good care of Mum and Dad.'

'That's just it. I think he steals from them.'

'Oh, come on, Alan. It's that suspicious copper's mind of yours working overtime again.'

'No. It's more than that.' Banks told him about the short change.

'Could have been any reason for that,' Roy said. 'A genuine mistake. You don't always have to think the worst of people, you know.'

'He's got their PIN number. They give him their Abbeylink card.'

'He takes care of their finances. For crying out loud, *somebody's* got to do it. I mean it's not as if you're around much, is it?'

Banks realized he was fighting a losing battle. Roy didn't want to believe that Geoff was anything other than a godsend, and he would resist any evidence to the contrary. 'He's got a criminal record,' Banks went on nevertheless, pissing against the wind. 'Swindling old folk out of their life savings.'

Roy just laughed. 'Mum and Dad haven't got anything worth swindling. You know that. And besides, don't you believe in rehabilitation? I assume he's paid his debt to society?'

'Yes, but—'

'Well, then.'

'For Christ's sake, Roy. I caught him red-handed.'

'Listen, big brother. So what if he's pocketing a bob or two here and there? He practically does all their shopping for them, house cleaning, too. Isn't it worth it?'

'That's not the point. If he wants paying for what he does, that's different.'

'Maybe it's just his way.'

'It's a funny bloody way.'

Roy shrugged and laid his arm across Banks's shoulders. 'Like I said, it's not as if you're around to do it, is it, eh? I say count your blessings and let sleeping dogs lie. Look, there's Uncle Ken. See you later.'

Banks muttered to himself under his breath. He should have known approaching Roy was a waste of time. Anybody suspected of swindling a penny out of *him* and he'd probably put a contract out on them, but his own parents . . . On the other hand, was Roy right? Was Banks making too much out of all this? Being a party pooper? He looked at his parents. They seemed happy enough – his mother did, anyway – what right had he got to challenge that? What gave him the moral justification to come down here once in a blue moon and spoil what little good fortune they had going for them? His mother clearly adored Geoff – he could tell by the way she looked at him and talked about him – and having him around made life a hell of a lot easier for his father, too. Roy was right. Banks had been interfering too much, and it was about time he backed off and left people to get on with their lives.

'Penny for them?'

Banks turned. It was Kay. 'I didn't hear you come in,' he said. 'Nice to see you.'

She smiled and touched his arm. 'Nice to see you, too. I was just talking to your mother. She offered her condolences.'

She was wearing a lemon summer dress, which fell to just below her knees and she had her hair tied up and held in place with a patterned leather barrette.

'You look wonderful,' Banks said.

Kay blushed. 'Thank you. How about a drink for the lady?'

'Of course. Vodka and tonic?'

'That'll do nicely.' She took hold of his arm. 'And don't go too far away. I don't know anyone else here.'

'Of course you do,' said Banks. 'You know my parents.'

'I haven't seen them for years.'

'And my brother Roy.'

'He was just a little kid when we were together. Around too often, if I remember correctly.'

Banks nodded. He remembered being blackmailed into giving Roy money to get lost on more than one occasion. 'You know Geoff Salisbury,' he said, nodding to where Geoff stood by the fireplace talking to some cousin whose name Banks couldn't remember.

Kay gave a little shudder. 'Yuck. I don't know about you, but he gives me the creeps.'

They got their drinks.

'Come on,' Banks said to Kay. 'Let's get some fresh air.'

They went out to the back step. Banks could hear music next door, but only softly. The rain had stopped earlier that afternoon and it had turned into a pleasant evening. The sky was already darkening and the stars coming out. There was even a pale quarter moon low in the sky. Banks leaned against the wall. Kay stood quietly beside him.

'Last night—' he began.

But Kay hushed him, putting a finger to his lips. 'No. Don't say anything. That was marvellous. Special. Let's leave it at that, shall we?'

'If you like,' Banks said. He'd been thinking the same thing. What had happened had been about the past, unfinished business, passing magic. It had been time out of time. Tomorrow they would both go back to their real lives and probably never see one another again. Banks thought about how their relationship had ended all those years ago, and how he had believed he would never see her again after he went to London. This was enough. This was more than enough. It had to be.

They went back inside. The party went on, as these things do. Banks and Kay talked to Mrs Green for a while, and Banks promised not to be such a stranger. Aunt Florence regaled him with her cataracts, and Aunt Lynn went on about her gall-bladder operation. He also heard about Cousin Patrick's prostate problems, Uncle Gerald's haemorrhoids and Cousin Louise's manic depression. It was enough to make him want to kill himself before he got old. Then there was Cousin Beth's divorce, Nick and Janet's third baby, a girl they had named Shania, Sharon's promotion, Gail's miscarriage and Ayesha's boob job. All the while Kay stood politely by, asking questions and making sympathetic comments or noises. Roy continued to work the room, seemingly indefatigable.

Inevitably, Uncle Ted fell asleep. Cousin Angie had too much to drink and was sick in the kitchen sink, dislodging a nose stud in the process, which she nearly inhaled. Uncle Gerald and Uncle Frank almost came to blows. Aunt Ruth wet herself, and young, lovely, anorexic Cousin Sue, with all the self-esteem of a blade of grass, became tearful and made a pathetic attempt to seduce Banks.

All in all, it was just another typical family do.

Roy and Corinne left early. They sought out Banks and Kay to say their goodbyes, and as usual Roy invited Banks to the South Kensington house, said they really must see more of one another and that he hoped Banks could make it to the wedding next year. Banks promised he would try, gave the blushing bride-to-be a chaste kiss on her pale, cool cheek, and they were gone.

When Banks looked around, he noticed that Geoff Salisbury had left too. Only one or two relatives remained, and they were either very close or very drunk. Banks found his mother having a heart-to-heart with her sister, Flo, and said he'd see Kay home and be right back.

The street was quiet, the evening air cool. They only saw only a few people as they walked the short distance to Kay's house.

'I'd better not come in,' he said at the doorstep.

'No.'

He wondered what would happen if he leaned forward and kissed her on the lips. Would their resolve melt? Somehow, he didn't think it was very strong.

'Anyway,' he said, 'if you're ever up Eastvale way—'

'Of course I will.' She gave him the sort of smile that said she never would be, then after a quick kiss on the cheek, the door opened and closed and Banks was left standing there alone.

He didn't want to go back to the dregs of the party immediately, didn't want to face the drunken relatives desperately sobering up for the drive home, didn't want to face the mess of spilled drinks and food smeared on the carpets. He knew he would have to – he owed it to his parents to help clean up at least – but he could put it off for a little while longer.

The moon was higher now and Banks could see stars, planets, constellations even, beyond the amber glow of the street lights. He wandered the quiet Sunday night streets of the estate feeling oddly melancholy, past the maisonettes where he used to deliver newspapers, past the house where his old, late friend Steve Hill used to live. Steve had kept toads in a bell jar at the bottom of the garden, Banks remembered, but he was forgetful, and one summer he neglected them for so long that they shrivelled up and died. They looked like dried mushrooms. That was what happened to living things you were supposed to love and care for but neglected.

His melancholy was probably something to do with Kay, he realized, though he hadn't really wanted to repeat last night, either. Last night had had a magic about it that any attempt at repetition would fall well short of. He remembered how their relationship had fallen apart all those years ago. His fault.

It had all started to change when Kay left school at sixteen and got a job at Lloyd's bank in the town centre. She made new friends, had money to spare, started going for drinks with the office crowd regularly after work on a Friday. Banks was still at school, having stayed on for his A levels, and somehow a schoolboy had less appeal than these slightly older, better dressed, more sophisticated men of the world at the office. They had more money to flash around and, even more important, some of them had cars. One pillock called Nigel, with a plummy accent and a Triumph MG, particularly got up Banks's nose. Kay insisted there was no hanky-panky going on, but Banks became tortured with jealousy, racked by imagined infidelities, and in the end Kay walked away. She couldn't stand his constant harping on about who she was seeing and what she was doing, she said, and the way he got stroppy if she even so much as *looked at* another man.

The irony was, given that his A level results weren't good enough for university – the first bone of contention between him and his parents – he might as well not have bothered staying on. He'd spent far too much time with Kay, away from his studies, listening to Hendrix, Dylan and Pink Floyd, reading books that weren't on the syllabus.

Shortly after the break up, Banks moved to London and went to pursue business studies at the poly. A year or two after that and several brief, unsatisfactory, casual relationships later, he met Sandra.

A dog barked as he reached the edge of the estate by the railway lines. A local train rattled by, one or two silhouettes visible through the windows. Banks started towards home. He had only got a few yards when the mobile in his pocket rang. He had forgotten to turn it off.

'Alan? I hope I'm not disturbing your party.'

It was Annie Cabbot. Banks wondered how he would have felt if he had gone in with Kay and the phone had rung just as they were . . . it didn't bear thinking about.

'No,' he said quietly. He happened to be passing the telephone boxes at the end of the street, so he decided to stand inside one and take the call. That way he didn't seem like one of those silly buggers walking around talking to his girlfriend on his mobile phone.

'I'm sorry to call so late,' Annie said.

'That's all right. Aren't you off duty?'

'Yes, but I was waiting to hear from DS Ryan in Loughborough. He was out at the pictures.'

'DS Ryan? So this is about Geoff Salisbury?'

'Yes. What's wrong, Alan? You sound funny. Distant.'

'So would you if you were standing in the middle of a council estate talking on your mobile.'

Annie laughed. 'Oh, I don't know. I'm not quite as conservative as you are.'

'OK. Point taken. What did this DS Ryan come up with?'

'It's interesting, actually,' said Annie. 'At least, I thought you'd want to know.'

'Fill me in.'

'As Winsome told you, Salisbury was actually convicted of fraud. It was a neighbour, an elderly woman, and he started by helping out around the place, that sort of thing.'

'Sounds familiar,' said Banks. 'Go on.'

'Seems he managed to come between her and her children and get himself written into her will. She didn't have much. Only a few hundred quid and an insurance policy, but he copped for most of it.'

'What happened?'

'The family contested it. Undue influence, that sort of thing. Hard to prove. Anyway, in the end Mr Salisbury won out.'

'Where does the conviction come in?'

'Just getting to that. During proceedings, it came out that Geoff Salisbury had persuaded the woman to invest in a non-existent business venture of his. A garage.'

'Ah-hah.'

'Again, it wasn't much. Only two hundred quid.'

'Doesn't matter,' said Banks. 'Is a man who preys on the poor any less guilty than one who preys on the rich?'

'I'm afraid that's a bit too philosophical for me at this time on a Sunday evening, but at a guess I'd say even more so, wouldn't you?'

'I would. Thanks a lot, Annie. Above and beyond, and all that.'

'Oh, that's not all.'

'Really?'

'Really. While all this was going on, Mr Salisbury's mother died. Well, she was old and—'

'Sick?'

'How did you guess? She had diabetes. Anyway, she died. Or—'

Banks felt a tingle go up his spine. 'Or what?'

'Or he helped her on her way. Nothing was ever proven. There weren't even any charges. But DS Ryan was one of the investigating officers, and he says he was suspicious enough to ask for an autopsy. Negative. The woman was old, she went hypoglycaemic, and that was that.'

'What's that?'

'Hypoglycaemic? It's something that happens to diabetics, apparently, caused by too much insulin or low food intake.'

'He gave her an overdose of insulin?'

'No evidence of that.'

'But someone could have brought it about, this hypoglycaemic coma?'

'Yes. Hard to prove, though.'

'What did DS Ryan say?'

'DS Ryan said that his older sister is a diabetic and she always keeps her bedside drawer full of Mars bars or chocolate of some kind for just that sort of eventuality.'

'But I thought diabetics had to avoid sugar like the plague?'

'So did I. Apparently, they do. Unless they go hypoglycaemic. Then they need a hit of sugar.'

'Or?'

'Coma. Death. And in this case there were other complications. Weak heart, for example.'

'And DS Ryan says?'

'DS Ryan says the doctor didn't find any traces of sugar products close to Mrs Salisbury's bed, and he found that in itself suspicious. In his opinion – DS Ryan's, that is – Geoff Salisbury was responsible, knowing it was just a matter of time before she'd need a sugar fix.'

'He killed his own mother. Is that what you're saying?'

'Mercy killing, but killing all the same.'

'Bloody hell,' said Banks. 'This changes things.'

'It does?'

'I'd been thinking of leaving well alone.'

'But not now?'

'Not now. Thanks a lot, Annie.'

'My pleasure. See you tomorrow?'

'OK. And thanks again.'

Missing Mars bars. A faulty oxygen-tank valve. Banks wondered who else Geoff Salisbury had assisted in their final moments on earth. He also wondered how long it would be before his own father suffered that fatal angina attack and was unable to find his nitroglycerine tablets in time. Putting his phone in his pocket, he headed straight for Geoff Salisbury's house.

20

'Look, I can see you're not going to let this drop, are you?' said Salisbury when Banks had told him he knew about the conviction.

'So I've been to prison. It's nothing to be ashamed of. I served my time.'

'As a matter of fact,' said Banks, 'it is something to be ashamed of. But those who've been there rarely seem to think so. Innocent, were you, like everyone else?'

'No. I did it. I was desperate and she didn't need the money, so I conned her. I'm not saying I'm proud of *that*, what I did, but like I said, I served my time, paid my debt to society.'

Debt to society. Roy's words exactly and an odd phrase when you really thought about it. 'Would that it were as simple as that,' Banks said. Salisbury's living room wasn't quite as clean and tidy as he had expected, but perhaps he used all his energy on other people's homes and had none left for his own. Dust gathered in the corners, the carpet was threadbare and lumps of mould floated on the half-empty coffee cup on the table.

'All right,' said Salisbury, 'suppose, just *suppose* that I was ripping people off. Some people might actually believe I'm a power for good around here.'

'What do you mean?'

'An estate like this, the old folks need someone on their side, someone to look out for them. They die off, you see, and when they do it's mostly young 'uns come in off the waiting list. You know the sort. Young lasses barely out of school with three kids and no father in sight. Or that lot next door to your mum and dad's. Scum. Now you're a copper, Alan, you tell me if he doesn't have prison written all over him. And as for the kids, well, it'll only be a matter of time. And if it's not scum like that it's foreigners. Gyppos. Darkies. Pakis. Them with the turbans. All with their funny ways, slaughtering goats in the street and whatever, not giving a toss for our customs and traditions and way of life. See, the old folks, they get frightened when everything around them starts to feel threatening and *unfamiliar*. Their world's changing so fast and their bodies can't do what they used to do, so they end up feeling lost and scared. That's where someone like me comes in. I reassure them, do odd jobs, give them a friendly and familiar face to relate to. So what if I make a few bob out of it? Hypothetically.'

'I'd say, hypothetically, that it makes you a thief.'

'Words, Alan, just words.'

'Actually, no. Legal concepts.'

'Well, you would say that, wouldn't you?'

'Here's another one to try on for size. *Murder*.'

Salisbury blinked and stared at him. 'What?'

'You heard me, Geoff. Oh, you might have a more fancy name for it, something high-sounding and moral, such as *mercy* killing, but in my eyes it's murder plain and simple.'

Salisbury sat back in his chair. 'I don't know what you're talking about.'

'Oh, I think you do. There was your own mother for a start. Don't tell me a woman who's been a diabetic for a good part of her life doesn't know to keep some sugar on hand in case she goes hypoglycaemic.'

Salisbury banged his fist on the chair arm. 'That's over and done with,' he said. 'I wasn't there. Nobody ever proved anything against me!'

'I'm not saying you haven't been clever, Geoff. You never were there, were you? Mr Green's faulty valve, for example. Wouldn't be difficult for a car mechanic, would it? And what about Mrs Summerville, Geoff, gentle pillow over the face as she slept, was it? Nobody would ask too many questions. Or perhaps a little too much morphine? She was alone. You had a key. They always give you a key, don't they? And what about the hundred quid you drew out with her bank card the day she died. Mistake, that. She couldn't get it herself, remember - she was bedridden - and her daughter could find no sign of the money.'

Salisbury got to his feet. 'You can't prove a damn thing. Get out of here! Go on, get out!'

Banks didn't move. 'You don't get away with it that easily, Geoff, especially not when it's my parents you're playing with now. I saw the piece of silver paper you folded and dropped in the bin at Mrs Summerville's house. I'll bet it has your prints on it.'

'So I went there. I helped her. Like I helped the others. So what? That doesn't prove anything.'

'I'll bet if we exhumed the body, though, we'd find some evidence of tampering, some evidence of what you did. She hasn't been dead as long the others, Geoff. There'll be forensic evidence. In the house, too.'

For the first time, Banks saw Salisbury falter and sit down again. He knew he had been guessing, taking a stab in the dark, but it seemed to have touched a nerve. 'She had cancer and a weak heart,' Banks went on. 'All it took was a little pressure. She didn't even have the strength to fight back, did she?'

'What do you mean *forensic* evidence?' Geoff asked. 'They'd never dig her up.'

'Oh yes, they would. On my say-so. And you know exactly what they'd find, don't you?'

'But the doctor signed the death certificates. There wasn't even an inquest, nothing suspicious at all.'

'Why would there be, Geoff? Don't you know how it goes? All your victims were medically attended during their illnesses, they'd all been seen by their doctors within fourteen days of death, and they were all terminally ill, likely to die at any time. There were no grounds for a coroner's inquest. And remember: none of them was alone with family members when they died. Not even your mother. You made sure you were out of the house that night, didn't you?'

'This is absurd. They'll never open up her coffin.'

'Yes, they will. We'd just better thank the Lord that she was buried and not cremated, don't you think? What will they find? Tell me.'

Salisbury licked his lips, staring at Banks, and said nothing for a long time. 'You think you're clever, don't you?' he said at last. 'You don't know nothing about it.'

'About what?'

'Suffering.'

'Tell me about it, Geoff. I want to know.'

'Why should I? You wouldn't understand.'

'Believe me, I'll try. And it'll go better for you if you do. If we don't have to exhume the body. That's a lot of work. And messy. Nobody wants to do it. I think we'd be able to prove a case against you, Geoff, I really do, but if you help us, if you tell me about it, it'll go a lot easier for you.'

'Why do you think they let me cheat them, take their money?'

Banks frowned. 'Come again?'

'You don't think they didn't know what I was doing, do you? They knew all right and they let it go on. Payment. That's what it was. They just couldn't come right out and say it. What they really wanted me to do. But it was their way of paying me, of letting me know what they wanted me to do.'

'Hang on a minute, Geoff,' said Banks. 'Let me get this straight. Did you kill Mr Green and Mrs Summerville?'

'Yes. No. I put them to sleep. I ended their suffering.'

'And your mother?'

'It was what she wanted. It was what they all wanted. It was beautiful.'

'What was?'

Salisbury's eyes shone. 'The transformation. From pain to peace. Suffering to grace. It was like being God.'

'Did either Mrs Green or anyone from the Summerville family suggest that you do what you did?'

'Not in so many words, no.'

'But that was how you interpreted their actions in letting you get away with stealing money?'

'Like I said, they knew. It was their way of paying for what they wanted done. Close family couldn't do it, could they? They'd soon be suspects, or they didn't care enough and were never around, like you and that Summerville girl. You don't see their suffering. I do. Day in, day out. I was their saviour. Somebody had to be.'

Banks got up.

'What are you doing?'

'I'm going to ring the local police now, and I want you to tell them what you've just told me. Tell them everything. Maybe you're sick. Maybe you need help. I don't know.' All I do know, Banks thought as he took out his mobile, is that I want you off this estate and as far away from my parents as possible.

21

It was about an hour later when two uniformed constables and one detective sergeant, grumpy at being dragged out of the Sunday night pub darts match, arrived at Geoff Salisbury's house.

'You know, with all due respect to your rank and all, sir, we don't particularly appreciate North Yorkshire CID poking around on our patch, doing our job for us,' said the surly DS, whose name was Les Kelly and who was going prematurely bald. Luckily, Banks hadn't encountered DS Kelly on his last trip to Peterborough.

Banks smiled to himself. It would probably have been his reaction, too, had Kelly come up north. At least it would have been *if* he had been a DS and ten years younger.

'Believe me, DS Kelly, it wasn't my intention,' he said. 'I just came for the party.'

'You what?'

Banks sighed. 'I was brought up around here. Down the street. I came home for my parents' golden wedding and this is what I found going on.' He gestured towards Salisbury, who was giving his statement to the uniformed officers.

'How about we go outside for a minute?' said Kelly. 'The uniforms can deal with his statement, and I fancy a smoke.'

Banks and Kelly stood on the path. Kelly lit a cigarette and Banks craved one. A few locals had noted the arrival of the police and a small crowd had gathered just beyond the patrol car. Not that police cars were a novelty on the estate, but it *was* nearly bedtime on a Sunday.

'I was winning, too,' said Kelly.

'What?'

'The darts match.'

Banks smiled. 'Oh. Sorry.'

'Never mind. We never sleep. Always ready to bring another wrongdoer to justice. I just transferred here from West Midlands, myself. You say you're from around these parts?'

'Uh-huh. Long time ago. Came here when I was twelve. Grew up just down the street. Used to go out with the girl whose mother that bastard killed.'

'They'll put him in the nut house.'

'Likely. As long as he's locked up.'

Kelly looked around and sniffed the air, then he took a deep drag on his cigarette and blew out a long plume of smoke. 'I grew up on an estate pretty much like this one,' he said. 'Barrow-in-Furness.'

'Not a part of the world I know.'

'Don't bother.'

'Look, while you're here,' said Banks, 'there is another small matter you might be able to help with.'

'Oh? And what's that?'

'The family that lives next to my parents,' said Banks. 'I don't know their names but the bloke looks like Fred West—'

'Ah, the Wyatts.'

'Is that their name?'

'Well, it's easier that way. To be honest, though, I think he's the only true Wyatt there. She's a Fisher. Had kids with a Young and Harrison and a Davies. Need I go on?'

'How many of them are there?'

'According to the council, only five. That's all the place is big enough for.'

'I saw a sleeping bag on the staircase.'

'You were in there?'

'Noise complaint.'

'Ah, yes. Well, our latest estimation is about twelve, give or take a couple.'

'Can you do anything?'

'About what?'

'Drugs, for a start. And I wouldn't be surprised if some of those kids are being sexually abused.'

'Nor me.' Kelly finished his cigarette and stamped it out on the path. 'It's only a matter of time,' he said. 'You know how these things can drag on. But we've got an eye on them, and the social's investigating them, too, so sooner or later one of us will come up with something.'

'And then?'

Kelly laughed. 'And then? You know as well as I do. Then the farce just begins. They'll end up on another estate much like this one, most likely, and it'll start all over again.'

The uniforms came out with Geoff Salisbury, slump-shouldered, between them. 'Done,' one of them said. Salisbury gave Banks a look that was half pleading for understanding and forgiveness, and half pure hatred. Banks didn't know which half he liked less.

'Right.' Kelly clapped his hands. 'Let's go see what the custody sergeant has to say, shall we? And I'll say goodnight to you, for the moment, DCI Banks. We might need you again.'

Banks smiled. 'I'm only a phone call away.'

22

By Monday morning, when Banks awoke to sunshine and the sound of birds beyond his thin curtains, news of Geoff Salisbury's arrest had spread around the entire estate. When he went down for breakfast, he found his parents sitting quietly at the table. He poured himself a cup of tea. His mother wouldn't look at him when he walked into the room.

'You've heard, then?' he asked.

'About Geoff?' she said, tears in her eyes. 'Mrs Wilkins came to tell me. That was your doing, wasn't it?'

'I'd no choice, Mum,' said Banks, resting his hand on her arm. She jerked it away.

'How could you do that? You know what he meant to us.'

'Mum, Geoff Salisbury was a murderer. He killed Mr Green and he killed Kay's mother.' Not to mention his own mother, Banks thought. 'I don't see how you can defend him. You *knew* those people. They were your neighbours.'

Mrs Banks shook her head. 'I don't believe it. Not Geoff. He wouldn't do anything like that. He's gentle as a kitten.'

'He admitted it.'

'You must have forced him. Interrogated him until he didn't know what he was saying.'

'I don't work like that, Mum. Believe me, he did it. He might have thought he was doing good, doing the families a favour, but he did it.'

Banks looked at his father, who caught his eye. He knew right away that they were thinking the same thing: who was next?

Banks stood up. 'Look, Mum, I've got to go now.'

'All you brought was trouble. It was supposed to be a happy occasion. Now look what you've gone and done. Spoiled it all, as usual. I wish our Roy was here.'

Banks's heart felt heavy, but there was nothing more he could say. There was as much point in telling his mother that Roy didn't give a shit as there was in telling her that Geoff Salisbury was a cold-blooded murderer.

'I'm sorry, Mum,' he said, then dashed upstairs to throw his few belongings in his bag. He looked at the boxes of records and exercise books again and decided to leave them. All he took was the poetry.

Let go.

He was standing at the door of his room when he saw his father come slowly up the stairs. They stood on the landing facing one another. 'She's upset,' said Arthur Banks. 'She doesn't know what she's saying. I'll take care of her. I'll make sure she knows what's what.'

'What *is* what, Dad? I'm not even sure I know. Did I do the right thing?'

'Only you know that for certain, lad. But you did your job. You'd no choice. You're a copper and he was a bad 'un. Your mother'll get over it. She really liked him, that's all. He was useful around the house. And he could be a right charmer.'

'I know,' said Banks. 'His type usually is.'

'You know she never likes admitting she's wrong about people. But if he killed those people, you were right. You were only doing your job. I don't mind a bob or two here and there – and don't think I didn't notice, I just kept quiet for your mother's sake – but I draw the line at killing.' He laughed. 'Who's to say it wouldn't have been me next, eh?'

They both knew there was a lot more truth in that fear than either cared to explore.

'Bye, Dad,' Banks said. 'I'll be in touch.'

'Don't be a stranger, son. And don't worry. Your mother'll get over it. I'll tell her to ring you in a day or so, shall I?'

'Please do.'

His father smiled. 'Or send you an email?'

Banks moved forward impulsively and hugged him. It was quick, and he felt only the slightest pressure of his father's hand on the back of his shoulder, but it was enough.

Banks dashed down the stairs and walked down the path to his car, tears prickling his eyes. He felt a weight in the side pocket of his jacket and realized it was Kay's copy of *Lady Chatterley's Lover*. Now he decided he might as well keep it. Maybe he would even get around to reading it, over thirty years after he'd borrowed it.

When he got to the driver's side of his car, he cursed out loud. Some bastard had taken a coin or a nail and made a deep scratch along the paintwork all the way from back to front. He thought he saw someone watching from an upstairs window of the Wyatt house.

Bugger them. Bugger the lot of them, he thought, and got into his car and drove away.